PRAISE FOR **THE SPY'S WIFE**

"Marriage is a mystery. Add to the mix a chaotic, unconventional family, and we're in for a wild ride. This is a story of one woman's strength to walk through betrayal and lies while also navigating her pain and anger with grace and composure. Part heartbreaking, part joy—this book kept me guessing until the very end."

—MAAN GABRIEL, author of *After Perfect*

"Unraveling secrets, multiple identities, and scandal, the heroine of this fast-paced novel is trapped in a web of lies she must untangle. I was caught up in her world as she holds her family together while trying to find meaning in her own life. *The Spy's Wife* is a fun read that made me think about my own life entanglements."

—KAREN GERSHOWITZ, author of *Travel Mania: Stories of Wanderlust*

"The protagonist in *The Spy's Wife* is a very engaging, compassionate super-mom whose world is upended when she starts to learn about her husband's secret life; this forces her to assess her own choices. I could easily identify with her. Entertaining, surprising, a bit of a romp . . . a very fun book to read."

—AMES SHELDON, author of *Eleanor's Wars*, *Don't Put the Boats Away*, and *Lemons in the Garden of Love*

PRAISE FOR **THE LONG-LOST JULES**

"Hughes offers up a contemporary mystery/thriller with a strong helping of historical fiction and romance. . . . An enjoyable globe-trotting adventure and investigation."

—*Kirkus Reviews*

"A sharp, engrossing international thriller with twists that will keep you turning pages."

—Lindsay Cameron,
author of *BIGLAW* and *Just One Look*

"With a satisfying ending that resolves all of its mysteries, *The Long-Lost Jules* is an absorbing mystery novel . . ."

—*Foreword Clarion Reviews*

THE
SPY'S
WIFE

THE
SPY'S
WIFE

A NOVEL

JANE ELIZABETH HUGHES

SPARKPRESS

Published by SparkPress, a BookSparks imprint,
A division of SparkPoint Studio, LLC
Phoenix, Arizona, USA, 85007
www.gosparkpress.com

Published 2022
Printed in the United States of America
Print ISBN: 978-1-68463-135-3
E-ISBN: 978-1-68463-136-0
Library of Congress Control Number: 2021923640

Formatting by Katherine Lloyd/The DESK

This book is dedicated to my sisterhood: Kim, Laurie, Mary Rose, Tina, Melissa, Beth, and Sarah. Where would we be without each other?

Part I

THE
CHARGES

CHAPTER ONE

To Do:
Take new cat (name?) to vet
Neil & Marisa re: Friday dinner
Auction kickoff meeting
Nonfat Greek yogurt
Bills
Schedule mammogram
Call Dani back

ON TV, MY HUSBAND DIDN'T LOOK ANYTHING like the man I'd woken up next to for the past twenty years. He looked like a tall remote stranger hurrying away from the cameras, waving an impatient hand at the reporters who clustered around him. Maybe that was because he was supposed to be in Cleveland—but the dateline on CNN read "Moscow." Or maybe it was because he was supposed to be a dullish management consultant. Not a spy.

And the day had started out so benignly. It was the Tuesday after Labor Day, and the kids were blessedly back in school—my sister's kids, that is, the seventeen-year-old twins who called me Mommy-Shelley and their biological mother

Mommy-Marisa. I had just settled down at the kitchen table for a glorious moment to myself, switching on CNN for the eight o'clock news and opening a Diet Coke. I was even considering the blueberry muffin that Sasha had left untouched—after all, blueberries are healthy, right?

I stretched luxuriously in the warm September sun streaming through the bay window, reveling in the quietness. No Sam asking me to go over his college essay because Mommy-Marisa was too busy; no Sasha loudly refusing to discuss *her* college essay and invading the kitchen with a hungry horde of hunky boys. It was just me and the cats.

I took a long swig of my soda, thinking about the week ahead, as the two newscasters exchanged quips. There was a membership drive at the synagogue that I had, in a moment of sheer lunacy, agreed to spearhead; a fundraising drive at the twins' school that I somehow seemed to be running; the new cat had an oddly hairless spot on his back; and I was supposed to be mediating the divorce from hell this week at work. I had dialed back on work over the summer when the twins were out of school, but now it was exploding again.

I added a few more items to my to-do list.

Suddenly one of the newscasters said breathlessly, "This just in from Moscow: David Harris, a top CIA officer also known as Peter Brooks, has been revealed as the source for leaks to the BBC about British intelligence officers supplying weapons and information to the terrorist group Hamas. . . ."

I choked on my soda, spewing it across the kitchen table and startling two cats into flight. David Harris? *My* David Harris? As the camera focused on his frowning face, the tilt of his head and the width of his shoulders confirmed it.

The newscaster continued, "Harris named as the source for Mia Holloway, the BBC correspondent who broke the story two weeks ago that has rocked the intelligence establishment. Sources confirm that Harris has been a top CIA officer for over two decades. Operating in Europe and the Middle East under deep cover, he had access to most closely held information and was apparently so frustrated with his attempts to halt the operation that he provided information to Holloway." The ticker on the screen read, "CIA Superspy Harris Was Secret Source."

I remembered shaking my head in dismay over the story about British agents secretly providing support to Hamas, apparently in an attempt to force Israel to make concessions. And I remembered commenting on it to David, who gave his usual disinterested shrug when the discussion turned to Mideast affairs. "Not my problem," he'd said. He had been negotiating a deal in Akron, Ohio, at the time. Or so he said.

My phone started ringing. Dazed, I forced my eyes away from the TV screen and picked up the phone as the newscaster moved on to the next story.

"Shelley?" my best friend gasped. "Are you watching CNN?"

Rachel Lowenthal and I had been best friends since we met in an infertility group eighteen years ago. Either her doctor or her body was better than mine; she had given birth to two healthy babies while I gave birth to none—but we still managed to be best friends. She knew my habits better than my husband did, and she knew that I got my morning news fix from CNN.

"Yes," I said numbly. "It's on now."

"Is it true? Is David really a—I can't even say it!—is he really a spy? And you never *told* me? I can't believe you kept that from me!"

My thoughts were spinning too fast. "It must be some crazy mistake," I said. "It's ridiculous."

"Of course—silly me." Loyal friend that she was, she tried to hide the doubt in her voice. "Have you talked to him?"

"Not yet," I replied. "You know how hard it is to reach him when he's out of town." Unbidden and unwelcome, a memory popped into my head of the day eight-year-old Sasha fell off a swing at the school playground while her parents were in Puerto Rico. For hours I tried frantically to reach David on his cellphone, at his office, even on the sacred Blackberry that was only supposed to be used for work. His cellphone—as usual—went straight to voicemail; the anonymous man who answered his office phone promised to pass on the message; and his Blackberry gave me a recorded "out of service" response. By the time he finally called me, explaining that he lost his cellphone and had left his Blackberry in his jacket pocket, Sasha's broken arm was in a cast and Rachel had taken charge of Sam.

"Yeah," Rachel said. "I know."

"I think it might be true," I burst out, possibly surprising myself even more than Rachel. "I mean, if he's really a spy, he couldn't tell me—could he? And you know how he is. . . ."

"I know," Rachel said again. We both knew how David was—a warm and loving surrogate father to the twins (when he was in town), a pleasant husband—but always a little removed. Even on the increasingly rare occasions when he was physically here. Sudden tears sprang to my eyes at the sympathy in her voice, and I shook my head impatiently.

"No," I said firmly. "It can't be true. I would know if he was working for the CIA. Wouldn't I?"

I could almost feel Rachel fumbling for an answer, trying to quiet my fears and suspicions while tamping down her own. If we talked any longer, I really would fall apart.

"Sorry, Rach, my caller ID's going wild," I said quickly. "It's probably David. I'll call you later."

My caller ID *was* going wild, but my older sister Marisa's name and number were on the display. I breathed in and out while I let it go to voicemail. The phone rang again almost immediately—the temple president this time. More voicemail. My brother-in-law, his kind voice sounding worried. Marisa again. My younger sister, Dani. I sat numbly and watched the numbers flash on my caller ID as the messages grew—eighteen, nineteen, twenty, twenty-one. And then Unknown Caller appeared.

I snatched up the phone. "David?"

"Shelley," he said.

I couldn't think what to say. Suddenly I burst out, "Why doesn't your name ever come up on caller ID? Why does it always say Unknown Caller?" As soon as the words came out, I couldn't believe it—with so many questions waiting to be answered, all I ask him about is caller ID?

He paused, then said, "Because I switch cellphones all the time, and they're encrypted. They're never registered to my name."

And that's when I knew my husband had been lying to me for twenty years.

CHAPTER TWO

"I don't understand," I started but was cut off by the insistent ringing of our doorbell. Looking out the bay window, I saw several news trucks blocking the driveway and more than the usual collection of reporters on the street. Being near Embassy Row, our neighborhood was accustomed to a fairly constant flow of human rights and Free Tibet protestors on parade, with the inevitable media brigade on their heels.

But this was for us.

How had they found us so quickly?

"David, there are millions of reporters here, and they're not the usual ones. I think they're here for you." Loud and strident, my doorbell and landline phone both rang simultaneously.

"Don't talk to any of them," my husband said sharply, his tone as clipped as if he were giving orders to a new recruit. "Don't use the landline or your cell, and don't let anyone in the house. I have to clear up a few things here, but I'll be home in a few hours, and I can explain. *Don't talk to anyone until I get there.* Understood?"

"Yes, sir!" I snapped, a wave of anger sweeping away the numbness. "Does that include the twins?"

But he had already hung up, and I stared at my phone, watching the caller ID display light up once more. My auction cochair. Rachel again. Good lord, the veterinarian?

Like a tired kindergartner, I put my head down on the table and closed my eyes. How could he be home in a few hours? Didn't CNN say he was in Russia? He had trained me well; aside from the (apparently fictitious) itinerary on our fridge, I never bothered asking him about his constant business trips. He said his time at home was too precious to waste it talking about work.

Then I realized that the news segment could have been taped yesterday, so he could be anywhere in the world right now. London? Prague? Langley? Almost certainly not Ohio, at any rate.

I wanted to go back to bed, pull the covers over my head, and pretend this morning had never happened. I wanted to restart this day—have a do-over, like in *Groundhog Day*—with life going back to normal. David would be my unruffled, unmysterious husband who went to work every day in a dark suit and tie and advised multinational corporations on how to restructure their management teams.

But the memories kept rolling in, and I couldn't silence my rebellious thoughts. The news report had said, "David Harris, also known as Peter Brooks. . . ."

I suddenly snapped to attention. Peter Brooks! I *had* heard that name before. It was several years ago; I was still in bed, and David was in the shower. His iPhone wouldn't stop ringing, and finally I roused from my half-slumber to grab the phone and mumble, "Hello?"

A man's voice demanded, "Peter Brooks, please!"

"Sorry, wrong number," I said and clicked the phone off, but it rang again almost immediately. Inside the bathroom, I could hear the water raining down on David's oblivious head, so I picked up the phone again.

"Palmer? Is Mitchell Palmer there?" asked a woman's voice.

"Wrong number!" I shouted, and threw the iPhone down.

When it rang yet again, I grumblingly dragged myself out of bed to pound on the bathroom door.

David emerged, a towel wrapped around his lean hips and his damp hair forming dark blond ringlets on his glistening neck. Looking at the still-ringing phone, he asked, "Who are they asking for?"

"I don't know. Peter or Mitchell somebody. Why?"

He shrugged, and droplets flew from his broad shoulders to the wide-beamed oak floor. Now, besieged by doubts and worries, I could still remember how I felt as I looked at him that morning. My mind had momentarily gone blank in a haze of heat and passion. David had taken a step toward me, his eyes dancing with sudden interest, but I'd forced myself to meet his gaze with one of cool disinterest. He stopped short and reached for the buzzing iPhone instead.

On autopilot now, I got up and started tidying the kitchen, dumping Sasha's untouched muffin in the disposal and sopping up my spilled Diet Coke. I could make a chicken Caesar salad for dinner tonight if it was just me and the twins . . . or would David be home for dinner as he'd alluded? Was he even on this continent? And what in God's name would I tell the twins? Please, don't let them hear about this until they get home. . . .

The number of phone messages kept mounting. Why had I never wondered about his calls showing up as Unknown Caller before? I'd just assumed that, as a management consultant who worked on lots of confidential projects, he didn't want to be trackable to outsiders, but—Sam's name popped up on the caller ID, and I quickly picked up the phone.

"Hi, sweetie," I said, trying to sound normal and cheerful.

"Mom? Shelley, I mean? I don't know if you've seen the news, but one of the guys said David was on CNN? So I Googled it, and you're not going to believe this, but they're saying that he's a spy? And he told some BBC reporter about Hamas and the British? Mom? Are you there?"

Sam's voice, normally so calm and confident, was much higher and faster than usual. "I saw the story," I said.

"So did you talk to him? What the hell is going on?"

A senior in high school, Sam was still young enough to expect that David and I would make everything right again for him.

"I don't know," I told him. "He's on his way home now so we can figure all this out. But don't worry, sweetie. . . ." I stopped. David had said not to talk on this line, in that brusque tone that meant I needed to pay attention.

Not like when my neighbor's landscaper dumped the scruffy orange cat in the trash, and I rescued her and realized she was pregnant, and David insisted we couldn't keep her. And when the five kittens were born in his underwear drawer, he just sighed and helped me bottle-feed the tiny runt, and let the others sleep on our bed until we found homes for all but one. The former runt now weighed nineteen pounds and terrorized the other cats in our household; he still thought David was his father.

But this time I couldn't ignore his wishes. So I said, "As soon as David gets home, I'm sure he'll explain everything. Until then, there's no point in speculating."

"Okay. But, Mom—Shelley, I mean—"

"Sam, I really don't know what's going on; I'm in the dark as much as you. We just have to wait for David to get home." I wouldn't lie to Sam; this was David's mess to clear up.

Uncertainly, he said, "Is it . . . is everything okay?"

I bit my lip. Not lying was one thing; frightening him was another. "It's fine," I said firmly. "Now, I've got to run. Bye, Sam. Love you."

"Love you too."

As I pressed the End Call button, the caller ID lit up again. Damn, this time it was Sasha. I could let everyone else's calls go to voicemail, but not the kids. I pressed my hand against my forehead, where an ominous ache was starting just above my left eye, and picked up the phone again.

"Mom? Shelley, I mean?"

I smiled a little. When the twins hit puberty, they decided that the childish names of Mommy-Shelley and Mommy-Marisa should be relegated to babyhood along with the stuffed animals and blankies. They fumbled around for a while trying to figure out what to call us, and finally dropped all titles in favor of simply "Marisa" and "Shelley." But in moments of extreme stress, they reverted back to the Mommy-Shelley habit.

"Sasha," I said calmly. "How are you, honey?" A cracked fingernail could be high drama for Sasha; my job was to bring her down to earth.

"Shelley, you won't believe this, but my Latin teacher just told me that David was on TV this morning, and they said he was a spy! Is that true?"

I paused, debating. If I told her it was all a misunderstanding, she would believe me—for the moment—but then, what if it wasn't? Finally I admitted, "I just don't know, Sash."

Her voice rose several octaves. "You don't *know*? You mean it might be *true?*"

"I don't know," I repeated. "David's on his way home, and we'll figure it all out then. Now, you're not allowed to use your cellphone in school, are you? You'd better hang up; I don't want another conversation with that dean of students."

She giggled. My pretty, flighty Sasha—all bouncing taffy-colored curls and blue eyes and sparkling nail polish—took after no one in the family that I could see. She and a group of her field hockey friends had called in sick on the first beautiful beach day the previous May and headed for the shore; the dean of students, no dummy, had uncovered the plot and gotten the girls' car turned around before they had gone thirty miles. I had been dismayed, but the dean told me privately that if that was the worst mischief they got up to, I should count my blessings. I wasn't counting yet.

"Oh, Shelley, you know we learned our lesson. Anyway, I'll skip practice today and come straight home after school, okay?"

"Of course," I said abstractedly.

"See you later. Bye, Shelley. Love you."

"Bye, sweetie. Love you too."

Two down. I looked at the phone and wondered if I should just sit there and wait for the rest of the world to call. Maybe not. With a sigh, I got to my feet to make sure Sasha's and Sam's rooms had clean sheets. We had put an addition on the house years ago, when it became clear that the twins would be dividing their lives between us and my sister, so they could have their own rooms. David had painted the rooms himself.

David. Suddenly overwhelmed, I stopped flicking sheets over the frilly canopied bed that Sasha had chosen when she was eight. *Was* the news story true? *Could* he have been lying to me for the entire time I'd known him? He had brought Sasha the collection of Barbie dolls that still stood on her dressing table, the dolls dressed in costumes from all over the world. I regarded them thoughtfully. Had he really gotten them at the Walmart at Tyson's Corner, as he claimed? Or had he actually bought the Thai Barbie in Bangkok, and the Brazilian Barbie in Rio, and...?

And then I thought about how little I knew of his work. I knew that as a consultant to some of the biggest companies in the world, his work was often highly confidential. Anyway, he said, the details would bore me to tears. I thought that was

—

13

probably true; and besides, I was always juggling work and soccer practice and field hockey games and "volunteer" work (which felt an awful lot like unpaid labor) and . . . and besides, he traveled so much.

Many, many eons later—late afternoon by the clock—the reporters had stopped ringing the doorbell and phoning, but they had multiplied until their numbers overwhelmed our small side street, and the DC police had arrived to set up barriers and direct traffic. I had canceled my work appointment, broken my no-weekday-drinking rule, and was opening a bottle of wine when I heard a renewed frenzy outside. The reporters' shouting mounted to a dull roar of anticipation, then frustration, as our garage gates opened and closed.

David was home.

When I heard his footsteps behind me, I turned around and met his gaze evenly.

"Hi," he said cautiously.

He was still my David, my husband, the same man I raised my sister's children with, the same man I made love to, the same man who held me after my miscarriages and coached Sam's Little League team. Tall and strongly built, he was good-looking in a quiet, unobtrusive, preppy kind of way. His dark blond hair was always conservatively cut, his dark blue eyes often hidden behind the wire-rimmed glasses he wore even though his vision really wasn't that bad, or the dark sunglasses he always wore outdoors.

For the first time in our lives together, I couldn't think what to say.

CHAPTER THREE

He sat down at the kitchen table, pulling his tie loose and unbuttoning the top button of his shirt. When I still didn't reply, he stirred uneasily, pushing the salt and pepper shakers around with his finger. It was unheard of for him to fidget; he was the most controlled, self-contained person I'd ever met.

My eyes snagged on the dark blond chest hair that curled through his open collar. Part of me longed to throw myself against him, run my fingers through his hair, and remind us that he was still mine; another part of me wanted to punch him in the face.

"Don't look at me that way," he said, a little sharply. "Nothing has changed—nothing between *us*, I mean."

"Then you'd better tell me what *has* changed, hadn't you?" I was proud that my voice wasn't shaky.

He took a deep breath and blew it out slowly. "I went to work for the CIA right out of college. I am—*was*—what they call a nonofficial cover agent. Remember the NOC list that Tom Cruise was trying to recover in *Mission Impossible*? The list of CIA officers under deep cover? That's me."

I shook my head. "I don't understand." What I really meant was, I couldn't believe it.

"Most CIA officers work under official cover: the State

Department, Treasury, something like that. But a very few work under nonofficial cover."

"Like a management consulting firm?"

"Yes, exactly. If the official cover guys are caught out, they have their wrists slapped, and they're sent home. If we're exposed—well, we're on our own. No diplomatic immunity."

I half-smiled at the absurdity of it all. "So the Department will deny all knowledge of you? David, for heaven's sake, this sounds like James Bond!"

He shrugged. I looked at him again, trying to picture him in a foreign country, slipping through fetid alleyways and running through darkened buildings, gun in hand and eyes sharp with knowledge. Astonishingly, for a second, I could see it. Then I blinked, and the image was gone.

"Surely you could have told *me*, though?" I asked.

"Yes," he said slowly, "I could have. But by the time I met you, I'd been doing this for five years, and the habit was pretty tough to break. Nobody knew except my brother. And I figured it would be easier on you if you didn't know. Maybe easier on me too."

His twin brother—of course. Daniel was the only person in the world he truly trusted, aside from me. Or maybe the only person, period. I felt a familiar rush of jealousy and guilt when I thought about Daniel, who looked and acted nothing like David but shared an almost mystical bond with my husband that I could never hope for. Daniel had embraced Orthodox Judaism in college and moved to Israel soon after graduation. He lived in a village near Jerusalem with his Israeli-born wife, Rebekah, and their five daughters; the last family picture he'd sent us showed a giant of a man, blond-gray beard trailing down his chest and a gun strapped to his belt, surrounded by five stair-step daughters and his plump dark wife. Of course David had confided in Daniel, and not me.

I stared at him disbelievingly, anger starting to replace my determined calm. "You thought it would be *easier*? To live a lie? To *lie* to me all the time, every day, every night? You thought that would be good for our marriage?"

Our marriage. Long-suppressed tendrils of worry flickered through my brain: the increasing distance between us, the increasingly routine and less frequent sex, the ever-decreasing amount of time that David and I actually spent together. . . . I hadn't wanted to think about it—the very notion that our long-lasting, comfortable family life could be on shaky ground was simply too terrifying to process. My parents' divorce had destroyed my mother and shaken us girls to the core; I would never do that to the twins.

But now I wondered: Was it all based on lies?

He looked away.

"Who's Peter Brooks?" I asked.

"One of my aliases. I use—*used* to use it—a lot. Now it's useless to me," he said, a little bitterly.

"What else have you lied about?"

"Nothing," he said quickly.

Ha. But instead of pressing him again, I busied myself setting out plates for dinner. "So what are you going to tell the kids?"

He looked back at me with a wry half-smile. "I thought you could handle that. You're so much better at that kind of thing than me."

I thought about throwing a plate at his head. "You must be kidding!"

He sighed. "Honestly, Shelley, right now I'm more concerned about picking up the shreds of my career than with what to tell the kids. Hopefully, they'll understand—obviously, I'm not going to trust children with a secret that literally means life or death to a lot of people. I think they'll understand that."

But I wasn't a child. Couldn't I be trusted? The unspoken words hung uneasily between us.

I cleared my throat. "Why did you leak the story to the BBC, then, if you're so worried about your career? You must have known what would happen."

He pressed his lips together. "I thought my role would be kept quiet, and I could handle things within the Agency—I never thought it would break publicly like this." He shook his head. "I can't believe Mia did that to me."

Mia? Oh yes, the BBC correspondent. I pictured her strong, striking features and wavy dark hair, and my lips tightened a little. "She's very pretty. Is she American?"

"Her mother's Spanish," he said absently. "Her father's English."

I started to ask another question, but the front door slammed and Sasha burst in. I braced myself.

Sasha threw her backpack on the floor and flung herself on David, just as I'd longed to do. She looked up at him beseechingly, tears trembling on her long dark eyelashes. "David!" she cried. "It isn't true, is it? Tell me it isn't true!"

David hugged her close, and for a moment I could see his vulnerability as well. But when he spoke, his voice was as calm as ever. "What isn't true, honey? Tell me what you've heard, and I'll tell you what is and isn't true."

Sasha knelt at his feet and looked up into his face. "They say you're a spy," she whispered. "With the CIA. And that you told reporters that the British were working with Hamas, giving them rifles and bombs to use against Israel. And that you tortured people, and killed people, and. . . ." She stopped, unable to go on. All the world was a drama to Sasha; this, a real-life drama, was almost too much.

"Now, Sasha," I said in the firm, no-nonsense tone I used

so often with her. "You know David would never hurt anyone. Grab a snack and start your homework. David will explain everything at dinner tonight when Sam's home—no sense in telling the story twice."

Her face cleared, as I had known it would. Like Sam, she still believed in my magical powers to make her world right again. "So it's not true?" she asked, her voice still trembling.

I didn't want to lie to her, either. "You know how people exaggerate," I said. "Remember when you fell at field hockey practice, and by the time you got to school the next day, your teammates had convinced everyone you were in a coma? Now eat your snack, please, and get to work." Her guidance counselor had warned me that Sasha absolutely had to get her grades up in this crucial fall semester of senior year.

She took a fat-free yogurt out of the refrigerator and started out the kitchen door. "I'll be up in my room."

"Okay," I started to say. But David cut in quickly, "No, Sasha, you'll do your homework at the kitchen table in front of us."

"But—"

"Right here." He pointed at the corner, where her back-pack—with all her schoolwork inside it—sat lonely and discarded. "How were you going to do your homework without that?" he asked quietly.

Sasha pouted. I was even more chagrined; I hadn't noticed the forlorn backpack. Christ, did nothing get by him? And for the first time, it occurred to me that maybe he'd been trained to notice everything.

CHAPTER FOUR

September 11, 2001, 9:03 a.m.

"Goddamn it!" David shouted. "Goddamn those fucking bastards all to hell!" Something crashed into the wall and shattered, and I dropped my toothbrush into the sink and rushed into the bedroom.

"David," I cried. "What's the matter?" He was standing in the middle of the room, still shirtless, glaring at the Blackberry in his hand. His bedside lamp was in a thousand sparkling pieces on the floor.

He glanced up, and for a moment it was as if he didn't even see me. He was seeing something else, and his eyes flickered black with some emotion too powerful to name. Then it was gone, and he drew in a deep, ragged breath.

"Sorry, Shells," he said. "We just lost an account at work, that's all." He dropped the Blackberry into his pocket and shrugged into a shirt. "I have to go out of town; don't know when I'll be back. Sorry," he said again.

I stared at him. David never shouted, never cursed.

"I have to go," he said quickly, before I could react. "Oh, and Shelley? I'm really sorry, but you'll need to stay in the house all day today; I arranged for painters to come in. I know I should have told you earlier, but—"

"Stay in all day! David, it's such short notice, and I really have to be at work. Why didn't you tell me earlier?"

Perfectly in control now, he gave a final tweak to his tie and came over to kiss me good-bye. "I know, I'm an idiot and I owe you big. If I get a better idea of when they'll be here, I'll call you—but otherwise you'll have to stay in all day. Promise me?"

I shrugged and promised. I didn't see him again for almost a month. And the painters never showed up.

I COULDN'T MOTIVATE MYSELF TO COOK DINNER, so I told David to facilitate a pizza delivery from Uber Eats and took refuge upstairs in a very long, very hot shower. I figured it would take him forever to negotiate the complicated food requirements of our family: plain pizza for me, meatball and sausage for Sam, veggies for Sasha, green pepper and onions for himself. So I lingered in our bedroom, dressing with unusual care in the designer jeans that Sasha had insisted I buy after finally losing that last pesky five pounds last spring.

I picked up our wedding photo from the bureau, trying to reassure myself that everything was still the same. My shoulder-length hair was the same deep chestnut, almost auburn (with a little assistance from Marcello at Capelli Salon every six weeks); my eyes brown; my build small and reasonably slim. Funny how everything could look just the same on the outside but feel so different on the inside.

Down in the kitchen, teenage noise reigned. Sasha was on her phone with a friend, while Sam was opining into his phone with increasing volume about the president's decision to send warships into the Persian Gulf. David shouldered open the kitchen door, almost invisible behind the pile of pizza boxes in his arms, and Sam leaped forward to help him—skidding on a furious cat along the way. The cat screeched and spat, Sam grabbed at the counter to steady himself and knocked over Sasha's glass of pomegranate juice instead, and David cursed as the pizza pile tilted ominously.

"You knocked over my juice!" Sasha cried indignantly.

"Stop talking to the other field hockey ditzes and grab the pizzas before David drops them!" Sam ordered his sister.

David groaned and looked at me. "Can't you control them?" he asked pathetically.

"Sit down and eat!" I snapped in the resolute tone that never failed to gain their attention. I never yelled, having learned that my "Mom voice" was much more effective. David wasn't a yeller either, and my friend Rachel often commented wistfully on how calm and civilized our household was, especially considering that we had twins (most of the time, that is).

They sat.

I concentrated on getting the right pizza into the right hands while David poured drinks and handed out napkins, while Sasha—who hated eating with her fingers—set out knives and forks, which no one but her would use. Just a typical dinner in the Harris household.

Or not. Sam took a huge bite of pizza and said, "So what the hell is going on, David? We're all together now; time to 'fess up."

"Don't talk with your mouth full," I said automatically.

"Language," David said at the same time. Our eyes met.

David put down his pizza and looked around the table at his family; I could almost see his mind working. Was he preparing another lie? Was he deciding how much of the truth he could tell?

"I joined the CIA right after college," he began, as he had with me. "I was a deep-cover officer. No one except a few people at the Agency knew my real identity. My cover job at Hanson is a real job; I really do consult with multinational companies. But

I've been doing two jobs, and people would have been in a lot of danger if my cover were broken. Spies who I ran, other officers I worked with . . . their lives literally depended on my cover. So that's why I couldn't tell you guys." He paused, measuring his words. "I would say I'm sorry for not telling you about any of this, but the fact is I'm not. I couldn't have done it any other way. So I'm sorry you feel betrayed, but it's the job I chose and the job I did—and I'm not sorry about that."

There was a silence as everyone digested this. Predictably, Sasha was the first to speak. "Is it dangerous?" she asked.

David shrugged. "Not usually."

"But sometimes?"

He shrugged again and didn't answer. I felt my throat close up momentarily. If someone had "broken his cover" and he'd died a terrifying, lonely death in some hellhole, what would they have told me? Would I ever have known the truth? Would he have become one of those brave, anonymous stars on the wall of the CIA headquarters that I'd seen in movies—one star for every nameless, faceless agent who died undercover?

Sam asked, "What will you do now? I mean, I assume you can't go undercover anymore." He laughed a little. "That sounds so funny; I feel like I'm in a movie. But it's real life, isn't it?"

David smiled. "It's real, all right. Well, I was planning to come back to Langley anyway, and I guess I can tell you now—I was just promoted to Director of Clandestine Operations." His smile faded. "Though now I probably won't be named anything but defendant."

Defendant. The lawyer side of me woke up, and I realized for the first time that he could be in serious legal trouble. I filed that away for a later, teenager-free discussion.

Sasha asked tremulously, "Is it true that you tortured people? K-killed people?"

Sam put in excitedly, "Do you carry a gun?" and Sasha gasped.

David held up a hand. "People, settle! Sasha, of course I never tortured anyone. Good God, I'm still the same man I always was. If I can put up with those horrible cats that Shelley keeps taking in, I can put up with anyone. Besides, I don't need to torture people to get them to tell me the truth—right, Sam?"

Sam looked chagrined, and I guessed he was thinking about his aborted excursion to a strip club in Silver Spring. He'd casually told us that he and some friends planned to go bowling that night, but something had tripped David's internal lie detector alarm, and it only took a few artful questions before the truth came out. He'd probably been trained in that too.

And I wondered if anyone else noticed that David hadn't answered the other questions.

I looked at Sasha, who was toying with her pizza, pushing it around the plate and poking at the cheese on top with her fork. Obediently, she put a small bite in her mouth and started chewing.

Sam swallowed a huge bite of pizza. "You're not even interested in the Mideast," he said accusingly. "You never wanted to talk about world affairs or Israel or anything like that."

David nodded. "Part of my cover. Anyway—" he pushed a clean napkin over to Sam, who took it automatically "—I really don't want to talk about world affairs when I come home. I have enough of that at work, believe me."

Sasha asked, "So when you told us you were in—I don't know, somewhere boring like Chicago—where were you really?"

"Well," David said, "I started my career in Pakistan. Then I had a few other assignments, including a two-year assignment at Langley, which is when I met your mother—Shelley, I mean. Let's see . . . Beirut, Yemen, then Langley again, then Cairo. I was station chief in Riyadh for a few years, but spent a lot of time traveling."

I remembered that period; he had only been home for one weekend every month. He'd told me he was working on a huge multiyear project for General Electric's California division, and he was away so much, I'd asked if we should move to California so we could be together. But he'd said that he worked such long hours, he wouldn't really get to see us even if we were there; and besides, we couldn't leave Sasha and Sam. Better to stay in Washington, where the kids could be settled and secure. It had seemed to make sense at the time.

And by then, I was used to doing without him.

David continued, "Then I had a temporary assignment at Langley—that was your sophomore year in high school—and for the last couple years I've been running operations in the Middle East."

My pizza caught in my throat, and I put it down. "Iraq?" It was the first question I'd asked him in front of the children.

"Iraq, Iran, Qameen . . . other countries. All the Middle Eastern stations report to me."

"Holy shit," said Sam. I couldn't even find the energy to reprove him.

I asked, "Then what were you doing in Moscow?"

"A meeting," David said briefly.

Sasha hadn't said a word. I glanced over at her and saw that her eyes were wide with horror as she watched her uncle. "Sasha? Are you all right?"

She got up and backed away from the table. "I can't believe this," she said, her voice shaking. "I can't believe that David was doing this—these horrible things—the prisoners at Abu Ghraib—these horrible wars—I just can't believe it."

"Oh, for cripes sake," David said impatiently. "I was never

within a hundred kilometers of Abu Ghraib, and I agree that all wars are horrible. You know that. Let's try to curb the melodrama, okay, Sash?"

It was the wrong approach, as I could have told him. Sasha turned and ran from the kitchen, her long hair flying out behind her like a doomed princess in one of those Elizabethan period dramas she loved to watch.

"Well," said David dryly. "That went well."

I was debating going after her when the doorbell began to ring insistently, as if someone was leaning on it.

"What the hell—?" I began; then there was a terrific pounding on our door.

"FBI!" a man's voice shouted. "Open up! Federal agents!"

CHAPTER FIVE

To Do:
Call criminal lawyer

"DAVID!" I CRIED.

He carefully placed his napkin on the table and strolled over to the door, tucking his shirttails into his jeans. "Federal agents," he mused. "Well, well." He flung open the door. "Gentlemen," he drawled. "Do come in."

There were only four of them, but they managed to give the impression of an invading army as they burst into our comfortable home, darting sharp, suspicious glances around the cream-colored living room and treading with heavy black shoes on our delicate Tibetan carpet. They looked almost comically identical, dressed in ill-fitting dark suits that stretched across their wide shoulders with close-cropped hair, tight-jawed faces, and earpieces snaking down under their collars. All had a suspicious bulge in their jackets—guns, I realized, and I was suddenly frightened. I hated guns.

David stood in the middle of the room, his arms stretched wide. "You'd better come and frisk me," he suggested. "I'm a dangerous character."

The youngest of the men actually took an uncertain step forward, but then the grayest man snapped out an order and he backed away.

"Mr. David Harris," the gray man said, "aka Peter Brooks. We'd like you to accompany us to FBI headquarters for questioning."

David stuck his hands in his jeans pockets and smiled genially. "Ask whatever questions you want."

"We'd like you to accompany us to headquarters," the man repeated stiffly, as though he were reading from a script. "Sir," he added.

"Well, I'm busy right now. Special Agent . . . what is your name?"

"Special Agent Harney, sir."

"Harney, go back and tell Brian we can talk tomorrow. At *my* office."

"Sir, I have orders to bring you in right now. We don't want to use force, but we will if we have to."

David just shook his head in disbelief.

I looked at him. My vaguely-recalled criminal law class came into my head, and I knew this wasn't the right way to deal with FBI agents who storm into your house. "David," I said, "You should go with them, but don't answer any questions. I'll call a lawyer."

He didn't even look at me.

"Mr. Harris," the man started again.

David took his hands out of his pockets and flexed them. "Why don't you guys give force a try?"

None of the men moved. And amazingly, shockingly, I realized they were afraid of him. Four armed men versus one unarmed man in bare feet and shirtsleeves—and they were afraid of *him*.

"Mr. Harris, we will bring you in tonight," Harney said. "Whatever it takes."

"Oh, you will not!" David snapped impatiently. "You can't use your guns against an unarmed man in his own home, so stop pretending that you will. And we can have one hell of a brawl here if you want—but get ready to justify a twenty-thousand-dollar bill for damages when we're done."

The FBI agent pressed his lips together.

"Call Brian," David suggested. He held his hands up to show that they were empty, then slowly pulled an iPhone out of his back pocket and held it out to the man. "I have him on speed dial. Press 666."

The youngest man grinned and nudged his partner. "Sign of the devil, right? Who's Brian?"

"Brian Secor," Agent Harney said slowly. "Attorney general." All of a sudden he looked deflated.

David sighed. "You guys are seriously tasked with bringing me in tonight? Who sent you?"

"Sir, I'm not at liberty to—"

"Oh, for God's sake," David said. "You really are trying my patience, Harney. And just when I was starting to feel sorry for you."

"Special Agent Lamberti sent us. Sir."

David grinned. "My old buddy Marty? This evening, gentlemen, marks a new low in the Feebie-Agency rivalry. Well then, by all means, let's go and have a chat with Special Agent Lamebrain." He slapped Harney on the back and started rolling down his shirtsleeves.

"David," I said warningly. The scene had turned from fearful into farce, but I knew he shouldn't answer any of their questions. I was a divorce mediation lawyer, not a criminal lawyer, but I had learned that on my first day of law school.

For the first time, he flicked a glance in my direction. "I'm going down to FBI headquarters," he said, relaxed and debonair in his bare feet and rumpled shirt. "Don't wait up for me."

And they were gone.

I sat down and stood up again, unnerved and wondering at the little scene. Had they really been afraid of him, of my David, unarmed and amused as he was? But then I realized he had been an un-David, superbly connected and superbly capable, and I sat down again. This was ridiculous. It was only David—not some superhero. Only David.

My David.

I went to bed at my usual time, determined to treat this like any other night in the Harris household. The twins, unsurprisingly, had been deeply shaken by the invasion and refused to go to sleep; it took me forever to get them settled down and focused on their homework. Eventually, I managed to doze off, but I woke at dawn, just as delivery trucks and early commuters started to grumble along our street. I lay in our big comfortable bed and pondered the recent events. And then I heard sirens blaring through our open window, and I rushed to look out onto the street. A cavalcade was pulling up in front of the house—DC patrol cars in front, two stretch limousines in the middle, more patrol cars, and police motorcyclists bringing up the rear.

I hung out the window, staring, as the cavalcade came to a stop. A driver hurried to open the door of the first limousine and, inevitably, out stepped David. A tall, gaunt man with silvery hair got out behind him, and as they stood talking on the street, I recognized Brian Secor, the attorney general. He slapped David on the back, they shook hands, and David waved to the accompanying policemen. As he strode into our front hall, I saw that he was still barefoot.

Trying to untangle my emotions, I waited in the living room. "What happened?" I asked when he caught sight of me on the couch. "Did they question you? I hope you didn't answer anything! Was that really Brian Secor?"

He smiled at me, the cavalier facade still in place. "We went down to the Feebies' headquarters, I talked to Brian, everyone apologized profusely, and they sent me home with a parade. Your taxpayer dollars at work."

Then he sighed, and just for a moment I glimpsed weariness and frustration behind the mask. "Christ, I'm tired," he admitted, running a hand through his hair.

Surprising both of us, I put my arm around him and guided him into the bedroom. "Get into bed," I said. "I'm going to bring you a Tylenol PM and you're going to sleep."

"I can't, Shells; I have to be at the office at—"

"Get into bed! The world will just have to survive without you for the next eight hours."

He sighed again and rubbed a hand over his face. "Okay," he said. "Just for a few hours, though. Set the alarm."

He tossed his clothes on the floor and pulled on a pair of boxers and a soft, worn UCLA T-shirt; obediently, he swallowed the pills and water I handed him and climbed into the warm, welcoming bed. "Thanks, sweetheart," he murmured, and then fell fast asleep.

Old habits run deep. I pulled the comforter up around his shoulders and tucked it in around his cold feet. "Sleep well," I whispered. "You lying bastard."

The twins were reassured to learn that David was home safe, so they went to school without the usual protestations and delays. That evening, Sasha fed the cats without being nagged, and David and Sam retreated to the garage to change the oil in

Sam's car. I was left alone in the kitchen, staring at the detritus of dinner. Tinky-Winky the ex-runt jumped onto the table and started browsing among the leftovers; I halfheartedly told him to get down but wasn't really in the mood for an argument. The other cats, less bold, lined up wistfully on the floor and watched him eat a meatball.

I cleaned up the kitchen and retired to what the kids called "Shelley's secret clubhouse" on the second floor, a small sunny room that we had once hoped would be the nursery; eventually I furnished it with a desk, a squashy sofa, and a TV, so I could escape when I needed some time away from the rest of the household. There, I ignored the blinking message light on my phone and tried to read a book.

Later that evening, Sam wandered in and ran a hand through his dark curls.

"Sharona and I had a fight."

This was familiar ground. "Again?" I took a sip of my Relax Riesling, which wasn't living up to its name tonight.

"She wants to go to a party with her friends on Saturday night, and I want to go to a party with the lacrosse team, and she said they were all bros and she hated going to their parties. So we had a fight."

"Oh, dear." I sighed. Sam had met Sharona during the previous spring and he'd fallen hard, for the first time in his life. She was extremely pretty—too pretty, I fretted—small and delicate, with long very black hair and snapping black eyes. I didn't like her for Sam, but I didn't want her to break his heart, either.

"Did you make up?" I asked.

I could almost hear him shrug. "Sort of," he answered. "We agreed that I'll go to my lacrosse party for an hour, then meet her at her party. But I'm co-captain of the team this year; I really should stay with my teammates."

"Yes, you should," I said in a neutral tone. "Maybe Sharona has to learn to compromise a little more."

Instantly his guard went up. "She compromises all the time!" he said indignantly.

Oh God, I'd forgotten Rule Number One of Dealing with the Son's Girlfriend—he can say whatever he wants about her, but I have to be supportive of him without breathing a word of criticism about her. For a moment I was nostalgic for the good old days, when kids refused to speak to anyone over thirty, especially their parents and surrogate parents. Sam, like all the other high school kids I knew, gave us almost daily reports on his life and loves. It was wonderful, I supposed—but now and then I wondered if my life would be less worrisome if I didn't know so *much* about his life.

"You're always so critical of her," he went on defensively. "And she thinks we're terrific. She's planning a mani-pedi day with Sasha next weekend."

"I think Sharona is lovely," I said diplomatically. "And it's really sweet of her to hang out with Sasha. I just want to make sure you're happy, that's all."

"I am happy with her," he insisted. Very strongly.

Okaaaaay. To be continued, I thought, and he slumped his way out of the room as I felt my stomach cramp with anxiety for what I feared would be his first heartbreak.

I had loved—and worried over—Sam and Sasha since they first entered the world. My sister Marisa had suffered from severe postpartum depression after the twins were born. Terrified to be alone with the babies, she brought them to my house as soon as her husband Neil left for work in the morning, and he collected them on his way home at night.

The timing was fortuitous for me—the twins had been born a few months after my sixth miscarriage. Every three months, regular as clockwork, I got pregnant—and just as regularly, lost the baby I was carrying before another three months had passed. I had even taken a leave of absence from my job since I had to be on bed rest for every second of the failed pregnancies. After number six, the obstetrician bluntly told us to stop trying; I would never carry a baby to term. And a week later, David came home early one day and collapsed onto the sofa with an ice pack on his groin. He hadn't even told me he was thinking about a vasectomy—but it was done.

And then my sister fell into a deep depression, leaving me in sole charge of the sweet, precious babies she had produced with such incomprehensible ease. I was only too happy to prolong my leave of absence to mother Sasha and Sam . . . so as soon as she was able, Marisa got her real estate license and went back to work, leaving the babies semipermanently in my care. After a time, we told the adoption agencies we'd contacted to toss our applications; our home was full with the twins. When they entered school, I returned to work part-time, so I could be home with them in the afternoons and evenings; it wasn't surprising that when my brother-in-law's job was transferred to Delaware during their freshman year in high school, the kids elected to stay with me and David rather than move to rural Delaware.

With that kind of childhood, I suppose the twins should have grown up hopelessly confused. Instead, they had defied the odds and emerged remarkably whole—loving their biological mother with a kind of tolerant, amused affection for the charming, mercurial person she was, and loving me as the mother who scolded them, nursed them, chauffeured them, nagged them, fed and clothed them, and listened to them. If I was sometimes boring and annoying compared to their real mother, I was always there. Amazingly, it all seemed to work.

So the house that we'd bought in Northwest DC for our

hoped-for brood of children absorbed the twins just as naturally as we absorbed the abandoned kittens that neighbors kept leaving on my doorstep. David had once told me that it really wasn't necessary to mother the whole world—but he said it with a wry grin and an affectionate arm around my shoulders. I think he was holding at least two cats and one twin in his lap when he said it.

David peered around the doorframe at ten o'clock. "Coming to bed, Shells?"

I didn't look up from the TV. "In a bit. I'm watching a special on life in Iran."

"Well," he said with a smile in his voice, "if you come to bed, I can tell you a lot more about it than CNN will ever know."

"Maybe later," I said, my eyes glued to the screen.

He waited a moment, but when I didn't say anything more he sighed and left.

I let out my breath. I was much too stunned and much too angry to deal with him yet; the most important thing was helping the kids deal with this—my needs could wait.

CHAPTER SIX

To Do:
Buy yogurt (fat-free)
Call vet re: sore on Luna's shoulder
Schedule mammogram
Temple: new prayer books?
Auction raffle meeting
Email class parents re welcome parties
Call Dani back!

I STAYED IN MY CLUBHOUSE MAKING TO-DO lists until almost midnight, when I was sure David would be asleep; then I crept into bed beside him. Only then did I allow myself to relax, listening to his even breathing and taking warmth from the closeness of his strong, solid body against mine. He was away so much that I never allowed myself to think about how much I missed him when he was gone. But the comfort of having him in my bed always helped banish the worries and tensions of even the most tumultuous day.

He stirred against me, sighed, and turned over to face me, his arm automatically sliding under my body to pull me close. I couldn't pull away. "Shells," he murmured, "I never wanted to hurt you. I wanted to protect you."

I stiffened, thinking of all the lies. Years and years of lies. Decades of lies!

He sensed it and lifted his other hand to brush the tangled hair back from my face. "I needed you not to know anything," he whispered. "I needed to live in a sane, normal place where I could pretend to be going to a sane, normal job every morning instead of going to—well, to hell. I needed you not to know."

"I thought you were trying to keep us safe," I said, not yielding to his touch. "Which is it, David?"

"Both. I swear to you, it was both."

He'd sworn lots of things to me; how much of it was lies?

"Are we safe now?"

He stirred uneasily. "Internal Security has a team on the house. We're fine."

"Well, that should be convenient—they can blend in with the journalists." I hated the band of journalists who continued to throng our sidewalk. It wasn't hard to avoid them by just keeping my windows rolled up as I pulled in and out of the garage, but I couldn't miss seeing their greedy faces and hearing their shouted questions: "Will your husband go to jail?" "Shelley, over here!" "Shelley, how much did you know? Are you going to be charged as an accessory?" Even worse, they hounded Sam and Sasha as they raced in and out of the house; I wanted to beat them all with a club.

I turned so I could see his face in the dim room. "Do you carry a gun?"

"Always. When I'm not at home."

"Have you ever shot at someone?"

"Yes."

"Killed someone?"

He paused. "Do you really want to know?"

"I think so," I said uncertainly.

"Yes."

It was impossible. This was just David, my quiet, neutral husband who never yelled at the children or the cats. Who was this un-David, anyway?

My mind racing, I turned over and pressed my hot face into the pillow, signaling an end to our conversation.

It took Sasha two false starts before she finally got on her way to school the next morning—first she couldn't find her car keys, then she forgot her Latin homework and had to race back. Then Sam lost his cleats, and Sasha dropped her yogurt on the floor. By the time everyone was gone, I was ready to banish them all to the innermost rings of hell. So I headed for my friend Rachel's house for a prework coffee.

They'd moved just over the line into Chevy Chase when her husband made enough money to buy a bigger house in a better school system. I dropped my keys onto the kitchen counter and collapsed into one of the hand-painted chairs that we'd found together at the Torpedo Factory in Alexandria.

Rachel put a Diet Coke in front of me and gave me a hug. "So what the hell is going on?"

I told her all that I knew, which wasn't much, I realized. When I was done, she stared at me. "Are you kidding?" she asked. "Are you making this up?"

I shook my head. "I don't have that good an imagination."

"And that's all you know? Didn't you ask him about what exactly he's been doing all these years? How he got away with it? Where he's been?"

"The kids started asking him some, but he was pretty evasive—you know how he can be. Then Sasha got upset, and we stopped talking about it with the kids. And I was too upset to ask him later."

Rachel looked incredulous. "I can't believe you didn't pin him down and make him tell you everything. I would have," she declared.

"I'm still just . . . taking it in, I guess." I bit my lip, thinking. "It's all so bizarre—thinking you're married to Ward Cleaver and then finding out he's James Bond. It's just . . . I just can't believe it."

"I can," Rachel said, surprisingly.

I stared at her.

"I don't mean I ever suspected," she amended quickly. "I just mean that now that I know—well, it does seem possible. David's always been the strong and silent type, hasn't he?"

Maybe. Maybe it *was* possible. Rachel had always had great instincts about people; the first time she met Sam's girlfriend Sharona, she shook her head and lamented, "Why do the nicest boys always fall for the meanest girls?"

I thought about a few clues that I had missed with David over the years.

There was the time that my friend Francie had asked me what kind of business David had at the CIA. I had answered "none," but she told me that her husband had seen David's car turning into the gates of CIA headquarters at Langley the day before. When I asked David about it that night, he gave me a long and detailed account of a client's IT presentation at Langley that he was supposed to critique—something about 4G networks and turbo burners. I fell asleep in the middle of it.

And then there was the time I found foreign currency in his wallet when I was looking for money to tip the deliveryman. "When were you in Singapore?" I had asked David. He had looked at me blankly and said he'd never been to Singapore. "Then why do you have Singapore dollars in your wallet?" He'd laughed and said it was a running gag at work; his colleagues kept slipping foreign money into his wallet, knowing how much he detested foreign travel. I didn't get the joke.

And then, finally, there was the Unknown Caller and the constant travel and the refusal to discuss work or socialize with work colleagues. The ever-present, ever-buzzing Blackberry and iPhone, the dark sunglasses, the refusal to vacation abroad despite my constant pleas.

So I asked her, "What should I do?"

She got up and put her arms around me, and I let my tired head fall onto her shoulder for a moment. "What do you want to do?" she asked.

I picked up my head and looked at her. "Huh?"

"That's all that matters now—what do *you* want to do? You can be mad as all get-out—I would be!—but how do you want this to play out? Do you want to take a break from him? I wouldn't blame you. . . ."

Horrified, I shook my head. My parents' divorce had just about killed me and my sisters; that was why my life's work was mediating divorces so they were amicable and the kids were protected. (At least that was the hope.)

"Well, then," she went on, "Maybe, it's just possible, maybe he really couldn't tell you and the kids—so maybe you want to let him explain and work it out together." She drew away and took a sip of her coffee. "That's marriage," she added, a bit grimly.

Suddenly I needed to change the subject, to bring everything back to more comfortable ground. "So how's Ben doing? You think Ritalin might help?"

Rachel launched into her usual litany of woes about her son's impossible behavior and clueless teachers and insensitive classmates, while I listened with half an ear. This was how our relationship was supposed to work—Rachel worried, and I soothed; she had crises, and I helped her though them. It felt much better that way.

Just as the Ben conversation was winding down, my cellphone dinged with a text, and I glanced at it, expecting one of the kids ("I got a run in my tights!" or "Sharona wants to have lunch with her ex-boyfriend," for example). But it was from Unknown Caller, and my palms suddenly felt clammy.

The text was brief: "Sorry, Shells, but I'm getting on a plane now and will be out of touch for a bit. Bad timing, I know, but urgent business. Please forgive. D."

In silence I showed the text to Rachel, and in silence she read it and handed the phone back to me. I wondered if he would be in danger—a plane for *where?*—my shoulders slumped, and I picked up my pocketbook. "Well," I said. "See you later."

She put her arms around me again and hugged me close. Wordless, close to tears, I eased myself away and went to work.

When I got home that afternoon, I went right back up to my clubhouse and sat down at my desk. The voicemail display was still blinking furiously and my email had forty-eight new messages, but I ignored them all and pulled out a yellow legal pad.

Hindsight Is 20-20: Top Ten Clues

1. *He said that the house and cars and everything else should be in my name, and I should have my own credit cards.*

2. *Our phone is unlisted, and he makes us change the number every year.*

3. *He never wanted to travel abroad for vacations. He says he's hopeless with foreign languages, but once when I did persuade him to take us to Europe and we missed our connection in Paris, he managed to get us on another*

flight that left barely an hour later—in first class, no less! I always wondered how he accomplished that minor miracle without a word of French.

4. *He hates having his picture taken.*

5. *He won't use anything with monograms. I bought him a briefcase once with his initials monogrammed on it, and I don't think he ever used it. I haven't seen it in years.*

6. *Why couldn't he ever get an assignment in Washington? Do all management consultants travel ALL the time?*

7. *He never brings work home. No laptop, files, nothing. Never talks about his work or his colleagues. Says he just likes to relax when he's home. I've never met any of his coworkers.*

8. *Despite being the least vain man in the world, he exercises fiercely and is a champion at the Krav Maga studio in Chevy Chase. When I asked him once why he works out so much, he told me that it could save his life one day. I thought he meant his heart.*

9. *He keeps a gun in the house, even though he's passionately pro gun control. (The twins would die if they knew.)*

10. *Peter Brooks????*

Looking at the list, I thought that hindsight is truly twenty-twenty. Knowing what I knew now, I could see all these trivialities as clues—but at the time, they added up to exactly nothing. And he always had a perfectly reasonable explanation: All women should have their own independent credit history; it takes telemarketers about a year to find your new phone number; his brother Daniel had given him the gun when he was in Israel. . . .

No, I couldn't fault myself for not putting the pieces together. And perhaps I couldn't even fault him if his job, and other people's lives, depended on complete secrecy.

—

But now—as Rachel had said—now it was all too believable. I remembered finding out about the gun. It was the middle of the night, and we were fast asleep when the cats started rustling nervously. We heard the sound of glass breaking and, even more heart-stopping, muffled footsteps downstairs. David was up and out the bedroom door in an instant; he was so quick that I almost thought I had dreamed the dark, gleaming gun in his hand. "Lock yourself and the kids in our bathroom," he snapped over his shoulder. "I'll call the cops."

Shaking so hard I could barely get my limbs to function, I gathered up the confused twins and we huddled in the master bathroom, which had a businesslike security bolt on it that David had installed to keep Sam from playing in our huge tub when he was little. Or so he said.

After what seemed like an eternity, I heard David's voice from outside and I unlocked the door with trembling hands. Sasha rushed into his arms and he hugged her tight. Sam, trying to be manful, cleared his throat. "Everything okay, David?" he inquired, but his voice almost broke on the last word, and David and I exchanged brief smiles. The gun had disappeared.

"Everything's fine," David assured us. "Some kids tried to break in, but we have the attack cats to protect us. Tinky was very brave, Sasha."

I looked around. "Where are the police?"

"I'll go by in the morning and fill out a report," David said. "Nothing they can do now."

When I asked David about the gun after the kids were back in bed, he admitted that he did feel safer in Washington, DC, with a gun. Yes, he knew all the statistics and he believed in gun control, but he still felt better with the gun, and yes, he had a permit and kept it safely locked up. The next morning a team of tight-jawed, slightly scary-looking men arrived from a security company downtown—or so he said—and a new alarm system was installed, along with dead bolts on all the doors and bars on the basement windows. Ever since then I worried about us accidentally setting off the damned alarm and locking ourselves out of the house, but not about unwanted burglars getting in.

Now I stared out the window onto our sun-dappled lawn and the ever-present throng of reporters beyond, and pondered. If the gun was so safely locked up, how did it get into his hand so quickly? Had he really called the cops? Were those security guys CIA? And most important, was it really just a petty burglary, or did he think it was someone from his other life—the un-David's life—going after him at home?

CHAPTER SEVEN

To Do:
Dani: birthday present
Sasha—homework tutor?
Call vet re: Morton (psoriasis???)
Schedule mammogram
Barnes & Noble: return Middlesex
Raffle items!
Call CIA???

IT WAS HARD TO FOCUS ON WORK the next day, especially since I really hated this case. Mr. and Mrs. Farrell were a hardworking, careworn couple who didn't have the money for divorce lawyers so had agreed on mediation—probably the one and only thing they'd agreed on in the past two decades.

What I really hated, though, was the fact that they had fourteen-year-old twins, a boy and a girl—the same age that I was when my family fell apart, and just a few years younger than the twins that I shared with my sister.

I *really* hated this case.

I was pretty sure of my decision, which would make everyone hate me—the fate of the mediator—but I wanted to hear from the teenagers themselves before I delivered my finding. The father and I waited in silence; then the door opened, and Mrs. Farrell walked in with the twins. The boy hung back, but the girl ran straight to her father and threw herself into his arms. She sobbed, "Daddy," and heavy tears ran down his gray face; he looked, in that moment, twenty years older than his real age. My heart tightened.

But I said, briskly, "Minnie, please sit down."

"I haven't seen her in two weeks!" Mr. Farrell protested.

"I understand. I'm here to help all of you work this out. Now let's all sit down."

I nodded at the steno occupying her quiet corner and she nodded back, flexing her fingers over the keys of her machine.

"Let's get started," I said.

As I had expected—and feared—the boy wanted to live with his mother, and the girl wanted to live with her father. The twins sobbed in each other's arms and I watched, seeing the closeness that twins so often share.

Feeling nauseous, I made the Solomonic judgment that the teenagers' guardian ad litem (who was appointed by a judge to protect the children's interests) and I had already agreed upon: The twins could not be separated. So I gave the parents joint custody, one week with one parent and the next week with the other—and the sad ex-family left in furious silence. At least now all their fury was concentrated on me—better than on each other, I thought.

The steno and I, veterans of these small wars, nodded at each other again and fled the scene.

Tomorrow would be another broken family, another battlefield.

Why had I ever thought that divorce mediation would be a helping profession? Sometimes, the job was like a rasp on my soul.

—

The next morning, I woke up with a new sense of mission. Desperate for information and frustratingly unable to interrogate my Unknown Caller (who had not called or texted since leaving on his "urgent business"), I sat down and Googled Central Intelligence Agency. Who knew there was an Office of Public Affairs! Without giving myself time to think, I dialed the phone number and took a deep breath.

Mary Ann could not have been more pleasant. Once I had navigated my way through phone menu hell and spoken to a real person, Mary Ann took my call immediately, and we arranged to meet that afternoon. I had visions of a safe house deep in the bowels of a naval base, or at least a hidden cottage in West Virginia—but she suggested the Starbucks on Connecticut Avenue. It was disappointing.

And I was even more surprised when I walked into the Starbucks and saw two frumpy-looking, thoroughly nondescript middle-aged women sitting together at a corner table. One of them waved to me and I asked dubiously, "Mary Ann?"

"Mrs. Harris, it's a pleasure to meet you. I'm Mary Ann and this is Dr. Lillian, a staff psychologist. She works with a number of our families."

A psychologist. Our families. I digested that.

"Please sit down," said Dr. Lillian. I wondered if that was her first name or her last name. Or her name at all.

I sat.

Mary Ann offered me a scone and a latte, but I shook my head; food would only stick in my dry mouth. Both women were fortyish and plumpish, with graying hair and grayer pantsuits. Mary Ann's eyes were a lovely gray-blue, and she looked like she smiled a lot. Both were eminently forgettable; I doubted that I could pick either one out of a lineup.

Dr. Lillian said sympathetically, "This must all be a great shock to you, Mrs. Harris. Or may I call you Shelley?"

I resented her patronizing sympathy and wanted to cling to my married title. But, "Shelley is fine," I said. The habits of politeness die hard.

"How did you feel when you learned about your husband's work?" she asked.

Was she kidding? How did I *feel*? I thought of TV "reporters" shoving microphones into the faces of shocked refugees and asking how they felt when their houses burned down. How did she think I felt?

Instead of answering, I asked my own question. "Is my family safe?"

"We have an Internal Security team on your home."

"What about when we're not at home?"

"We don't believe there's any danger to you," she said.

"What about my . . . my niece and nephew? And my husband?"

"Please don't worry," urged Dr. Lillian. "You can trust us to take care of our own."

Trust them! Why, the woman had a sense of humor after all.

"Why couldn't he tell me the truth?" I asked. "Does the CIA order its agents to lie to their own families?"

The two women exchanged glances. Mary Ann said, "It's true, we used to strongly warn our officers against confiding in their spouses. But we found that that resulted in a very high divorce rate—"

No shit, I thought.

"—So we changed that policy and now encourage officers to read in their spouses."

"When did you change that policy?"

Dr. Lillian said, "About ten years ago. But some long-time

officers, like your husband, found it difficult to change their modus operandi, so to speak. It's quite understandable."

Maybe to her. I was still trying very hard to understand.

Mary Ann leaned forward. "Mrs. Harris, your husband has had a highly distinguished career with the Agency. More than highly distinguished—extraordinary. He is one of our most decorated officers in history."

"Really? What has he won awards for?"

Another exchange of glances.

"Unfortunately, those operations are classified. We can't reveal anything about them."

"And where are the awards?"

"Locked in a safe at Langley."

"Well, that's helpful," I said, surprised that I'd actually spoken the words out loud. I couldn't remember the last time I had been rude to anyone. Perhaps I was morphing into the un-Shelley too.

The psychologist said gently, "Of course you must have a lot of questions and feelings about this, Shelley. We're here to help you in any way that we can."

"Then can you tell me where my husband is right now?"

"Uh . . . no," said Mary Ann.

"Is he in danger?"

"I really couldn't say."

"Then what can you say? What's the point of this meeting, anyway?" I exploded. I hated these women, and everything that they stood for; I hated that they knew secrets about my husband that I couldn't even comprehend, and I hated their patronizing sympathy.

Dr. Lillian said encouragingly, "Our officers are highly trained, Shelley, and your husband is one of the most—"

"I don't care if he's double-oh-seven on steroids! I just want to know what continent he's on! Is that too much to ask?"

"I'm afraid so," said Mary Ann. "But he is a truly superb officer; you should be proud—"

I got up and walked out.

Shellshocked by the useless meeting, I sleepwalked through the next few days. Unknown Caller texted once: "Don't worry, all fine. Sorry but business still urgent."

"A matter of life and death?" I texted back, sarcastically.

"Yes," replied my no-drama husband.

CHAPTER EIGHT

THE NEXT DAY I HAD ANOTHER MEETING, one that would have no need of my mediating skills. For Rachel's fortieth birthday, our book group had decided to surprise her with a special treat. Instead of discussing the eight-hundred-page *Middlesex*, which poor Rachel had labored through while the rest of us giggled among ourselves, we'd hired a "sexpert" to come and talk to us about how to keep our marriages hot. Considering the state of my marriage at the moment, I wasn't too sure I wanted to take part—the very last thing I wanted to do was dwell on its sorry state—but we had planned the evening months ago, and I couldn't chicken out now.

"I can't believe you made me read that horrible book!" Rachel screeched. "Eight hundred pages! Eight hundred miserable, lousy pages while you all were studying up on your *Kama Sutra*! How could you?"

Even I was laughing. The "sexpert," a surprisingly ordinary-looking thirtysomething woman with a feathery blond bob and blue eyes, looked amused. "You can discuss *Middlesex* if you'd rather," she suggested.

Rachel shuddered. "God forbid. Anyway—" she had the grace to look ashamed—"I gave up after five hundred pages. I read the online Spark notes for the rest."

Petra, our sexpert, smiled. "Good for you. Well, ladies, we're going to start with a questionnaire. There are ten of you, so we won't have any trouble maintaining anonymity. Take your time and answer all the questions as fully as possible, then hand them back to me and I'll give suggestions based on the results. Any questions? Good."

Oh, boy. I took the innocent-looking sheaf of papers she handed me and held them carefully, as if I were handling a bomb. But really, there was nothing to worry about. Until the recent revelation, David and I had a great sex life. Well, good, anyway. Passable. I looked uneasily at the questionnaire.

How often do you have sex? Well, that was easy. Confidently, I wrote "once a week" in the space provided. More or less. When he was in town, anyway.

How many orgasms do you have during sex? I blinked at the piece of paper. How *many*? Was she serious? I wondered if fake orgasms counted. "One," I wrote, a little less confidently. Sometimes. Occasionally.

Do you ever fantasize during sex? Yes, I fantasize that he'll be done in time for Stephen Colbert. "No," I wrote.

Do you buy fancy lingerie for you and your husband to enjoy together? Uneasily, I shifted in my seat, glad that Petra couldn't see under my jeans and sweater to the three-for-ten-dollars cotton panties I wore. Maybe my bra was black. Did that count? "No," I wrote.

Do you and your husband engage in oral sex?

Rachel, sitting next to me on the couch, was scribbling furiously on her questionnaire—how could she have so much to say? I tried to peek at her answers, but she covered her paper, glaring at me, and I returned to my own questionnaire.

"No," I wrote again. When we were first dating, I told David that Jewish girls didn't give blow jobs, and he shrugged. The subject had never come up again.

Do you always have sex in the same position? How many alternatives could there be? Suddenly I flashed back to those early years when we were trying so desperately to make a baby that would "stick," as my obstetrician once put it. I'd read online that the pregnancy would be stronger if I lay on my back for half an hour after sex with my legs up in the air, so David dutifully propped me up on pillows afterward while he lay beside me and watched the news. It didn't stick. And at some point, sex and miscarriage became inextricably linked in my mind. Then, of course, there were the twins, who didn't sleep through the night until they went to kindergarten, especially Sasha, who liked to sleep between us in our big bed. "Yes," I wrote down. We always have sex in the same position.

Do you ever fake orgasm? I bit my lip and looked around. "Yes," I wrote in my smallest, neatest handwriting. Didn't everyone?

Where is the most unusual place you're ever had sex? Umm . . . our bed? I left that one blank.

What do you and your husband talk about when you're alone? "The children," I wrote. And . . . uh . . . I put the pen down, thinking. What *did* we talk about? And when were we ever alone? Sam's unfortunate infatuation with Sharona, what college would be gullible enough to accept Sasha, my sister Dani's latest boyfriend. I sighed. Surely we talked about other things. I just couldn't think of them right now. Thank God, only one more question to go.

Do you still find your husband sexy? I drew a deep breath and closed my eyes for a moment, letting myself feel instead of think. Did I still find David attractive? I thought about the dark blond hair on his chest that sometimes curled up under the collar on his shirt, and about his broad shoulders and strong, muscled forearms. Astonishingly, I felt a rush of desire so powerful that I hastily opened my eyes, afraid that someone would read it on my face. I picked up the pen once more. "Yes," I wrote quickly. Then before I could think any more, I folded up the paper and handed it to Petra.

The first questionnaire she read was Rachel's; even though they were supposed to be anonymous, I recognized her large loopy handwriting halfway across the room. Petra looked up and smiled after she scanned through Rachel's responses. "Well, this marriage is highly sexualized. This couple has sex three or four times a week, and she has at least two orgasms when they make love. Congratulations!"

Startled, I couldn't help a sideways glance at Rachel. She must have exaggerated to spice things up a bit. But her face was becomingly flushed and her eyes were sparkling, and suddenly I wasn't so sure.

"She likes to wear lacy lingerie when they're alone," Petra went on approvingly, "and oral sex is a big part of their sexual repertoire."

This time I glared at Rachel. She didn't give blow jobs, either—I was sure of it. Or almost sure, anyway. It wasn't something we'd ever talked about. Petra went on, making some suggestions for Couple A (sex in the shower, surprising him with a "dirty weekend" away); by now Rachel was nodding happily, clearly having forgotten that we weren't supposed to know who Couple A was. Petra tossed a handful of chocolate candy kisses to the room and moved on to the next questionnaire.

By the time she got to mine, I was praying that it had gotten lost. Either my friends were the biggest liars since Donald Trump or everyone else was having much more—and much better!—sex than me. Couple G once had sex in her in-laws' kitchen while Mom- and Dad-in-law were hosting a dinner party in the dining room. Couple D used strawberry-flavored lube, and Couple F claimed to have done it in an airplane. I squirmed uneasily in my seat, willing the evening to come to an end.

"And finally," Petra announced, "we have Couple J, our last couple. I saved Couple J for last because they may have slipped into a bit of a rut. They seem to have routine sex—I don't feel much excitement or pleasure here—and yet Wife J still appears to be attracted to her husband. Any suggestions, ladies?"

My friends were full of helpful ideas. A trip to Victoria's Secret. A romantic weekend away, without any kids. Dance classes. Watching a sexy movie together. I suggested a couples massage myself, so that no one would realize I was the poor, pathetic Wife J. This is so lame, I thought, waiting impatiently to be released from my seat.

And yet, even after my escape, I was uneasy. I lay awake into the early hours, thinking about—and trying not to think about—David, and me, and our life together. Could it really be this arid? How had this happened to us?

CHAPTER NINE

Remarkably, the rest of the week passed without any more drama. I still couldn't wrap my mind around the fact that my best friend Rachel—whose husband was a tax attorney!—was having much better sex than me and my James Bond. We had dull, routine, occasional sex, while Rachel and Mark were swinging from the chandeliers. I told myself that I was just upset because it was so embarrassing; how would I ever look Mark in the face again?

But I knew it was more than that; the questionnaire and the sexpert had forced me to face something I had shoved below the surface for too long. I remembered someone once saying that all marriages have peaks and valleys; sometimes everything he does irritates you, and sometimes you shiver with pleasure at the slightest brush of his hand. Well, we were in a very deep valley right now—and it seemed we'd been there for quite a while, even before the news of his secret life.

Was my marriage in trouble? Or just in a rut?

The possibilities were too frightening to consider. I had never heard from my father again after he left, and my mother had disappeared almost as completely into her despair. I had been four years younger than Sasha when my parents left me.

But in a way, hadn't David already left us? His lies and his deceptions, his other life, his long absences—wasn't that a form of desertion? And what if he went to jail over this?

It was too frightening to consider.

Rachel forced the issue on Saturday morning, when we met for coffee while our kids were either sleeping in (Sasha and Sam) or at soccer (her Ben and Madeleine). "I knew that was you," she said without preamble, wiping lemon cake crumbs from her mouth.

"Who?"

"You know. Couple J. I knew that was you."

"Well, I knew the first couple was you! But you and Mark—really? He's a tax attorney, for heaven's sake!"

For all our closeness, Rachel and I had never discussed our sex lives with our husbands; it was a secret, private part of our lives and a place where we never ventured.

Now she blushed, like a schoolgirl with a crush on the math teacher. "Tax attorneys have sex too," she said.

"Apparently that's quite an understatement," I said dryly.

She grinned.

I had to ask. "Were you exaggerating? Or is . . . all that . . . really true?" They'd been married even longer than me and David; I willed her to admit that she'd been engaging in some wishful thinking. With all my heart, I willed it.

But she said, indignantly, "Of course it's true."

I couldn't help myself. "But . . . how?"

She understood what I was asking. "Maybe it's because I slept around so much in college—I got used to lots of good sex. Really good sex. And Mark . . . well, no matter how annoying he can be, with Ben and everything . . . in bed, I always want him."

"How?" I asked again, thinking of her husband Mark with his receding hairline and expanding waistline.

She shrugged, but a small smile was playing around her mouth. "I don't know why or how, Shelley. I just do."

I sat back and toyed with my napkin, shredding it into tiny flakes that littered the table like small teardrops. "I don't," I said finally. "And David doesn't, either."

Rachel wasn't surprised; I wondered if she had sensed something even before the sexpert session. She was so damn good at reading people. "I know lots of mothers who are too exhausted after a long day with the kids to want sex," she commented. "But I've never heard of a husband who didn't want more, and hotter, sex."

I shrugged. Who knew what David wanted? He kept himself to himself; mostly, I liked it that way. I didn't need another needy person in my life.

"But you used to," she went on. "Didn't you go to bed with him on your first date?"

"It wasn't even a date. . . ."

September 1998

I can't believe I slept with him. How could I have done that? Not even our third date—our first! And not even a date: one minute we were being introduced in the synagogue playroom, and by dinnertime I was naked in his bed. Me! It was incomprehensible.

Still . . . I stared at the blank computer screen on my desk, uncomfortably aware that a silly smile was creeping over my face. He was so calm, and self-possessed, and he seemed so dependable . . . reliable . . . grown-up. Nothing like the guys I usually met. Nothing like my father. And those broad shoulders and dark blue eyes . . . I lost myself in a daze of remembered pleasure, until the beeping of my "you've got mail" icon jerked me back to reality. From david@hansen consulting.org, it read. Subject line: About last night . . .

I cleared my throat. "Anyway," I said. "It hasn't been like that for a while."

"And you think that's because . . . ?"

"I don't know! All the miscarriages, and then suddenly the twins—and they were such terrible sleepers. . . ."

"But that was years ago," Rachel pointed out.

"And he's never *here*! He's always somewhere, on 'urgent business.'" My tone was bitter, but I didn't care.

"And even when he's here. . . ?" Rachel probed.

"He's still not here! We're like independent operators; he goes to work, and I go to my work, and my meetings, and when he's home we're dealing with the kids, and then he's gone again."

"I'm sorry," said my best friend. "I didn't know things were so bad."

Neither did I.

As soon as I got home, I called Mary Ann. "I need to speak to my husband," I said,

"I'm sorry, I—"

"I know, you can't tell me where he is. But you can get a message to him. Tell him he needs to call me. It's urgent business."

Take that, I thought!

"Well, I can try, but—"

I hung up.

So I was primed and prepared when Unknown Caller called just before ten that night. "Are the kids all right?" he asked quickly.

I should have felt guilty for alarming him—of course he would think of the kids first—but I didn't. Maybe I was going through the stages of grief; denial was gone, and all I felt was anger. "They're fine," I said coldly. "Aside from wondering where their uncle is, and if he's safe, and what he's doing."

"Then what's your 'urgent business?'"

"What's yours?" I retorted childishly, and he laughed. Even I had to smile, and for just a moment I felt the warmth again.

Then it faded, and I said, "According to my new friend Mary Ann, CIA officers are encouraged to tell their spouses what they do."

He waited. Finally he said, politely, "Is that a question?"

In that moment, I almost hated him. "Why didn't you tell me?" I snapped.

"In the late 1990s when we first met, officers—especially nonofficial cover officers—were *not* encouraged to tell their families. In fact, we were strongly warned against it."

"But later?"

"Yes, later the policy changed. But by then—I told you this already!—it was a habit, and I saw no reason to rock the boat."

Rock the boat! Why, that self-righteous bastard!

He interpreted my silence correctly and added, "Also, my work is especially . . . delicate. I have some assets in grave danger now and—"

"What's an asset?" I interrupted.

"Oh. An asset is a foreign national who cooperates with me. Gives me information, at great risk to himself and his family."

"Where?"

"Where what?"

"Where are these 'assets?'"

He hesitated. I waited. "The Kingdom of Qameen," he said finally. "Mostly Qameen these days."

Qameen! I shuddered. Racked by an obscenely bloody civil war for almost three years now, Qameen had become one of the worst places on earth. Over a hundred thousand people had fled the fighting, only to find themselves in refugee purgatory—hellish camps and detention centers. Nobody wanted them, and nobody knew how to stop the atrocities.

"What on earth do you do in Qameen?"

"Shelley, I really can't—"

"David, I'm not going to run to CNN with breaking news. Don't you trust me?" And that, I realized, was the crux of the matter.

He must have realized it too, for he muttered something indistinguishable under his breath. "I'm not in the habit of trusting anyone," he said.

"And that may be the truest thing you've ever said to me," I replied, feeling unexpected tears well up in my eyes.

There was a brief silence. Then he said, "I also operate in Iran."

"Iran?"

"That's where some of my assets are too."

Suddenly I wanted to end the conversation. David had never really trusted me, and he had this whole other life—a life with "assets," and danger, and knowledge of places like Qameen and Iran that I only knew as foreign, hostile images on the news. Where did that leave me? And our marriage? Rachel had said to "work it out," but what did that mean?

I said abruptly, "I have work to do."

"Good," said David. "So do I." And we hung up, going our separate ways.

The twins kept their own counsel. I shooed them out the door to school a few days later and sank down at the kitchen table for my morning Diet Coke, realizing that it was exactly a week since the bombshell hit.

I switched on the TV and settled back, my eyes noting the

remains of Sasha's whole-wheat English muffin. It was like an instant replay of the previous week: everything exactly the same, except that nothing was the same. I looked back at the TV, and there was my husband's face *again*. Except that this time he was with a woman—and this time the headline read, "Superspy Harris Romantically Linked to BBC Correspondent."

Oh. My. God.

CHAPTER TEN

THIS TIME NO ONE CALLED ME, not my sisters, not even Rachel. Everyone knew this was really bad, and they were mercifully leaving me alone. The news stories were very thin, a collection of rumors and nuance, but according to the usual "unnamed sources," my husband David (aka Peter Brooks) and the BBC reporter, Mia Holloway, had a "very close personal relationship" while she was covering the refugees in Qameen and he was traveling in the Mideast on CIA business.

Over and over, CNN showed two photographs of David with a tall dark-haired woman. In the first, he was wearing crumpled chinos and a light polo shirt; the blond hairs on his forearms glinted in the sunlight of a hot Middle Eastern day. He was half-turned away from the camera, listening to the woman—but his stance, his frame, his strong shoulders—it was all David. In the second, the camera had caught him in the act of turning away; his face was indistinct, but his arm was around the woman and her dark head rested on his shoulder. It was obviously a candid shot; they were so absorbed in each other that a dozen paparazzi could have flashed bulbs in their faces, and they would have been oblivious. "Harris and Holloway in Beirut," the CNN banner read.

Unknown Caller called just before noon. I picked up the phone, my palms moist and my heart beating fast. "David?" I said.

"Shelley. We have to talk."

"Yes." My voice was perfectly steady.

"I'm sorry. I'm really sorry. But I'm out of town right now, and I can't get home until—"

"Where are you?" I interrupted.

He paused. "I can't tell you that."

"Well, are you in the United States?"

Another pause. "No," he said finally.

I licked my dry lips. "When will you be home?"

"Friday."

I hung up the phone.

When the kids got home, I was perfectly calm and composed. "I talked to David," I told them. "You know how the press loves to go wild on this kind of thing. There's absolutely nothing to it."

Sasha looked at me worriedly, but I could see that she simply couldn't imagine her beloved uncle doing such a thing. "Are you sure?"

I laughed. "Of course I'm sure! Would I be standing here making dinner and arguing with the cats if I were worried? Now, eat this cheese before Tinky does, and get ready for field hockey practice."

"Okay," she said a little dubiously. But she wanted to be reassured so badly that I thought I had convinced her.

Sam was a little more difficult. "Why isn't David at home?" he demanded that night. "I want to talk to him. Where the hell is he, anyway? Shouldn't he be home at a time like this?"

Yes, he certainly should, I thought. But I couldn't say that to our beloved Sam. "He'll be home as soon as he can," I said instead. "He's out of town on business; I told you that. He'll be home this weekend."

He stomped off, and I felt sick.

But I had gotten very good at pushing my own needs away so that I could concentrate on everyone else's, and right now I was very glad for those skills. I hadn't thought about David once since hanging up on him this morning, and I didn't intend to think about him again for a very, very long time. Maybe never. So I was perfectly calm . . . practically comatose.

That afternoon I took the new kitten, which I had decided to name Albatross, to the vet. Albie had joined our family a few weeks before, when a woman from the next street over had knocked on my door and practically thrust the filthy, shivering bundle into my arms. "I found him lying in the yard under the weeping willow and we can't keep him, my husband's allergic," she babbled nervously. "But I just can't let him die, so naturally I thought of you."

Naturally. Why didn't I just put up a sign: all abandoned cats, find hope here? After just two weeks, Albie had reverted to the natural arrogance and ingratitude of his species; obviously considering himself to the manor born, he expected to ride around all day on my right shoulder, which infuriated Luna, the dainty Siamese who believed that shoulder to be *her* personal property. The vet, who knew me embarrassingly well, burst out laughing when we proceeded into her office at the stately gait that Albie preferred.

"Shelley, I think the ASPCA lights candles in your honor every year! How many does this make, six?"

"No, five; Tabby died last year."

"Oh, right—I think he was the longest-living cat I ever treated."

"All of my cats are long-living," I said, a little grimly. I set

Albie down on the table, and the vet bent down for a closer look.

"Well, aren't you a handsome one," she cooed.

I smiled proudly. "Look at his paws. He's going to be a big guy, aren't you, little one?"

As Dr. Reiner opened his mouth to examine his teeth, she asked me, "How are you holding up? I keep seeing your husband on the news."

I shrugged. "It's all nonsense. You just have to ignore fifty percent of what you hear."

She smiled, clearly not believing me for a second. "Of course." She deftly inserted the syringe into the skin on his neck, so quickly that he didn't even flinch, and ran skilled fingers along his belly and down his legs. Then she tried to hand the kitten back to me, but he escaped and scampered up to my shoulder, snagging his claws in my new cashmere sweater as he ran.

"Sorry," she said.

I shrugged again, obediently reaching up to steady the kitten and stroke his back. "So you'll come to the house next month to give the others their shots, right?" I asked as I slung my bag over my other shoulder. "Tinky refuses to get in the cat carrier, which incites the others."

She laughed as she held the door open. "In my next life, I want to come back as one of your cats."

So did I. In fact, I wanted to come back as anything other than David's wife.

On Friday night David came home, striding comfortably into the kitchen as if he'd never been gone. He weaved his way around Albie, Luna, and Tinky with the ease of long practice and dropped a bag on the table. "Picked up Chinese for dinner," he said.

I wondered if he thought that would make me melt a little. "I don't feel like Chinese," I said coldly. "I'll just make a salad."

"Okay."

Sasha and Sam came thundering into the kitchen and began throwing questions at David, their words running over each other in their haste. "David, who is that woman they showed you with on TV?" "David, what the *hell* is going on?" "My friends all said you and that woman were—" "Did they Photoshop you into that picture?"

"Let's all—" I began, when the phone rang.

Sasha leapt to answer it and handed it to me after a moment, her face puzzled. "I can't understand what they're saying."

I took the phone. "Hello?"

The line crackled with static. "Hello?" I said again.

A woman's voice came through, breathless, sobbing, and high-pitched with emotion. "Is this Peter's house? Please, I have to talk to Peter!"

CHAPTER ELEVEN

WORDLESSLY, I HELD THE PHONE OUT to my husband.

He put the phone to his ear, frowning. "Hello? Sorry, I can't understand you—hello?" Then his voice changed. "Mia. Honey, calm down, I can't help you if I can't hear—uh-huh. Okay. Wait a minute, I have to get to my computer."

Mia. Honey. Something in me shriveled and died.

He got up and strode out of the kitchen, the phone still pressed to his ear. Sasha and I watched him, our faces frozen. Then I pushed my chair back from the table and followed David.

He was in his small office, scowling at the screen of his laptop and listening intently to the phone. Even from across the room, I could hear the woman's quick, frantic voice and I could see the effort he was making to will her into calm. "Mia," he said again. "Listen to me, honey. I can't help you if you're hysterical. Can you answer questions? Are they in the room with you now?"

He glanced up and saw me standing in the doorway, watching him. Something crossed his face that I couldn't identify—guilt, sorrow, annoyance?—and then his expression was under control once more. He turned his attention back to the laptop.

"Okay, I've got a reading on it now," he said into the phone. "Mia? Can you still hear me? Mia?"

But the connection was apparently dead. He cursed savagely

and threw the phone to the floor—David, who never lost his temper, never threw things, never lost his cool control—and reached into his desk drawer for a clumsy-looking black telephone that I'd never seen before. He plugged it into a wire in the drawer of his desk, not looking at me, and pressed some buttons. I walked away.

I was staring sightlessly at the pages of my book in bed when he came upstairs well after midnight. I had tried to make our bedroom into a cozy, warm nest for just us—the private world of David and Shelley—with the deepest down comforter and pillows I could find. Colorful rugs brightened up the wide oak floorboards, and rich green curtains across the big windows kept the darkness outside at bay.

But it wasn't working tonight. I had heard his voice downstairs barking out questions and orders over the strange-looking phone, and his footsteps pacing the floor as he spoke. Twice the house phone rang, and each time he picked it up instantly. Once I heard him fling something against the wall in frustration.

He was still angry when he strode into the bedroom. In silence he stripped off his suit jacket and pants, tossing them into a heap on the bathroom floor; he went into the closet and came out again in worn jeans and a UCLA T-shirt that he usually used for sleeping. He dragged his battered leather carry-on from the laundry room and began throwing clothes into it.

Finally I said, "David? Are you going to talk to me?"

He turned his head, seemingly noticing for the first time that I was in the room. "Sorry," he said automatically. "I have to catch a flight at oh-three-hundred hours from Andrews Air Force Base. If I miss that one, I'll have to fly commercial, and that would be a problem."

Well, that certainly explained nothing. *Mia. Honey.* I hated him.

—

He shoved aside a pile of shoes and athletic gear on his side of the huge walk-in closet and leaned in to press his fingertip to a patch of wall. Silently, a safe door slid open.

David drew a shoulder holster and a small mean-looking gun out of the safe, shrugged into the shoulder holster, shoved the gun into it, and pulled on a well-worn gray flannel shirt. Then he picked up a stack of passports—different colors, different countries, I realized—and selected one. He tossed the others back into the safe and slipped the chosen one into his hip pocket. He was ready.

And for one stark moment, standing there in the middle of our warm, cozy bedroom, he didn't look like my David at all, but a stranger—a dark, dangerous professional who looked at me through cold eyes I couldn't even recognize. A man who called another woman "honey."

I pulled the warm comforter around my shoulders in a vain attempt to stop my shivering. "Where the hell are you going?" I hissed at him, suddenly angry beyond control. "Are you off to play superspy again, leaving the wife and kiddies behind?"

He turned on me, his eyes blazing. "Do you think this is all a game?"

"I don't know *what* to think, since you don't tell me a damn thing!" I shot back. "You get a mysterious phone call from your hysterical girlfriend, then you come up here and pack up to leave again. I'm sorry your boring family doesn't provide enough excitement for you, but—"

"Shut up!" he shouted at me. "Just shut up! You don't know what the fuck you're talking about, so—"

"How *can* I know what I'm talking about?" I blazed back at him. My whole body was shaking uncontrollably and tears were streaming down my face. Never had David spoken to me that way; never would I have thought he could. It felt like a physical assault. "Everything I know about you, I learned from CNN! Now you're off on some mysterious mission with your girlfriend, and what am I *supposed* to think? What do you want from me?"

"She's not my girlfriend!" he shouted. "She—"

There came a timid knock on our door.

"What!" we both shouted.

Sasha poked a frightened, pale face in the door. "Mom, David, I heard you yelling at each other—"

"Go back to bed!" I snapped. I was incapable of being kind to anyone at the moment.

Sasha stared at me. "What? Is everything—"

"Everything is fine," David said curtly. "Go back to bed and close the door."

Sasha's lower lip trembled, but she obediently backed out of the room. David and I looked at each other, silent and spent.

"You were pretty close," he said quietly. "Mia's in trouble. She went to interview the leader of a drug gang in Colombia— or resistance fighter, depending on your point of view—and they decided to take her hostage. The damned idiot," he added dispassionately.

I asked just as quietly, "And you have to go rescue her? You don't even speak Spanish." I paused. "Do you?"

He shrugged. "Not really. I had one temporary assignment in Mexico right after training, before I met you. So I know some very basic Spanish—where's the bathroom, drop the gun, that kind of thing."

Yes, that would be everyone's definition of basic Spanish. "So why you?" I asked.

He sighed. "It's not an official mission, so I can't ask anybody else to take it on. And I'm not going to be doing a Rambo-style rescue, despite the weaponry. I'll be negotiating with the little pricks, waving thick wads of cash in their faces until they hand her over. Hostage-taking is a very lucrative profession."

Then why the gun? Suddenly too exhausted for words, I said, "Fine. Go."

He studied me, and I dropped my eyes, recognizing that underlying his cold mask was a thick layer of strong emotion. Anxiety? Fear? Love? Anger? I just couldn't tell.

And he wouldn't tell me, either. He stood there for a moment, uncharacteristically indecisive, and then pressed his lips together and straightened up. He picked up the worn leather case, tossed a jacket over his shoulders, and then stopped again at the door, his hand on the handle. For the first time in our lives, he asked me, "Will you be okay?"

"No," I said.

His face went blank; then he lifted the door handle and left me alone in the big bedroom.

CHAPTER TWELVE

To Do:
Raffle: free cruise??
Remind Sasha re picture day
Mediate picture frame

I FINALLY FELL INTO AN UNEASY DOZE sometime before dawn. When the alarm woke me, I rolled over to stare at the ceiling, feeling leaden. I was meeting with a new client that morning, and I had to browbeat Sasha into swallowing a few mouthfuls of yogurt and collecting the schoolbooks that lay scattered in her untidy wake, but I felt unable to move, my body aching as if I'd been physically beaten. I wondered where he was at this moment—flinging open Mia's cage doors so she could fly into his arms for a romantic reunion? Drawing his gun and firing blindly into a miasma of dust and fire? Maybe they would die wrapped in each other's arms. It didn't matter to me. Nothing mattered.

Dimly I wondered if David was really gone this time. Did he realize that our life, our marriage, was at stake? Did it matter to him? We had never talked to each other like that, never parted like that. I rolled over on my side and drew my knees up to my chest, hugging myself in a futile attempt to warm my frozen body. If he was gone, I was done. That was it. Someone else would have to take care of Sasha's homework and Sam's broken heart and my warring couples and the stray cats. I was done.

I couldn't cope without him. I was terrified of a life without David. But then, why was I thinking this way? I was horrified at the thought of a life *with* him too.

Somehow I managed to get Sasha and Sam off to school.

Then I went to work and mechanically, on autopilot, met with my new clients. They were in the early, agonizing phase of their divorce, unable to make eye contact with each other, practically hissing and spitting. If I could ease their misery just a little bit, I told myself, it would be worthwhile.

When I entered law school, I thought I wanted to be a divorce lawyer so that I could help families—especially children—who were going through this trauma. But after a few years of practice, I realized that divorce lawyers, at least in my firm, were all about fighting World War Three rather than trying to find a peaceable outcome for these shattered families. The lawyers thought they were being paid to charge out of their corners, fists swinging and boots kicking, and aim straight for the jugular.

That wasn't what I wanted—quite the opposite, in fact. So I left my high-paying job and joined a small, much lower-rent divorce mediation firm. My cases generally started with a husband and wife who hated each other, and hated the situation in which they found themselves, and ended up—hopefully—hating each other a little less, and comfortable with the equitable division of money and children that I had hammered out. Sometimes it even worked out that way. Sometimes it was agonizing.

At the beginning, divorce mediation was almost a calling; now, I had seen too much pain and misery.

Clients often inquired curiously if I was divorced, and I always said no—while thinking, *never. Never ever. Never.*

So when the meeting ended, and no one was in tears, I thought, "mission accomplished"—until I remembered my own situation. Still on autopilot, I drove over to Rachel's house. When she opened the door and saw me, she gasped. "What happened? Are you all right? Are the kids—?"

"The kids are fine. Me, not so much."

She pulled me inside. "Sit down. Do you want some nice hot tea? You look like you're freezing. Here, put this afghan around you."

I was still shivering; it seemed like years since I'd been warm. I didn't know if I'd ever be warm again.

Rachel sat down next to me and put her hand over mine. "What happened?"

I cried and talked and cried some more, crying until I thought there couldn't possibly be any tears left in my body, but still they kept seeping down my exhausted face. Rachel listened, made some tea, and forced me to take a few sips. Finally I was done and rested my head against the back of the sofa, feeling drained.

"Okay," Rachel said slowly, feeling her way. "So this woman—the one he had the affair with—"

I shuddered, and Rachel continued more quickly, "She calls him from Colombia, where she's been kidnapped, and he races off with a gun and fake passport to rescue her."

I nodded.

Rachel smiled. "He couldn't just have a boring fling with his secretary like everyone else?"

I smiled weakly.

"So—don't get me wrong here—but what exactly are you most upset about? I know you; you're determined to stay with him. So does that mean you could come to terms with the original affair? Are you worried now because he's in danger? And what could he have done—told her to have a nice life with the kidnappers and hung up?"

I couldn't tell her that I had realized David's priority was his job, not us. I should have realized it long ago.

"I don't know if I can explain it," I said, thinking aloud. "Everything is so *wrong*. David losing control, yelling at me, cursing at me. It's just so wrong! It's not us, not Shelley and David. I don't know *who* we are anymore!"

"It's still David," Rachel said, a little uncertainly.

"No . . . I mean, who the hell *is* David? What would have happened if he'd died in the field? Would I ever have known who he was? What would they have told us? Would we ever have known that we were burying and mourning a complete stranger?"

Rachel was silent, but I couldn't stop my raging thoughts. Of David—the man who kept guns and fake passports in a safe in our closet. Who flew to the rescue of another woman and called her "honey." Who looked like a stranger in the middle of our safe, familiar bedroom. I was afraid that his other life would catch up with us and endanger the twins; I was afraid that he was more comfortable lying than telling the truth.

Most of all, I was afraid of this Other David—afraid that he wasn't the man I had married, and that he wouldn't be able to love safe, familiar me. I was afraid of the sexual thrill that coursed through my body when I looked at my husband and saw instead a stranger—a tall, dangerous, remote stranger. I was afraid of the passions that were boiling between us. And I was afraid that I could never trust him again.

Finally Rachel said, "You're still Shelley and David. He's still your husband, and you want it to stay that way. Maybe—I don't know—maybe this will do some good for you. You two have always been all about the kids, and you're amazing with the twins. But sometimes it seems that that's all you are—parents."

Somehow I made it through the rest of the day. When Sasha got home, I didn't even tell her to clean up the trail of sketchpads, pencils, popcorn, and hairbands scattered through the house in her wake. I just crawled fully dressed under the thick comforter on my bed. I wanted to stay there forever.

But that wasn't the way life worked. The next day our top raffle item for the school's spring auction fell through, and I had to talk my panicked cochair into begging her travel agent for a free cruise instead; my new divorce clients had a monumental battle over a picture frame and demanded that I mediate; and Sasha called me from school because she'd forgotten about school picture day, and could I please, please drop off her blue turtleneck so she could wear it in the picture.

Around lunchtime my phone chirped again; I glanced at it wearily, then snapped to attention when I saw Unknown Caller in the display. I bit my lip and watched unblinkingly as the chirps went on—one, two, three—and then the caller hung up. I continued entering the new couple's assets into the computer, my hand trembling slightly. But then the phone dinged, indicating a new text message, and I reached for it automatically.

The text was a link to a website with a long address string that I didn't recognize. Reluctantly, with pounding heart and shaking fingers, I clicked on the website and watched it load.

It was lyrics from the old love ballad, "You Are My Sunshine."

CHAPTER THIRTEEN

To Do:
Insurance forms
Research Qameen
Set up Google Alerts

WHAT THE F*&%?

I sat staring at the words on the tiny screen for a long time, fighting the tears—the rage—the love—that were all battling to emerge. How dare he? What was he thinking? And God, was he all right? Was he coming home?

The phone chirped again, and I lunged for it. "Hello?" I gasped.

"Is this Mrs. Harris?"

My stomach clenched. It didn't sound like a telemarketer. "Yes," I said unsteadily.

"This is Officer Probst in Chevy Chase, Maryland. Your niece Sasha has been in an accident here, and she says her parents are out of town. Can you come to the scene?"

My mind cleared instantly. "Where are you?" I asked steadily. "Is she hurt?"

"We're at the corner of Connecticut Avenue and Catlin

Street. Northwest corner. And I think she's fine, ma'am, just shaken up. The medics are on their way, but I don't think she'll need to go to the hospital."

"Okay, thank you. I can be there in fifteen minutes."

When I pulled up behind Sasha's car, I wasn't surprised to see that "shaken up" had been an understatement. My poor Sasha was huddled into a quilt, her small shoulders shaking with her sobs and her pale face drenched with tears. A policewoman stood next to her, ineffectively patting her on the back and looking helpless.

I marched up to them. "Sasha, deep breaths," I said briskly. "This isn't a crisis, so take it down a few notches."

The policewoman looked shocked, but I knew how to handle Sasha in a crisis. "Ma'am, she's very shaken up—" the woman began reprovingly, but I interrupted.

"She'll be fine," I said bracingly. "Now, Sasha, does the police officer have some forms for me?"

He did. Sasha, who had only gotten her license the previous month, had been on her way to the health food store for lunch. She claimed that the car in front of her had stopped abruptly, and Sasha had rear-ended it so that both cars were damaged and an insurance claim would be necessary. Wonderful.

I dealt with the police officer, called AAA, and handed Sasha a granola bar while we sat on the curb waiting for the tow truck.

"What am I going to do for a car now?" Sasha asked, sniffing piteously in between little nibbles at the bar.

"You'll have to share with Sam, I guess." I put my arm around her, and she leaned against me for a long moment.

"I'm sorry, Mom," she murmured.

"It's okay," I soothed her. "That's why it's called an accident. Nobody plans it; it just happens."

I wished I could call David and tell him what happened. Even though she was all right, and I was handling things, it was the sort of thing a wife wants to share with her husband. But I didn't know how to reach him. I realized that this was the way our marriage had always worked: I never knew how to reach him. And he never let me find out.

Back home, I tucked Sasha into bed for a badly needed nap and collapsed on the sofa. I couldn't stop thinking about the Unknown Caller's message, scarcely daring to believe it was from David. When he was in town, our normal emails and texts were brief exchanges about the kids and whether we should renew the termite service plan. When he was out of town, I barely heard from him at all. For a wild moment, I wondered if I had a secret admirer—it almost seemed more likely than that my husband, after twenty years of a pleasant if decliningly passionate partnership, had suddenly sent me a love song. My cheating, treacherous husband.

Still, knowing that David had been thinking of me in such a way warmed me, and the longing for him, unwelcome yet no less intense, came rushing back. I closed my eyes and leaned back, dreaming about him. Then I remembered that he had raced into danger to take care of another woman, with barely a word of explanation to me.

I had never felt so conflicted in my life.

David came home three days later, shouldering open the kitchen door to find me at the table, spooning up cereal with one hand and sifting through a mound of papers with the other. "I brought bagels home," he said. "What are all these papers?"

"Insurance," I said, a little unsteadily. Were we really talking about car insurance, as if nothing had happened? My gaze drifted over him as he shrugged out of his jacket; he was wearing a dusty-gray, long-sleeved T-shirt that proclaimed him to be a fan of the Toronto Blue Jays. When he rolled up the sleeves to his elbows, I noticed streaks of dirt along his muscled forearms. He wasn't wearing the shoulder holster.

"Why?" he asked.

I blinked. "Why what?"

"Why do you have insurance papers?" he asked patiently. He paused to push his hair off his forehead and run a hand over his stubbly cheeks. He looked tired.

I sighed. "Sasha had a car accident. She's fine; it was just a fender-bender. But she rear-ended a car, so technically it's her fault, so the insurance. . . ."

"Technically and really," he said.

I shrugged.

"She's really okay?" he asked again.

"Yes."

He grimaced. "All right. Leave the papers for me; I'll take care of it. Is there any coffee, Shells? I haven't slept more than four hours in the past few days. I'm running on empty here."

I got up quickly and busied myself at the stove, glad to have something to do. "So what happened?" I threw over my shoulder.

David went over to the sink to wash his hands. "Well, I found Mia and spent a few days wrangling. It was messier than I expected, but she's safe in Mexico City now. All done."

All done? What did that mean? Was he speaking in code?

"How was it messier?" I set down a plate of scrambled eggs and toast buttered with a thin glaze of cinnamon, just as he liked it, and handed him a steaming mug of black coffee. He nodded his thanks and dug in.

"They were after a little more than just money," he said briefly.

I waited. "So?" I asked finally.

He glanced at me. "So it took more effort than I expected. But I got her out, in the end."

I couldn't stop the words from tumbling out. "And did you and Mia enjoy your reunion after you rescued her?" I asked.

David grunted, then looked up and saw my face. "Of course not," he said.

I wanted to tell him there was no "of course" about it, but I bit my lip. It was bad enough already.

He swallowed a big bite of egg and put the fork down, suddenly looking too exhausted to make the effort of eating.

Through my anger and hurt, I felt a little flutter of anxiety. "You'd better go to bed. You look terrible."

"I feel terrible," he admitted. With a visible effort he rose from the table, steadying himself against the wall before he started walking.

Hastily, I put the dishes in the sink and followed him up the stairs. When we got to the bedroom, he turned and gave me a small smile. "I don't need an escort. Really, I can handle this on my own."

But some instinct led me to walk over to him and gently, carefully, ease the dirty T-shirt over his head. I caught my breath in shock as his bare chest was revealed, spattered with blood and dust, with a long grimy bandage running from his shoulder all the way down to his belt buckle. I gasped. "What happened?"

He shrugged, trying for insouciance but not quite making it. "Work-related injury."

I stared at him. "Was it . . . a bullet?"

"Knife. Fortunately, he was even worse with a knife than me—I didn't do too well on that part of the training course. So . . . well . . ." he tried for a grin, "you should see the other guy."

"David!" I exclaimed. "You need to go to the hospital."

"No hospital," he said briefly. "Don't fuss, Shelley, it looks a lot worse than it is."

I set my lips and hurried into the bathroom to start a shower. I threw at him over my shoulder, "You need to get that cleaned up so I can put on a fresh bandage, and then we'll see about a doctor. Come on—the twins will be home soon."

When he was finally clean and bandaged, I led him to the bed. Though I could hear the twins knocking around the kitchen downstairs, David's need was greater. I wouldn't leave my worst enemy bloodied and in pain.

"Go on, help the kids," he urged weakly. "I'm fine."

"I want to get you tucked in," I said adamantly. I didn't know what I was afraid he'd do, but I didn't trust him one inch.

He sighed. "Then don't look," he advised. He took a hypodermic needle out of his worn toiletries kit, swabbed a spot on his thigh, and expertly jabbed the needle into his leg without a wince.

"Antibiotics," he said briefly in response to my questioning look.

Was there anything the man couldn't do?

"Get into bed," I ordered.

"Yes, ma'am."

He climbed between the cool white sheets, and I gently tucked their softness around his weary body. I could almost feel the relief with which he settled into the clean, comforting bed. "Thanks, Shelley—thanks for everything."

I headed for the door, where I turned for one last look at him. His damp dark lashes stuck together in clumpy crescents against his bruised, dark-stubbled cheeks. He almost looked vulnerable.

Part II

DISCOVERY

CHAPTER FOURTEEN

To Do:
Discovery

DAVID WAS BACK TO HIMSELF THE NEXT day, striding around the kitchen chiding Sasha for leaving her damp skates out overnight and chivying her into eating a piece of wheat toast.

"Are you going to work today?" I asked.

"Of course," he said. "Why wouldn't I?"

I pressed my lips together. We both knew that vicious slash on his chest, now an angry red and purple around the primitive stitches that someone (surely not David?) must have put in to stem the bleeding, wouldn't heal overnight, and when he got dressed that morning I'd seen the other cuts and bruises on his body. He looked like he'd survived a minor war. But it was mostly hidden underneath his clothes, and he moved with his usual easy grace when the kids were watching. Only I knew how much effort those movements must be costing him.

"I'll take the insurance papers into the office with me," he said.

"Okay." I didn't thank him and couldn't question him, but watched unblinkingly as he went out the door. Who *was* this man?

It was long past time for me to take matters into my own hands. I reminded myself that I was a lawyer and an expert in "discovery," the essential and eye-opening gathering of facts that precedes a trial. In my mind, David was on trial—for adultery and treason. I was desperate for knowledge of this un-David, and even more desperate to know what had happened in Qameen. Such an unlikely place for a tryst; and steady, reliable David was such an unlikely partner in a tryst. After all, wasn't that why I had married him?

Maybe it wasn't true. How could it be true? What were the facts?

To Research:

1. Credit card records.

Our Visa and MasterCard bills yielded nothing interesting, but my online research informed me that NOC officers usually had several aliases, with full personal credit records in each alias. Well, I knew of one alias—Peter Brooks—and I guessed that some of "Peter's" stuff was at our house to enable last-minute travel.

I called a locksmith. Three hours later, I was staring at a battered faux-leather wallet that had been stowed in the locked bottom drawer of his desk.

Peter Brooks had a California driver's license, a social security card, and his mother's maiden name was Ruth Brier. Primed with this information, I had no trouble persuading Citibank to email me the last six months of Peter's bills; Verizon was more troublesome but eventually offered up his phone records, and I was in business.

Yet I found myself oddly reluctant to open the computer files. Even if David had been home, would I have asked him about Mia Holloway? Plausible deniability—wasn't that what they called it? As long as I didn't know anything for sure, I could believe that it wasn't true. I needed to preserve the illusion of our perfect family for as long as possible, so I preferred the safety of silence. Though I was realizing how much of an illusion that had been, and how unsafe it actually was.

I sat staring at the email icon until my eyes started to sting. The computer clicked, signaling that it was ready to go to sleep, and I finally hit Enter.

Peter Brooks got around. He flew from Washington to Tel Aviv on July 7, then somehow ended up with a $20,352 bill from the Hilton Hotel in Amman, Jordan. In Amman he went shopping; bookstores showed hefty charges, as did two electronics game stores. He flew back to the US on July 17th, arriving in Tampa. There was a July 22nd $2,836 bill from a steakhouse in Atlanta. Yet my personal calendar confirmed that he'd been home for my birthday on July 20th.

The next two weeks showed no travel, although my calendar showed that he was supposedly in Cincinnati and Cleveland. Another alias, perhaps? Peter was a busy boy again in August—Paris, Cyprus, Miami, Vancouver. (David was in Chicago then, according to my calendar.) He bought a lot of wine in Vancouver.

I was thoroughly befuddled. I scrolled through the rest of the bills, seeing no patterns except for a lot of random travel, expensive meals for large parties, and luxury purchases. Plus the occasional miscellaneous item (Ahava factory store in Masada, Israel; Giuseppe's Glassblowers in Cyprus). But there was one recurring charge in Reston, Virginia: B&J Storage. Peter paid $79 every month to B&J for storage locker number 149. I leaned back in my chair, a smile finally starting to curve my lips. Time for a field trip.

2. B&J Storage

"Hi, I'm Bunny—B. My husband's J," said the woman at the front desk, giving Peter Brooks's driver's license a cursory glance and returning it to me. "I don't think I ever met your husband," she continued, peering interestedly at me. "Travels a lot, does he?"

"Sometimes," I said, visions of Marrakech and Masada dancing in my brain.

"Want a coffee?" she inquired. "Cold day out there, isn't it?" She seemed in no hurry to give me access.

"Yes—I mean no. It's pouring rain, but I'm afraid I don't have time for coffee."

"Yeah," she drawled. "In a hurry to get in there?" Her eyes were shrewd.

I swallowed, afraid that she could see right through me. I had no backup plan if she refused to let me into the locker. I hadn't been able to find the keys, and this was my last lead.

"It's all right with me if you want to check up on your husband," she said, reaching into a drawer for a set of keys. "We gals gotta stick together. Here it is."

With a sigh of relief, I signed the register as Julianne Brooks—I had planned to name our first daughter Julianne—and two minutes later, I was inside the tiny cell-like room with cement walls and no windows. Rubbing my cold arms briskly, I set to work perusing my husband's past.

I started with his Andover prep school yearbook, jolted every time I found his picture. (*My* David had supposedly gone to a big public high school in Long Beach, California.) Young David had been good-looking, blessed with wavy blond hair and athletic prowess; he played varsity tennis and football in his senior year. His tennis coach wrote in his yearbook, "David, you were the best captain I've ever known. Good luck in all your future endeavors—I think you'll make Andover proud!" Most interestingly to me, he had apparently dated a girl named Muffy Petite (I kid you not). Muffy wrote, "Dear David, I can't believe I'm writing in your yearbook. I'll never forget Bells Night; thank God old Wurster never found out what we did with her nightie! I will always always love you, and I know we'll stay together; Princeton isn't that far from Wellesley. Don't forget C.W. and PeC and all the other great times! I love you love you love you! Muffy."

Princeton! What the hell? My David had gone to UCLA, the diploma hung proudly on his study wall.

And what had happened to Muffy and C.W. and all the other figments of his past? Had he buried them so deep in his brain that even he couldn't recall them, or did he dredge up their ghosts sometimes when he lay alone in bed in hostile foreign cities?

I moved on to his Princeton records, where there was no mention of Muffy. He'd joined an eating club called Ivy; photographs showed a sea of perfectly groomed, improbably handsome young white men being served by a small army of Black waiters (again, I kid you not). There was a large photo of David impeccably turned out in tuxedo, on his arm a tall, lovely dark-haired girl clad in shimmering cream satin; I turned over the photo and it read, "David and Dylan, Houseparties 1993." She reminded me a little of Mia.

Musing, I paged through his yearbook and found that Dylan DuPont (could it possibly be *the* DuPonts?) had played varsity lacrosse at Princeton and majored in economics. Dylan wasn't the sort to write adoring messages in his yearbook though. Instead, I found a brown envelope holding a pair of lacy red thong panties, a key, and a note: "Waldorf Astoria, Room 1327. DD." I wondered if David had ever used the key; somehow, I suspected that Dylan had been left waiting.

I sorted through boxes of athletic equipment and old clothing. Two trunks yielded barely worn, custom-made Savile Row suits and dinner jackets in David's size. Who on earth was the man who wore these clothes? Surely not my buttoned-down, Brooks Brothers husband.

One small box in the farthest corner held a well-worn Hebrew prayer book and ceremonial tallis, undoubtedly from his childhood. Thoughtfully, I lifted out the tallis and ran a gentle finger over the soft, shimmery old silk, picturing it across a young David's shoulders. Perhaps he had worn this at his bar mitzvah?

I put the prayer book and tallis into my bag.

My research at a dead end, for the rest of the week I tried to keep myself too busy to think about him—working on volunteer lists for the spring auction, negotiating with the temple board on budget cuts, ferrying the twins to their various appointments, coaxing my soon-to-be-divorced couple to divvy up their shot glass collection, advising Sam on the latest flare-up with Sharona, and cooking meals that a carnivorous male and a health-conscious teenage girl would both eat. My older sister Marisa called every day to ask my advice on her various plastic surgery options, and my younger sister Dani called every day to complain about her authors. I stood over Sasha while she did her homework and coached Sam for his college interviews.

But the CNN photo was burned into my brain, as firmly and vividly as the kids' baby pictures. David and Mia, I kept thinking. Not David and Shelley. David and *Mia*.

It was impossible. Unbearable. Unthinkable.

CHAPTER FIFTEEN

STILL, I HAD TO KEEP MYSELF GOING. Luckily, the press seemed to have lost interest in the story after the initial flurry of publicity. A country music superstar, bless his soul, had a massive public meltdown at the Grammy Awards, and my (phi-landering?) husband was forgotten for the moment. So when the phone rang that afternoon, the last thing I was expecting was another bombshell.

"Ms. Harris? Michelle Mendelson Harris?"

The caller ID read Beecham, Ward, and Connell, which had piqued my interest; it didn't sound like a telemarketer.

"Yes," I said guardedly.

"Ms. Harris, I'm calling from the law offices of Beecham, Ward, and Connell. We represent the estate of Aviva Tellerman, and Mr. Beecham would like to meet with you as soon as possible. Could you come in on Monday morning? It's rather urgent."

Aviva! I almost dropped the phone. She'd been a young lan-guage arts teacher at the twins' school, whom I barely knew until the morning last winter when I went to the bathroom after a PTO meeting and found her huddled in a corner, crying as if her heart would break. After much patting and soothing, she confided in me that she was pregnant. The father didn't want anything to do with the baby; he was moving to Los Angeles to put as much distance between them as possible. She said that it was just as well that he was leaving—she didn't want him to have anything to do with the baby. But she was terrified that one day he would reappear and try to assert some parental rights.

"I'm done with him," she explained, wiping her tears and sitting up straighter. "I want this baby. But what if he comes back and ruins her life? You should have heard the things he said when I told him I wouldn't get an abortion." She shuddered and I sighed, seeing all the potential problems that could lie ahead.

I reminded her that I was a family lawyer and asked if he would be willing to sign away his rights. She shrank away, tears welling up again.

"I couldn't. . . ."

"Why not?"

"He hit me," she said softly. "He drinks and does coke and . . . he beat me when I told him I was pregnant and I wouldn't get an abortion. . . ." She turned her face to look straight at me, and I caught my breath sharply at the sight of her swollen, discolored cheek and cut lip. Wordlessly she pushed up her long sleeves, and I gasped again at the angry purple bruises that ringed her slender arms.

I begged her to let me take her to the hospital and the police, but she was terrified. Finally, distressed and depressed, I admitted defeat and gave her my card. "Please, please," I said. "Please reconsider this and let me help you. I can draw up the papers and have him served and—"

But she was too frightened; *he must be a monster*, I thought.

After that I invited her for dinner regularly and gave her several boxfuls of Sasha's old baby clothes, as well as her cradle and highchair. When Aviva developed preeclampsia and was put on bed rest, I organized a dinner chain of parents from the school to bring food and check on her every day.

So it was a horrible shock when the head of school called me one day in April, her voice heavy with sadness, to tell me that Aviva had died. Apparently, the parent who was assigned to bring food to her that day found her collapsed in her apartment and called an ambulance, but it was too late; poor Aviva had died before the baby could be born.

Despite her insistence that she wanted to live alone, I still felt guilty for not insisting that she stay with us until the baby was born. I knew it was a high-risk pregnancy, and I still felt sick with sorrow every time I thought of her—so I tried to push it to the back of my mind along with all the other sorrows of the world that I couldn't fix.

I couldn't imagine what her lawyer would be calling me about now. "Aviva?" I said after a moment. "She died six months ago; why are you calling me now?"

The woman's voice was prim and cautious. "The estate was complicated, but now it's important that Mr. Beecham see you as soon as possible. Monday morning at ten?"

Numbly, I agreed and hung up. I didn't think Aviva had any money, but she'd had some pretty hand-painted furniture that I'd admired. Maybe that was it? I wasn't sure I wanted anything of Aviva's here, though; it would just remind me of my inability to take care of her. Maybe I would donate it to the Salvation Army.

My mood wasn't lightened by another phone call later that afternoon—Sasha's homeroom teacher saying ominously that we needed to talk. So when David texted (the coward!) to say that he wouldn't be home until Monday night, I put my head down on the kitchen table and cried. The universe was clearly conspiring against me.

As I walked down K Street on Monday morning, I wasn't surprised to find the lawyer's office in a hypermodern new building

high above K Street, overlooking the masses of people pushing their way into the Metro, Starbucks, and People's Drug.
Predictably, the decor was the standard dark, heavy furniture,
massive Persian rugs, and sweeping fresh flower arrangements
that I would expect of Washington power lawyers. But when
the receptionist ushered me into Mr. Beecham's palatial corner
office, there was something very nonstandard: the unmistakable,
never-forgotten cry of a tiny baby.

CHAPTER SIXTEEN

To Do:
Stroller, jumper seat, formula

I SWALLOWED, GUESSING EVEN BEFORE I FACED the young social worker and the squirming bundle held in her arms. "I heard that Aviva's baby was stillborn," I told the lawyer who rose to greet me.

He held out his hand to shake mine. "Malcolm Beecham. Thank you so much for coming in, Ms. Harris. We've been looking forward to meeting you. And no, the baby was not stillborn."

My eyes had already returned to the small mewling baby girl. The blanket that she was kicking with infuriated vigor was pink, as was the tiny cap on her head. Her eyes were squinched tightly shut as she gathered breath for another shriek, her cheeks were bright red with rage, and her hands were curled into small fists.

"This can't be Aviva's baby," I said, numb with shock.

"It is," the lawyer replied. "This is Amelia."

Finally, I looked at him. "And this is what Aviva left me, isn't it?"

He nodded. "Yes. She made a will when she was diagnosed with the preeclampsia. Just in case."

Just in case. Just in case she died all alone, leaving this precious child to fare for herself? Could Aviva have even considered that possibility? I pressed my lips together to keep from crying out and sank into the upholstered chair opposite Mr. Beecham's massive desk. The baby continued to wail.

"I've raised two children," I said dazedly. "They're getting ready to go off to college. I'm forty-two years old and my husband is forty-six. I can't raise a baby now. Where has she been for the last six months, anyway? Who's been taking care of her?"

Beecham shifted uneasily in his chair, the baby's crying clearly jangling his nerves. As the young social worker jiggled the baby and murmured ineffectually in her ear, I stifled the impulse to grab the baby and rock her until the tears stopped.

"She's been in foster care," Beecham said. "It took a while to settle the estate and make sure that the biological father was out of the picture."

I stiffened at the mention of the baby's biological father, picturing Aviva's swollen face and bruised arms. Thank God he *was* out of the picture.

"Of course, you're under no obligation to take her," Beecham said briskly. "There are many potential parents eager to adopt healthy infants. The state would have no trouble placing her if you feel that you don't want to take this burden on. It would be entirely understandable."

A burden. Yes, that's what she would be. And God knows I had enough of those, I thought, the photos of David and Mia flashing in my mind like a warning sign. I nodded decisively. "Well then, Mr. Beecham, that's what we should do. What do I have to sign?"

The baby, perhaps sensing her rejection, drew a deep, quivering breath and let out an earsplitting shriek. Beecham and I shuddered in unison. He quickly said, "We can draw up the papers renouncing your parental rights and turning her over to the state in just a few minutes. I'll have my paralegal get them ready. . . ." Clearly glad to escape, he hurried out of his office. I rose too and walked over to stare out the window, watching the pigeons fighting over crumbs and a homeless man sleeping on one of the benches, a protective hand over the battered shopping cart that held all his bits and treasures.

Reluctantly, I turned to gaze at the baby once more. She was crying in a more quiet, resigned, almost hopeless way now, and I felt desperate to escape. As I paced back and forth like a caged animal, the social worker avoided my eyes, helplessly jiggling the baby on the couch.

But as I waited for Beecham to return, the baby's hopeless sobs soaked into my soul, and I couldn't bear it any longer. Not when I had the power to make it stop. Succumbing to the inevitable, I walked over to the social worker and held out my arms.

"You can't sit still and soothe a crying baby," I said quietly. "You have to stand up and keep moving, like this."

I expertly put the baby on my shoulder, where she snuggled with an almost perceptible sigh of relief, and I gently rubbed her back as I swayed side to side. A blessed silence descended over the room.

Beecham walked in a couple of minutes later and watched me cautiously. "Do you still want to sign the relinquishment papers?" he ventured.

I sighed. "No, I'm not going to sign those damn papers. I'm going to sign the other papers. Do you have her things? Medical records, clothes, toys?"

I can't believe this, I thought. I cannot fucking believe this. I go out to run an errand, and I come home with a baby. Nobody will ever believe this.

I signed the sheaf of papers that Beecham thrust hurriedly

into my hands, perhaps afraid that I would change my mind again. The social worker retrieved a pink diaper bag from beside the sofa and slung it over my other shoulder. "All her records are in the bag," she said. "We'll do a home visit in a few weeks to see how she's getting on, but I'm sure you'll be great together."

I snatched up my handbag and marched out the door, the social worker close upon my heels with a car seat clutched to her chest. Amelia chose this moment to puff up her cheeks and draw her brows together in fierce concentration. As we got onto the elevator, her tiny body tensed as she prepared for a giant push, and then her muscles relaxed; a distinctive, unmistakable aroma filled the air, and the Armani-clad man standing next to me drew back, looking pained.

"I think your baby needs to be changed," he said stiffly.

I can't fucking believe this, I told myself.

The social worker and I manhandled the massive seat into my car, where I fumbled through changing my first diaper in more than fifteen years. Then I drove straight to the giant Walmart in Chevy Chase. I wandered the aisles in a daze at first, overwhelmed by the multitude of selections and all the new baby technology that had appeared since the twins arrived, nearly eighteen years before. Finally I pulled myself together and started filling shopping carts.

By the time we got home, we were both exhausted. I rinsed out one of the new bottles—I'd never been a great believer in sterilizing, anyway, I told myself—and filled it with some of the new formula, and Amelia and I collapsed onto the family room couch. She sucked greedily at her bottle, one fist waving aimlessly and one reaching up to curl around my fingers. Her dark, slate blue eyes watched me intently, almost wonderingly, her eyes occasionally crossing with the effort of her gulps. When the bottle was almost empty, her lids drooped and she fell asleep, emitting tiny puffs of air through her delicately pursed mouth. I leaned my head back against the cushions and closed my eyes too.

We hadn't moved when the kitchen door slammed open and two sets of footsteps pounded into the house. "Shelley!" Sasha shouted. "Can you come with me to the Galleria? I want to get—" She stopped so abruptly that Sam practically crashed into her. "Whose baby is that?" she asked, cautiously advancing into the room. "Are you babysitting?"

Sam said, "What a cutie! How old is she? Why are you babysitting? Is someone sick?"

I should have prepared for this moment, I realized. But as I looked at the twins, my mind was still a blank. I didn't seem to be capable of thinking, let alone explaining. I simply said, "This is Amelia."

"Amelia who?" Sasha asked.

"Amelia Harris," I replied.

CHAPTER SEVENTEEN

To Do:
File adoption papers
Portacrib
Pediatrician
PACIFIERS!

SASHA SANK DOWN ONTO THE FLOOR as if her legs wouldn't support her and gazed from me to the baby. She said tremulously, "Shelley?"

I summoned all my resources and dredged up a smile. "Amelia is Aviva Tellerman's baby—you remember, Sasha, the teacher who died, from your school? She left a will naming me the baby's guardian."

Sam just stared.

Sasha's lips were stiff. "I thought the baby died too."

"So did I. But, obviously. . . ." I didn't need to finish the sentence.

Sasha crept closer and reached out to touch the baby. "Her skin is so soft," she observed. "How old is she?"

"Six months."

"Isn't she awfully small?"

"She's on the small side, but seems healthy." I hoped.

"Does David know about this?" Sam asked.

"No, not yet. But I'm sure he'll . . . feel the same way I do." Whatever that was.

Sam swallowed. "Where is her father?"

"Her biological father is an abusive alcoholic and cokehead. He's out of the picture."

Sasha pressed her lips together.

I suggested, "Sam, can you drive Sasha to the Galleria? I don't want to disturb the baby. She's had a hard day." Sasha was still leery of driving since her accident, so I'd been driving her around as much as possible.

"I wanted you to take me," Sasha complained. "I want to try on prom dresses."

"Well, why don't you pick out a few and bring them home? Then I'll return the ones you don't want," I suggested.

Grumbling, Sasha acquiesced, and the teenagers backed out of the room, their wide eyes still fixed on the baby. When they got into the kitchen, their voices rose in excited chatter.

David walked in just after dinner. Amelia had hated being bathed, and I was walking her up and down the kitchen floor trying to soothe her screams. Sasha was shouting useless suggestions over the baby's cries, the kitchen floor was slippery with water and soapsuds, and no one had cleaned up after dinner. One of the cats had thrown up on the braided rug in front of the kitchen sink. Sam, anxious to help, offered to run out and buy some pacifiers, and Sasha was on her phone Googling "crying babies."

David stood in the kitchen doorway and stared around him in patent disbelief. "What the hell is going on here?" The phone rang, and we all ignored it.

Sasha ran to him and flung her arms around him. "David,

thank God you're home!" she cried dramatically. "Shelley is taking care of Ms. Tellerman's baby, and all it does is cry, and Shelley couldn't take me to the Galleria, and she says she's *keeping it* and—"

"Hold on," he said. "Let's all calm down, shall we?" But such was the extent of our discombobulation that, for once, no one paid any attention to him. Amelia kept screaming, Sasha kept complaining, and Sam kept trying to tell me what to do. And the phone kept ringing.

"Everyone just shut up!" David finally shouted.

It was so extraordinary for him to shout that the room fell silent; even Amelia stopped crying to stare at him.

He let out a long breath. "Good," he said more quietly. "Now. First of all, when is this baby going back home, for God's sake? And whose baby is she, anyway?"

I smiled at him over Amelia's damp head. After all the emotional uproar that he'd put me through over the past two weeks, it gave me great satisfaction to turn the tables on him. "She's ours, David," I said sweetly.

He stared. "I don't think so."

"Oh, yes," I said. "Why, she even looks like you: She has your hair color, and I think her eyes are going to stay blue too." It felt good to needle him.

"And if I hadn't had a vasectomy, I'd be proud to claim her," he said ironically. "But seeing as it's physically impossible—"

"Yes, she is ours!" Sasha burst out. "She's Ms. Tellerman's baby—you know, my teacher who died—"

"And she left her to Shelley in her will," Sam cut in. "So she brought her home from the lawyer's office—"

"And she's going to take care of her now!" Sasha finished.

"Oh no, she's not," David said grimly. His eyes hard, his mouth tight, at the moment he looked every bit as I imagined a tough superspy to look—nothing like my David. A wave of pure hatred shot through me.

"Oh yes, I am," I snapped. Amelia chose this moment to start crying again, and I thrust her into David's arms. "Here. Take her while I get her bottle ready."

He automatically cradled her with a practiced grip, bouncing her so her wails died down into whimpers as she stared up into his face. "Kids, go upstairs now," he said without taking his eyes off the baby. "Shelley and I need to talk."

"Tell her this is ridiculous," Sasha begged. "We can't have a baby now. Please, David!"

"Just go," he snapped, and they hurried out of the room.

As soon as the door swung shut behind them, he turned to me. "Shelley, this is ridiculous," he said calmly. "You must know we can't keep this baby. I'm sure she'd be adopted in no time, and she'd be better off with younger parents."

I set the bottle of formula in a warm bowl of water to heat it up. "Aviva wanted me to raise her," I said equally calmly. "She's my baby now."

He pulled me around to face him in the middle of the kitchen, the baby held between us like a shield. Her dark blue eyes went from one face to another, and she gave me a tentative toothless smile. "Shelley, she's not your baby," David said, kindly but firmly. "She's an orphaned child who needs a home and will have no trouble finding a family that's dying to adopt her. Good God, are you crazy? I'm forty-six years old; I'd be sixty-five by the time she goes to college!"

"Let go of my arm," I said coolly. "I have to get her bottle."

He leaned back against the counter and watched as I settled myself in the kitchen rocker and gave Amelia her bottle. She sucked eagerly, her eyes seeking mine and her fingers once again reaching out to curl around mine. Abruptly she let go of the nipple to give me a milky-sweet smile, and I smiled back.

David scowled. "Shelley," he said warningly, "this is crazy. We can't go back eighteen years. We're done with all this, remember? And she's not even ours, for God's sake."

"Neither were Sasha and Sam," I reminded him. "And that never mattered."

"That's what I mean!" he exploded. "God Almighty, it's not enough that we raised your sister's children! Now you have to take in a stranger's baby too?"

I rocked back and forth, smiling at Amelia as she nestled against me and her eyelids began to droop closed in sleep. The sight seemed to madden David.

"Fine!" he snapped. "Are you punishing me? Because if it's about the damned photographs, I can explain—"

I looked over at him. "Why, is there something I should be punishing you for?" I asked innocently. "Actually, you did me a favor—I'm thinking of starting an online support group for wives who learned that their husbands were cheating on them from the TV news."

"Shelley," he started, but I cut him off.

"There's Eliot Spitzer's wife—remember, he was sleeping with a high-priced call girl," I continued brightly, "and Rudy Giuliani's wife—oh no, I think she only found out he was divorcing her from the news. And wasn't there a governor from New Jersey whose wife found out he was gay when he announced it at a news conference? I think I'd be doing a great service for—"

"That's enough!" David threw his jacket onto the floor, where it landed in the cat vomit I hadn't had a chance to clean up. "Fuck!" he yelled. At that moment, the new kitten wandered into the kitchen, and David tripped over him as he backed away from the mess on the kitchen floor. "And where the hell did this cat come from, anyway?" he roared.

I couldn't hold back a semihysterical giggle.

David gazed at me and suddenly his own face cleared, as well. He grinned.

I grinned back. "I named him Albatross. Albie for short."

"Appropriate." He bent down to pet the cat, who immediately swarmed up his good khaki slacks and onto his right shoulder, purring enthusiastically. David looked back at the baby. "And what's her name?" he asked.

"Amelia," I said. "I think I'll call her Amy."

He nodded. "That was one of our names if we had a girl, remember?"

I nodded and our eyes met. Just for a moment, it was hard to keep hating him.

He picked up his coat from the floor and held it out at arm's length. "I'll dump this in the washing machine and get the Portacrib out of the attic. You didn't set it up yet, did you?"

I shook my head.

"Where do you want it? Our room?"

"Yes. Later we can make the guest room into a nursery. But for now Amy can just sleep in our room."

"Until we figure out what we're going to do."

"There's nothing to figure out," I said. "She's ours."

David shook his head and started to leave the kitchen but stopped at the door for one long, last look at me and the baby in the rocker. She was asleep, her long dark lashes resting gently on her rounded cheeks and her mouth slightly open in a satiated stupor. "I can't fucking believe this," he said.

Amy, it turned out, slept like a baby—she was up every two hours demanding food, company, and entertainment. When I started to throw back the covers at four in the morning, David pulled me back onto the bed, none too gently. "I'll get this one," he said, and I sank back against the pillows in a dreamless fog.

The next thing I knew, the sun was streaming through the windows; it was seven thirty, and Amy was screaming again.

That afternoon I took her to the pediatrician. Dr. Meyerson handled her gently, but Amy still wailed like a banshee when the doctor took off her diaper to examine her body.

"She doesn't like getting undressed," I explained apologetically.

"I noticed," the doctor said dryly. Pathetically, Amy reached up her arms toward me as if she were being nailed to a cross, and I picked her up and cuddled her against my breast. Instantly her screams stopped.

Dr. Meyerson started filling out forms. "Amelia . . . Harris," she muttered to herself. "What's her middle name?"

Embarrassed, I admitted that I didn't know.

"Well, it must be in here somewhere," the doctor said, riffling through the medical forms the lawyer had given me. "Oh, here it is! Joy. Amelia Joy. That's a pretty name."

Amy Joy and I spent the rest of the day shopping. I was surprised at how quickly I remembered the tricks of mothering a young baby. I strapped her to my chest in the Snugli when we returned to Walmart for the thousand and one items I'd forgotten the previous day and pushed her in her new stroller for the trip to Gymboree and BuyBuyBaby for tiny blue jeans and matching, pink-striped shirts. We even made a quick stop at the grocery store, where I introduced her to the wonders of a crumbly, soggy Zwieback biscuit as we whizzed through the store. By the time we got home, she needed another bath, and I needed a day at the spa.

I had barely finished lugging all our purchases into the kitchen when there was a knock on the kitchen door, and Rachel sauntered in. She looked about at my normally spotless kitchen, and her eyes grew round.

"Holy shit," she said. "What is *that*?"

"That, as you so elegantly put it, is Amy Joy."

"And who is Amy Joy?"

I gulped. "My new daughter."

Rachel blinked. "Your new what?"

"I'm—we're—adopting her. She was Aviva Tellerman's baby."

Rachel shook her head and sank down on the kitchen rocker. "I leave you alone for one weekend, and this is what happens. Shelley, what the hell have you done?"

CHAPTER EIGHTEEN

To Do:
Tina—clean twice a week???
Nursery school signup

WHAT INDEED?

But David and I had not a moment to talk about anything—not the photographs, not Amy Joy, not our marriage; hostility emanated from me in such palpable waves that I was surprised it didn't engulf him, and yet we were immersed in the demands of our ever-expanding family and his "urgent business." After a couple of days I realized he was avoiding me, leaving for work before I was awake and getting home after I was in bed. On day three, I set my cellphone alarm for five in the morning to entrap him.

"David, we have to talk."

Caught in the act of shaving silently in the darkened bathroom, he turned a surprised face to me.

"Is Amy Joy up? I have to get to—"

"Work. I know. But we're going to talk first."

Carefully, he set the razor down and wiped cream off his face. I averted my eyes from his bare chest, the intimacy of the scene slashing away at my nerves.

"Okay," he said cautiously.

Suddenly I realized that I still couldn't, after all, ask him about The Woman. My father had left when I was a young teenager, and now we had Amy Joy. I didn't want to know what David had done. I didn't even want to care. I hated him with every bone in my body—but I needed my family. If I knew, then I would have to do something about it. I swallowed.

"Where were you?" I asked instead. "What was so important that you couldn't be with your family when all this news was coming out?"

"Amman," he said, surprising me with a direct answer. I had gotten so used to evasions and half-truths.

"Why? What were you doing there?"

"Working with an exfil spesh to get some of my assets out of Qameen."

"Huh? Speak English, please." Mary Ann and Dr. Lillian would have understood him, I thought bitterly. Maybe even Mia. But not me—I'm the one who's excluded from his world.

"A specialist in exfiltration—getting people out of dangerous places."

Like Ben Affleck in *Argo*, I thought. I had liked that movie.

"Thanks to those bloody news stories, some of my best people were in imminent danger. If their governments knew they were in contact with me, they'd be. . . . And I had to hang back in the safety of Amman and direct operations instead of going in myself," he said disgustedly. "Trust in someone I barely know and didn't even train, to get my people out. *My* people!"

We were his people too, I thought.

"Why?"

"Why what?"

"Why did you have to stay in Amman?"

"Oh. Those fucking photographs. Even in disguise, Langley

doesn't want me in the field any more than I have to be," he said bitterly, and I realized he was as angry as I was. For different reasons, though.

But I could see he was telling the truth about one thing; he trusted no one, not even his highly trained fellow CIA officers. It should have made me feel better.

"Finally I just went in and did it myself," he added.

Went into the hell of Qameen! I shivered.

"But—how?"

"Heavily disguised. It worked." He paused. "Mostly."

I wondered what that meant.

"David," I began, then stopped.

He waited, and in the silence we heard Amy Joy's wake-up wail.

"You'd better get her," David said. "Before she wakes the kids up."

I just couldn't ask him. I walked over to Amy Joy's crib and lifted her up, nuzzling her soft head and breathing in her sweet scent. This baby needed a family. She needed a mother and a father. So I said, "I guess you had to think of your 'assets' first? Not your family?"

"They were in danger," my husband said evenly. "You weren't."

Maybe not then. But I was terribly afraid that we were now.

And suddenly, I had to ask. The words flew out of me as if they'd been stoppered up for years: "What about that woman? That reporter?" I couldn't bear to say her name; maybe he had murmured it when they were entangled together, their bodies melding into one. My skin prickled as if needles were shooting through my veins.

"When we—before those pictures were taken—we were in Qameen together. It was bad; she was upset."

"*She* was upset?" My voice had risen, but I couldn't control myself—didn't want to try, either. "What about me? Do you think maybe I was upset?"

"Shelley, it was a . . . it was unspeakably horrible. Like nothing you could imagine."

"No, I never could imagine my husband fucking another woman!"

His face closed up and he opened his mouth to say something we would both regret when Sasha's sleepy face peeked around the bedroom door.

"Shelley? David? Why are you yelling? And why don't you give Amy Joy a bottle?"

Her tremulous, frightened tones quieted us both instantly. Temporarily united again, David and I spoke in unison.

"Sorry, sweetie, we didn't realize we were so loud. Guess my hearing's going in my old age," David said.

I added, "I was hoping Amy Joy would go back to sleep. Sorry we woke you, sweetie."

Dubious, Sasha looked back and forth between us, and David put a reassuring arm around my shoulders. "Can you please do us a favor, Sash? Shelley and I want to go out for a quick breakfast before work. Can you take care of Amy Joy for an hour or so?"

She shook her head, long taffy curls swirling in the early morning light, but David just took the baby from me and put her in Sasha's arms; she retreated in a huffy silence. He dropped his arm from around me as if I were poison, and I jerked away from him.

"Get dressed, Shelley. You wanted to talk? Let's talk."

Quickly but with trembling hands, I pulled on my clothes and closed my ears to the shrieking Amy Joy and indignant Sasha. Together in tight-lipped silence, we slipped down the stairs and out the garage door.

As we drove down the quiet streets, I just couldn't stand it anymore—the deceit, the hateful silences, the doubts, the questions—and something inside me snapped.

"Tell me about Mia."

His face was a mask. "Shelley. . . ." he said.

I clasped my trembling hands together in my lap. "I want to know. Tell me about her."

He sighed. "Do we really have to do this?"

So it was true. I think I had always known that. "Yes," I said steadily.

CHAPTER NINETEEN

ABRUPTLY HE SIGNALED FOR A TURN AND swung the car across two lanes of traffic to bring it to a halt in the parking lot of a giant Staples.

David turned the car off and tried to take my hand, but I pulled away from him and turned so my back was against the door, as far away from him as I could get inside the car. He drew a deep breath and let it out slowly. "I hoped we wouldn't have to do this," he said, half to himself. "But . . . Qameen truly is hell, Shelley. It's hell like I've never seen before and like I never hope to see again."

This wasn't quite what I'd expected to hear. I nodded, waiting for him to go on.

"I was traveling with Mia. It's good cover; she's a well-known reporter, and if I sling a camera over my shoulder, anyone would take me for her photographer. I've known her for years—I have relationships with a lot of journalists; they're good sources—but there was never anything else."

I was biting my lip so hard it drew blood.

"We spent the day at a hospital in Qameen City. Shelley, I just don't have words to describe. . . ."

He paused for a moment, a muscle in his jaw working. "Nothing can describe it. She was reporting on the children—tiny bodies with head injuries so all you could see was a sea of bandages and a pair of dark eyes staring out—and gunshot wounds; one little boy was shot while he was trying to cross a street to get bread for his family. He lost both legs. Every day a few kids died, and no one had the energy to bury them, so they just tossed the bodies into this pit and every week or so set it on fire so the smell didn't get too bad. There wasn't much to burn; those tiny bodies had less meat on them than Amy Joy's."

"Why were *you* at the hospital?" I asked. My voice was dry; I had to clear my throat to get the words out.

"I had an asset there, a young doctor named Noura. I had finally gotten a visa for her and her son to come to America—and I wanted to give her the good news myself."

Already I could sense what was coming, and I didn't want to hear it. I was silent with dread.

"We left the hospital and traveled in a convoy to Beirut. Mia and I were having drinks in the hotel bar with a few other journalists when we got the news—the hospital had been bombed. Most of those children were dead. Noura's son, who spent the night with her in the hospital, died immediately, but she took hours to die."

"My God," was all I could think of to say.

"Everyone else went to file their stories, but Mia couldn't do it; she was shattered. *We* were shattered. So we just sat at the bar and drank, and drank, and then. . . ." He couldn't finish the sentence, couldn't meet my eyes.

It was true, then.

"And you. . . ." I couldn't say the words. Slept with her? Had an affair? Fucked her?

"Yes."

I nodded. David stared out the windshield, his face distant and remote, and I looked down at my lap. I felt almost numb.

I had seen this scene in so many movies; it was so trite and cliched. So why did it hurt so much?

David turned to look at me again. "Shelley," he said, almost pleadingly. David never pleaded. "Sweetheart, don't look like that. Please. It never would have happened if not for Qameen, and it will never happen again."

"How many others?" My voice sounded dry and rusty.

"What?"

"How many other women have there been?"

"Christ, Shelley! What do you think I am?"

I almost laughed. "Actually, David, I have no idea *what* you are. A management consultant? A spy? My husband? Mia's lover? Why don't you tell *me* what you are?"

"I'm your husband," he snapped.

"You didn't answer the question."

"None! There's never been anyone else."

"And have you seen Mia since . . . Beirut? Before you ran off to rescue her in Colombia, I mean."

He hesitated for a moment. "Yes."

My calm numbness was beginning to shatter, but I fought to hold it together. "Where?"

"New York, London . . . I ran into her in Tel Aviv last month . . . Our paths cross, but it's nothing, Shelley. She's doing her job and I'm doing mine. I slept with her one time and one time only. It was a terrible mistake."

"Really."

"Yes, really."

"Do you want a divorce?" I sounded calm, even detached.

His iron control shattering, he shouted, "No, I don't want a fucking divorce! Haven't you heard a word I've said?"

It was at least the second time he'd shouted at me since the news stories broke—and not the way we ever communicated before this. "I heard you," I said quietly. "That's why I'm asking."

He instantly throttled himself down. "No, I don't want a divorce. I love you, and I'm sorry for what I did—more sorry than I can ever say. I was . . . shattered, after Qameen. I didn't know what I was doing." Almost as an afterthought, he added in a low voice, "I've seen bad things happen to people before—but they were usually people who were up to their necks in bad shit already. Not children."

"And Mia helped put you back together again," I said ironically.

He didn't say anything. I studied his face, the dark blue eyes behind his wire-rimmed glasses, the lean cheeks stubbled with early morning whiskers, the dark blond hair growing a little too long. I didn't know if I could ever touch him again without thinking of another woman between us. Had she stroked his hair? Run her fingers down his body to touch him? Clung to his back as he . . .

All at once, I knew I was going to vomit. I wrenched open the car door and fell out to retch miserably onto the pebbly black pavement. David got out and came around to hold my head and pull my hair back from my face. "Here," he said gently, handing me a tissue. "Wipe your face."

Tears were streaming down my cheeks and I made no attempt to brush them away as I sobbed. Passersby stared curiously but veered away; I wondered if someone would call in a domestic disturbance to the police. David must have had the same thought. "Get back in the car," he said. "Lean back and close your eyes for a minute."

I was crying so hard, I couldn't even find the car door. David put his arm around my shoulders to guide me, but I shook him off violently. "Don't touch me," I hissed. I would throw up over and over until I was empty inside if he ever tried to touch me again.

—
118

He silently held the door open for me and closed it when I climbed in; then he went around to the other side.

I looked at his hands on the steering wheel and thought about them on another woman's body. Nausea rose in my throat again, and I wanted to wound him as badly as he had wounded me. "Did you get tested?" I asked, clearing my throat so I could speak.

That jolted him. "What?" he asked, his hands tightening a little on the wheel.

"Did. You. Get. Tested. God only knows who else she's been with."

"She hasn't. . . ." he began, then stopped. "No, Shelley, I didn't get tested."

"Did you use a condom?" I couldn't believe I had to ask these things of my husband.

"Yes."

"Every time?"

"That's enough, Shelley," he said in a dangerous tone.

"Really? Because if you didn't use a condom every time, then I need to get tested too."

"Jesus, Shelley! I told you it was one time! Would you stop?"

"Fuck you!" I screamed. The small, claustrophobic interior of the car was an echo chamber of fury and pain. "You know why I was throwing up? Because I was thinking about you touching me with those filthy hands, that filthy body that's been inside another woman. . . ." I couldn't continue because I was sobbing too hard.

"And what about us? You and me? If I came home to you, I'd have to get in line behind your crazy sisters and your sister's children and your PTO meetings and your goddamn cats and everyone else in the fucking world who needs you! At least Mia paid attention to my needs!"

My tears stopped cold. "You hypocrite. You self-serving, hypocritical bastard! How the *hell* did you expect me to take care of your needs when you've never once told me what they were? Or where you've been? Or what you've been doing? You shut me out *entirely*, David." I stared straight ahead. "I want to go home."

"Fine." We drove home in silence, broken only by the sound of my sobs and his fingers tapping against the steering wheel. It started to rain just as we pulled into the driveway.

CHAPTER TWENTY

To Do:
Continue Qameen research

I DON'T KNOW HOW I GOT THROUGH the next few days. Thankfully, David was away, so I didn't have to see his cheating, lying face, and he had the good sense not to call or text me. At dinner I talked to the kids as naturally as ever so they wouldn't know. And Amy Joy had a cold that turned into an ear infection, so her misery demanded all my attention and provided an excuse for my weariness and haggard eyes.

The truth was, I was paralyzed. Now that I knew, did I have to do something about it? And if so, what? I played and replayed the car conversation over and over in my head, until I could recite it from memory. David and the woman had been through a trauma together; I tried and failed to picture myself in a similar situation. Surely I wouldn't hop into bed with the nearest warm body?

And yet . . . I tracked down pictures of the bombed-out hospital online and saw the horror for myself—babies burned beyond all recognition, frantic parents scrabbling through the blackened rubble, a Red Crescent worker in tears. And how much worse it must have been for David, who had known some of the victims, who had talked to them just hours before their agonizing deaths. Who had gone to bring the good news of her long-awaited escape to America to Noura and her son. Noura, who had "taken hours to die."

The week passed, and eventually David came home again from wherever he had been. His wounds were healing, but every time I saw his scarring naked chest or watched him wince in pain at an unexpected movement, I thought of Mia—"honey"—and how he had leaped to her assistance, regardless of the consequences. When he got into bed at night, I turned my back to him and drew my knees to my chest in an almost fetal position so I wouldn't have to touch him; he slept deeply and peacefully by my side. During the day, I avoided him and focused all my attention on Amy Joy and Sasha, delighting in the former and gradually coaxing food into the latter.

Clearly sensing my mood, David avoided me too—but he began to spend more time with Amy Joy, who responded with happy gurgles and giggles when he tickled her tummy and played peekaboo. I wondered if he was feeling guilty, or if he was genuinely growing attached to her, but I didn't really care. Nothing could erase what he had done. Nothing mattered.

I couldn't avoid him forever though. On Wednesday morning we had to meet with the DC Department of Child and Family Services (DCFS) together about the adoption, so I dropped Amy Joy off with a delighted Rachel, and we walked down a quiet side street toward Connecticut Avenue together; he shortened his strides to match my slower gait.

I filled in the cold silence by telling him that I was a little apprehensive about meeting with DCFS, since I had made a few enemies there. In a recent divorce case, I was puzzled to find both parents charging that the other had abused their one-year-old baby. It was odd enough that I called in DCFS, but the team of investigators assigned to the case—Skip Henley and Fred Heaton—found no evidence of abuse. Unconvinced, I ordered the parents to hire a private investigator, who found that the nanny routinely shouted at and slapped the poor child. I reported the findings to the investigators' superiors at DCFS, who disciplined Henley and Heaton—only to receive a vicious email from Henley that stopped just short of threatening.

David said, "Don't worry, they won't be assigned to our case," and I was starting to respond—when a man stepped out from behind a parked van and pushed his way between us, elbowing me so I stumbled and almost fell. A flash of fear shot through me as I veered sharply away, seeking the shelter of David's hard body. But he was quicker; before I even saw him react, David had the man's arm twisted behind his back so that his mouth set into a rictus of pain.

"Let me go," the man panted. "Just trying to do my job. Please, let go of my arm!"

"Not until you show me what's in your hand."

"Paper, that's all! I swear it!"

"Open your hand very, very slowly, and show me."

The man's hand opened, and I watched a sheaf of papers drift to the ground. David released his hold only slightly and dragged the man back into the shadows between two apartment buildings. His movements were so smooth that no one on the street even noticed what was happening.

"What the fuck were you doing?" my husband demanded, shoving the man against the brick wall.

"I'm just doing my job! Can I pick up my papers?"

David let him go, and the man scooped up his papers and handed them over. "Here's a subpoena, asshole. You've been served," he said, a slight smirk creeping across his face. "Next one'll be for your pretty lady here. That'll be even more fun; I can—"

David's face went blank. He picked the man up by his shirt front and threw him against the dirty brick wall. "What are you doing?" the man yelped.

"Deciding whether to break your arm or just your collarbone." With a vicious swipe, David knocked the man to the ground. "Stay away from my wife," he said quietly. Then he took my arm and walked us away.

Staggered and a little frightened by this glimpse of the un-David—not to mention the subpoena—I was almost mute in the DCFS meeting (without Henley and Heaton, thank goodness) and on the way home. When I asked David about the subpoena later that day, he said it was just a legal game of chicken, and not to worry about it.

Of course, as a lawyer, I knew better than that.

After that, it was frighteningly easy to avoid each other in the days that followed, as Hurricane Amy Joy had engulfed the entire household. The twins, absurdly, were showing some signs of childish sibling rivalry ("You never pay attention to me anymore," Sasha whined); I recognized it for what it was and patiently waited it out. Sam was a little better, but clearly mystified and a little alarmed by the baby's usurpation of the entire household. I had forgotten how much space one tiny baby occupied, with her Pack 'n Play and diaper bag and toy basket and bouncy seat and baby swing and. . . . Baby gear littered the kitchen and family room, since I was too exhausted at the end of the day to restore the house to its usual pristine condition. (The silver lining, though, was Amy Joy's unceasing demands; she kept me so befuddled and besieged that I couldn't spare even a moment to think about David and Mia and the photographs—and I loved her even more for that.)

David said little; mercifully and surprisingly, he seemed to have accepted Amy Joy's presence in our lives with the same equanimity that he displayed toward my collection of homeless cats. I wondered if he might be afraid of my reaction if he challenged me on this. And he would be right; a nuclear explosion would be nothing compared to what would happen if he dared to suggest that Amy Joy was not ours.

Or maybe he knew that he owed me, after having betrayed me so unforgivably.

At any rate, he stayed home from work one morning to set up the new nursery. He got up once every night to give Amy Joy a bottle so I could get one four-hour stretch of sleep. Albie had transferred his fickle attentions to David and followed him around the house, jumping into his lap as soon as the poor man sat down and purring hysterically whenever David obediently scratched his ears. The other cats kept an awed distance from the now-dominant Albie.

Our relationship was in an odd state of stalemate. I pressed myself against the wall when he walked by so I didn't have to brush against him, and I didn't know if I could ever bear to have him touch me again. I knew that we couldn't live like this forever, but I was terrified of what the future would reveal. I needed, absolutely *required*, our family to stay together—so I was grateful for Amy Joy's all-encompassing need of me; it served as an even more effective barrier against David than my anger or fear could have done.

Only with Rachel, it seemed, could I be honest. A couple of weeks after my early-morning confrontation with David, I packed up Amy Joy and met Rachel at the same Starbucks where I had met Mary Ann and Dr. Lillian. Anger welled up again when I thought of them, and I had to stuff it down before I could greet Rachel civilly.

"What's wrong?" she asked immediately, reaching out to take the baby and smile into her sweet face.

"What do you think?" I retorted.

Loyal friend that Rachel was, she didn't respond to my sharp tone.

"Well—have you talked to David? About the woman?" She unwrapped Amy Joy's coat and handed her a set of toy keys to suck on.

"Well, yes. Sort of."

"What does that mean?"

"It means that we talked—he said they were together in Qameen and that she was upset—it was really bad there. . . ."

"That's probably true," said Rachel, and I glared at her.

Quickly, she said, "I saw the pictures. You're *much* prettier than she is. She has a hard face, don't you think?"

I shrugged. The woman's face was too strong and angular for real beauty, but there was a certain something that I thought men—David—might react to.

"What else did he say?" Amy Joy threw the keys on the floor, and I handed her a cloth book.

"That it's true. He slept with her."

Rachel's face registered shock at my bluntness. I sat in silence, letting my words sink in. Finally she said, "And? What are you thinking?"

"Nothing. I'm thinking nothing."

"Shelley—"

I interrupted her. "Is there a stage of grief called avoidance?"

"No, and you've never been a shrinking violet! Jesus, Shelley, take control of the situation! Figure out what you want, and then—you know. Deal with it."

I opened my mouth and closed it again as my best friend regarded me with doubt and worry. I started talking, thinking aloud, fears tumbling out that I had never even known I harbored.

"I don't have to do anything. I don't have to deal with it."

Rachel shook her head in incomprehension.

"You know about my father, right? How he left us, and my mother fell apart?"

She said nothing, but her arms tightened protectively around Amy Joy, who was sucking on a cloth book in near ecstasy.

Rapidly, I went on, "If only he'd stayed around . . . the truth is that I don't care if he slept with a thousand women—if only he'd stayed with us."

Rachel said quietly, "But your mother might have cared."

"I don't think so, Rach. I really don't think so. She was incapable of driving us to school for six months after he left. Of going to the bank. Of paying bills or buying groceries. Jesus, Rachel, she was *broken!*"

"You're not your mother. You wouldn't be like that. You're the strongest person in the world, and you can handle anything."

But I wasn't sure. Somewhere inside me lingered that terrified teenage girl, terrified that another man would sail off into the sunset and leave me in charge of a desolate family.

"And David's not like your father. He would never do that," Rachel added. "Even if—you know—even if the worst happened—"

Numbly, I noted that she couldn't bring herself to use the D-word: divorce.

"He would still be around for you and the kids. You know that."

The rational adult part of me did know that. But it didn't matter as long as the abandoned teenager was in control. I sat in silent misery, thinking thoughts that I couldn't share even with Rachel. Of course I knew that David wasn't anything like my father! Wasn't that why I had married him? He seemed so steady and reliable, so grounded, not a man who would ever run out on his wife and family.

And I needed him to still be that man—stable, even a little dull—not a mysterious superspy who jetted around the world with strange women and with a hard, brusque edge that I'd never seen before.

But I didn't say that. Instead I gathered up Amy Joy and wiped her little face and said my good-byes. For the moment, David seemed as happy to avoid me as I was to avoid him. Maybe we could make that work.

That weekend, Sasha and Sam went "home" for a visit with their "real" parents. I felt bereft, even uneasily guilty, watching their car pull out of the driveway. The kids had heard the shouting between me and David in the bedroom on that early morning, and it had upset them. We weren't a shouting family, and they'd never heard such acrimony between us before. Not even when we took them to Disney World, and the hotel lost our reservation and all of us had to stay in a cramped, miserable single room—with one single bed—at the Holiday Inn. I had tripped over Sam's sleeping form on my way to the bathroom at two in the morning and broken my toe; then David got a vicious sunburn, and we lost Sasha in the Magic Kingdom because she was flirting with one of Pooh's handlers and didn't see us leaving the ride. Even then, David kept his cool, and we managed to make light of the string of disasters.

But this was different, and I knew the children were frightened by the tension in the house. I couldn't afford to blow up at David again, so instead I kept my distance. It seemed to work.

Later that afternoon, he wandered out of our bedroom with a bemused expression on his face. "You broke into my desk," he said, sitting down across from me on the floor of our living room where I was playing with Amy Joy.

"Not me, exactly," I said. "A locksmith."

He groaned. "Tell me you didn't let someone else see inside that desk," he begged. "Please tell me that."

"Of course I didn't," I said indignantly. "I didn't open a drawer until he was gone."

He leaned back and sighed. "So what did you discover about Pete Brooks? I always thought him a dull chap—all work and no play."

"Not exactly," I said, watching him. "Peter has expensive tastes in wine and Venetian glass."

For a split second, I saw that I had surprised him. "Peter does enjoy his little luxuries," he agreed.

I reached into my pocket and tossed him the old Sony Walkman I'd discovered among his Princeton papers. "I see that you like Jimi Hendrix," I said.

He shrugged, wary again. "John Mayer gets boring," was all he said.

"Why did you say you went to UCLA, when you went to Princeton?" I had wanted to ask him about all of this ever since my little spying mission into his desk and locker, but somehow the time had never been right.

"Princeton is too closely associated with the Agency, both past and present. Nobody thinks of spies and UCLA in the same sentence."

"What languages do you speak?"

"Arabic and Farsi. They wanted me to learn German, but I refused."

"Why?"

"Because my parents would be spinning in their graves if they thought I spoke the language, let alone went there."

"Why *do* you go to Germany?" I asked.

"Terrorist cells in Hamburg. I go in, do my business, get out."

Modern Germany had come to terms with its role in the Holocaust, though, and most Jews had long ago abandoned such attitudes. So it was surprising and a little endearing to hear that David still had such an emotional—even childlike—reaction.

"When I was in college," he went on, "some friends and I spent a few weeks backpacking through Europe. I refused to go to Germany—my parents were still alive then—but we had to take the train from Vienna to Amsterdam."

I edged closer; he'd never talked about his college days before. His real college days, that is.

"It was before the EU and open borders," he went on, "so when we got to the German border, the train stopped and some German officials got on and started going from cabin to cabin, checking passports. I was in a cold sweat, shaking from head to toe."

"You had a panic attack," I said sympathetically.

"I don't have panic attacks."

I said nothing.

"But I stayed up all night," he went on, "staring out the train windows until we were out of Germany. You know, Shells, my parents had fucking numbers tattooed on their arms! My mother hoarded food until the day she died; when we were sitting shiva, Daniel and I had to go through their apartment and find all her stashes. Dried apricots behind the radiator, roasted peanuts under the freakin' sofa cushions. . . ."

He was practically throwing the words at me, and I had to fight the urge to put my arms around him and hold him close.

"I know what it's like to protect a damaged mother," I said instead.

"So you do." He sounded surprised. "I guess we do have some things in common, after all."

Amy Joy shrieked suddenly and I got up automatically, like a marionette on her strings. "Jesus," said David. "Are you really sure that you want to be saddled with another baby, after all these years?"

"Yes," I bit out, hating him again—and hating myself for having fallen into the old familiar trap of easy conversation. I turned my back on him and ran to pick up my crying baby.

One step forward, two steps back.

CHAPTER TWENTY-ONE

To Do:
Buy tissues with aloe, mint green tea, organic honey,
Evian for Dani
Put on hypoallergenic sheets for Dani
Schedule mani/pedi for Dani
Call Javier at Save Qameen

AFTERWARD, I WAS FURIOUS AT MYSELF and at him; I hadn't learned much, and still I hadn't asked the right questions. The next morning, David packed a bag. "I'm going overseas," he told me. "I'm not sure when I'll be back. Maybe Friday, but don't count on it."

I wasn't sure I could ever count on him again. Evenly, I asked, "Where are you going?"

He looked as if he wasn't going to answer, but then shrugged. "Qameen."

I gulped, momentarily unable to maintain the frozen wall of silence between us. "Really? Qameen?"

"Yes. I've been there before, Shelley. I know what I'm doing."

Suddenly I wished he hadn't told me; now I'd be terrified the whole time he was gone. "Oh, my God."

He frowned. "This is why I never told you about my job before."

It stung, and I turned away, my eyes clouded by sudden tears. David sighed. "It'll be all right," he said, trying to put his arm around me and draw me close. I almost let him, my eyes swimming with tears, and he bent his head down to mine. But all at once I saw that photo of my husband's dark blond head bending down to that other woman's, and I wondered if she'd be in Qameen too.

I pulled away, hating him, and his arms dropped to his sides.

"Wait a minute," I said. "How can you go to places like Qameen, now that your picture is plastered all over the Internet?"

"I know what I'm doing, Shelley."

Fury rose in me again. "You bastard, can't you even answer a simple question? How the *hell* can you be undercover overseas, after all that's happened?"

"In disguise," he said briefly.

"But—"

"Shelley," he said. "Have a little faith in me."

"You must be kidding," I spat at him, and he recoiled.

"Okay, then. I'll be back in a week or so. Maybe less." He stood for a moment, then shook himself and picked up his bag. "And while I'm gone? Why don't you think again about whether you really want a new baby?"

"I want her a whole lot more than I want you!" I flung after him, and without another word he strode out of the room.

A wave of sheer pain washed through my entire body, and I almost sank to my knees, but Sasha burst into the room wailing that Tinky had peed on her homework, and I heard Amy Joy start making noises in the crib behind me.

I straightened up. I couldn't afford the luxury of falling apart; too many people were counting on me to hold them together.

———

"Let's see if we can clean off your homework," I told Sasha. I picked up Amy Joy from her crib, smiling as she snuggled into my shoulder and gave me a sleepy good morning smile, and we went down the stairs together.

With David gone again, I decided to continue my research. So the next afternoon when Amy Joy was napping, I set to work searching through all his possessions. I was looking for clues, souvenirs—anything that might illuminate the glimpses of the un-David(s) I kept seeing.

But there was nothing. No receipts, no wadded-up notes, not even a stray business card. Every pocket was empty, every drawer innocent.

And then I remembered the gray safe in our closet.

So I called the locksmith again. Eyeing me a little dubiously this time, he admitted that he'd never seen a safe like this one, and that it was beyond even his prowess.

"Can't you drill it open?" I begged. "Please?"

"Sorry, ma'am," he said, shaking his head. "I reckon you'd have to get one of those secret government types—CIA or FBI or one of them guys—to open this here contraption."

My younger sister, Dani, came to visit that weekend. I hadn't heard a word from David aside from a brief email on Thursday that informed me that—surprise!—he now wouldn't be home until the following week. I deleted the email with a quick swipe, wishing I could wipe him out of my mind with equal ease.

Dani's train was delayed, so Amy Joy and I sat in the car together outside Union Station for over an hour as the sun dipped below the horizon and the rush-hour crowds slowly dwindled to a crawl. By the time Dani finally appeared, looking freshly made-up and sprightly in her little miniskirt and sleeveless cashmere vest, I was sweating like a pig, and Amy Joy's face was bright red with anger. Just as Dani climbed into the car and leaned over to kiss me, Amy Joy let loose with a howl.

"Ouch!" Dani cried, falling back in her seat with an exaggerated gasp. "That child has one healthy set of lungs!" She twisted around for a good look at the baby, who was howling with all her strength and flailing her tiny fists in frustrated fury. "She's cute," Dani added unconvincingly, and I almost grinned. With her fortieth birthday just ahead of her, Dani had never even contemplated the ticking of her biological clock; she was not a babysitting, adoring aunt—although now that Sasha was a teenager, Dani loved to take her shopping at their favorite stores. God knows, Dani dressed in the same clothes that Sasha wore.

As Amy Joy squirmed and fought against the straps on her car seat, Dani bestowed a frown on me. "I hope you know what you're getting yourself into," she called over Amy Joy's shrieks and twisted around for a more assessing scrutiny. "She has David's coloring. Are you sure she isn't his love child?"

"He got snipped, remember?" I shouted back. "After all the miscarriages? Anyway, what's new with you? Are you going to London for the book fair?"

Dani nodded. "Can't you give her a bottle or something?" she yelled. "Yeah, I'm going to London, and then I'm stopping in Paris for a long weekend with some friends. Too bad you couldn't get away and go with me."

A long weekend in Paris! I almost laughed. "Well, it would be pretty difficult for me to get away right now."

"So I see," my sister said a little dryly.

I didn't think I could go as far as Baltimore without my whole family collapsing. I was barely holding them together as it was. Sasha was still struggling through sibling rivalry and Sam was vacillating between fear and despair, parsing every conversation with Sharona to reassure himself that she still loved him (as she obviously did not). I was ashamed to find myself sometimes resenting their seemingly endless need for my advice, sympathy, energy . . . it was probably just the sleep-deprived nights. But still, Sam's travails with Sharona and Sasha's feud with the team captain seemed a bit petty compared to Amy Joy's urgent needs and my disappearing marriage.

"So did you read that manuscript I sent you?" Dani asked.

I forced my mind away from Amy Joy's escalating shrieks. We were past Dupont Circle now; only a few more minutes and we'd be home. "Sorry," I said. "Which manuscript?"

"The new *Teenage Trauma!*" Dani shouted. "Didn't you read it yet? People would kill for that manuscript, and you haven't even read it?" She sounded horrified.

"Sorry," I yelled. "I've been a little busy."

She muttered something disapproving, and I sighed. Dani's needs were always more important and more pressing than other people's; now I remembered that she'd sent me the manuscript a couple of weeks ago with a note asking me to take a look and let her know what I thought. My little sister was an editor at one of New York's top publishing houses, and the *Teenage Trauma* series was her huge moneymaker—but my time wasn't my own right now. Right now, my only priority was getting home and getting poor Amy Joy out of that blasted car seat.

The whole gang showed up for dinner on Saturday night— Sasha, Sam, Marisa, her husband Neil, Dani, and Sharona. I was exhausted from another sleepless night with Amy Joy. She'd caught another cold, and her runny nose and constant wails of misery were like nails on a blackboard.

"Would you please take the baby for a minute!" I snapped at

Sasha. "I'm trying to make a complicated dinner and clean up after the damned cats and keep her from crying—would it kill you to be helpful?"

Sasha took her from me gingerly, staring down into the tiny face as she walked over toward Sam's girlfriend. Amy Joy stared back. I waited for an explosion of screams, but the baby remained blessedly quiet, possibly stunned by being handed into another set of arms. Usually I kept Amy Joy all to myself, mesmerized by the miracle of her presence, but it was time to let the older kids in on her care. Sasha cautiously touched her cheek, and Amy Joy gave her a tentative smile.

"She's smiling at you!" Sharona exclaimed. "Oh, she's so cute—can I hold her now?"

Sasha glanced down at the baby in her arms. "She doesn't really like strangers. I think I'd better keep her."

Astonished that Sasha knew that—let alone that she wasn't trying to hand Amy Joy off to the first willing set of arms in sight—I hurried into the kitchen and pulled open the oven door.

Sharona followed me. "Can I help you with anything, Mrs. Harris?" she asked.

I wished I could like her more. But something about her slightly sharp face—not to mention Sam's naked, vulnerable adoration of her—always made me want to bar the door against her and festoon the gate with ropes of garlic. "Please," I said, maybe a little snappishly. "It's Shelley."

She nodded. "Shelley, can I help you?"

Sam, who was always close upon her heels, came into the kitchen. He lifted a strand of her long, gleaming black hair and let it run through his hands, seemingly mesmerized by its glossy perfection. "Have you ever seen anything so beautiful?" he said to no one in particular.

I winced and turned away to stir my grilled asparagus on the stove. "Sharona," I said over my shoulder, "maybe you could take some drinks out to the table. Thanks."

I served up the meal—kosher chicken for Sam, who had suddenly decided to be more observant, veggies for Sasha and Sharona, oven-roasted potatoes for Marisa's husband Neil, who was still a meat and potatoes kind of guy, salad for me, mashed applesauce for Amy Joy, bread and olive oil for all. It took a while for everyone to get their required food.

Sam said a blessing while Sharona rolled her eyes, and we dug in.

"So, Shelley," Neil said. "Where's the superspy these days?"

CHAPTER TWENTY-TWO

"QAMEEN," I SAID, SPEARING A FORKFUL of red leaf lettuce.

Sam choked on his chicken. "What?" he gasped.

"Qameen." I turned to spoon some applesauce into Amy Joy's eager mouth.

"What the hell is he doing there?" Dani demanded.

I shrugged. "Whatever it is that spies do. I don't know."

There was a brief silence. Sasha asked, "Aren't you worried, Shelley?"

"Not at all," I said airily. Maybe he and the BBC reporter would die in each other's arms. I couldn't care less. Amy Joy squawked, and I gave her another spoonful of applesauce.

Marisa declared, "Well, I wouldn't let my husband go anywhere near that godforsaken place. Don't start getting any ideas, Neil."

Neil, an accountant who didn't even like traveling to Pittsburgh, stared at her. I stifled a laugh.

Dani, never shy, asked, "And what's the story with the BBC reporter? Mia Holloway? She's gorgeous, isn't she? I'd love to find out who does her hair."

"I know," Sharona said eagerly. "And did you see the cocktail dress she was wearing at the BBC awards? They had it on CNN...." A little belatedly, her voice trailed off as she realized that this might not be the most tactful area of discussion. "Uh, sorry, Shelley," she muttered, her face turning pink.

"Don't worry about me," I said quickly. "It's just the press exaggerating a . . . work friendship."

"But they were in Qameen together, weren't they?" Sam asked. Of all the children, he was the most likely to follow in David's footsteps. He never let go of a question until it was resolved, and he never forgot anything. Probably great attributes in an interrogator; not so great in a teenager.

"I think so," I answered. "But it's not exactly a romantic atmosphere, you know. They were working. Qameen is a hellhole, I've been reading about it. The plight of the refugees is just—"

They weren't interested in hearing about Qameen.

"But there was that other picture," Dani interrupted. "Where were they, anyway?"

"Beirut," said Sam. "I looked it up."

There was an expectant pause. I bit my lip, furious at David for getting me into this position and wishing he was here to see the consequences of his actions. But that was just the point, wasn't it? He was never here.

Marisa shrugged. "Oh, who cares, anyway?"

Well, I did, quite a bit. But I was glad for her interruption.

"What's much more interesting," Dani put in eagerly, "is the fact that I have a new boyfriend! Don't you want to know all about it?"

Sasha leaned forward eagerly, while Marisa groaned. Sharona looked amused.

"Not another loser," Marisa said. "What's wrong with this one? Does he live with his mother? Collect exotic tarantulas? Talk to his orchids?"

"No," Dani snapped, stung. They had tortured each other as children, and I guess you never grow out of some habits.

I said quickly, "Just ignore her, Dani. So what's he like? What does he do?"

Satisfied, Dani settled back. "Well," she said dramatically, "you're never going to believe this. Guess what he does!"

"Lawyer?" I suggested.

"Investment banker?" Neil said hopefully. A rich husband would be a very good thing for Dani, whose sartorial requirements regularly exceeded her salary; Marisa and I had been subsidizing her for years.

"Writer?" Sasha tried.

"Artist?" Sharona.

"Spy?" This was Sam's contribution, along with a sideways grin at me.

"No!" Dani said. "I told you you'd never believe me. He's a . . ." she paused dramatically then said excitedly, "a rabbi!"

A dumbfounded silence settled over the table. Finally I said weakly, "A rabbi?"

"Isn't that wonderful?" Dani exclaimed.

"Cool," said Sam. Everyone ignored him.

"How in God's name did you ever meet a rabbi?" Marisa wanted to know.

"His mother set us up," Dani said smugly.

"Oh. My. God. The rabbi's mother set you up with her precious son?" Marisa was choking with laughter. "That's the funniest thing I ever heard."

"Marisa," I said warningly.

"Yes," Dani snapped. "His name is Josh Leibowitz, and he's assistant rabbi at Stephen Wise on the Upper West Side, and his mother is best friends with one of my writers. And he's wonderful!"

"Just like the performance artist?" Marisa suggested. "And the personal trainer, and the Reiki master, and the waiter-slash-actor, and the. . . ."

"Shut up!" Dani hissed.

"That's enough, Marisa," I said firmly, and Neil put a gentle hand on his wife's arm.

"I'm telling you, he's The One," Dani insisted.

"How long have you been seeing him?" I asked gently.

"We've had two dates so far, and he's absolutely perfect. I tried to tell you all about him last week, but you're always too busy to talk to me!"

"What does he look like?" Sasha asked eagerly, drowning out Marisa's snort of derision.

"I think that's enough on the rabbi," I said hastily. "Let's move on."

Dani left on Sunday evening, having spent most of her time criticizing my wardrobe and cringing every time Amy Joy cried—which was painfully often; her tiny nose was still swollen and totally stuffed up. With a fretful Amy Joy perched on my left hip and my constantly chattering sister raising her voice to be heard above the baby's complaints, my ears were ringing by the time that her Uber arrived.

"Bye, sweetie," I said, hugging her tightly for a moment. She was wearing Paige jeans that fit as if they'd been molded to her thin, wiry body, and I wondered briefly what a rabbi's salary could possibly be. Probably not enough to finance $195 jeans. "Take care of yourself."

She drew back as Amy Joy's snot-smeared face threatened to brush against hers. "Ugh," she said. "That baby is a walking germ factory. I hope you know what you're doing."

Aside from the brief dinner table discussion, we hadn't talked at all about David or Amy Joy or any of the other things that were going on in my life. Dani dominated the conversation with tales about wild-eyed authors, lying agents, grasping lawyers, and lecherous personal trainers. It was just as well.

"I know what I'm doing," I said firmly, tightening my grasp on the squirming baby as she reached curiously for the gold necklace swinging free on Dani's blouse. Maybe if I said it often enough, it would come true.

CHAPTER TWENTY-THREE

To Do:
Diapers
Infant Tylenol
Send Dani everything she left behind (gold-leaf mois-
turizer, Prada shoes, Vineyard Vines sweater)

AND THEN, FINALLY, DAVID CAME HOME. I was trying to get a
fretful Amy Joy to take her bottle when I heard his footsteps on
the stairs. Her nose was so stuffed that she could barely breathe
when she was sucking on the bottle, and the frustration made
her furious. She was shaking her head back and forth, whimper-
ing, as David came into the bedroom.

"Here," he said, dropping his bag on the floor and rolling up
his sleeves. "I'll take her."

I remembered his parting words: Why don't you think about
if you really want a new baby?—and hugged her closer to my
chest. But he held out his arms and I was exhausted enough to
hand her over, marveling that she didn't put him in the dreaded
"stranger" category despite how little she saw of him. Croon-
ing gently, he settled down in my abandoned rocking chair and
slipped the bottle between her lips. "She still has a cold?" he
asked without looking up.

I nodded wearily. "Since forever."

"That must have been fun this weekend," he observed. "And I'm sure that Dani was a big help."

"Oh, yeah. You know how much she loves babies with runny noses."

He grunted. "I'm sorry for what I said about her," he said, looking down into Amy Joy's tiny face. She beamed back.

"You should be."

"She's part of our family now."

"You're damned right she is."

He nodded and stroked her wispy dark blond hair with a gentle finger. Then, briskly, he got up. "Have you been suctioning her nose out?" he asked, heading for the bathroom.

"Yes, but she hates it."

"I'll do it." At the door, he turned around and glanced at me over his shoulder. "I really am sorry, Shelley," he said.

For which sin? I wondered.

That Sunday David took Amy Joy out for the morning, and I didn't get out of bed until almost noon. When they got home, he put her down for a nap and spent the afternoon repairing the garage door, which Sasha had backed her car into a few days before.

Sasha wandered through the kitchen in a tiny miniskirt and skimpy top. "Whoa," I said. "Where do you think you're going in that outfit?"

She scowled at me. "I'm just going over to Tessa's."

"Not wearing that—"

The kitchen door slammed shut and David strode in. He headed for the sink to wash his hands but stopped short at the sight of Sasha. "You must be kidding," he told her.

"What?" she demanded.

The rest of the discussion was predictable. Sasha stormed up to her room, sobbing that she hated both of us. Amy Joy woke up and started crying, and David turned to me.

"She's just acting out a little," I said. "A lot has happened in her life recently; she'll be fine."

"I understand," he said. It was the first real conversation we'd had since the car, and I could sense him lingering behind me, not wanting to let it go. "Shelley. . . ."

I pushed past him, calling over my shoulder, "I have to get Amy Joy; she's crying."

When we came back down to the kitchen, Amy Joy was still fussing. But she broke out in a smile as soon as she saw David and held out eager hands toward him.

His face cleared and he took her from me. "Did you have a good nap, sweetheart?" he murmured, holding her up so she could look into his face.

The little wretch actually giggled, and I turned away.

Late that night, when David was in bed and Sasha was out with her friends, I logged onto my laptop. I idly contemplated the screensaver, a sunny, windblown photograph of the kids on the beach in southern Florida the previous winter, and realized that I needed a new picture of the kids with Amy Joy in it.

I hadn't expected to fall in love with her so immediately and thoroughly. We hadn't sought her, or even welcomed her arrival into our life. She'd seemed like a burden when we were finally beginning to shake free of the chains of child-raising.

We should have resented her—instead, we fell in love. Even David had fallen for her charms, I suspected. Perhaps the gift of Amy Joy was payback for those years of miscarriages. Perhaps she was a lost baby finally returned to me at a time when I really needed her.

I gave myself a mental shake and saw a Google alert in my

email from the Drudge Report, which had compiled an entire dossier on David. I remembered setting up Google alerts when I first started my research on him; it seemed so long ago now. Before I knew.

I scanned the dossier, finding little that I hadn't already discovered, but Drudge had managed to dig up some sources who were willing to talk, now that David was out of the closet, so to speak. Apparently he was almost killed in Karachi a few years ago; the details were murky, but it had something to do with an al-Qaeda cell and a hostage situation. When he was station chief in Riyadh, he was reputed to have recruited a top Russian industrialist and a deputy minister of state for the CIA; he was also the first to identify and break a Hezbollah cell in Hamburg. There were also rumors that he had predicted a massive al-Qaeda attack in the US just three weeks before 9/11, and had practically torn Langley apart demanding a meeting with the President—which was never granted.

His career was spotless, until the current mess. For the first time, I pushed aside my personal woes and started wondering about the facts that David had risked his twenty-five-year career to expose. That subpoena was much more than a "legal game of chicken"—it put his life's work on the line. And yet . . . the British were passing information to Hamas? Arming them with weapons? Working secretly with terrorists to pressure Israel? No wonder he had been so outraged.

At two in the morning I heard footsteps behind me and felt his presence. "Come to bed," David said. He glanced over my shoulder. "What the hell are you doing?" he asked warily.

I didn't turn around. "Researching you," I said. "Matt Drudge knows far more about you than I do."

"That's mostly crap." He reached around me to scroll up the page, speed-reading and muttering under his breath.

"Well?" I asked when he was done.

"I'd love to have a word with his sources," my husband said grimly.

I shrugged and turned off the computer. I have to admit, a tiny part of me was impressed and a little intimidated. Had he really done all those things? But most of me was just exhausted, weary beyond words at the realization of how little I'd actually known about him. "You go to bed," I said. "I'm going to read for a while."

The next week brought Amy Joy's social worker for the first of three required home visits. When I opened the door, I was relieved to see a woman around my age, not the hapless girl who had handed the baby over to me at the lawyer's office or my archenemy team of Henley and Heaton. This woman frowned at me over her reading glasses.

"Is your husband here too?" she asked.

"No, he couldn't miss work today," I answered.

"We like to see both adoptive parents," she said disapprovingly.

"I'm so sorry. He was very sorry to have to miss you," I said automatically. Long experience had taught me that bully bureaucrats like this were best handled with extreme deference and frequent apologies.

She sniffed. "And this is the Tellerman baby?" She turned her attention to Amy Joy, who was perched on my hip, chewing on plastic teething keys while staring suspiciously at the social worker.

"Legally, yes," I said. "But in our hearts she's a Harris."

The woman settled onto my family room couch and pulled a clipboard out of her overflowing tote bag. We went through her checklist: how many bowel movements does the baby produce in a twenty-four-hour period; is there any watery discharge from her eyes, ears, or vagina; has she spoken her first word. (At six months??)

We got along swimmingly.

Finally she heaved herself up and stuffed everything back into her tote bag. "I guess I can submit a satisfactory report so far," she allowed grudgingly. "But next time I'll also have to meet with your husband to assess your relationship. A stable marriage is very important in cases like this."

Suddenly alarmed, I turned to put Amy Joy down on her blanket to hide my reaction. "What do you mean?" I asked as I turned back, trying to sound casual. "It's not an issue for us, but I'm wondering because Amy Joy's mother was single—her biological father was never in the picture."

The woman eyed me narrowly. "Even though he's renounced his rights, if the biological father should ever change his mind, it would be important for you to be able to demonstrate a stable marriage."

It had never even occurred to me that Amy Joy's biological father would reappear. "That won't happen," I said confidently. "He was abusive; he did drugs—he could never win custody." Amy Joy whimpered and I bent to pick her up again, holding her small, warm body against mine more tightly than usual.

"The courts are very disposed to favor the biological parent," the woman warned.

I looked down into Amy Joy's dark blue eyes and felt a chill run through me. Never, I promised her silently. But after I showed the social worker out, I couldn't dispel the unease that had gripped me, and I ran to the phone to call David.

He didn't answer, of course. It was just as well; I told myself to stop being foolish and took Amy Joy upstairs to find a pretty pink dress to wear.

David had left for somewhere in the Middle East the day before, and I hadn't spoken to him since. I tried not to think about him.

—

I didn't ever want to think about him again—it hurt too much. Twice I saw Unknown Caller come up on the caller ID, and twice I let the calls go unanswered. I knew he wouldn't leave a voicemail; he never did. Probably too easy to trace.

But he showed up on Thursday night as we were sitting down to dinner, shouldering open the kitchen door and tossing his bags on the floor so he could loosen his tie and grab Sasha for a hug. "Hi, honey, I'm home!" he said in his best Ricky Ricardo imitation.

Sasha and Sam looked at me uncertainly. The kids had just as stubbornly refused to talk about David, not questioning me again about the Mia Holloway photos or the damning news reports that followed. We were all suffering from a deplorable lack of curiosity—or courage, I supposed. And none of us was willing to jump up and welcome him home tonight. Everyone was waiting for my lead.

And I needed to keep the family peace. Though I probably hated him, I said evenly, "David. I didn't expect you, but I think there's enough chicken. Sasha, would you set another place, please?"

He looked at the row of eyes firmly fixed on their plates, and pained understanding crossed his face. I steeled myself, determined not to feel any sympathy for him. "Sorry I couldn't call," he said cautiously. "It was almost impossible to get cell-phone service."

"Where were you?" Sam asked, just as cautiously. Sasha set down an extra plate and silverware, careful not to brush against David as she leaned down.

"The Middle East."

Sam was clearly dying to ask more questions, but just as clearly conflicted about how to treat this beloved uncle/father who had suddenly morphed into a mysterious, possibly hateful, stranger. He fell silent.

Finally I suggested, "Maybe if you tell us whatever you can about your work, we'll all be able to understand better."

David swallowed a big bite of chicken and got up to pour himself a glass of wine. "I was meeting with some tribal leaders," he said as he sat down again. "We're trying to pick off some Taliban sympathizers, get them to cooperate with us or at least to stop fighting us."

Sam shot a glance at me, and I nodded slightly. He leaned forward. "Is it dangerous?" he asked eagerly. "Do you go into the tribal areas or the training camps?"

Clearly, Sam too had been doing some research. David smiled and looked at me to share the moment, but I refused to meet his gaze. "I do go into the tribal areas," he told Sam, "but no, it's not dangerous."

I doubted that very highly.

"But you're armed, aren't you?" Sam persisted.

"Oh, yes."

"What do you carry?" Sam, again. Even Sasha was interested now, though she was playing with her food again and pretending to ignore the conversation.

"A Glock and a Beretta."

Sam forgot to be cool. "You carry two guns?" he breathed.

David nodded. "And a mountain knife."

I stood up. "I think that's enough on the weapons," I said briskly, ignoring Sam's look of disappointment. "We get the picture. Sam, it's your turn to clear the table."

As I picked up Amy Joy and headed for the stairs, David followed me. "I know this is a bad time," he said. "But I need to ask you for a favor."

I pressed my lips together and waited.

"I'm sorry to ask this of you," he began.

"Oh, for heaven's sake! When will you realize that 'I'm sorry' just isn't enough?"

"But it's . . . important."

I stared straight ahead in silence.

"Shelley, I need to go to Paris and London for some meetings. It's very important."

"A matter of life and death?" I suggested.

"Yes, it is. I need to travel in my true name in Western Europe now; it's an understanding that we have with their intelligence services once an officer has been burned. Since I can't hide the fact that I'm making the trip, all I can do is hope to disguise its purpose. That's where you come in."

I swallowed.

"I need you to come to Europe with me. I need you to pretend that we're on a second honeymoon—a trip to heal our marriage—so that I can take meetings without being watched every second of the day."

Pretend that we're on a second honeymoon? Is that anything like pretending that we still have a marriage?

He waited. "Shelley? Did you hear me?"

"Yes."

He waited some more. Finally, he said impatiently, "Yes you heard me? Or yes you'll come? For God's sake, Shelley, could you just talk to me?"

I heard the urgency in his voice and wondered, with a quickening pulse, what the source of his passion was. *Did* he care for me after all? Was there more than a business favor in his plea? Was he still invested in us? *Why?*

But I was still shellshocked; I wasn't ready to ask those questions. Instead I said, "I don't understand why you're still working for the CIA at all, let alone making important trips for them. Aren't you in some pretty serious legal trouble? After what you did. Leaking information to the BBC."

His lips tightened. "What I did—as you so nicely put it—is more complicated than the news stories suggest. Yes, I still have my job, and they still need my contacts and my experience. Anyway, no changes will be made until the Senate investigation is over."

I stood up and smoothed my linen skirt over my knees. It was almost time for *Grey's Anatomy*; I wanted to brush my teeth and get into bed before it started. I was so numb inside that I felt half-dead. "I'll think about it," I said, and walked away.

I did think about it. I thought about what a fool I'd be to let David use me—exploiting our battered marriage to hide some "meetings." I thought about how liberating it would be to get out of Washington, away from the prying eyes of my neighbors and coworkers and friends. I thought about the one and only trip we'd taken to Europe after I lost the fourth baby, when we really were trying to heal our marriage.

And most of all, I thought about my questions. About why David wanted to stay married to me even after all the losses, and why he wanted to stay married to me now. Maybe—just maybe—away from our natural environment, forced together, I could begin to explore some answers.

"All right," I told him. "I'll go."

CHAPTER TWENTY-FOUR

To Do:
Visit Maison Goyard
Prada sunglasses??

I HAD FORGOTTEN HOW DELICIOUS A COOL, breezy morning in France could be. Our one and only trip abroad together had been to Provence, almost eighteen years ago; my keenest memories were of David's atrocious efforts to communicate in his pidgin French, and my atrocious efforts to pretend to enjoy our lovemaking, so close on the heels of my "procedures." Now I looked back and realized: That was the start of our noncommunication, the start of our decline. It was such a long time ago.

So as our taxi barreled through the gritty suburbs on the outskirts of Paris into the city proper, I found myself leaning forward eagerly to absorb its richness. The wonders of first-class travel had left me remarkably refreshed, and my spirits rose at the sight of the wide, tree-lined boulevards and the swarms of Parisians hurrying to work. There were impossibly thin, chic women with stylishly gamine short haircuts and elegant high heels; equally thin young men in motorcycle leathers or slim-cut suits; silvery-haired grandes dames of mature elegance with small dogs tugging at the end of their leather leashes. . . . Forgetting that I had planned to remain cool and distant, I cried, "David! Do you think we could stop and pick up a baguette for breakfast?"

He glanced up from his iPhone, seeming to take in his surroundings for the first time. "Sure," he said distractedly. "Just tell the driver to stop whenever you want." And he returned to furiously tapping at the tiny keys.

The taxi swerved abruptly, throwing me against David's shoulder. He didn't seem to register the sudden contact and fended me off with a casual arm; we were crossing the Seine, and I gazed out the window again. But now the gaily colored tourist boats and the timeless line of used-book and poster stalls abutting the crumbling stone riverbanks had lost their appeal.

I thought I knew why David had come to Paris. He had explained that he planned to meet with various contacts he had developed over the years, and to begin transitioning them to other "handlers." It may even have been the truth.

I was less sure why I had come to Paris. Washington was still a glaring fishbowl for me, so in part this trip was an escape from my friends, sisters, temple board, auction cochairs, neighbors, and everyone else who eyed me with an unholy mixture of voyeuristic curiosity and suspicion.

But I knew there was more to it than that.

Another violent swerve and we swept into the curving driveway of the Ritz. "Arrive incognito and be assured now, as always, of absolute discretion," the hotel's website claimed. How fitting for a twenty-first-century spy!

I barely had time to admire the ancient Place Vendôme, with its cobblestoned surface upon which Marie Antoinette's silken slippers must have trodden, before a small army of hotel officials descended upon us. There was one to help me out of the cab, another to whisk my carry-on bag from my arm, and at least three to welcome David and take our luggage.

The concierge joined our parade as we paced solemnly across the marble-floored entrance and proceeded up the wide sweeping staircase to the main lobby. Forgetting myself in the absurdity of it all, I caught David's arm and pulled his head down to mine. "Do you think any of these guys are spies?" I whispered.

He glanced at the elegant fair-haired man, whose shoulders were so stiff under his perfectly cut dark suit that he could have been a mannequin. "Sure," he said. "Probably Afghan."

I stifled a giggle before I remembered that we weren't supposed to be laughing together. I would have to guard against that; being so far from home seemed, already, to be releasing some of the control we usually relied upon. Perhaps that was why David had claimed to hate foreign vacations.

After settling into our sumptuous, spacious room and admiring the view of the lush gardens behind the hotel, David suggested a stroll, and we walked down one of the side streets ringing the Place. I gazed eagerly through the windows of the *pâtisseries* at the *tartes aux fraises* gleaming with fresh strawberries, the buttery-soft *pains au chocolat* oozing with warm chocolate, and the mountains of crusty bread and baguettes. We stopped at the best-looking pâtisserie and filled a bakery box with the fragrant, still-warm pastries.

Then we arrived at our apparent destination, a small café that seemed indistinct from the many others we had strolled past. Fascinated by the vibrant, bustling Parisian street, I insisted that we sit at one of the small tables that clung precariously to the narrow sidewalk; David smiled and agreed. As we settled into our spindly, wire-backed chairs, I was rocked by a sudden sense of déjà vu.

February 2001

"*Who goes to Provence in February?*" *David demanded, brushing the pellets of icy rain off his jacket and trying unsuccessfully to shield me with his body.* "*Look, there's a café. Let's go in and warm up a little before we head back to the hotel.*"

"*It wouldn't be so bad if the cabdrivers and buses weren't on strike at the same time,*" *I volunteered inside the café as I unwound a few outer layers from my frozen body.*

"*Avignon is a city for walking, anyway,*" *David said, visibly cheering up in the warmth of the café.* "*I think I'm getting some feeling back in my toes. Are my lips blue?*"

"*A lovely shade of lavender,*" *I assured him.* "*Can you ask the waiter for some hot cocoa?*"

"*Do you have the phrase book?*" *he countered back.* "*Uh,* garçon, una tassa de chocolate? *Please?*"

The waiter looked mystified. "Pardonnez-moi, monsieur?"

David pantomimed holding a hot cup in his hands and blowing on it. Uncomprehending, the waiter shook his head and motioned over a friend.

"*Oh, this is ridiculous!*" *I snapped, cold and hunger making me pettish.* "*Didn't you tell me you took French in school?*"

"*My high school French isn't holding up very well,*" *David admitted ruefully. Once again he pantomimed the hot cup and both waiters imitated him, chuckling and blowing on their pretend drinks.*

"*Oh, forget it!*" *I exclaimed impatiently. I picked up the menu, pointed to the drawing of a cup of hot chocolate on the front, and dredged up the one French phrase I knew,* "S'il vous plaît?"

Now I dragged myself back into the present, as a young waiter sidled up to our table and clumsily poured water into our glasses, splashing some on the cloth and David's lap. "Oh! Monsieur! *Je m'excuse*! Sorry! Sorry! *Mon* . . . my firstest day."

David gave him a friendly smile. "*Pas de problème*," he said in a pitch-perfect French accent. "*D'où venez-vous?*"

I gaped at him.

The young man licked his lips. "De Bordeaux, monsieur."

David leaned back. "*Ah, quelle région magnifique! Je voudrais bien visiter vos entreprises vinicoles et manger vos Madeleines célèbres. J'imagine que votre vin ait le meilleur goût là-bas, si c'est possible!*"

The waiter, now looking almost as relaxed as David, responded eagerly, "*Oui, c'est possible. Il n'y a rien de plus délicieux qu'une gorgée de vin de Bordeaux quand on soit là.*"

David ordered some food—at least I assume that's what he did; he could have been discussing peat farming in Bolivia for all I knew—and our now-smiling waiter departed. I stared at my husband. Suddenly he spoke French?

He stared back at me, equally surprised. "Now what?"

"Last time we were here you couldn't even order hot chocolate. Now you're chatting with the waiter in what sounds like perfect colloquial French," I said coldly. "What happened?"

"Oh," he said, not at all discomfited. "Actually, my French isn't all that perfect. I speak it with a strong Irish accent." He grinned at me, clearly not comprehending my anger. "And that wasn't easy to acquire, let me tell you. Hours and hours with those bloody language tapes—"

"You're Irish when you're undercover?"

"Shh," he said, glancing around. "Usually, except for when I'm in Ireland. My accent would never hold up there. I'd look a right *eejit*."

"You told me . . . you told me you speak Arabic and Farsi," I said.

"I didn't count French, as you knew I could speak some."

The last sentence came out in what sounded to me like a perfect Irish lilt. I gazed thoughtfully at him, wondering about all the other men he was. It was like suddenly discovering that you were married to someone with multiple personalities: One day he was the mild-mannered management consultant you thought you knew, and the next day he was a stranger who thought he was Superman.

But I couldn't deny that this tiny glimpse of the un-David was fascinating. Clinging to my last shreds of pride, I forced myself to bottle up the questions that I was longing to ask: How do you pretend to be a different person all the time? Do you have an entire pretend background? Pictures of a pretend family and kids? How did you learn to do all of this? Aren't you scared sometimes? Lonely? And how did I feel about the un-David who was emerging from behind the mask?

I swallowed. "Could you please order me a glass of wine?"

"Monsieur, *puis-je regarder votre sélection de vins? Lequel suggérez-vous?*" my husband asked his devoted waiter.

The next morning David left early for his mysterious meetings, so I lingered over croissants and chocolate in our hotel room while poring over brochures and deciding on my plan for the day. The smell from a nearby pâtisserie wafted onto our tiny terrace; the Paris pavements were calling to me.

As I descended the wide marble staircase, accompanied by the ghosts of Proust, Princess Diana, and Coco Chanel, I realized that I felt better than I had in weeks. I couldn't imagine why; nothing had changed. I was still the woman whose husband had lied to her for their entire marriage . . . whose husband had cheated on her and let her discover his betrayal from CNN. Yet foolishly, I was feeling a little better. It was a clear, crisp fall day in Paris, and I was going to start my day with Monet's water lilies.

The Orangerie museum was spectacular, and Monet's huge, room-size paintings enveloped me in their bluish-greenish haze of color and splendor. I sat mesmerized until a marauding horde of French schoolchildren descended en masse, and then I took a cab and strolled up the steep, narrow streets toward the artists' quarter of Montmartre, barely even aware of my surroundings.

But while I was daydreaming, the weather was changing. When the first drop hit my nose, I looked up to find that the sky had darkened to a threatening shade of coppery brown, almost black, and I felt the first stirrings of unease as I looked around. This mean, menacing quarter looked nothing like the tourist-clogged squares of Montmartre. I glanced over my shoulder uneasily, hoping for a fellow tourist.

Instead I saw two men leave an alleyway and fall into step behind me, their grim silence and set expressions a threat in themselves. I realized that the same men had been on the street when I emerged from my hotel that morning, and my heart began to race. Incredibly, unbelievably, this was danger.

CHAPTER TWENTY-FIVE

I QUICKENED MY PACE, HOPING TO FIND a less deserted street with an open café or office lobby where I could find shelter—and people. A low, ominous rumble of thunder frightened me into a near run, and I risked a glance behind me. The men were closing in.

I opened my mouth to scream, and they were upon me. One of them held a gun in his hand, and I thought, for one crazy instant, that this all must be a joke; it couldn't possibly be real.

But it was, and the other man grabbed my arm before I could jerk away and pushed me into an alleyway, so dark and narrow that it wasn't much more than a dark slit between two tenements. With the rain starting to pound down and growling thunder alternating with jagged streaks of lightning, I could barely see two feet in front of me. My arms brushed against the filthy, rain-soaked sides of the buildings that dwarfed our narrow passage. Instinctively I shrank back into my thin jacket.

We stopped in a garbage-strewn courtyard behind the building, and my captor let go of my arm. I was trembling so hard, I could barely stay upright. The man with the gun aimed it at my stomach and I staggered back, too frightened to plead. But then there was a whirl of movement from the shadows, and, unbelievably, my husband emerged. He sauntered into the fetid space and surveyed the scene, grinning. My breath caught in my throat.

David waved one of the two champagne bottles he was carrying at the men. "Wanna drink?" he asked.

The two men exchanged glances.

"See, 'cause I got some terrific champers here," he went on, and I realized he was using his Irish accent. "Right good stuff, if I do say so, and I dunna mind if—"

"Shut up!" one of the men snapped. To his partner, he muttered, "I heard Brooks was off his game, but I didn't know it was this bad."

David weaved a little, and one of the champagne bottles swayed dangerously close to my head.

"Step back from her," the man ordered. "Get lost, Brooks."

"But she's just a girl," David whined. "A lady. You know, brutha—"

He swung a champagne bottle smack into the gun-holder's face and spun around to aim a deadly kick right into the other man's groin. Both men collapsed into groaning heaps on the muddy ground. His face running with blood, the gunman tried to get up, and with brutal efficiency my husband stamped on his gun hand viciously enough to send the weapon skittering uselessly off into the shadows. "Still want to get up, brutha?" he taunted.

Cradling his broken hand against his chest, the man sank back down onto the ground.

David turned to me and grinned. "Terrible waste of good champagne, isn't it?" he said. "At least I didn't have to use my hand; I hate to get it wrapped after a messy takedown. Let's head back to the hotel."

I stared at him disbelievingly, not sure whether to vomit or burst into tears.

David said, "Come on, Shells. These two are just rookies, but I can't guarantee they don't have some friends around. I really don't want to use my other bottle."

His insouciance was infuriating. I tried to swallow but gagged instead.

David took my arm and told the gunman still writhing on the ground, "Son, never try a leapfrog surveillance in a neighborhood like this. I picked you up at the Métro." And he propelled me down the rain-slicked alley and onto the street again.

Without a word, David ushered me toward a shabby black Renault perched precariously on the sidewalk. As I was getting into the car, I felt an ominous rustle in the muddy leaves at my feet and couldn't suppress a small scream as a rat scampered over my ruined loafer.

David glanced over at me. "It's okay, Shells. You're okay," he said, and the calm in his voice served to calm me as well. He put the car into gear, and I felt it leap forward; the shabby little car had a deceptively powerful engine. He switched gears and I watched his strong hands expertly guiding the car through the rain-drenched streets as another memory surfaced in my dazed brain.

Avignon, February 2001

"Why can't we rent a car?" I demanded again. The prospect of dragging our suitcases to the train station and switching trains twice on our way to Nice was unappealing. "If we rented a car we could drive through Provence and stop at some of the châteaux. . . ."

"I told you," David said patiently. "I don't know how to drive a stick shift, and it costs a small fortune to rent a car with an automatic transmission in Europe. Besides, I'm not all that comfortable driving in a foreign country. I can't read

the road signs, and I don't know the rules . . . it's intimidat-
ing." He smiled at me. "Cheer up, the train will be fun."
  I groaned.

Now, David effortlessly switched gears again and eased the car into what seemed like a seven-way merge as I watched, mesmerized.

"Are you feeling better?" he asked, not without sympathy. "I'm sorry that happened; I'm sorry you were frightened. But honestly, those guys were just rookies. It wasn't a serious attempt."

Rookies? It had seemed serious enough to me; I remembered the hand grasping my arm, and the gun pointed at my belly, and a long, painful shiver ran through my body. I was freezing cold, my teeth were chattering, and I felt as if I would never warm up again, despite the car's heater.

He glanced over at me. "I'm sorry," he said again. Almost to himself, he muttered, "I forget what it's like when you're not used to it."

"How did you find me?" I asked, unclenching my teeth.

"I was tracking you on GPS, and when you headed into this area I figured I'd better check it out."

"Tracking me?" I rasped. My voice sounded strange.

"I put a GPS chip in your bag. Much more efficient than putting a team on you."

"More efficient," I echoed.

"Shells, you didn't really want agents following you around, did you?"

"Why would I need anyone following me? You knew I was in danger? You knew, and didn't *warn* me?" The heat was finally seeping into my frozen bones, and I felt my icy hands curling into fists.

For the first time, David seemed uncomfortable. He checked his rearview mirror, neatly shot the car across four lanes of traffic, and pulled into the circular driveway in front of the Ritz. A valet instantly surfaced to open doors and shelter us under an umbrella.

"I didn't know, and I would never let you walk into danger," my husband said, and suddenly I realized that beneath his casual exterior, he was even more angry than I was. "But I swear this to you, Shelley—it will *never* happen again."

CHAPTER TWENTY-SIX

October 1998

I had dressed carefully for our third date. A snug pull-on shirt and my front-closing bra, just in case I decided to let him . . . I looked at David, driving carefully as always with both hands securely on the wheel, and suppressed a smile. He was always so buttoned-down; my nerves tingled as I remembered him naked and sweaty and hot.

He caught my glance and smiled. Embarrassed, I cast around for something to say. "Oh, listen!" I exclaimed. "It's my favorite song." I turned up the radio as Paul McCartney sang the Beatles' tune "Michelle."

"Really?" he asked, still smiling. "Why is it your favorite?"

"It's my name. Shelley's my nickname."

"Ah," he said. "Then it's my favorite song too, ma belle Michelle." And he sang along lustily, in a hilariously execrable French accent.

"Your French is awful," I said, laughing.

"I'm a lover, not a linguist," he retorted, and I tingled all over in anticipation.

NOW IT APPEARED THAT HE *was* a linguist—certainly not a lover. Didn't *know* I was in danger? I barely managed to restrain myself until we were in our room.

As the door clicked shut, I tore off my rain-soaked, filthy jacket that the man had grasped with his terrifying hands and threw it across the room. I kicked off my sodden, muddy loafers and threw them across the room too, then wrapped my still-shivering body in the thick wool quilt from the foot of our bed. "You didn't *know* I was in danger, so you didn't bother warning me?"

"Shelley," he said. "Let me explain."

But I cut him off. "Let you explain? God give me strength, *let you explain?* Where should you start—with the BBC girl that you fucked? With all the lies you've told me?" I mimicked a whiny male voice: "Sorry, Shelley, I can't speak foreign languages; sorry, honey, foreign countries make me nervous, let's just take a vacation in Florida; sorry, sweetie, I never learned to drive a stick shift, and I'm too wimpy to learn."

He looked as if I'd hit *him* across the face with a champagne bottle. Never in all our years together had I talked—shouted!—at him like this. "Shelley—"

"Shut up!" I screamed at him. "Just shut your filthy, lying mouth! I hate you, you filthy, lying son of a bitch! I can't even think of anything bad enough to call you! How could you *do* this to me? Do you hate me? Is that it? Do you hate me because I couldn't have any children, and you're stuck with me? Why don't you just divorce me? Get rid of me? Why did you decide to torture me instead?" I started to sob uncontrollably, tears streaming down my face and my body shaking with rage and pain.

"Shelley!" David looked horrified. "Of course I don't hate you! How could you say that? You're my wife. How can you even think such a thing?"

"How could I *think* it?" I shouted. "Are you kidding me? You cheat on me, you lie to me, and you let me find out from the *news?* God Almighty, every news anchor in the Western world knew that my husband was a liar and a cheater before I did!" He moved to put his arms around me, and I warned, "Don't touch me, you bastard! Don't you ever touch me again!"

Stung, he retorted, "Well, that won't be any great loss."

I shot back, "No, it won't—I'm tired of faking it all the time!"

An awful little silence fell; the room seemed to echo with my helpless rage and his anger. David opened his mouth and closed it again.

I turned away. "Get out."

"I can't. We're on our second honeymoon, remember? I'll sleep on the couch."

"Get *out*." Unable to bear the sight of him for another second, I grabbed his jacket, trying to forcibly shove him out of the room. "Get out! Get out! *Get out!!*"

"Stop it!" my husband shouted. "I can't get out; I have to protect my mission! I have people to protect!"

"Like you protected me?" I shouted back at him. I grabbed a heavy vase from the bureau and swung it blindly, furiously, at his head.

David grabbed my hand and forced my fingers apart so the vase fell harmlessly on the thick carpet. I struck out at him, wanting to batter his face, tear at his eyes, but he imprisoned my flailing hands in his. "Shelley!" he shouted. "Get a hold of yourself! People are in danger because of this fucking leak— serious, life-or-death danger, and I'm trying to save lives! Can you understand that?"

"How *should* I know that?" I screamed at him. "I don't even know your fucking name half the time!"

David took a deep breath, visibly trying to collect himself. "Well, let me explain this to you. When the news stories revealed my identity, that endangered—"

I tried to twist free of his hands, but his grip was like iron. "I don't give a shit about your explanations."

But he ignored me, continuing, "—every person I'd been in contact with over the past twenty-five years. Every intelligence agency in the world is scouring my travel records, my 'business' partners, everyone I've met with in foreign countries—and all those people are under suspicion. The Iranians, Hamas, ISIS, Hezbollah—some really bad people are rounding up all of my contacts. Do you understand?"

I wanted to say that I didn't give a shit, but I couldn't quite bring myself to say it.

"Having your cover broken like this is every CIA officer's worst nightmare," he went on in the same even tone.

I snapped at him, "You know what's my worst nightmare, you son of a bitch? Every time I close my eyes at night, I see you in bed with that fucking bitch *Mia!*" I spat her name at him like a foul taste that I needed to expel from my mouth. "So don't lecture me about your nightmares—I have plenty of my own, thanks to you!"

He exploded, "Well, *sweetheart*, I know that sucks, but I have nightmares about an ancient history scholar at Teheran University named Nasir, who's probably hanging from a meat hook in Evin Prison right now because of me! I am truly, deeply sorry about what I've done to you—and I'm even sorrier that I failed to protect you and the kids from all of this—but—"

I wrenched free of his grasp and swung at his face, but again he was too quick for me and grabbed my hands before I could connect. "Listen to me," he said, his voice low and urgent. "Just listen, for once. Please?"

The "please" caught me and I stopped fighting his hold. I drew a deep, shuddering breath.

"Thank you," David said formally.

Suddenly, every bit of the furious energy deserted my body, just as quickly as it had flooded me. I sagged against his grip and would have fallen had he not been holding me. Carefully, as if I were a sleeping baby, David eased me onto the bed and arranged the down comforter around my shoulders. I was shivering hard again. "David," I said through chattering teeth, "I don't feel well. I feel sick."

Gently, he stroked the damp hair back from my clammy forehead. "You're okay," he told me. "It's just the adrenaline crash. Breathe in and out—that's right, nice and deep—while I get you something to drink."

I concentrated on breathing while David rummaged through the minibar, then handed me a glass. It was whiskey neat, and I chugged it down like a sailor on shore leave. "Better," David said, smiling, as I handed the glass back to him and leaned back on the soft pillows with a sigh. I felt as if I could sleep forever.

He stretched out on the bed next to me; I was too wrung-out to protest. I wondered if there really was a Nasir, or if he'd made that up just to disarm me. Anything was possible with this new David.

"Nasir is real," he said quietly, reading my thoughts uncannily. "So is Salwa, who works for one of Hezbollah's community organizations in Gaza, and works with me because I got her son out of the Strip and into Andover on a full scholarship. God knows what will happen to her now."

"Are all of your sources pure and noble?" I inquired, finding my voice again.

He smiled, a little bitterly. "God, no. Most of them are snotty little buggers who would trade their mothers in for a fistful of American dollars. Throw in a pipe full of crack and you could have their kids too."

I was silent.

"But even the worst bastards don't deserve what'll happen

to them when the Iranian secret police catch up to them," he said wearily.

For the first time, I really looked at him. He was visibly tired; the lines around his mouth were deeper than usual, and his eyes were smoky with fatigue and . . . regret, maybe? Pain? I steeled myself against caring.

With a jolt of surprise, I realized that he wasn't wearing the clothes he'd put on that morning. The khaki slacks, gray blazer, and black wing tips had been replaced by scruffy jeans, a Manchester United T-shirt, and heavy workman's boots. No wonder that groin kick had been so effective.

"Where did you get those clothes?" I asked. I was sure that he hadn't packed—had never even owned—a Manchester United T-shirt.

He glanced down at himself in surprise. "Oh, that. I keep stashes of work clothes in lots of cities. Much easier than trying to plan out who I'll be next week in Prague."

Work clothes. "So you find some convenient phone booth and change from your ordinary clothes into your Superman cape?"

He grimaced. "More likely a grotty loo somewhere down in the Tube."

I noted the British turn of phrase with interest. How much time did he spend being Irish, anyway? Who *was* this man?

Of course David read my expression again. "Sorry," he said briefly. "Must be because I'm back on the auld sod again. Or nearer to it, anyway."

I shrugged to show my unconcern. Suddenly another thought leaped into my head, though. "You *are* American, aren't you? I mean, you weren't really born in Ireland. Right?"

He laughed out loud. "Michelle, ma belle, I am American through and through. Born and raised in—"

—

171

He stopped short, and my head came up sharply. "Born and raised where, David?"

His California-boy grin faded, but only slightly as he told me with a touch of pride, "New York City."

CHAPTER TWENTY-SEVEN

THE REVELATION THAT MY HUSBAND had been born on the opposite coast from the California home he'd always claimed set me back on my heels. It mattered that he had maintained his facade even in the privacy of marriage. He had woven his web of lies so artfully that I hadn't had a chance of piercing it; he was a master. It was an alarming realization. "Why California?" I asked weakly.

"It's all about the cover, Shells. Everything is about maintaining the cover."

April 2010

There was no warning. One minute we were shuffling off the Metro at Dupont Circle, packed closely together with the heaving Saturday afternoon tourist crowd. The next there was a scream and a shove and another scream. David grabbed my arm and pushed his way through the panicked crowd so that we could get to the escalator. And then I saw the blood, dark red blood streaming across the dirty subway platform. A man lay motionless, the blood pouring from his gaping head wound, and two other men faced each other across his body, crouched, long ugly knives at the ready. One knife was wet.

David pushed me onto the escalator and pulled out his cell phone, punching numbers into it. 911, I supposed. Our faces were only inches apart, pressed together as we were by the escaping crowd. I cried, "Why didn't you do something? Why are you just running away?" He didn't answer.

Then we were on the street, and screaming sirens heralded the arrival of the police cars. Even before we hit the pavement, a police van had screeched to a halt, and police officers with guns drawn were racing down the stairs and into the station. I was shaken by David's cowardice; surely he and some other men could have done more than run away. Why had he taken all those Krav Maga classes? "See how quickly the police got here?" I said to him. "Couldn't you and some others have done something? Kept those men separated until the police arrived?"

"Do you think I'm Superman?" my husband asked.

Now I looked at him with sudden comprehension. "That's why you didn't do anything at the Metro station!" I exclaimed.

His brow knitted.

"You know, the knife fight? At Dupont Circle?"

"Oh, right."

"You could have separated them, couldn't you?" I asked, thinking about his fast, sure moves in the alley. "You could have stopped the fight."

"Two street punks?" he said contemptuously. "I'd like to think so."

I remembered accusing him of cowardice, and fell silent.

"It wasn't worth being on the news that night. Blowing my cover."

I digested that.

"But I did cheat a little," he added. "I may have accidentally punched in the number for 'CIA officer in trouble' instead of plain old nine-one-one."

Well, that explained the police officers' lightning-fast arrival on the scene.

"GPS locator chip is in your sunglasses so I can track you. Also, I put a panic button in your wallet. Please take it with you. D."
I was tempted to crumple up this affectionate little pillow note the next morning so I could throw it in his face, but on second thought I tore it into small pieces and flushed it down the toilet, feeling like a Bond girl. Or at least, a spy's wife.

Lost in thought, my day passed slowly. I walked to the Louvre and spent six hours within its safe and hallowed walls before walking back to the hotel, peering over my shoulder every five or six strides for possible followers or attackers. Under the lowering gray sky, the bustling Parisian streets seemed narrow and sinister rather than charming and alive.

Needless to say, I saw no one—and I saw everyone. Was the tall, bearded man watching me too closely? How about the chubby Asian man? Hadn't he been behind me for the last block? I couldn't even enjoy the sidewalk cafés brimming with people or the pâtisserie windows with their tantalizing displays.

The constant anxiety was exhausting, and I collapsed onto the bed again when I returned to our room, wondering how David managed it. When he returned that evening, dressed once again in his Clark Kent khakis and sport jacket, I asked him.

"You get used to it," he said, shrugging out of his jacket and tossing it toward the closet.

"How?"

He looked at me, probably trying to assess whether I was really interested. I was. "Well," he said, "you just operate at a certain level of watchfulness. Always."

"What do you mean?"

He bit his lip, thinking. "Well," he said again. "Okay. Tonight's doorman was new; I'd never seen him before. He looked at me a second too long when I came in, so I snapped a picture and I'm going to have someone run him through the system. When I walked through the Métro station, a couple of guys caught my eye. Probably just a drug deal, but I'll have someone check that out too. And three different teams tried to tail me today, but I shook them all on the Métro. That's what I mean."

Métro? Tails? "I thought you were in meetings all day," I said.

"I was."

"Then why were you. . . ?"

He smiled slightly. "I never go in a straight line from A to B; I usually go via W. And public transportation is an officer's best friend. The first thing you do when you arrive in a city is memorize at least three different ways to get out."

"And doesn't that wear you down? All the tension, worrying all the time?"

He looked surprised. "It's not worry," he tried to explain. "It's just my job. Hey, remember I told you about Nasir last night?"

Nasir. Oh yes, the Iranian professor whom David had been worrying about. "Yes," I said.

"Well, he and his family showed up at the US Embassy in Beirut today." David tried to hide his grin, but he wasn't entirely successful. "They'll resettle him wherever he wants to go. Probably California; he has family there."

"And the Iranians just let him out of the country? I thought you said he was probably in prison."

The smile disappeared. "He was—in Evin Prison in Teheran; it makes Abu Ghraib look like Disneyland."

"Then how. . . ?"

"Shells," said my husband. "That's my job too." He kicked off his neat, tassel-tied loafers and strode into the bathroom to wash off the dirt and grime of the day.

The next few days passed uneventfully, and on Saturday we found ourselves on the Eurostar train headed for London. I had taken to clutching the panic button in my hand every time I ventured out alone; irrationally, I believed that it would summon David to my side in an instant. Perhaps he would swoop in like Batman or descend a silvery web from the sky like Spiderman.

London was noisier than Paris. Flashier, grittier, and infinitely more fun and exciting. The streets seemed wider and the alleyways less threatening; illogically, I was relieved by the constant chatter in a language I could understand. Even the pushing throngs on the underground seemed familiar.

Feeling safer, I wandered the open sidewalks of the city, eventually transferring the panic button from my hand to my jeans pocket, no longer looking over my shoulder every few steps for menacing strangers. I visited Harrods and had tea in one of its dozens of eateries; I stood among hundreds of wide-eyed tourists and squirmy children for the ceremony of the Horse Guards; I visited Churchill's War Rooms and marveled at the dank underground rooms from which the British had defeated the Germans.

Gradually, as I strode the crowded sidewalks and mingled with the other guidebook-toting tourists, I began to relax. David also seemed less tightly strung. Perhaps Nasir's escape had buoyed him, or perhaps it was something else entirely. Needless to say, I had no idea. He went to endless meetings with unnamed British associates, and once I spotted him in the hotel lobby in earnest conversation with a Middle Eastern man in full Islamic garb.

David and I had retreated to a polite state of détente. We scrupulously avoided brushing up against each other, even in the crowded environs of the hotel elevator; we slept with our backs to each other, curled into ourselves on the far sides of the big bed; we exchanged pleasantries about the weather and the food like courteous strangers. But I was watching him constantly, observing him as I never had before. And now that my eyes were opened, I was starting to see him more clearly.

The next morning David said to me, "I'd like to take you somewhere very private."

I looked at him in surprise. "What for?"

"To talk. I realize that I've been evasive."

Evasive! To put it mildly. But then, I hadn't been a very eager interrogator either, preferring to research him in private rather than questions and confrontations. Each of us beset by our own demons, I thought.

So I followed him obediently, first mystified, then amused, then understanding as we took three taxis and two underground rides, circling back upon ourselves and dodging in and out of shops and hotels. It was exhausting; I said to him, "Do you do this all the time?"

He grimaced. "*All* the time. It's not all martinis shaken not stirred and Halle Berry frolicking in the surf, you know."

The latter hit a sour note, and I turned away from him. "Come on," he said. "We're clear."

Our odyssey wound up very close to where we had started, in a basement room of the Israeli Embassy. David explained that it was the most secure room in all of London, and he nodded his thanks to a very serious-looking Israeli soldier as he ushered me inside the windowless room.

Finally seated, David studied me for a moment. I avoided his gaze, fanning myself with my hand and uncapping the bottle of water that sat on the table. I wondered if this was where Israeli agents interrogated spies. Terrorists? Slipped away for an afternoon tryst?

"I know you've got lots of questions that you're not asking, and I know that I'm having trouble telling you anything. Both of us, it seems, have some bad habits to overcome."

I swallowed some water and looked at my hands.

"So I'll start. Yes, Shelley, my work is dangerous and ugly. I carry lethal weapons, and sometimes I've even used them. I remember the names and faces of every man I've shot at, and I'll remember them until the day I die."

I was staring at him now, spellbound. "Go on," I said.

"And I desperately wanted—no, I *needed*—to keep you and the kids out of it. Safe . . . safe from my nightmares as well as my enemies. I needed you to be untouched by my world."

I nodded.

"And then in Paris, I failed. I failed to protect you, and you were frightened, and that was inexcusable. It will never happen again."

I nodded again, realizing that, on that at least, I believed him. I even trusted him. I gazed at the bunched-up muscles of his bare forearms—his sleeves were rolled up to his elbows, as always—and, surprisingly, for the first time since I learned about that woman, felt a jolt of desire course through me. I lowered my eyes again.

"But the woman," I said. "That's different."

His sigh was almost a groan. "I know it's different, Shelley. I understand that. But it's also part of the same piece—if I can just explain it . . . I'm sorry, I'm just not used to explaining myself."

Or telling the truth, I thought.

"But at that moment, she was the only person in the world who understood where I'd been, what I'd just experienced—"

"How could I possibly understand?" I shot back at him. "You never let me—"

"I know, that's what I'm saying!"

We both fell silent for a moment. I saw that he blamed himself, not me, for the distance between us—but I wasn't sure if he regretted it.

"If you hadn't been outed, would you have ever told me?"

For the first time in this strange, tense conversation, he almost smiled. "I was going to tell you on the day I retired. I had it all planned out—you would be able to come to Langley with me and see all my awards . . . maybe you would even be proud of me. I thought I could make you understand." Another awkward pause. "I hoped so, anyway."

I shook my head.

"I still have nightmares," he said conversationally. "I dream that it was Sasha in the hospital. Sasha in the flames."

I shuddered.

"And there are other things I've done, other things I've seen—"

"Women?" I asked, quickly.

"No, not women! I told you, that was one time. Never before, never since. No, I mean other things that I never want you and the kids to know about. My life is dark sometimes, Shelley."

His other life. Not our life.

"And I need you and the kids to be untainted by it."

But now we had been tainted; our marriage had been poisoned.

I didn't know what to think. I couldn't forget the woman, though I appreciated the obvious effort he had made in opening up to me like this.

Finally I asked, "And now?"

"And now . . . I'm in the middle of something really big,

something so big that it could literally change the course of history. Or at least the next decade."

David was not one for overstatement, quite the opposite. Finally I understood the need for the tradecraft tactics and the Israeli safe room.

"What is it?" I asked, and was surprised when he answered. "I have an asset very high up in the Iranian Revolutionary Guard. Only you and the director know about this, Shelley; I've been developing him for years. And we're working together to neutralize Iran's nuclear program." He paused and took a drink from his water bottle. "We're so close I can taste it. But this damn fucking leak!"

I wondered what "neutralize" meant, and then I thought about a world safe from Iran's nuclear weapons.

"I know you and I are in trouble," he said. "And I know a lot of that is my fault. Maybe all of it. But right now—I'm sorry—but right now, *we* are not my priority. The Iran op is." He studied me, trying to catch my eye, but I refused to meet his. "Can you understand that, Shelley?"

I could, and I couldn't.

He tried for a smile. "Remember Casablanca? The problems of two little people don't amount to a hill of beans in this crazy world? Or something like that."

They were *my* priority though, and they amounted to more than a hill of beans for me.

"So that's the deal?" I asked.

"That's the deal. For now. Once I get this settled, then we will work all the rest of it out, I swear. But—Shelley—please give me some time. For now."

I accepted his hand as he helped me stand up, stiff from the uncomfortable folding chair, and we walked back to the hotel in silence, our heads bowed in thought.

And what was my life? I was forty-five years old and had devoted the last thirty years of my life to my family, if you included the years caring for my sisters—and I did. What about the next thirty?

I was still thoughtful as we prepared to go out for our last night in London. The concierge had procured the hottest tickets in town: a revival of *Hair* had just opened in the West End and, despite the twenty years that had elapsed since its original run, it was a smash hit. I wasn't feeling very festive, but we had the tickets (at enormous cost), and it was better than sitting in our silent hotel room with the huge empty bed between us.

From the moment the play opened, I could see why it was such a hit. We were lost in its psychedelic colors and tones; the sometimes haunting, sometimes clashing melodies; and, most of all, the personal stories of these tormented, funny, passionate young people. They wanted liberation—they wanted to let the sunshine in—they wanted to strip everything away and live in the open, unmasked and unclothed. Their struggle to free themselves resonated deep within me and, looking over at David, I saw that he was as enthralled as I.

When the actors swung into their final song, "Let the Sunshine In," I jumped to my feet along with the rest of the audience, clapping and singing and swaying. David grabbed my hand, laughing. "Come on," he shouted in my ear. "Let's go on up!"

A ramp from the orchestra was flooding with spectators who were running onstage to dance and sing with the actors. For just one moment, my husband and I weren't estranged but deep in the Summer of Love, united by the irresistible draw of the music and the light and the beat.

I flung my arms around David's neck and kissed him on the mouth, demanding and insistent. He kissed me back, hard. Hand in hand, we pushed our way through the still-dancing crowd and ran back to the hotel. The elevator ride was torture, but the press of other passengers kept us close. I needed to touch him so badly I almost ached with it.

I practically fell into his arms before our room door closed and kissed him again, drowning and glorying in passion. "Michelle, ma belle," whispered my husband. "Take off your clothes."

As I tore at my shirt he laughed deep in his throat. "Need help?" he teased. I nodded, too breathless for words. Deftly, David unbuttoned my shirt and unclasped my bra; his fingers brushed against my breast and I shivered, leaning against him for support as he reached for my skirt zipper. Then we were naked and falling onto the floor, too urgent to get to the bed. "Shelley," David murmured. "Oh, my God, Shelley."

"David," I gasped. "David, David, my David. . . ."

And then he entered me, and my body rose to meet him in a whirling frenzy of passion and need and, ultimately, fulfillment.

CHAPTER TWENTY-EIGHT

THE NEXT MORNING, OF COURSE, I was appalled. I refused to look at David as we packed our bags; in near silence, we descended to the marble-clad lobby, and he walked over to the desk to check out while I pretended to admire the massive arrangement of lilies and baby's breath by the doors. My silence seemed to amuse him.

Inevitably, my eyes were drawn to him again, and an electric thrill coursed through my body as I recalled the night before. While I was admiring his tall form and thinking about the hard leanness underneath his clothes, a tall dark-haired woman walked toward him. She gave him a casual glance, then did a classic double-take and whipped off her massive Prada sunglasses.

"Peter!" she cried. "Or should I call you David now?"

"Mia," he said, his tone wary and his face expressionless. He must have spotted her earlier, I realized; even he wasn't that good at hiding his surprise.

Or was he? Was this all a setup? Had he planned to meet her here all along?

Suddenly my breath was coming in short gasps. I shrank back, behind a marble pillar, all my attention concentrated on the pair.

"What are you doing here?" she asked, smiling up at him. "I thought they'd have you under house arrest, at the very least." Now that she was over her initial shock, her low, throaty voice was cool. Amused. She was much prettier, and darker, than she looked on the TV screen. Long legs. Slim.

"Thanks to you."

She smiled at him, her teeth blindingly white. "Now don't sulk, Petey. It doesn't become you."

Petey? Oh yes, Peter Brooks. I was riveted to the spot, my heart pounding.

David signed the credit card slip and began to turn away. She put her hand on his arm to detain him. "We should talk, don't you think?"

"I don't think we should be communicating. I'm under Senate investigation."

She moved so close that her breast brushed against his upper arm. I moved closer too, to catch every syllable, but they were too intent upon each other to notice me. "Oh Peter—I mean, David—we both know how that will turn out. Sooner or later someone will tell the truth."

He smiled slightly. "And you think you know what that is?"

"Why don't we have a drink tonight and you can explain it to me?"

"Actually, I'm here with my wife, and we're heading out today."

Would he have said yes if he were alone? I was icy cold.

"What a waste," she murmured. "Perhaps some other time?"

My husband nodded—in agreement or dismissal?—and walked away.

Numbly, I followed him into the car he'd booked to take us to the airport. I couldn't tell if he had seen me witnessing the scene with Mia or not; as usual, his face betrayed nothing.

—

I kept replaying the brief exchange in my mind, over and over again. Her teasing, flirting tone; "Petey" (seriously?); "what a waste"—presumably, that was me; he was wasted on me. His final, enigmatic nod. She was so pretty.

And yet he was still my husband, and I still had some knowledge of him—more with every passing day. And I could swear that the cool edge to his tone when he spoke to her was real . . . that his nod was a resounding "no," and that he had not enjoyed the intimate contact that she had forced upon him.

Perhaps I was a blind fool, but I didn't think so.

Besides, there was last night.

The silence between us drew on as the car gathered speed and accelerated onto the highway.

"You're going to have to talk to me sooner or later," David said finally, leaning back and stretching out his long legs. He looked rested and relaxed (three fabulous orgasms will do that for you, a little voice in my head remarked), more relaxed than I could ever remember seeing him. He hadn't bothered to shave this morning and his beard was stylishly scruffy. With his hair also longer than usual, he looked almost boyish. No wonder Mia had had such a predatory gleam in her eyes.

"Did you know that Mia would be there?"

"Of course not. She's always on the road; you never know where she'll turn up."

How comforting. Especially since he was always on the road too.

Reading my mind, David said, "We run into each other occasionally, Shells. It's nothing. Nothing to do with you and me."

My mind, once again, was blank. I refused to feel anything.

"And don't make the mistake of thinking she's interested in *me*," he added. "She's interested in making a big name for herself and breaking big stories for the BBC. So she'll flirt with me if that gets the job done—but it's the job that counts."

He might be underestimating his appeal. But I, too, had seen her eyes sparkle with excitement when he suggested that she didn't know everything, and I thought he might be half right about her motives.

Uncertain, I leaned my head back against the black leather seat and closed my eyes. Not even noon, and I was already exhausted—seeing your husband's mistress will do that to you. But I hadn't gotten much sleep last night either, and, annoyingly, treacherously, my body tingled in memory.

When we arrived at the airport, a dark-skinned man in a dark suit and darker sunglasses approached our car and opened the door for me. David reached across me to shake hands with the man. "Nathan. Good to see you."

"Nathan" paid our driver, hefted my bag with the ease of an athlete, and led us past the check-in counter, security lines, and X-ray machines. The security officers were expressionless as they watched us pass, and David tossed me a grin. "I could get used to being outed," he remarked. "Makes travel a lot easier."

We parted ways from Nathan at the gate. As we settled into chairs in the first-class section to wait, I glanced up at the flight board and frowned. "David—this flight's going to Bermuda, not Washington. What's going on?"

My husband grinned. "Surprise!" he said, and dropped a kiss on the top of my head.

Well! It was starting to seem as if being married to a spy carried some advantages, after all. My mind raced as I tried to figure out when David had decided to take me on a real vacation. Had he even had time after our—well, last night—to put this all together? Had he planned to surprise me all along? Had he always intended to make our fake second honeymoon into a real one?

"But . . . the kids," I protested halfheartedly.

"Don't worry. It's all taken care of. Dani and Marisa have the kids under control."

Dani and Marisa—Good God!

"When—" I started.

But a flight attendant came over to us then and leaned down so that her ample breasts were about an inch from my grinning husband's face. "Mr. and Mrs. Harris?" she asked. "If you'll come with me now, we'll get you boarded before everyone else."

Yes, I could get used to this.

As soon as we'd settled ourselves in our spacious first-class seats, David reclined his armchair and put in his AirPods. "One of the best things about my job," he confided, "—my real job, that is—is that I can't bring paperwork home with me. See you in Bermuda, babe." And he closed his eyes.

I couldn't stop looking at him. Since we were in first class, the flight attendants kept offering me food—breakfast? Dinner? Snack, perhaps?—and I kept declining. All I wanted to do was look at my husband—and, yes, touch him too. I watched him slip easily into a light waking doze, his fingers still tapping intermittently in time with the silent music; I watched his long dark eyelashes rest against his cheeks, and I watched the lines around his mouth relax into contentment. But even in repose he was alert; when a passenger brushed against him as the man reeled up the aisle toward the bathroom, I saw David's eyes following closely from behind his lashes. I wondered if he ever really relaxed.

And all the while I was remembering last night—his knowing hands on my body and his hard, strong body driving into mine—so familiar, and yet so new. Every nerve ending was atingle with memory and yes, with anticipation, as I thought about the nights ahead. His Bermuda surprise felt like a warm hug, another sign of the healing that we so badly needed.

So when the plane landed, I turned to him and shyly put my hand over his. "This is really wonderful of you, David, and I want you to know that I'm going to try too—"

My words died away as his face showed confusion, and then regret.

"David?" I asked uncertainly.

"Mr. and Mrs. Harris?" the flight attendant said. "If you'll follow me, there's a car waiting for you on the taxiway."

"Let's go," he said briefly. "I can't keep them waiting."

He shouldered our bags and led the way down the stairs and into a black limousine waiting by the nose of the plane. As we sped away I glanced back and saw our fellow passengers with their noses pressed to the windows, doubtless wondering and speculating about who we were.

"Mr. Brooks," said our driver. "It's a pleasure and an honor to work with you, sir."

I fumbled in my bag and pulled out dark sunglasses to hide my sudden tears. I was so stupid, so gullible. How could I have let myself believe that David had planned this as a second honeymoon? Of course it was work.

David was talking to the driver, perhaps giving me time to pull myself together. "We're going to drop Mrs. Harris at her hotel first," he said. "Do you have a protection team for her?"

Her hotel, I thought dully.

"Yes, sir, they'll meet us at the hotel."

Well, that will be a pretty sight at poolside. Me and the Navy SEALs.

David turned to me. "You'll be at the Elbow Beach, a beautiful hotel. I'm sure you'll like it there."

Not *"we'll"* be at the Elbow Beach. "Where will *you* be, then?"

"I'll try to join you at some point. I booked you into a double."

"Don't do me any favors," I snapped.

David pressed his lips together, glanced pointedly at the driver's back, and put on his dark sunglasses. Now his eyes were as veiled as mine.

The hotel *was* lovely, and I spent the next two days on its fabled pink sand beaches, sipping margaritas and plowing doggedly through one romance novel after another. Sometimes I thought I could spot my "protection team" when I saw a particularly well-muscled man with mirrored sunglasses, or a hard-bodied woman in a businesslike one-piece bathing suit and barely visible earpiece. Sometimes I had no idea where they were. I spoke to no one except the waiter.

On the third night David "joined" me. I had taken a sleeping pill and didn't even hear his soundless entry into the room; I only jolted awake when he slipped into the bed next to me and I found myself mindlessly drawn into his warm, hard body. Instantly I jerked away again and heard him sigh into the darkness. There would be no more passionate, unthinking sex between us; the *Hair* interlude had been a one-off, I told myself. I would never trust him with my body again—let alone my heart.

The next morning David came to the beach with me, looking almost like a caricature of a husband on vacation with his giant bottle of sunscreen, baseball cap, sunglasses, and John Grisham novel. When we were settled in our beach chairs and my well-trained waiter had brought me my first margarita of the day, somewhat to David's surprise (it was only ten o'clock), he said, "Look, Shells, I'm sorry about all of this."

I shrugged. "It doesn't matter."

"But it does. You thought—"

"Please, David. Forget it." I didn't want him to air my pathetic, schoolgirlish flutterings in the open. It was humiliating.

"Well, anyway," he said. "I wish—"

"Just shut up about it," I snapped. "Enough." I opened my book at random, but since I hadn't taken in a single word that I had read in the past three days, it hardly mattered.

David opened his book too.

That afternoon an older man walked past our chairs, then stopped and did a double take. Was it a little too theatrical? A little too rehearsed? I wasn't sure.

"Max Wilder!" the man exclaimed. "Imagine finding you here, of all places! How are you?"

David stood up and shook hands with the man, slapping him on the back. "Well, Andrei! I didn't know you ever took vacations. Fancy a drink?" he said in a crisp British accent. And off they went to the poolside bar.

It was only after they left that I understood why David had not introduced me, had not turned to me and said, "I'll be right back" or "Can I bring you something?" or even "See you later." I realized I had been staring vacantly into space and looked over at the bar, but they were nowhere to be seen. It was as if they'd disappeared into thin air.

But I guess his mission was accomplished because the next morning we went home.

And this time I had no dreamy, sex-tinged illusions as I sat next to him in the cushiony first-class seats. The Bermuda getaway hadn't been a second honeymoon or a chance to repair our marriage; it had been work—part of his "dark" side. And what else had I expected? After all, he had warned me, during that crazy secret conversation in the Israeli Embassy. I was *not* his priority—"for now"—the mission was.

Still, it felt like a third betrayal. Three strikes and you're out?

CHAPTER TWENTY-NINE

To Do:
Kosher supermarket
Sasha: COLLEGE ESSAY
Clothing for Qameen family
Books for Qameen family
Furniture for Qameen family
Mosque for Qameen family

ONE STEP UP AND TWO STEPS BACK: An apt description of my relationship with my husband right now.

But back at home, there was no time to brood, for another small tragedy soon erupted.

Sam, excited about sending in his early decision application to Brandeis, was animatedly tapping away at his cellphone while I pulled yet another kosher chicken out of the freezer. Suddenly his face closed up and he thrust the phone into his pocket, hunching over into himself. David, who was giving Amy Joy her dinner bottle in the kitchen rocker, looked at me over her blond head and we exchanged glances.

"Hey, sweetheart," I said, reaching up to put my arms around Sam's tall body. He broke down as soon as I touched him.

"Sharona broke up with me," he sobbed into my shoulder. "She doesn't even want to be friends, she thinks we should have a clean break . . . oh, Mom, what am I going to do without her?"

That little bitch, with her self-centered little brain! How dare she do this to my son? And via text??! Any girl in her right mind should be thrilled to get my sweet, sensitive, kind, loving Sam! I wanted to drive a knife right into her heart. Instead I hugged my tall grown-up boy, my heart aching with unshed tears.

David handed Amy Joy to Sasha and put his arm around Sam's shaking shoulders. "It's your first love, son," he said, his voice deep with sympathy. "You never forget your first love."

I shot my husband a sharp glance. Who was his first love? Muffy? Dylan? Me?

"But you move on," he went on, unaware. "There's a whole world of wonderful girls out there for you, much nicer girls than Sharona."

Sam straightened up and wiped his cheeks, embarrassed at crying in our kitchen. "There'll never be anyone like Sharona," he said, with all the wisdom of a seventeen-year-old.

Sasha volunteered, "I never liked her. She borrowed my lululemon top and didn't give it back."

"I'm sure she just forgot," said Sam, instantly defensive.

I held back a sharp retort. "Let's go out to dinner," I said.

Dinner was a quiet affair. There were so many taboo topics—David's job, David's affair, Sam's love life—that we found it hard to sustain much interest in the dull topics we did manage to settle on.

There was a TV on over the bar, and I found myself watching a golf match, trying to keep myself from yawning, when the bartender switched the station to CNN. Suddenly Mia Holloway's striking face, with its cloud of dark hair and strong features, gazed gravely at me from the TV screen, the UN head-quarters in the background.

I interrupted David and Sam, who had been manfully trying to maintain a conversation about college algebra. "Sam, did you know that David actually went to Princeton?"

Sasha jumped, and Sam snapped to attention. "What?" they both said in unison.

David said, "Well, yes."

"Dad, you went to Princeton?" Sam demanded. "Not UCLA?"

David shrugged.

"Why did you say you went to UCLA?" Sam asked, frowning.

"It was part of my cover," David explained. "An Andover–Princeton–Woodrow Wilson School pedigree is very common for Agency officers. I needed to construct a different past to live my cover."

The kids were silent.

I thought, *so he practiced his lying skills by lying even to his family.*

Sam said indignantly, "You mean I could've been a legacy at Princeton?" and Sasha turned on him.

"You're so selfish," she accused. "He's been lying to Mom—to Shelley, I mean—to all of us—for all these years, and all you can think of is that maybe you could've gotten into Princeton?"

"I was just kidding," he retorted.

"No you weren't, you were—"

I took a deep breath and interrupted, "It's okay, Sasha, he had to do it for his job."

Sam glanced away and I saw him staring at a thin black-haired girl near the door. "Doesn't that girl look like Sharona?" he asked wistfully, and I sighed.

Back at home, the kids safe in their rooms, David took out a bottle of brandy. "So what do you think about Sam?" he asked as he handed me a snifter-full and we settled ourselves at the kitchen table. The kids were always a safe space for us.

I grimaced. "That little bitch Sharona. I always knew she would do this to him."

He nodded. "Maybe he'll learn something from it, though."

"Like what? How to get your heart broken?"

"Well, how to get your heart broken and survive it. Maybe he won't be so vulnerable next time."

I sipped my brandy and considered. "Is that how you operate?" I asked. "You don't let yourself be vulnerable?"

Suddenly I realized that some of David's appeal for me had been his lack of vulnerability, his lack of neediness; he required virtually no emotional investment from me, unlike everyone else in my life. What's the opposite of needy? Self-contained? Detached?

And especially after all the lost babies and all the procedures—six miscarriages in barely two years!—his touch, his very presence, brought me back to that time of shared misery when I couldn't bear his sadness on top of mine.

So that was how we became roommates rather than soulmates, I supposed.

Now he said, "You have to harden yourself to a lot in my business. Lots of times we're dealing with the scum of the earth, and there's a lot we have to ignore. That was what went wrong in Qameen—I couldn't ignore it."

I knew what he was trying to tell me, and part of me even understood. By now I had done enough research on Qameen that a dim realization of what he must have witnessed was dawning. Perhaps those horrors were enough to *explain* what he had done, but did they *justify* it? I didn't know.

"I've been reading a lot about Qameen," I said instead. "It's horrifying—like another Holocaust, or another Rwanda. I know this sounds silly, but . . . is there anything I can do to help?" The tragedy was so titanic, so earthshaking, that I felt foolish even asking—but then again, how could I not?

"Even you can't fix Qameen," David began. Then he stopped short, and I swore I could see a thought bubble magically appearing above his head. "You know what? Actually, there is something you can help me with."

"Really?"

"Yes." He shook his head, running his hand through his dark blond hair so that, for a moment, he looked years younger. "I don't know why I didn't think of it earlier. There's a family of Qameeni refugees here in Maryland that's really struggling. Father can't find work, mother afraid to go outside, kids traumatized . . . Social services has tried to help, but they're so overstretched."

"Well, sure," I said, but I wondered what he thought I could accomplish if the social workers had failed—and why he was focused on this one family, out of the millions of refugees.

"See, the thing is, I knew them in Qameen. They couldn't leave for a long time because the grandma was sick and took a while to die; their eldest son was killed . . . anyway, I'd like to figure out how we can help them."

Oh. Now I understood. He "knew" them in Qameen; they must have been "assets" of his, so even this was work-related. Still . . . "How many children do they have?" I asked, and we both knew I was hooked.

David again left for "somewhere in the Middle East" the next morning. "I'll be home for Thanksgiving," he told me as he tossed balled-up socks into his worn leather carry-on.

"Not before?" Thanksgiving was three weeks away.

"I don't know. Probably not."

I watched him snap the case shut and set it on the floor. "Do you travel with guns?" I asked, suddenly curious.

He glanced at me. "I check a bag with my weapons. It's at the office. I travel on an Irish diplomatic passport."

"Oh," I said. "So if you get caught—"

"I don't get caught."

"But *if* you did . . . would the CIA claim you? Or would they deny that they know you?"

"I don't get caught," he repeated, amused. "But, Shelley—the Agency doesn't leave its people behind. We take care of our own." He bent to kiss me. "I'll be home for Thanksgiving. Love you."

"Mm," I said, and got up to heat Amy Joy's morning bottle.

A few days later, Marisa drove up to have dinner with the twins and came into my office after they had settled down with their homework. With characteristic bluntness, she asked, "What's going on with David?"

Suddenly I realized I could talk to Marisa—really talk to her. Rachel was wonderful, but she was constrained by her kind tactfulness and her unspoken fears; if David could cheat, then anyone could.

But Marisa, who had no tact and had learned from years of therapy after her postpartum depression to drive straight to the heart of the matter, had no such compunction. And her husband still thought it a miracle that he had won her; Marisa was supremely confident that Neil would never, ever stray. So was I.

"It's like I'm catching these glimpses of a totally different David—the un-David, I call him." I swallowed. I didn't want to admit that the un-David both intrigued and attracted me. Powerfully attracted me.

"Well, I don't care how many Davids you think there are; it's your husband David who slept with that woman."

"There were extenuating circumstances. . . ." I started to tell her about the children, and the hospital, but she interrupted.

"Are you making excuses for him? Standing by your man? Honestly, Shelley!"

"I know, I know. But here's the thing . . . I just don't want him to leave. I need this family to stay together."

Marisa's face softened. Awkwardly, she patted me on the shoulder, and we sat in silence together, two survivors of a ship-wrecked family. Of all people, Marisa understood.

"Well," she said. "It was a one-off? He and the woman?"

"He says so."

"And you believe him?"

"Yes." I paused. "I think so."

"Well, then. . . ." She shrugged. "Shit happens."

I nodded in fervent agreement.

"But, Shelley—if you stay with him—you can't punish him for the rest of your lives. You have to get past it."

"How?"

She shrugged again. "You have to start doing something different, I think. That might help."

"What do you mean?"

"I mean your job. Don't you ever get tired of marriages breaking up around you? I know you supposedly help with the mediation, but still, isn't it depressing?"

Yes, sisters were special; of all the people in the world, only Marisa could really know how I felt about working with divorces, day in and day out. I had gone into the field to help families and children—but was I really helping? Or just making money out of the tragedy of broken marriages?

"And you run the PTO, and the temple, and the kids (thank God)—but geez, Shells, isn't enough enough? Get away from that depressing job, and all that volunteer stuff, and the kids, and do something different! I think that would help."

Astonished, I stared at her. We had made different choices in life; Marisa had gone back to her work as a very full-time real estate agent when the twins were only a few weeks old, while I had elected to work part-time to raise her children. Neither of us had ever questioned the other's choices before, and I wondered why on earth she was bringing this up now.

"But Amy Joy—" I began.

"Oh, please. That's why God created the au pair."

I flinched, and she got up. I stood up too and hugged her. "Thanks, Marisa," I said. "I love you."

"Love you too."

The days until Thanksgiving plodded by. Sam was in mourning for his lost love; Sasha refused to write her college essay. My sisters called every day with their usual list of complaints, while Rachel vented to me about her son's new medication and *her* daughter's college applications. Unknown Caller phoned only twice; each time I struggled to listen to what he didn't say, between the usual chat about our struggling Wi-Fi network and Amy Joy's new tooth. All I learned from the phone calls was that he was still alive at that moment; the darkness hadn't swallowed him up yet. I was furious at myself for worrying about him—and couldn't wait for him to get home.

And then it was Thanksgiving. We all gathered around my expanded dining room table—the kids; a jet-lagged, bleary-eyed David; Neil and Marisa; Dani; and last-minute additions Rachel and her family. Their flight to Palm Beach, where her parents lived, had been canceled due to a late-season nor'easter, and I couldn't let them be alone on Thanksgiving. We overflowed into the living room, and I had to set the highchair at the corner of the table. Amy Joy kept kicking it gleefully with her new slippers until David plucked her out and sat her in his lap.

As usual, we went around the table saying what we were thankful for this year. "Nothing," Sam said mournfully.

"Oh, come on," said Sasha impatiently. "You must be thankful for something."

He shook his head, and I wished I could have unleashed a hitman on Sharona. Then he redeemed himself. "I'm thankful that David is home safe and sound," he said. "And I'm thankful that Shelley is strong and brave." He smiled at me, and I gave him a watery smile back.

"I'm thankful that I'm getting all Bs," Sasha proclaimed. "And I'm thankful for Amy Joy." She beamed at the baby, who beamed back at her. Sasha was definitely her favorite.

"I'm thankful that I was born a Jew," Sam said solemnly. He had recently undergone a religious epiphany and decided to be observant; Sasha groaned and threw a dinner roll at him.

"And I'm thankful that Sam is free of Sharona and can move on," she added, and Sam scowled.

"No controversies, please," I said. "Marisa?"

She sent a beaming smile around the table. "I'm thankful that my family is all together on this wonderful day. I'm thankful that I lost three pounds last week. And I'm especially thankful that I didn't have to do any cooking today!"

We were all grateful for that; Marisa's cooking tasted like straw or wallpaper, depending on the consistency.

Neil, always conventional, said, "I'm thankful for my beautiful wife and children."

"Good one," David said agreeably. He exchanged an amused glance with me until I forced my eyes away. I didn't want to be linked with him in silent understanding—and yet, I was.

"I'm thankful for our dear friends and neighbors, who took us in for this holiday," said Rachel's husband Mark.

"Me too," Rachel agreed.

"I'm thankful for that too," her daughter exclaimed. "I'm especially thankful that I love Brandeis, and I think they're going to accept me because they're looking for art history majors."

She cast a shy glance at Sam, and I felt a sudden rush of hope—was it possible that these two beloved children, who took soothing baths together when they were three and had chicken pox, could become something more to each other now? What a wonderful idea! I gazed over at Rachel and saw the same thought taking hold in her head. She nodded back at me and I settled back, satisfied. Back in the shtetl, the match would be done by now.

Rachel's thirteen-year-old son Ben looked rebellious. "I don't have anything to say," he declared.

"How about that you're thankful for your soccer team?" his father suggested.

Ben shrugged. "Whatever," he said.

Rachel rolled her eyes to heaven and I gave her a sympathetic smile. Then I looked around the table. "Has everyone gone already? Is it my turn?"

"You and David," Sam said, a little warily. I couldn't blame him.

"Well," I said, "I'm grateful for . . . all of my children. Sam and Sasha and precious little Amy Joy." Hearing her name, the baby looked up and beamed at me. I beamed back.

David said, "I'm also grateful for all our children. I'm thankful that I don't live in Pakistan, or Iran, or Qameen. And—" he hesitated, "and I'm grateful for Shelley, who is the true love of my life, and who doesn't . . . who doesn't deserve what I've put her through." He looked directly at me, and I wanted to tear my eyes away but couldn't. "I'm sorry, Shelley," he said simply.

Shit. Everyone looked at me expectantly, and I gulped; I wasn't ready for public forgiveness. Not yet, anyway. Finally Amy Joy broke the silence with an indignant shout; David had stopped spooning mashed potatoes into her mouth. Everyone laughed uneasily as David picked up the tiny spoon again, and soon everyday chatter filled the room. Thanksgiving was back on course.

CHAPTER THIRTY

When I went downstairs the next morning, the twins were already at the table and David was cooking breakfast, expertly flipping pancakes with one hand while balancing Amy Joy on his hip with the other. Some skills you never forget. She held out her arms to me and I took her from David, dropping a kiss on her soft hair. "Chocolate chips or strawberries in your pancakes, Shelley?" David asked.

"Both," I said, sitting down so I could play pat-a-cake with Amy Joy. "Has she eaten already?"

"At six o'clock," my husband said. "You were dead to the world."

"Oh. Thanks."

He shrugged and handed me a plate with my pancakes on it. "I thought we'd go to Langley today."

Sam put an enormous bite of chocolate chip pancake into his mouth and asked, "We? What do you mean?"

"Don't talk with your mouth full," said David.

Sam swallowed. "We?" he repeated.

"Yes, I got approval to take all of you in so you can see CIA headquarters. There's a terrific spy museum there, and even a gift shop. Now that I've been outed, there's no reason why you can't see what it's like."

"Wow," said Sam slowly. "That's really cool." He glanced over at me, gauging my reaction.

I thought it was pretty cool too but was loath to admit this to David. Maybe he thought I could forgive and forget—maybe I even could—but if we were going to "work this out," I wanted different terms than before. I didn't want to be roommates anymore.

"Okay," I said.

David said, "So it's settled. We'll leave after breakfast."

We walked into the CIA headquarters through its fabled main entrance, with a huge seal of the Central Intelligence Agency embossed on the floor, and a wall with stars for every agent who died undercover to the right. David flashed a pass and we all presented our driver's licenses, and the guard motioned us in. A thrill went through me as we crossed over the seal and I gazed at David; this was his life's work, his second home. Or maybe his first home?

The children were wide-eyed and silent, looking down the huge empty corridors and pausing to study the photographs on the wall.

David said, "What would you like to see first?"

"The spy museum!" exclaimed Sam.

"Your office?" I suggested.

"The gift shop." Predictably from Sasha.

David grinned. "All of the above."

So we started in the museum. We had visited Washington's International Spy Museum a few years earlier when it opened, but this seemed so much more immediate, knowing that this was David's life. Or the un-David's life, at any rate.

Sam was transfixed by an exhibit on spies who had lost their lives undercover, and I joined him as he stood silently by the glass case. "That guy," he said, pointing to one grainy, dark photograph, "died in Lebanon after twenty-seven years undercover. And that one too. They tortured him but he never gave up any information."

David joined us, looking over our shoulders. "Torture is inefficient."

Sam glanced at him.

"Do you mean it doesn't work?" I asked, intrigued despite myself.

"That's right," said my husband. "People under torture will say anything to make it stop. Not necessarily the truth."

I swallowed. "Let's move on," I suggested, before Sam could ask him how he knew this for sure.

I paused to consider a tattered poster entitled "Moscow Rules." The placard accompanying it explained that these were the rules devised by CIA agents operating behind the Iron Curtain during the cold war.

Moscow Rules

1. Assume nothing.

2. Never go against your gut.

3. Try to blend in; go with the flow.

4. Everyone is potentially under opposition control. Everyone.

I stopped reading, struck by a sudden thought. Was that how David saw the world?

Then we trooped up to the seventh floor, where David's office was. Or at least that's where he told us his office was—all we saw was a blank door with a number, 701J, and a silver keypad to the right. "This is as far as I can take you," he said with a grin.

"Are you kidding?" Sam demanded.

"Afraid not."

"So this could be anyone's office?" I asked.

"It could. But it is my office."

"So you're 701J," said Sasha solemnly, and he nodded.

"That's me," he agreed. "701J."

We weren't allowed into the famous "Bubble" auditorium either, but we saw the surprisingly ordinary-looking cafeteria and a magnificent gym and workout facility before winding up our tour in the gift shop. While Sasha splurged on CIA-logo tchotchkes from notepads to T-shirts, I found my way to the books and paged through a history of the CIA.

David approached and glanced over my shoulder. "I'm in there."

"Really?"

"Yes, they talk about several of my operations. Buy it; I'll show you when we get home."

"Okay," I said, a little uncertainly. I wasn't sure how much I wanted to know.

But that night, when we were in bed and the lights were out and the house was quiet, I thought about Marisa's words: If you're going to stay together, you have to find a way to get past it. And I thought that the more I understood—the more I knew of this un-David—the more that might be possible.

So I turned over to face him. "Tell me stories," I said.

He knew what I meant, and I could sense his hesitation. "Do you really want to know?"

I wasn't sure. "Yes," I said firmly.

"Well. Okay. Let's see . . . remember when the twins were in their freshman year, and we went to San Diego on vacation, and I had to leave suddenly and miss the last two days?"

"I certainly do," I said, a little grimly.

"I left because one of our operatives had been captured in Iran. I went to get him out."

"And how do you do that?"

"They'd already tried bribery—usually our first line of defense—but that wasn't working. So I set up a sting. I speak good Farsi and have some contacts among drug dealers in that part of the world. So I offered to introduce my contacts to a money laundering ring in Nigeria that I also had good relationships with. They needed new bankers; we'd just rolled up their old ones in Russia. In return, I demanded to see the prisoner so I could get my CIA handlers to back off. I had told them I was a double agent, you see."

I was getting confused. "You'd told *who* you were a double agent?"

"The Iranians," he said, as if it were obvious. "They'd never believe I had no Agency connection, doing business in that part of the world. So I told them I was a freelance informant, but that I usually gave the Agency false intel. After a few . . . operations . . . I managed to convince them."

Jesus. I decided not to ever ask for the details of those operations.

"So anyway," he continued, "they took me to see the guy. Christ, that was bad." He paused, and for a moment I could almost see what was in his memory—a dark underground cell; the thin bearded prisoner in chains on a filthy, rat-strewn floor; the weight of dank earth above and the constant threat of more torture, more beatings, more humiliations.

"I knew him," David said. "We'd worked together before. So when I looked into the cell, he recognized me. He started shouting in Yiddish—the one language that his captors would never know. It sounded like he was cursing me, but he managed to tell me the guards' schedule before they . . . shut him up." He was silent another moment. "After that, it was easy," he finished. "I got him out, we walked across the city, and a helo picked us up."

"What do you mean, it was easy?" I asked. "You just grabbed the keys and took him out?"

"Pretty much."

"How?"

I felt him smile. "You really want the gory details?"

I really did.

"I sneaked back just before dawn, got the gun off one guard, shot two others, released Frank. Tossed him a gun off one of the dead guards, he shot two more, I unlocked his shackles, and we left."

I was silent for a while, trying—and almost succeeding—to see my David in this impossible, movie-like scenario. The same man who had been flipping pancakes that morning with our baby perched on his hip. The mixture of familiarity and mystery, or closeness and remoteness, was heady . . . almost intoxicating.

It was with an effort that I turned over again and said good night.

CHAPTER THIRTY-ONE

To Do:

Schedule mammogram—really!!
Investigate Saturday mornings
Bring books to Sharif family
Call Uber re Abdal
Look for ESL classes

THE NEXT DAY, DAVID PUT THE STORM WINDOWS in and took Sasha to her final SAT tutoring class. I couldn't stop watching him, trying to match this familiar man doing such ordinary tasks with the daring, dangerous spy that I was beginning to realize he really was. He had told me he would be in Washington for the next few weeks, and I couldn't decide whether I was pleased or sorry that he would be around. I felt such a rush of mixed-up, conflicting emotions whenever I looked at him that it was easier for him to be gone. At times I believed that I hated him more than I had ever hated anyone in my entire life; at other times I believed that I was closer to understanding him than ever before. I couldn't decide which feeling was more frightening.

But one thing I was absolutely sure of—despite everything, if I had anything to say about it, we would stay married 'til death did us part. When David and I got married, I told him that I didn't believe in divorce; that he was stuck with me no matter what. He laughed and swung me into his arms, assuring me that was the whole idea of marriage. I never dreamed we'd go through such turmoil.

On Wednesday morning, CNN reported on the progress of the Senate investigation into leaks "originating from the senior undercover operative, David Harris, and his alleged lover, BBC correspondent Mia Holloway." Once again the photo of David and Mia in Beirut flashed onto my TV screen, and once again I gazed at her strong face and windblown hair as she stood in the arms of my tall husband. I watched the reports through unblinking, dry eyes. When David came home, all I said to him was, "How is the Senate investigation going?"

"Badly," he replied.

"Is that all you're going to say?"

He sighed. "Sorry. I'm just trying not to think about it."

"I've been thinking about it," I said. I might be a family court lawyer, but I was still a lawyer. "I think your attorney should move to quash the subpoena on the grounds of national security. And you might be able to claim executive privilege."

David nodded. "Thanks. I'll talk to him about that."

"If all else fails, there's always the Fifth," I added.

"That was my lawyer's first suggestion," David said. "I told him it's not going to happen. I have nothing to hide."

"Do you hear yourself?" I asked him. My eyes drifted over to the kitchen table, where the day's mail included an acknowledgment from David's fake alma mater, UCLA, for his contribution to the class annual fund.

David followed my gaze and smiled a little. "We're very good at what we do," he said.

For the rest of the week, David prepared for the Senate hearings; he left very early every morning in a dark suit and returned at night accompanied by a nondescript sedan driven by what were clearly bodyguards. The sedan sat outside our house all night long.

He so clearly did not want to discuss the investigation that I found myself unable to press him on it. And I was busy with my family of Qameeni refugees; they had greeted me with grave and formal courtesy when Amy Joy and I first arrived at their house. The communication gap was profound, since only the father—Abdal—spoke decent English. Amy Joy proved to be a wonderful icebreaker, though, and I felt that we were becoming friends.

But there was one more item on my research to-do list, and I determined to put it into action. As we were cleaning up the dinner dishes on Friday, I asked David, "Where do you go on Saturday mornings?"

For years, David had disappeared on Saturday mornings, claiming that he was doing volunteer work with his UCLA classmates. But it had occurred to me that since he didn't actually have any UCLA classmates, this was probably not true; I had considered trying to follow him but dismissed that notion quickly as sheer stupidity—he would pick up my tail within seconds.

He looked at me for a moment, assessingly. "Do you want to come with me? I'd rather show you than tell you." It sounded almost like a challenge.

"Well—sure."

"Okay, then. Wear a dress that covers your knees and shoulders. And comfortable shoes; it's about a mile walk."

Huh?

The next morning I dressed according to his specifications, and we walked together through the sleety gray morning. David was silent, serious, almost meditative, and I let him have his peace. Finally we turned one last corner and stood across the street from an unassuming gray stone building on the corner of Q and 28th. Above the large double-arched doorway was a simple Jewish star carved into stone and some Hebrew lettering.

We crossed the street and I read the English lettering to the right of the door: *Congregation Tehillath Israel, Traditional Orthodox services Friday nights and Saturday mornings. All invited.*

"David?" I said, my very tone a question.

"Do you want to come in? You'll have to sit on the women's side."

I hesitated. "I. . . ."

"That's okay. I'll see you at home." He paused, then added, "Shabbat Shalom."

I walked home in a daze. When I married David I was vaguely glad that he was Jewish too. But Orthodox services every week? I had been raised in a casual Reform Jewish household; we were so nonreligious, we were practically Unitarian.

But there was that well-worn Hebrew prayer book and the ceremonial tallis in the storage locker, and when I got home I paused at the door, gazing thoughtfully at the mezuzah that David had mounted on its right jamb. Could he possibly be an Orthodox Jew?

Well, this was an area where I had my own sources.

"Orthodox?" Rachel sounded stunned. She had grown up in an Orthodox household and rejected it for Judaism lite— Reform, that is—as soon as she left for college. "Are you making this up?"

"No, my imagination isn't that good. But he goes to Tehil-lath Israel on Saturday morning, and—"

"That's Orthodox," she said slowly. "Modern Orthodox, anyway."

"Well, what does that mean? Do I have to cut my hair off and wear a wig? Do I have to have two kitchens? Wear black dresses to the ankles?"

We both laughed at the thought. Then I said, "Seriously, is there anything I should be doing?"

Rachel paused. "I thought you were joking. Why do you have to do anything?"

I was momentarily stumped. "I don't really, of course. But . . . maybe I should try to support him. If he wants an Orthodox household."

"Has he asked you for that?"

"I just know that he wants it," I said stubbornly.

Rachel groaned. "Either you're the biggest chump in the Western Hemisphere, or he's fantastic in bed."

I jumped a little. "I'm trying," I said. "We're a family."

"Well, that's good," said Rachel, a little dubiously. "Do you think you can . . . you know, move past this together?"

Suddenly tears rose to my eyes. "I just don't understand. I mean, I get why he lied about the Agency and all that . . . but now it turns out that he lied about basically *everything*. He didn't just keep big important secrets; he kept stupid secrets! Why?"

"I don't know," Rachel admitted. "Maybe secrets were just a habit. He couldn't open up about anything."

Angrily, I dashed away my tears and burst out, "Why can't I even imagine life without David, after he betrayed me in the most public, humiliating way I can imagine? I'm such a fucking idiot!"

"No you're not," she cried, instantly sympathetic. "Jesus,

Shelley, I can't believe how you're holding it together. You're amazing!"

I didn't feel amazing; I felt incredibly muddled. I sighed.

After a moment, Rachel said, "The good news is that you don't have to do anything, really. You can pick and choose: observe Shabbat, but don't keep kosher. Or keep kosher in your home and eat whatever you want when you're out. There's about a thousand ways to be more observant—just go read a book. It'll tell you all the options."

"Okay," I said. "Thanks."

"But there's one really important rule."

"What?"

"Observant Jews have to re-consummate the marriage every Friday night."

"Very funny," I said.

"I'm serious. Go look it up."

CHAPTER THIRTY-TWO

To Do:
Read Judaism for Dummies
Buy Shabbat candles and challah for Friday night

WHEN DAVID CAME HOME FROM SERVICES, he seemed relaxed and peaceful. I didn't say anything to him about it, and he didn't say anything to me. After all, what was there to say? We watched each other assessingly, each trying to read the other's thoughts; I'm sure he was more successful than I was. As I watched him with the children, I recalled our early days together and our dreams for the future. We both wanted a big family. In fact, that's how we met—in the childcare room of Washington Hebrew Congregation.

September 1998
 I had volunteered to work during the Saturday morning Rosh Hashanah service that year—I hated the long, boring Shabbat morning Torah service but had been raised to believe that Rosh Hashanah was the one day of the year that I had to go to services. I'd asked Marisa to help me, but she refused (Neiman's was having a big sale.)

Then two of the other volunteers didn't show up, leaving me all alone to handle eighteen crying, bored children. I was reduced to standing on a chair and shrieking "Sheket, b'vakisha!" (Shut up, please!) when the door opened and in walked a tall, handsome man wearing his yarmulke rakishly tipped back. He stood for a moment with his hands on his hips, surveying the scene.

Then he turned to me. "The temple president sent me in to help," he explained gravely. "The rabbi has to use the microphone to be heard above all the noise."

One of the children chose this moment to pull a whistle out of his pocket and unleash a piercing blast that made me flinch.

The man reached out one long arm and plucked the whistle from the boy's mouth before he could draw another deep breath. "That's enough of that," he said. Then he took off his jacket, hung it up across the back of a chair, and rolled up his sleeves.

"Do you have any childcare experience?" I asked, suddenly very conscious of the sweaty hair straggling into my eyes and the fingerpaint smears on my white silk blouse.

"None," he said cheerfully. "But how hard can it be?" He looked around again. "I can't do any worse than you."

I snorted. "Well then, why don't you start by changing Leah's diaper? Think you can manage that?" I indicated a curly-haired moppet whose soaked diaper was creeping down her chubby legs; all the other children were giving her a wide berth.

"Well, I'm a management consultant," he said, "and my last assignment was in Detroit. I think I can figure out a diaper."

Half an hour later, all the other children were organized by age and interests into cheerful, contented groups. I looked

*at the tall man who was teaching a tight cluster of boys how
to play poker, as I sat on the floor cutting paper dolls with my
group of girls. "Will you marry me?" I asked him, jokingly.*

*"I think I will," he replied, not jokingly at all. "By the
way, my name's David."*

As I looked back now, it occurred to me that our whole life
together had been about children. We met over children, we
struggled to have children, we raised children. Had it always
been about the kids, never David and Shelley?

Another week passed quietly; I was spending more and
more time with David's former assets, the Sharif family. We had
progressed to the point where Fatima and I could actually have
primitive conversations while her young daughters played with
Amy Joy; the two older boys were learning English at an astound-
ing pace. I had gotten Abdal a temporary job as an Uber driver
while tapping into all my sources to see if he could return to his
real trade as an electrical engineer. I was close to finding preschool
spots for the two little girls. I loved spending time with them.

The peace was shattered, predictably, when Dani came to
visit on Friday afternoon following some meetings with Bos-
ton-based literary agents.

She spread the contents of her briefcase across the front
hallway and followed me into the kitchen, where I was putter-
ing around with Amy Joy perched on my hip. "What the hell are
you doing?" she asked.

I had decided that challah on Friday nights was the most I
could possibly do; *Judaism for Dummies* had convinced me that
Orthodoxy was not for me. "I'm making challah."

She stared at me. "Why?"

"Because David likes challah on Friday nights."

"Why?" She came over to the counter and poked her finger

suspiciously into the loaf of warm challah that I'd just pulled out of the oven.

"Stop that!" I snapped. "Because. That's why." Great, now we both sounded like toddlers.

"Christ, it must be contagious," Dani observed. "Josh does this stuff too, I think."

"Well, I should hope so," I said. "Him being a rabbi and all."

David strode through the kitchen door then and dropped his jacket on the chair. "The challah smells great," he said to me.

"Please," said Dani. "Tell me you're not into all this religious stuff too."

"Do you know the very best thing about Shabbat?" David asked. He winked at me and I groaned, trying to ignore the anticipatory butterflies in my stomach.

"Disgusting Manischewitz wine?" my sister suggested.

"Every married couple has to re-consummate the marriage on Friday night."

Dani laughed disbelievingly. "That's a good one."

"No, really," I said. "It's true; I looked it up."

"Really," mused Dani, the potential rabbi's wife. "Well, maybe there's something to be said for this Shabbat stuff after all."

I thought there might be something to be said for it too. Maybe. Someday.

The day before Christmas, David and I trooped down to Disney World with all three kids. Neil and Marisa wouldn't be caught dead in Disney World and set off for Miami; Sam and Sasha probably would have preferred that to Disney, but Marisa made it clear that they weren't invited. We had to rent a minivan with an extra-roomy trunk to transport us and our belongings to the hotel where we'd booked two rooms; when we finally had everyone settled into the van and I slammed the trunk shut, I felt as if I'd run a marathon.

"Keys?" David asked, holding out his hand.

Keys. Keys!! Oh, damn. Oh, shit. Oh . . . "I just locked them in the trunk," I said.

"You just what?"

I refused to repeat it.

The van erupted into pandemonium. "Quiet!" David roared. He rolled up his sleeves and started rooting through my pocketbook. "What are you—" I started.

"Okay," he said, straightening up with a sharp-pointed pen in his hand. "Time me. Ready? Go."

He bent over the trunk, frowning in concentration, and I obediently glanced at my wristwatch. The kids unbuckled their seat belts and twisted around to watch, exchanging glances.

The trunk opened with a polite click and David handed me my pen. "Time," he said proudly.

"Uh . . . twenty-seven seconds."

"Really? I can usually do a trunk in under twenty. Are you sure you—"

"Oh, for God's sake, David!" I snapped, still feeling like a fool. "Let's just get to the hotel."

Sam said eagerly, "Can you teach me to do that, David?"

David glanced at me.

"No," I said.

Once our entourage had settled into the hotel, we began discussing our plans for the day. "Let's go to Magic Kingdom!" Sasha cried eagerly. "I want to take Amy Joy on Small World."

"She can't appreciate that yet," her brother argued. "Let's go on Space Mountain."

Sasha looked apprehensive. "Maybe we should go to Epcot and see the countries. I don't like roller-coasters."

Sam said hopefully, "Can we go to that giant buffet for lunch? I'm starving!"

David looked inquiringly at me, and I shrugged wearily, still undone by the keys-in-the-trunk incident. "Okay," he said, "here's what we'll do. We'll all go to the buffet for lunch, then I'll take everyone to Magic Kingdom so the girls can do the kiddie rides and Sam and I will ride roller coasters. Mom will lie in a chair by the pool here and drink strawberry daiquiris. Any questions? We'll meet back here at eighteen hundred hours to assess dinner plans."

Everyone nodded. "Jeez," said Sam admiringly. "It's like being in the army."

Obeying my orders, I took a book down to the pool and drank strawberry daiquiris. By the time David got back with the kids, I was feeling rested and quite mellow, my cheeks pink from the sun and my limbs warm and heavy on the comfortable lounge chair.

"She's all yours," David announced, dropping a squealing Amy Joy onto my stomach.

The baby babbled happily at me and I dropped a kiss on her fine, wispy hair, astonished to realize that I hadn't even missed her during the past few hours.

"She was afraid of Mickey Mouse," Sasha reported, dropping onto the chair next to mine and pushing her hair back behind her ears.

"And Winnie the Pooh," contributed Sam.

"And the rides," said David wearily. "She didn't even like Small World."

"You didn't like Small World?" I cooed to the baby, who was now deeply engrossed in the wonders of my sunglasses. "Don't worry, you can hang out at the pool with me tomorrow."

"Damn right," grumbled David.

That night David and I left Amy Joy at the hotel with the kids, who had decided to have an in-room movie fest with popcorn and ice cream, and we walked over to Epcot for the fireworks. David took my hand as we walked over the bridge with magical fairy lights swinging in the light breeze. "Just like being in Paris," he said with only a touch of irony as we passed by the Eiffel Tower replica to our right.

"With two teenagers and a new baby," I reminded him.

He shuddered and laughed, depositing me on a bench by the lagoon for optimal fireworks viewing. We'd discovered this spot the first time we came here when the twins were babies; now we'd been here so many times that the bench should have an engraved plaque in our honor. "Save my seat," David said, and disappeared into the crowd.

When he returned, it was with a bottle of wine and a pastry box from the French pâtisserie. "Now this is why I married you!" I burst out, surprising us both and causing the elderly couple who were sharing our bench to give us a warm smile.

David sat down and put his arm around my shoulders. "I love you too," he said, and kissed me.

Damn. I turned away, examining the contents of the pastry box to hide my confusion. What was the matter with me, anyway? I forced the picture of Mia Holloway to the front of my mind, willing it to blank out the magnetism of the man sitting so close to me—my husband, my lover, the father of my children. But it was no use. His body was hard against mine on the crowded bench, and we fit together as well as we always had. Better, even. Why was everything so damn muddy?

With a sigh, I relaxed against him once more.

"How did we ever wind up with all these kids, anyway?" I asked dreamily, staring up at the star-studded sky as we waited for the fireworks to begin. David refilled my plastic wineglass. "I couldn't carry a pregnancy, and you had a vasectomy once we realized that. And yet we have three kids!"

"It's a miracle, isn't it?" David agreed lazily. "We've been so lucky."

With a start, I realized he was right. We'd been lucky to have the love of my sister's children, and now lucky to have this final, extra-beloved baby to brighten our lives.

"We've been through worse, you know," I said suddenly.

"Yes. We have," he agreed.

We both remembered so painfully those long months of trying to get pregnant, the multiple miscarriages, the doctors' final verdict. . . . Yes, we had been through worse times than Mia Holloway together, and we'd been very lucky.

For the first time since that morning when I saw my husband's face on CNN, I reached up and pulled his head down to mine for a long kiss. He murmured against my mouth, "Do we have to stay for the fireworks?"

"Yes," I said, as pinwheeling flashes of color started to explode in the darkness above his head. *Maybe our own fireworks were almost over*, I thought, optimistic for the first time in months.

On our final morning in Disney Hollywood Studios, we took Amy Joy to see the Little Mermaid show, which had been Sasha's favorite for over a decade. "It's a tradition," Sasha explained seriously, dressing Amy Joy in her new Little Mermaid T-shirt and putting a pink bow in her fair hair so it stuck up straight from the top of her head à la Pebbles Flintstone. "Doesn't she look perfect?"

David grunted.

"She looks like an idiot," said Sam.

Sasha smoothed down Amy Joy's fine hair and smiled at

her affectionately. "She looks adorable," she said, and exchanged pleased smiles with me.

David had procured FastPasses so we could bypass the Little Mermaid line, which snaked around the theater and overflowed into the courtyard beyond. "Good job, David," said Sam admiringly as we marched past the throngs in line and took our seats in the packed theater.

I settled Amy Joy in my lap and leaned against David's shoulder. I was always conscious of him these days; just the slightest touch of his fingers against my skin set my senses skittering and my breath into overdrive. It was almost like having a new lover, like the early days of a heady, sparkling new romance. I turned my head to glance up at him and he slanted a smile down at me.

Suddenly my seat shook violently, and I instinctively grabbed David's arm as a great bang simultaneously exploded from the back of the theater. The entire structure trembled, as if a gigantic freight train had run through the ground beneath us. My heart pounded as my terrified brain rushed through the possibilities. Bomb? Earthquake? Meteor?

Sirens rang out and alarms started to blare; I could barely hear David's voice as Sasha screamed. Frenzied throngs of people started shouting and pushing their way through the packed aisles, adding to the cacophony that was assaulting my ears from every direction. Sam cried, "David! David! What's going on?" as people jumped from their seats and rushed for the exits in a blind panic. Behind me I heard a woman screaming uncontrollably, and another man was praying aloud. Plaster rained down from the ceiling, and through the din of screams and sirens, I heard another explosive crash from the back of the theater. I clutched Amy Joy, terrified that we would be crushed in the panicked stampede.

CHAPTER THIRTY-THREE

David grabbed the screaming Amy Joy from my arms to thrust her into Sam's, the next biggest male in our group, and shouted, "Stay together! Go to the left! To the *left!*" Brutally, he forced his way through the screaming, jostling throngs who clogged the aisles, and then he jumped up onto the stage, grabbing a microphone from Ariel who stood frozen in the center of the stage, her mermaid finery covered with plaster and ash.

"Quiet in the theater!" he shouted into the microphone, drowning out the blaring of the emergency sirens. "Everybody silent! I want every person here to turn to your left and introduce yourself to your neighbor—*now!* Everybody take your neighbor's hand and walk—I said *walk*—to the end of the row. If I see any pushing, I will personally see to it that you're the last one out of this theater."

"I smell smoke!" shouted a terrified tourist in the back. "Fire!"

"No, you don't!" David yelled back. "That's just the fake fog from the stage. Now keep holding hands and keep walking! Tell your neighbor your name. Everybody make a friend. Quickly, quietly—that's right. See, the theater's already half-empty. Just walk quietly."

Sam pushed me—I too had been frozen, mesmerized by

David and his effect on the panicked mob—and I hadn't even realized that the row in front of us had emptied out, and it was our turn to go. Clutching Sam's hand as ordered, I started down the long aisle.

"But what about David?" Sasha whimpered.

Sam glanced back. "He won't leave until the theater is empty," he said briefly. "Keep moving, Sash."

She sobbed once, but Sam tightened his grasp on her arm and she moved down the aisle. Now I could smell smoke too. We walked quickly and quietly, holding hands, just as David had commanded. When we were halfway down the aisle, someone in the back called out, "Should we sing, mister?"

I glanced at David and could have sworn I saw him smother a smile, despite the growing heat in the dark, crowded theater and the scent of sweat and smoke that was beginning to permeate the heavy air.

But then a little boy near the front piped up, "Mister, we should sing a song, right?"

David nodded. "Knock yourself out," he said helplessly. And from the front of the theater came a voice, shouting more than singing, and almost immediately hundreds of eager voices joined in a loud rendition of "It's a Small World."

By the time we stumbled out into the sunshine, blinking our eyes against the sudden light and confusion, I was choking on a mixture of suppressed laughter and smoke. The last stragglers were coming out behind us, carried on a wave of the song and huddling in tearful, gasping groups around the building—from which flames were starting to emerge. And then David burst through the doors, supporting an elderly woman who struggled valiantly to keep up despite her twisted back and thin, blue-veined legs. He picked her up and swung her into his arms as flames licked the darkened theater behind him, then set her in the middle of the courtyard and surveyed the scene, frowning.

"Fucking amateurs," he said when he caught sight of us and hurried over. "Sam, take everyone back to the hotel now by the path. Walk along the lagoon; don't use Disney transport."

"But I want to—" Sam started.

"Why can't we—" whined Sasha.

"But what about you?" I asked anxiously.

He caught me by the arm, none too gently. "Get out of here," he said sharply. "Now. Get out of the park, don't use Disney transport, walk back by the path along the lagoon," he repeated. He gave me a hard kiss on the mouth and turned away, searching through the crowd once more. When I last saw him, he was showing some identification to a uniformed security guard on the edge of the crowd and barking out orders.

David was on the news again that night. "Good thing I'm not undercover anymore," he commented, watching himself on CNN with a cynical twist to his mouth. He picked up his bottle of beer and drank deeply.

"David Harris, newly appointed director of the CIA for Clandestine Operations," the newscaster said breathlessly, "happened to be on the site with his family and took charge of clearing the park in case there were secondary explosives in the area."

"Oh, *that's* what you were so worried about!" I exclaimed.

"Yes."

Oh, my God. That hadn't even occurred to me. But of course, that's what they do, isn't it—lure people outside with one bomb and then set off another. I shivered, thinking of the thousands of curious, unwary tourists massed together in the courtyard after the explosion. No wonder David had been so determined to get us away.

"Fucking amateurs," he said again. "They'll find it was some homegrown group of loner losers. Very inefficient bomb," he added scornfully. "Six hundred people in the theater, and not a single serious injury."

On the TV, an excited female reporter was cooing over David's successful evacuation of the theater and the good cheer of the Disney-singing crowd.

David shook his head and drank again. "That bloody song. If the guys at Langley get wind of this, I'll never hear the end of it."

Still, I thought he had been pretty amazing; the un-David was so much hotter than my old familiar husband; drawn like a moth to the flame, I feared getting hopelessly scorched as well.

At home again, my days filled up quickly with the usual family pursuits. I had found preschool spots for little Amira and Shura Sharif, and I assigned myself the task of teaching Fatima how to go food shopping for the family. On my last visit to their house, three other Qameeni women had shown up, with shy dark-eyed children clinging to their robes, and I guessed that I had been appointed head girl of the group.

David had surprised Sasha with a new set of skates for Chanukah, and she had been begging me to arrange ice dancing lessons; the weather had suddenly turned bitingly cold, and Amy Joy needed a snowsuit. My younger sister had left me three increasingly frantic messages while we were gone that I'd been putting off returning.

Fortified with a glass of wine, I finally called Dani after dinner one night.

"Shelley!" she exclaimed. "I've been calling you and calling you! Where have you been?"

"Disney World, remember? We were there when those survivalist nuts bombed the Little Mermaid show."

"Oh, right," said Dani, supremely disinterested in anything that didn't directly impact her precious self. "Well, I really need to talk to you! Remember Josh?"

I frowned. "Josh?" Her boyfriends came and went with such rapidity that I barely learned one name before she was on to the next.

"Josh!" she repeated impatiently. "I told you all about him when I was there in the fall. The rabbi, remember?"

I did, now, and was amazed to find that he was still in the picture. "Yes," I said cautiously.

"Well, you won't believe what we're doing this weekend! He's going to let me meet his kids! Isn't that amazing? Shelley, I really think this is it! He's never let another woman meet his boys since his wife died—he doesn't want them to get attached and start hoping for a stepmother—but he thinks it's time we start getting to know each other. Isn't that amazing?"

Amazing wouldn't even begin to cover it. Dani, whose maternal instincts approximated those of a fencepost, as a step-mother? "He has kids?" I asked weakly.

"Two boys. They're so adorable in the pictures!"

"Um . . . how old are they?"

Dani paused. "They're . . . I don't know, eight and ten, maybe? Or . . . maybe ten and twelve? Maybe around Sam and Sasha's age." She paused again. "Or younger?"

"Do you know their names?"

"Of course! Joseph and . . . um . . . Joseph and . . . why are you interrogating me, anyway? You know I love children!"

Heaven help those boys. Dani had babysat for us only once, when the twins were eighteen months old and David had per-suaded me to take a night off. She'd called six times during the evening to tell us that Sam was crying; when we finally got home at midnight, Dani and the babies were sitting side by side on the sofa, staring fixedly at Saturday Night Live on TV. I couldn't decide who looked more shell-shocked.

I'd picked Sam up and gasped at the soaked patch on the sofa under his bottom. His diaper was so heavy that he felt twice his normal weight. "Dani!" I snapped. "Didn't you change his diaper?"

"Well, no," she said guiltily. "He was crying so much that. . . ."

"He's soaked!" I accused.

Unrepentant, she'd grinned. "Well, I guess that'll happen when you drink six bottles of juice."

"Six bottles of juice!" I gasped.

"It was the only thing that would shut him up," she said defensively. "What else was I supposed to do?"

As she and the baby exchanged glares, David came up behind me to survey the wreckage. "Well, Dani," he'd said dryly. "I guess you've made your point."

As I'd headed for the bathroom with Sam, and David set to work on the urine-stained sofa, she gathered up her bag and flounced out. "I told you I don't babysit!"

"Stuart!" Dani now said triumphantly. "That's the other boy. See, I told you I know their names. So anyway, that's why I'm calling you. I want to do something really special for the first time I meet them. Do you think they'd like a book of Italian art? Or maybe a first edition of Lewis Carroll? I saw some beautiful first editions in Soho last week."

"No fancy books," I said firmly. "Listen, Dani, you can't really get them presents until you know a little bit about who they are and what they like." Or at least their ages.

"I have to get them something," she insisted.

I sighed. "Well . . . maybe something Harry Potterish?"

Dani was affronted. "That piece of trash? It's not even good literature! And the merchandising empire around it—why, it's enough to—"

Honestly, you would think she edited *War and Peace* rather than sluttier versions of *The Babysitters' Club*.

"Never mind," I interrupted. "Just get them some candy."

"Candy," said Dani thoughtfully. "Okay—there's a gourmet candymaker that just opened on West Sixty-Third Street. . . . Yeah, I guess I could do that."

I rolled my eyes, trying not to picture the boys' faces when they opened a beautifully wrapped package of hand-crafted, probably inedible Turkish truffles.

"Anyway," Dani went on cheerfully, "Josh is sure they'll love me. He says they need someone like me to brighten up their lives; they're all too serious. Don't you think that's a wonderful thing to say?"

"Actually, it is," I said, momentarily surprised. Maybe it would work out after all—stranger things had happened. Or maybe I'd end up raising these boys too, just like my other sister's children.

CHAPTER THIRTY-FOUR

To Do:
Fatima—supermarket
Mammogram!
AJ—snowsuit
Call Elie Wiesel Foundation
Call Temple Sinai
Meet with American Jewish World Service
Call Stephen Wise Synagogue

I SPENT THE REST OF THE WEEK lining up engineering job interviews for Abdal Sharif and working with my ever-expanding group of Qameeni wives on basic life skills (we were working on using ATMs and paying bills). When he got home on Friday, David asked me, "How would you like to go to a party tonight?"

I wasn't in much of a party mood. "I don't know—"

"It's a group of Agency officers. You can meet some of the people I work with."

Oh! "That would be good," I said.

"Good." He hesitated for a moment. "Just be prepared."

"For what?"

"For—well, it's hard to explain." He shrugged. "You'll see."

"*Pol–ly*! *Pol–ly*! *Pol–ly*!" Thirty or so conservatively clad, conservatively coiffed twenty- to fifty-somethings were jumping up and down, pumping their fists in the air and shouting. Who or what on earth was Polly?

I looked at David in confusion. So far it had seemed a standardly dull cocktail party, an endless stream of anonymous-looking people with professional smiles and vanilla-sounding first names (Mary, John, Linda, Pete). No last names. Then all of a sudden, the room had erupted.

David was grinning and shouting "*Polly!*" too.

"What's happening?" I yelled over the noise.

"You'll see. Boy, will you see!"

Apparently a victim had been selected. A youngish man with forgettable features and sandy-colored hair was dragged into the middle of the room and plumped down on a straight-backed chair. I watched in amazement as women pulled scarves from their necks and bands from their hair, then swarmed over the apprehensive man to tie him to the chair. Everyone else formed a circle around the chair as the women stepped back.

"Who's our first polygrapher?" the host, "Andy," called out.

A fortyish woman named Linda stepped forward, her face set in a menacing scowl. "Props!" she called.

The hostess dashed into the kitchen and returned with a wooden ruler and cellphone, which she thrust into Linda's hands.

Linda turned to the young man. "You understand that the polygraph machine will record your every emotion. You understand that I will know if you are lying." She tapped the ruler against her hand for emphasis.

Oh, poly*graph*! Now I understood.

The young man rolled his eyes.

"Sir? Do. You. Understand."

"Say yes, Toby!" someone called out.

"Yes," he mumbled.

"Good. Now let's begin. Is your name Toby?"

"Yes."

Linda paced back and forth. She tapped something into the cellphone and turned back to Toby.

"You are lying."

"Well, of course my name isn't Toby! You know that."

"Yes or no answers only!" a dozen people shouted in unison.

"What's the question?" "Toby" asked warily.

"Have you ever told a lie?"

"Yes!" the entire room shouted.

Linda ignored them. "Toby, have you ever told a lie?"

"Yes."

Linda frowned magnificently and made a great show of turning off an imaginary machine. Beads of sweat formed on Toby's brow.

"Now, Toby, tell me all the lies you've told in the past year."

"Tell her about your mother-in-law!" someone shouted.

An older man whom I hadn't met yet stepped forward. "I'll handle this from here," he told Linda.

She nodded. "Yes, sir."

The older man turned to poor Toby. "Have you ever engaged in homosexual activities?"

A great groan went up from the audience.

"No," Toby said.

The man looked at the cellphone and his brows shot up. "Really?"

"Yes. I mean no, sir."

"Really yes or really no?"

Toby paused.

"Have you seen a naked man in the past year?"

———

233

David was chuckling and I looked at him in amazement. This was fun?

"Um. Yes."

"So you do not deny that you had homosexual activities?"

Toby paused again, trying to untangle the double negatives. "It was at the gym," he protested finally. "In the locker room."

Now the whole room shouted. *"Yes or no answers only!"*

"Uh. . . ." said Toby.

Another man, tight-jawed and unsmiling, came up and whispered something in the interrogator's ear. "Toby," said the interrogator. "I'm sorry that you've been so uncooperative. I'll have to turn this over to Ray here."

Another chant went up. *"Ray! Ray! Ray! Ray!"*

The scary-looking Ray put his face about an inch from Toby's sweating one. "Young man!" he snapped. "Do you want to keep your job?"

"Yes, sir!"

"Do you want to be stripped of your security clearance?"

"No, sir!"

"When did you stop beating your wife?"

Toby gaped.

"When did you become an alcoholic?"

"I was never an—"

"Yes or no answers only!" roared the crowd.

"No?" Toby said hopefully.

"So you admit that you were an alcoholic?"

"No!"

"Do you admit that you speak French?"

"Uh . . . yes."

"Do you agree that only homosexuals speak French?"

"No!"

David was convulsed with laughter.

"Do you admit that you drink wine?"

"Yessss. . . ."

"Do you agree that only French-speaking homosexuals drink wine?"

"No, sir!" Toby shouted.

"Well, then." The man smiled suddenly and slapped Toby on the back. "Go back to work, son."

And he made a deep bow to the audience.

"So you play polygraph at your parties," I said to David, who was still chuckling. "What an . . . original idea."

"We all have to be poly-ed at least once a year to keep our clearance. Sometimes more than that. Sometimes they just pull you off your desk and bring you down for a random test. It's the most god-awful experience you can imagine."

Linda, who had been standing nearby, tried to explain. "Honey, I'd rather have a colonoscopy and root canal—without anesthesia—than a poly."

"Why?"

"Have you ever told a lie?" she asked me.

"Sure," I said.

"Well, you have to tell the polygrapher every single lie you've told since you started talking. Have you ever stolen anything?"

"No."

"Really? You've never taken a hotel towel home with you?"

"Well. . . ."

"You have to tell the polygrapher everything you've ever stolen too. Have you ever told a secret?"

"All the time—I have two sisters."

"Get the picture?"

I nodded. I was starting to.

"By the time they're done with you," David added, "you think you might actually be a drug-abusing pedophile who's

sold secrets to everyone from Karl Marx to Osama bin Laden."
Linda laughed and nodded.

Just then another shout rang out from the back of the room.
"*Fist trick! Fist trick!*"

A small, dainty blonde woman in a beautifully cut silk dress
stepped into the center of the room, blushing prettily.

"Are you sure, honey?" asked a man, apparently her husband.

"Sure," she said. "I'd like to." Her voice was low and gentle.

The chant went up again, and I watched with amazement
as the chic, dainty woman made her hand into a fist and slowly,
knuckle by knuckle, inserted her entire fist into her mouth. The
crowd roared with approval. She just as carefully slipped her fist
out and wiped it on the napkin her husband handed her, beaming with pride.

"These people are crazy," I said to David.

"Nah," he said. "They're CIA officers."

The next morning, the evening was still running through my
head while I surfed through Amazon.com picking up Hanuk-
kah gifts for the kids. I was surprised to find myself almost
jealous of David's obvious camaraderie with his coworkers; it
was truly a secret club of dark humor and knife-edge wits and
experiences that could be shared with no one. But at the same
time, I was starting to understand that the CIA wasn't just a job
for him—it was a life.

David came into the kitchen and asked, "Do you have the
insurance check for Sasha's car accident?"

Before I could stop him, he turned to my kitchen desk and
riffled through the stack of files there, seeing the one file I didn't
want anyone to see. My ideas were just in their germination
phase, still so fragile that I couldn't expose them to the harsh
light of day.

David silently leafed through the file's contents: the UN's Human Development Report on Qameen, the Senate Select Commission hearings on Qameen refugees, and American Jewish World Service's Qameen mission report. For a moment, his face drained of all color, and I had to look away from the remembered pain in his eyes; then the moment was gone. Without a word, he replaced the file on my desk, picked up the insurance papers, and left for work.

Quickly, I bundled together the rest of the ungainly file and hid it under a pile of blankets in the linen closet. If he had seen my impressive collection of business cards, old temple and school directories, and directors' lists from all the organizations in which I'd held office over the past twenty years—Hadassah, League of Women Voters, United Jewish Appeal, CAMERA— he would have forgotten his own demons out of sheer curiosity. But I wasn't ready to share this yet. And especially not with him; why should I share when he was so unwilling to do the same for me? Maybe the secrecy habit was contagious.

CHAPTER THIRTY-FIVE

THAT AFTERNOON I BUNDLED UP AMY JOY against the winter cold and took her to the lawyer's office downtown. His secretary had requested that I come in to sign some documents and discuss a new issue that had arisen, but I had no reason to expect any problem with the adoption. So I was completely unprepared when Mr. Beecham closed the door of his office and settled into his desk chair with a sigh. "We've run into a snag," he told me, steepling his hands together and looking grave.

My stomach clenched. "What kind of snag?"

"It appears that Amelia's biological father has decided that he would like custody of the baby. These cases tend to get—"

"What?" I snapped, jumping up from my chair and startling Amy Joy. "What do you mean, he wants custody? He can't have it! He never wanted the baby, he ran off to LA, and Aviva left the baby to me. It's all in your file!"

"Mrs. Harris, I'm afraid it's not that simple. You see—"

"Of course it's that simple!" I interrupted again. "He's a drug abuser, and he hit Aviva—he *beat* her!—when she said she wouldn't get an abortion. Amy Joy is *our* daughter now."

"Mrs. Harris," he said firmly. "I'm afraid Amelia is not your daughter until the courts say she is. And they tend to favor the biological father, especially in California, where the father is now living and has filed suit. I must tell you—I cannot guarantee a positive outcome."

I clutched Amy Joy to my chest until she protested, and I forced myself to loosen my grip. I gazed down into her sweet pink face, her cornflower-blue eyes gazing back at me so trustingly.

"Oh, no," I said, backing away from the lawyer. "She's our baby now. He's not going to take her. Why on earth would he want her, anyway? He wanted her aborted, for God's sake!"

"Well, it seems that he's read about you and . . . Mr. Harris . . . in the newspapers."

"So? What difference does that make?"

Mr. Beecham shrugged. "Possibly he thinks that now he can claim that it's not a stable household."

"Well, we'll fight it," I said fiercely. "It doesn't matter what it costs; we have plenty of money and I'm not giving her to an abusive man. DNA isn't what makes a family."

"I understand what you're feeling." He looked tired now, and a little bit sad. "And I'm sorry to be the bearer of such news. But this could be very difficult, and I cannot guarantee that Amelia—"

I cut him off. "Just fight it. Do whatever it takes. And, Mr. Beecham. . . ."

He looked up. "Yes?"

"Her name is Amy Joy."

My fear for Amy Joy had broken through my confused feelings toward David; I didn't trust him with me—maybe I never would—but I realized that I did trust him to come through for the children. Besides, our marital drama was nothing compared to the need to protect this precious child. So I called the central number for the CIA and told the operator that there was a family emergency and David Harris, in office number 701J, had to contact his wife immediately.

He called five minutes later. "Shelley, my God, what's happened? Are the kids—"

I started to cry. "You have to come home. Amy Joy's biological father wants to take her away, and the lawyer says there's nothing we can do, and the courts favor biological fathers, and he takes cocaine, and—"

"Jesus," he said. "Calm down, Shelley, we can handle this. Christ, I thought one of the kids, or you . . . I don't know what I thought."

"We *can't* handle it," I sobbed. "Mr. Beecham says—"

"Yes, I heard you the first time," he said. "I'll call Beecham and we'll figure out a strategy. I'm sure the courts won't award custody when they hear what the guy's really like."

I was crying so hard, I couldn't even answer.

"Shelley?"

I could only sniffle in response.

David sighed. "Do you want me to come home?"

It was the same tone he always used when he asked that question. I was expected to reply, of course not. I can handle the flood in the basement . . . the drunken teenager . . . the dead squirrel in the fireplace . . . the broken wrist . . . the broken heart. No, David, I don't need you. I can handle it.

"Yes," I sobbed. "Please."

"Okay," he said briskly. "I'll be there in half an hour."

When he got home, I was still crying. I'd reluctantly taken Amy Joy upstairs for her nap, despite my powerful need to keep her in sight, and I kept the monitor close so she didn't feel so far away.

"Come sit in the kitchen," David said.

When we were seated, he gently took my hand; quickly,

I pulled mine away. Just because we were allies in this didn't mean I'd forgotten everything else. "I talked to Beecham on the way home. Shelley, he's not optimistic. The courts have a strong preference for the biological father, especially in—"

"California," I said bleakly. "I know."

He studied me. "What do *you* think?"

National security law might not be my bailiwick, but family law was; I was trying to calm down and think like a family court lawyer, not a hysterical mother. "First," I said, "The judge will probably appoint a guardian ad litem for Amy Joy. A lawyer who will protect the baby's interests in all this."

He studied me. "Is that good or bad?"

I shrugged. "Depends. And I don't know California law, of course, but Mr. Beecham said there's a strong preference for the biological parent, which I think is probably true."

"So what are our options? Legally, I mean?"

I wondered what other "options" he had in mind. "Beecham will get us a California lawyer, and we'll fight it, of course. Our first step will be to try to move the case to Washington, DC."

"Will we win?"

I liked David's dependence on my expertise for a change— but I wished I didn't know so much about family law.

"Our chances aren't great," I admitted, tears welling up again. "There's been a lot of publicity about you—and us—" I bit my lip, then plowed on. "—And that could make us look like an unstable couple. And there's the Senate investigation too."

He was silent; for once, even he couldn't keep his face impassive. I saw pain and grief and guilt written all over it. Then he straightened his shoulders and nodded resolutely. "We have other ammunition," he said.

I stared at him. "Like what?"

"I have excellent contacts in LA. I can have the bastard

followed, night and day, and we'll collect enough evidence on him that no court in the universe would give him custody of a baby girl."

I gazed at him, hope and doubt flaring. "Really? You can do that?"

"Yes."

"But it may not be legally admissible in court."

"It'll give us leverage," he said. "Then we can deal with him."

"How, if we can't use it in court?"

There was a pause. "Don't worry," he said shortly. "I'll handle it."

How could I not worry? My lawyer instincts told me to be worried—to be very worried. But still, I felt a little comforted to know that David and his "contacts" would be on the case too. "Okay," I said.

Over the next few days, the tension began to affect everyone in the house. I spent hours on the phone with Mr. Beecham and our California lawyer, having expensive and depressing no-resolution conversations. With college applications finally done, the twins spent an absurd amount of time surfing websites and reporting depressing statistics about the odds of getting into their schools. And both Tinky and Albie developed gastrointestinal disorders that involved a horrifying volume of cat diarrhea and vomit on our sofa cushions and rugs (never on the easily cleaned tile floor). And poor Abdal Sharif lost his job at Uber when some drunken college kids accused him of being a towel-head terrorist, and he sideswiped a parked car.

One night, after a particularly chaotic dinner where David unexpectedly lost his temper again and yelled at Sasha, causing shock and tears I then had to soothe, I retreated to my "clubhouse" to take stock.

In a few short months, my life had turned upside down and inside out. I'd woken up one morning to discover that I was married to James Bond, and my placid, pleasant (boring?) marriage had turned into a stormy, tempestuous one. We had gone from a household that never shouted to one that was never at peace. The twins bickered endlessly for no possible reason that I could discern, except that the Internet outages were cutting them off from whatever they did online all night. My husband of twenty years was no longer a mild-mannered management consultant but an undercover spy with guns, aliases, and mysterious missions. He'd had an affair because I wasn't there when he needed me—me, the one who was always there for everybody, day and night.

And then he called another woman "honey" and raced off into danger, guns blazing, to rescue her. I wasn't sure we could ever put this splintered marriage back together again.

David came into the room. "What are you doing?" he asked.

"Nothing."

Before I could stop him, he reached down and sifted through the now-thick files on my desk. "Why are you reading about Qameen?" he asked.

"Because I want to understand."

He nodded. "I hear you're working with a bunch of refugee families now, not just the Sharifs. That's great, but be careful—even you can't save the world, Shelley."

I still wasn't ready to talk to him about it. "What do you think we should have done about Qameen?" I asked him instead.

He ran a hand through his hair. "Jesus. Send in a hundred thousand soldiers and a hundred thousand teachers. Then maybe—maybe!—we could have prevented the murders."

"The genocide," I corrected.

He sighed. "Just when I think I've done something good for

the world, when I've prevented a terror plot or brought down an ISIS cell . . . Qameen happens. And I ask myself, what can I really achieve?"

"But your Iran operation. . . ."

"Yes," he said. "I couldn't fix Qameen. Not a damn soul can fix it now, but I can stop Iran from raining death and hell on the rest of the world."

So I repeated his own words back to him. "David," I said, "You can't save the world."

He turned and walked out.

"How about a little break?" David emailed the next day. "I'd like to go visit Daniel and Rebekah; we could leave the kids and do some touring in Israel."

I stared at my iPhone and then at my to-do list, nonplussed. Touring in Israel! When I had just received a big fat envelope from the Elie Wiesel Foundation, and Amy Joy's mild stomach virus had cascaded into strep throat . . . when everyone was in an uproar over our wireless network's propensity for disappearing just before Sasha had saved her midterm exam and emailed it to her teacher.

And yet . . . I had never been to Israel before. David always visited his brother when he was overseas on "business," and I was always too busy with the kids to break away and join them. Maybe this would be another step in the discovery process. Maybe this would fill in the rest of the puzzle that was David. "Okay," I responded, surprising us both.

CHAPTER THIRTY-SIX

To Do:
Buy shekels

DANIEL, REBEKAH, AND THEIR FIVE DAUGHTERS—each more lovely than the next—lived in a small but thriving town just west of Jerusalem. When the cab pulled up in front of their house, I looked around in wonderment. "This isn't the house in your photos," I told David.

"Of course not."

This house was built of pale stone, on several levels to blend in with the uneven terrain, and brightly colored geraniums cascaded from the many balconies that overlooked the beautiful rolling Jerusalem hills. The entire town was built of such homes, both large and small, and clustered around a main square where children played with hoops and soccer balls.

"Where are the soldiers?" I asked. "The barbed wire?"

David laughed.

Daniel's wife Rebekah came running out of the house, her head scarf flying out behind her. "You're here!" she exclaimed. "Shelley, you're finally here!"

I had only met Rebekah once before, when she and Daniel

brought their third daughter to the US for medical treatment. She was a small woman, with dark hair modestly covered but hanging loose down her back. Like her daughters, she wore a long dark skirt that hung to her calves and serviceable brown shoes that I would have recoiled from in my pre-Amy Joy days. Now I just wondered if they were comfortable.

"Come in, come in!" she cried, hugging me. "Abba is so excited that you've arrived."

David reminded me in an undertone, "Abba means father, Ema means mother."

Rebekah and the eldest daughter, Miriam, whisked Amy Joy out of her car seat before I could protest, and our daughter, who disliked strangers, gazed up at them thoughtfully. But Rebekah cooed at her and Miriam murmured some nonsense, and to my astonishment Amy Joy smiled back. The younger sisters were more restrained at first, but Amy Joy soon won them over, and the youngest, Arielle, seemed prepared to clap hands with her for hours. With some shock, I realized that this could actually be a vacation.

"We'll have built-in babysitters the whole time we're here," said David, stretching lazily.

Maybe we should move to Israel, I thought, looking around at Rebekah's cluttered but sun-splashed kitchen. Five girls!

The next day we left our daughter in her cousins' excellent loving care while David took me sightseeing in Jerusalem. When we returned Amy Joy was napping peacefully, and Daniel had brought out an old photo album to show me. "This is the only photo of our mother in Poland before the war," he said, pointing to a grainy black-and-white shot of a slim young girl in white, smiling and leaning back against a concrete building.

I studied the photo curiously, searching for signs of her blond, blue-eyed sons. "She's so pretty," I said.

David reached across me and snapped the album shut, just narrowly missing my fingers. I jumped and stared at him. "David, what are you. . . ."

Rebekah took the album from him and replaced it on the shelf.

"Do you have anything to drink?" my husband demanded.

That night David got drunk. He never drank more than a glass or two of wine, or a bottle of beer. I couldn't believe my eyes when I saw him uncapping his seventh bottle of Israeli beer. "Vile stuff," he said cheerfully. His hair was hanging in his eyes, and he was sprawled across the sofa in the ungainliest pose I'd ever seen him in.

Daniel said something to him in a language I didn't understand, and David replied.

"Now what are you speaking?" I asked, a bit wearily. How many languages could one man speak?

Rebekah, coming into the room from checking on Amy Joy, told me, "It's their secret language. They made it up when they were just kids."

I stared at her. "They have a secret language?"

"It's not uncommon among twins," she said calmly.

Daniel said something else, and David burst out laughing.

"That's rude," I snapped, glaring at them.

"So what do you think of Israel?" Rebekah asked diplomatically.

"It's wonderful. Amazing. I can't believe—well, the history, and—just its existence is wonderful and amazing, isn't it?"

"That's why we're here," Rebekah agreed, exchanging glances with her husband. Daniel was a great bear of a man, his thick beard giving him something of a mountain man look.

David laughed again, for no reason that I could see.

"David, are you drunk?" I demanded.

"Of coursh not. I never get. . . ." his voice trailed away.

Daniel sighed. "Here, bro, have another beer," he suggested.

I didn't think he needed another beer. Daniel told me, "He does this when. . . . We never should have looked at the picture of our mother."

Uncomprehending, I stared at my husband. He had seemed so unmoved when we visited the Holocaust Memorial in Washington, dispassionately pointing to a photograph of Bergen-Belsen and telling me that was where his parents were interned. Now I asked tentatively, "David, what did your parents tell you about their experiences? You've never told me about it."

David waved his bottle at me. "Never will," he assured me, grinning as if I'd told him an especially funny joke.

"Our parents never talked to us about it," Daniel explained. "Never. We knew they were survivors, of course, and that they met in a refugee camp after the war, but—"

David interrupted savagely in their strange language.

"Don't mind him," Daniel said, with a reproachful glance at his scowling brother. "Anyway, they never talked about it. But our mother was just sixteen when the war ended." He added, almost as a non sequitur, "And she *was* pretty. Very pretty."

David exploded up toward his brother, but Daniel caught his fist before it connected—David's reflexes were slowed by the alcohol—and pinned his arms behind his back.

Rebekah removed David from her husband's grip. "Let's get you to bed," she soothed, steering my husband toward the stairs. "You're not feeling well, are you? I'll get you some aspirin and a glass of water and you'll feel much better. . . ." And she propelled him up the steps like a big, confused child until their voices died away in the darkness.

Shocked, I stared after them in silence. Daniel handed me a glass of wine.

"Sorry," he said. "I shouldn't have said that. Unlike my brother, I couldn't care less what our parents did to survive."

My mind flashed back to their slim, fair mother. Had a German soldier . . . "Did your mother—?"

Daniel shrugged. "Probably. Who knows? And probably our father blasted holes in the ground to bury dead Jews, or pulled the gold fillings from their teeth."

"And they never talked about it?"

"Never. We lived in a house of secrets . . . secrets and shame. It always made sense to me that David chose the life he did."

It made sense to me too. Maybe living in the shadows, in unobtrusive silence, was hard-wired into his ancestral memory. Maybe he was doing exactly what he'd been raised to do.

CHAPTER THIRTY-SEVEN

THE NEXT MORNING DAVID BEHAVED AS IF nothing unusual had happened the night before. I knew what he wanted of me, and I complied, as always, accepting his pretense just as I had always accepted it. Perhaps that was what I had been raised to do.

David had insisted that a visit to the shuk of Jerusalem was "part of the Israel experience," but at first I couldn't see why anyone would bother. From dark and crowded stalls, the Arab vendors sold "I Walked in the Steps of Jesus" pillows and 99-cent "silver" bracelets. The souks were dusty and monotonous and faintly sinister; sullen-looking Arab youths mingled uneasily with brightly dressed tourists and wary Israeli soldiers. After less than an hour, I was ready to leave.

"I think I've seen enough," I told him, shying back as yet another vendor blocked my path and begged "beautiful lady" to "just come in and look."

"It's our last day; let's do something more . . . meaningful," I suggested.

David shepherded me away. "Just a few more," he coaxed.

An Arab boy no more than fourteen touched David's arm. "Come look in my store," he whined. "Americans love my store. Cheap. I sell you anything."

Unexpectedly, David said, "Let's take a look."

Since he had warned me that stepping into an individual stall was tantamount to making an offer to buy, I looked at him in surprise. Avoiding my eyes, he pushed through the beaded curtains across the entrance and drew me in after him.

An older man, bearded and turbaned, followed us in and immediately started the usual patter. "Want to buy a T-shirt? Luggage?" he invited. "Need an extra suitcase to carry home everything you bought?"

I shook my head and edged toward the exit.

"Mezuzah? Bracelets? Cross?" he went on. "I have antique crosses, handmade by nuns in Bethlehem and blessed by the Pope."

David picked up a plastic cigarette lighter embossed with something written in Arabic. "This is nice," he said to me. "I bet my boss would like it."

I stared at him.

To the shopkeeper, he said, "How much for the lighter?"

Just as the shopkeeper opened his mouth to respond, the beaded curtains crashed against each other and four young Arab men strode in. They rapped out something in sharp Arabic and the shopkeeper hurried away, leaving us encircled by the heavily bearded toughs.

David spoke to them in Arabic and gestured casually toward the beaded curtains. As they all turned to look, he shifted his stance and let the lighter slip to the ground, where it slid across the dusty floor to my feet.

I froze. David, still calm, spoke to the men again. One of them answered him in rapid Arabic and David grimaced, then responded.

The biggest of the men shoved David against the hard stone wall and his voice rose in protest, but he made no move to resist. Another produced a business-like knife from under his robes and held it under my husband's chin. David's eyes didn't even flicker.

Before I had time to think about it, I dropped my sunglasses on the floor and slowly stooped to pick them up, scooping up the lighter along with the glasses. Slowly, slowly, I backed up to the entrance. No one glanced my way, but my heart was pounding so fiercely I could hardly draw breath.

David was arguing, holding his empty hands out in front of him in supplication, as one man held the knife to his throat while the other roughly went through his pockets. For one split second, David's eyes flickered to mine in a tiny, infinitesimal signal. I whirled and ran out through the beading, shouting at the top of my lungs in English. A troop of Israeli soldiers was sauntering through the souk, their ever-present weapons slung casually over their backs.

The Israeli commander rapped out an order, and the Uzis were in the soldiers' hands before I could move out of the way. They burst into the shop and barked out orders; I sank down onto my knees, trembling so hard I couldn't stand anymore. I would be a terrible spy.

David emerged from the stall in rapid-fire conversation with the young Israeli commander. The other soldiers surrounded them in a defensive stance, but I believed that the danger was over; the would-be assailants had fled through the back doorway. Attacking a lone man was one thing, but taking on seven battle-ready, heavily armed Israeli soldiers was quite another.

My husband glanced at me and said casually, "Got everything we need, Shells?"

Wordless, I nodded. Yes, I had the lighter.

David returned his attention to the commander, who was now in brisk conversation with someone on his cellphone. The commander snapped out another order to his men, who lowered their weapons and retreated to lean against the wall behind me. One lit a cigarette, and I realized with surprise that his hand was trembling. They were only teenagers, after all.

The commander made a final curt comment into his cellphone and turned to David. For a moment, I thought he would salute. Instead, he held out his hand and David shook it; then the young soldier threw his arms around my husband and hugged him. I watched, amazed.

Our now-devoted soldiers escorted us out of the souk and saw us into a cab. One handed me into the back seat with all the reverence that he would give his aged granny, and I thanked him, my head still reeling. The officer stuck his head in the driver's window and spoke a sentence or two.

As soon as we drove away, David turned to me and said, "Give it over."

I handed him the lighter. He pocketed it. Then he leaned forward and said something to the driver, who nodded and executed a U-turn, speeding off in the opposite direction.

I said, "Um, isn't our car parked over near Mamilla?"

"We're not going back to the car."

"Then . . . where are we going?"

David shook his head. I fell silent; life as a Bond girl wasn't all I had thought it would be.

The driver took us to the Hilton Hotel, where David told me briefly, "Go into the ladies room. When you come out in ten minutes, take this elevator back down to parking level two and wait for me there."

Pressing my lips together, I went into the ladies room and washed my hands free of the dust from the souk, then followed David's instructions. He swung up in a shabby gray Toyota.

I got in. "I thought this was supposed to be a Jaguar."

"What?"

"Doesn't James Bond always drive a Jaguar? Or at least an Aston Martin?"

Finally, my husband grinned. I leaned back and watched him, surprised to find my heart pounding now from excitement rather than fear.

We rolled out of the garage and proceeded at a sedate pace through the busy streets of Jerusalem, David's eyes constantly darting from the street before him to the rearview mirror. "What are you looking for?" I asked him finally.

"Our tails."

"Plural?"

"Well, we've got Mossad for sure."

"And. . . ?"

"Well," he said, "that's the problem."

I fell silent again, and David returned his attention to the rearview mirror, frowning. Finally, he sighed. "Since you're here, I guess I'll have to do this the boring way." He picked up his iPhone.

A few blocks later, we acquired an Israeli Defense Forces escort: two cars ahead of us, two behind, and a helicopter overhead.

"I'm sorry I cramped your style," I said.

David grinned again.

Our little parade proceeded onto the highway and followed the signs for Ben Gurion airport.

"David! Amy Joy is back at Daniel and Rebekah's—and all our stuff—"

"—Is being delivered to the plane. Amy Joy is fine. Rebekah and Miriam are bringing her under heavy police escort."

"We can't go back to the house?"

"No."

"Ever?"

———
254

He shrugged.

I bit my lip. "What went wrong?"

"What do you mean?"

"How did they find you in the shop?"

"Just bad luck. One bright young lad recognized me. My picture's been in the papers too many times."

"Then why did you . . . should you be doing this kind of work anymore? If any kid on the street can recognize you?"

"I absolutely should not be doing this kind of work anymore. But Ali insisted he would only deal with me, in person. And I was going mad after weeks and weeks of rehearsing my testimony in lawyers' offices, and then reciting my lines in Senate hearing rooms."

"And what did you get for all this trouble?" *It had better be good.*

He reached into his pocket and tossed me the lighter. "Go ahead and open it."

As if I were handling TNT, I twisted off the cap until the capsule sprang open, revealing a flash drive inside. I took it out. "What does this have on it?"

He shrugged again. "Hopefully, what he promised."

"And what would that be?"

"Detailed plans for the Iranian nuclear program."

I gulped.

"Don't you think that's worth a spot of trouble?" my husband asked.

Carefully, I reinserted the flash drive and screwed the lighter shut again. Then I handed it back to David. "Here. Take good care of it."

He glanced at me. "I take care of everything that's precious to me."

I nodded. I trusted him.

"By the way," he added, "thank you. You were absolutely perfect back there."

A warm glow spread throughout my body. Too brimful to speak, I smiled at him.

"You make one helluva spy's wife," my husband said.

Part III

TRIALS

CHAPTER THIRTY-EIGHT

To Do:
Kosher chicken stock: six chickens, fresh garlic, thyme,
    rosemary
DVR Qameen documentary on BBC
Arrange meeting at Elie Wiesel Foundation
Take Qameeni families to Holocaust Museum

ON MY FIRST MORNING BACK HOME, I felt like a Mack truck had hit me; jet lag was a bitch. I wondered how David managed it so well; he was up and dressed for work before I even staggered out of bed. I was still feeling prickly when Rachel came by for a cup of coffee. She handed me the three thick FedEx envelopes that had landed on my front porch and started to ask me why I was getting mail from all those synagogues, but I quickly distracted her by admiring her new tennis skirt and showing her Amy Joy's latest trick of clapping hands.

"How was the trip?" she asked.

"Amazing. Israel is amazing."

"And David? His family?"

"I think . . . I think I'm sort of there now."

"There? Where?"

I was fumbling for words; partly jet lag and partly because I was still figuring it out myself. "I think I've discovered the real David now." I paused. "I think. I think I know him enough, anyway."

Rachel looked hard at me. "And do you like what you know?"

I thought of all the Davids—hard, threatening, tender, loving, damaged, impossibly alluring—and swallowed. "Yes," I said simply.

There was a brief silence and then she said, "You know, this is really rude and inappropriate, but Mark asked me and then I just couldn't stop wondering. . . ."

"What?"

"Well, Mark asked me where does the money come from? How could you afford this house and vacations and stuff, on a government salary?"

I drew in a sharp breath. What a good question—where *did* all the money come from? Every two weeks a tidy sum arrived in our checking account from Hanson Consulting, and every December an even tidier sum bounced in—a bonus, I had always assumed. What other secrets was David keeping from me?

As soon as he walked in the door that evening, I dragged him into his bookcase-lined office off the front hallway, shut the door, and asked sternly, "David, where does all the money come from? You work for the CIA so you make—what, less than two hundred thousand dollars a year? Not hundreds of thousands as a management consultant? How did we afford this house? How come those huge deposits come into our checking account every two weeks? Where does the money *come* from?"

Unexpectedly, he laughed—a full belly laugh like I hadn't heard from him in quite a while. "I hope this doesn't disappoint you, ma belle, but the boring fact is that I inherited it."

I almost dropped Amy Joy. "From whom?"

"From my parents," he said, surprised.

His parents? They had been Holocaust survivors who met in a desolate refugee camp in Poland after the war and made their long, painful way to America where his father, as far as I ever knew, was a tailor and his mother a nurse's aide. A Holocaust survivors' foundation had financed the educations of David and Daniel, who had been miracle, change-of-life twin babies. Their parents never lost their heavy Yiddish accents nor spoke of their lives before America, hiding their concentration camp tattoos and their secrets under long-sleeved shirts and nearly unintelligible English.

David grew up in a house of secrets, I suddenly realized. Maybe living in the shadows, in unobtrusive silence, was hard-wired into his being. But still—

"How could your parents have scraped together enough money for an inheritance?" I stared at him, speechless.

"Well, it wasn't directly from them," he elaborated. "When Daniel got to Israel, he joined a survivors' lawsuit to reclaim the art and jewelry that was looted from our grandparents in Poland before the Holocaust. The suit was handled by an Israeli-French firm, Schlumberger, and it settled just after we were married. So I set up an automatic deposit to look like I had a high salary job."

I was nonplussed. Finally I said, "How much money do we—I mean, you—have?"

He shrugged. "With interest and dividend income—I don't know, around eight million, I guess."

I thought of his brother Daniel and his family, who lived very simply in a modest town of religious Jews near Jerusalem. "What about Daniel? Does he have—holy crap—eight million too?"

"Oh, no. Daniel put most of it into trusts for his girls. They'll have nice dowries when they marry," he added, smiling.

I still couldn't take it all in. Miriam, the eldest of Daniel and

Rebekah's girls, was almost twenty, ripe marriageable age for a religious girl in Israel. I knew they had already started looking around for a suitable boy. Miriam was very pretty and clever, a good match; now I realized she would bring money with her too.

As would our children. I gazed down at Amy Joy, who was intent on prying the button off my cashmere sweater with her tiny fingers. "You'll be an heiress," I told her. "Boys will want to marry you for your money."

And then I gazed at David again; my James Bond was now a multimillionaire as well.

Would I ever know all his secrets?

A few days later, Sam persuaded me to go to his wrestling match. I had managed to avoid them all so far, so I agreed to attend this one.

The match was in the sweaty, overcrowded old gym at Sam's school. Amy Joy gazed wide-eyed at the mass of boys around the thick wrestling mats; I pointed Sam out to her, and she squealed with excitement. David had said he might try to attend, so I craned my neck looking around but didn't see him.

Sam's bout was second, and I watched anxiously as he and the other boy grappled and fought, locked together in what seemed to me a very unseemly manner on the mat. Suddenly Sam's opponent twisted and heaved, and Sam's arm was wrenched back with a force that made him grimace in sheer agony. He tapped the mat with his free hand, his face a rictus of pain and defeat, but the other boy just increased the pressure. A tall, nondescript man in a baseball cap, standing by the door, shouted, "He tapped out! *Ref, he tapped out!*"

At almost the same moment, the other team's coach shouted, "Keep going! Break him! No mercy! No mercy!" The tall man shouldered his way through the onlookers and started for the coach; the other boy gave another yank and Sam's face contorted as if his arm had been wrenched from its socket. It was only then that I realized the tall man was my husband.

By the time I pushed my way through the onlookers, stepping awkwardly with Amy Joy clutched in my arms, David was face-to-face with the referee and both coaches, shouting. I ignored all of them and bent to Sam, who was lying on the mat, gasping and sobbing in pain; his arm hung at an awkward angle, and I was horrified to see bone poking through the reddened skin. His erstwhile opponent stood behind his coach, grinning pridefully. When he saw me kneel at Sam's side, the boy said quickly, "I was just doing the hold—I don't know what happened. Maybe he was holding his arm wrong. Is he okay?"

"Shut up!" I snapped, shoving him aside. I wanted to rip *his* arm off and stuff it down his throat. "Get out of the way!"

"Mom," Sam sobbed. "Mom, I think my arm's broken. Oh, God. . . ."

I stood up again and put my hand on David's arm; he calmed instantly at my touch and turned away from the other men in disgust. I couldn't go in the ambulance with them because of Amy Joy, but David could. I remembered to call Sam's real father too, and Neil also rushed over to the hospital. (Sam told me later, privately, that the hospital staff was confused at first by his "two fathers," but then one of the male nurses told him how cool it was, and that he and his boyfriend were hoping to adopt a baby too. Sam, mightily amused since the painkillers had kicked in, didn't set the record straight.)

His broken arm and dislocated elbow meant that he'd be needing a lot of TLC for the immediate future—which was fine with me. His needs were perfectly matched by my own burning need to wrap him in a warm, comforting blanket of chicken soup, constant fussing, and pain meds.

A week later, David came into our bedroom with the local newspaper as I was getting ready for bed. "Just thought you'd be interested," he said, pointing to a front-page article titled "Wrestling Scandal Implicates High-School Coach, Ref." I looked up at David and then down at the newspaper again.

"The long-time wrestling coach of St. Ignatius High School in Rockville, along with a first-year referee, have been suspended from their positions pending investigation of missing funds from the Northern Maryland Youth Wrestling Federation."

My gaze locked with David's. "Did you do this?" I asked, almost breathless.

"Yes."

"But . . . how?"

"Easy enough to move funds around. I'll make an anonymous donation to the Federation to make them whole again, plus a little extra. But that coach and ref are out of the business."

"David," I said. I didn't know what to say. "Thank you."

"You're welcome."

And suddenly, I was ready. One set of emotions took hold, burying everything else; this man was more electrifying, more exciting, than my management consultant husband had ever been, and I wanted him badly . . . more than I ever had in my life. "Can we go to bed now?"

His gaze snapped back to mine and his eyes sparked with keen interest. He walked over to the bedroom door and locked it.

"David," I breathed.

We didn't even stop to turn off the lights. I had already turned the bed down; its soft, yielding white sheets and lace-trimmed pillows were just waiting for our eager bodies. David unbuttoned his shirt, exposing his hard, muscled chest, and reached out for me.

"Wait," I said.

"You're not backing out on me, are you?" he teased.

"No, I'm just trying to think if I shaved my legs."

"Well, God knows I can't make love to you with hairy legs. Forget it, I'll just take a cold shower and—"

I threw myself at him and we tumbled onto the bed together, laughing. "You'd *better* make love to me."

"I plan to," he answered, and I closed my eyes and gave myself up to his familiar yet newly thrilling touch.

CHAPTER THIRTY-NINE

Afterward, I lay in his arms and he traced the line of my hip with a callused finger. Already I was questioning myself, but the heady mixture of familiarity and passion was so unexpected that I couldn't bring myself to draw away. "Stop thinking," he murmured into my ear.

I looked at him in surprise.

"You're worrying that we shouldn't have done this, and that I'll think you've forgiven me, but you're really still angry at me. Just stop thinking about it."

He knew me so well.

"Just because we had sex doesn't mean that—"

"I know," he said again. "But I love you, Shelley, and I'm not going anywhere. We can work this out."

I couldn't think of anything to say.

But there were two betrayals: his years of lying and the woman. The lies I was beginning to understand, but the other . . . I couldn't even bear to think her name, much less say it.

Unconsciously twisting my fingers into a painful knot, I tried to banish her from my mind. David pulled me closer and I melted into him, wanting him desperately. I wanted to know every inch of his body, to feel his hands on all my secret places, to feel him inside me, to become one with him again.

He knew. "Shelley," he murmured, bending to kiss my breast. And after that, I stopped thinking.

The next morning, of course, I was awash in confusion once more. My husband had cheated on me, had slept with another woman—and had both told me and shown me that I was not as important to him, right now, as his job. And what did I do? Why, I fell into bed with him at the first opportunity.

Well, maybe not exactly the first opportunity . . . I thought back to the past dreary months and the iciness between us. Did I really want to stay in that frozen hell forever?

And then there was that delicious, lovely, mind-jangling sex—no, lovemaking. . . . An involuntary smile curved my mouth as I spread the creamy duvet over our bed—*our* bed, David's and mine. It was really *our* bed again.

I was still lost in a dreamy reverie as I started the coffee-maker downstairs and David strode through the kitchen door. I jumped, aware that my cheeks were flushing red, and I saw his eyes darken in amused comprehension. "What are you thinking about, young lady?" he asked. "Could it have anything to do with last night?"

It had everything to do with last night, and he knew it. So I smiled, and he kissed me good-bye. I was still feeling languorous when Rachel stopped over for coffee.

She eyed me curiously. "Something you want to tell me?"

"Umm. Well . . . sort of." My cheeks blushed bright red once again, like a teenager caught out in the back seat of her boy-friend's car.

"Hmm," said Rachel. "So . . . things are better with you and David?"

I shifted uncomfortably. "Umm . . . yeah."

She looked at me closely. "What does that mean?"

"It means that—I slept with David," I burst out, startling both of us. "And I want to do it again."

It wasn't just sex; it was hot, passionate, meltingly intimate sex, like you read about in books. Maybe, I thought, this was the real David, and the one I'd been married to for the past twenty years was his pale carbon copy. I'd discovered that I was married to a passionate, slightly dangerous, achingly remote stranger—but a stranger who thrilled me to my very deepest core.

Rachel was stunned into silence. "Holy crap," she said finally. "That's not what I expected."

I smiled, a little uncertainly. "It's not what I expected, either. I'm wondering if I should be kicking myself."

"Well . . . how do you feel?"

Glorious, I thought. "I don't know. But it was . . . amazing."

She paused, obviously considering the value of amazing sex. "Wow. Good for you. God, marriage is mysterious, isn't it?"

David and I had a date that night—we left the kids at home and went out to dinner. I felt like I was dressing for a first date; I tried on three different blue sweaters and four pairs of jeans before returning to, of course, the first pair that I had tried on. I put in the sapphire earrings that looked great even if they made my earlobes ache, and the gold bracelet that David had bought me when I first became pregnant, so long ago.

We seated ourselves at a small bistro table, and I noticed David glancing around the room. "Close your eyes," I said suddenly.

"What?"

"Close your eyes," I repeated.

He shrugged but put his drink down on the table and closed his eyes.

"Now," I said. "Tell me about the people in the room."

He smiled. "I have to perform tricks for my dinner? Okay

. . . well, the German tourists in the far corner are trying to decide if the women at the bar are hookers—but they're not, so the guys are heading for disappointment. The bartender is scoping it out too, though, and he can provide some discreet contacts when the Germans crash and burn."

He paused, carefully lifting his martini for a deep swallow. "Go on," I ordered. "And no peeking."

He smiled again. "The guy in the Brooks Brothers suit to the right, with his overdressed wife? He's lying. Sweating like a pig, and lying like a trooper. He's a rookie though; he'll never get away with it. And the two suburban couples behind you—there's some bad chemistry there, but I can't figure out what it is. A lot of tension, though. And the heavyset guy two tables back is carrying a gun. Unusual in DC, so I'd keep an eye on him."

"Okay," I said, impressed despite myself.

"We used to do training exercises just like that at the Farm. Can I open my eyes now?"

"Yes." I watched him. "So if you were working right now, who would you be worried about? The guy with the gun?"

"No," he said immediately. "The guys in the corner with the baseball caps and beers."

I shook my head. "Why? They look so ordinary."

"Because they blend in so well, and they're only pretending to drink heavily. But I think they're probably Feebies."

His dark blue eyes took in everything, constantly assessing his surroundings even on a family weekend, and I wondered how I could have missed so much about him in the past. Of course this keen, unobtrusive man was not a management consultant; of course he operated in the darkest shadows and in the deepest secrecy.

His gaze snapped back to mine, and our eyes held for a long moment. "Thanks," he told the passing waiter, pulling two twenties from his wallet and tossing them onto the table. He got up and held his hand out to me. "Let's go, sweetheart."

The next morning I felt no confusion at all.

That afternoon I worked late, my mood lowering as I filled out paperwork on another ex-family that was united only in their anger at me, when I noticed a text from David saying "Call me." It had come in two hours before, but we had to turn off our phones while in the mediation session.

"Everything's fine," he began, and my stomach clenched. Clearly everything was not fine.

"But I'm at the pediatrician with Amy Joy—"

Oh. My. God.

"—but she's fine. The stitches will come out in two weeks, and the scratches aren't as bad as they look."

"David . . . what the hell?" was all I could manage.

"Sorry. Some boys were playing ball in the playground and one of them tripped over Amy Joy, and he fell on her and she cut her chin—that's where the stiches are—and she's got some scratches on her legs—"

In the background I heard Amy Joy's little voice saying, "Booboo," and my eyes welled up.

"Oh, my God," I said aloud. She was okay. She would be okay. But I felt nauseated at the thought of how much it must have hurt. . . . "Was the doctor gentle? Did the stitches hurt?"

"Well . . . I'm glad you weren't there. The worst part was putting in the lidocaine before the stitches."

Now I wished that he had lied to me; this would be a good time for that particular skill. Still, thank God for his calm steadiness; I knew he had been perfect with her.

"We're heading home now," he said. "Meet you there?"

When I got home, Amy Joy flung herself into my arms. "Boo-boo," she said over and over, seeming almost shocked that we had let something so terrible happen to her.

David said to me, "Shelley, I swear, it happened so fast . . . there was nothing I could do. I saw the big kids playing ball out of the corner of my eye and I thought they were too close to the little kids, but I didn't do anything. I should have chased them off, but then that woman who moved in down the street started talking to me—but I swear I never took my eyes off Amy Joy and by the time I saw—there was nothing I could do. I'm so sorry."

It was remarkable to see him so vulnerable. "I know that," I said gently. "Of course I know that."

He put his arm around me and kissed Amy Joy on the top of her soft head. "I'm sorry, sweetheart," he said. Was he talking to me or the baby?

Of course, Amy Joy's scrapes and scratches started to fade by the next day—babies heal so blessedly fast!—but much worse was to come. Three days after the accident, David strode into my "clubhouse" after Amy Joy was in bed and practically thrust his cellphone at me. "Look at this," he snarled. "Just look at this."

I took the cellphone and looked, while he paced and cursed. "Jesus Christ. Jesus *fucking* Christ."

"David," I said. "The kids can hear you."

He switched to Yiddish, but I knew he was still cursing.

I turned my attention to the little screen. It was one of those conspiracy-theory websites that equated all intelligence officers with torturers, and it had a banner headline: "Playboy Spy Investigated for Child Neglect."

"Jesus fucking Christ," I said.

Apparently someone had taken a cellphone video of the accident, and then someone else had photoshopped it; there was a still photo of David smiling down at a very attractive blonde while Amy Joy lay in a sobbing, bruised, bloody bundle at his feet.

"I swear to God, Shelley, I don't even know that woman!"

I did. She was half of a lovely gay couple who had moved in recently; her wife worked at the Treasury Department.

"And I picked up Amy Joy the *instant* the brat fell over her! They rearranged the time on the picture; I was talking to the woman *before* the accident, not while Amy Joy was lying there. My God!"

"David," I said calmly. "David, settle down." If the situation hadn't been so awful, I might have taken some pleasure in seeing him so shaken out of his usual sangfroid. "Of course I know that you were watching Amy Joy."

"Well, tell that to the District of Columbia," he said bitterly.

"What?"

"Keep reading."

After resurrecting David's liaison with Mia—I'm proud to say I barely winced over that—the article ended by reporting that the District's Child and Family Services department would be investigating us for child neglect. "Sources at the scene indicated that the child had older bruises at the time of this incident, and investigators are eager to look into conditions in the home," it concluded.

Older bruises? I searched my memory.

David read my mind. "From when she banged herself with the toy drum, remember?"

"That tiny bruise?" I looked at him disbelievingly, and he shrugged.

I reread the article while he paced some more.

—

"Is this anything?" he asked finally. "Will they actually investigate?"

We both knew I was the expert on family law. I looked away from his drawn face. "Yes."

"Really?"

"Definitely."

"Why?"

"Because she's a new adoptee, and some bureaucrats have decided that all new adoptees are at-risk; and because this is in the news, and there's so much terrible publicity about DCFS neglecting abused children; and because you're a big deal."

"But they won't find anything," he said.

I didn't disabuse him, but I knew better. If they wanted to find something, they might. I had a few enemies at DCFS.

CHAPTER FORTY

Two days later, just after dinner, there was a heavy pounding on the door. I plucked Amy Joy from her highchair and clutched her to me; the last time this happened it was the FBI. David came running down the stairs and pushed roughly past me to get to the door first.

Two men stood on our front stoop, wearing windbreakers that said, "DC DCFS."

"Oh, shit," I said under my breath. "David, this is Henley and Heaton, the investigators I told you about. . . ."

Henley smirked at me and said to David, "We have a search warrant for this residence. Please step aside and don't touch anything."

"The hell I will," said my husband.

"David," I said warningly, and quickly pushed *him* aside. I held out my hand. "Please let me see the warrant."

"It's all legit," said Henley. "Step aside and let us do our work."

I didn't move. "Let me examine the document."

He scowled ferociously. But his theatrics did not intimidate me as he clearly hoped; he reminded me of nothing more than Sasha in a sulk. I waited silently.

Visibly angry, he thrust a sheaf of papers at me, and I started reading. He was right; the search warrant was properly executed, and I couldn't see any grounds for contesting it. But I took my time and read it through carefully—twice. The inspectors moved around restlessly, practically pawing the ground in their eagerness to get inside, while David stood unyieldingly beside me.

Finally I nodded at the two men. "You can come in. I'm going to copy these documents, then I'll give them back."

Henley started to protest, but I cut over him, "If you object, that will give me grounds to have the search overthrown. Please, do me a favor—object."

He shut his mouth, scowled some more, and shoved his way inside.

David looked at me. "What do you want me to do?"

"Take out your cellphone and start filming them. Don't let them out of your sight."

The leader stopped, halfway up the stairs. "No fucking way. No filming."

You could cut the tension in the room with a knife. But this wasn't the FBI; these people weren't afraid of David, despite his powerful shoulders and clenched fists. He was afraid of them. They had the power to take away Amy Joy.

I thought furiously. In the District of Columbia, the video would not be admissible if one party objected to the filming. God damn it, why hadn't we chosen to live in Virginia?

"No filming," I said to David.

Amy Joy started to cry, and I thrust her at David. "Take the baby."

"No, I'll watch the inspectors."

"No!" I didn't know if he could control himself as they dug through our drawers and lifted our mattress and leafed through our books. "I'll watch them."

"Nobody watches us," said Heaton. "Unless you want this search to go on overnight, you'll leave us alone."

I could almost feel David's fury; he was powerless to protect me, his family, his home—everything that had meaning in his life. Thank God Sasha and Sam were at their parents' house that weekend. But the thought of Sasha's dainty underwear in their hands was sickening to me, and I leaned against David for mutual support. His body was stiff.

We stood together in the living room, listening to the heavy footsteps upstairs. Then the baby monitor in the kitchen crackled; they must be in Amy Joy's room. Of one mind, we raced into the kitchen, and I lifted up the little monitor so we could hear better. "Nothing here," Henley grunted.

What had they expected to find? Whips and chains?

"Let's make this exciting and plant some kiddie porn on the guy's computer," Heaton said.

"Or at least sprinkle some coke on his tighty-whities."

They both laughed.

David moved suddenly, and I grabbed his arm with both my hands. I held on tight until his muscles relaxed. "Don't worry," he said. "I'm not that stupid."

"This is a nightmare," I said.

"I'm a fucking idiot," he replied.

"What? Why?"

"I should have recorded that. This way, it's their word against ours. Why the fuck didn't I record them?"

He was furious at himself; he thought he'd failed me. Again.

"David," I said forcefully. "Stop. This is not your fault. This is an overzealous bureaucracy gone wild. I've seen it before. If anything, it's my fault; I've made enemies of these guys."

I don't think he even heard me. "I'm a fucking idiot," he said again.

I could barely breathe when our lawyer called a few days later to tell us that the preliminary hearing on Amy Joy's custody was scheduled for the following Monday. Acting on my suggestions, our lawyers had managed to move the case to the District of Columbia since that was the baby's domicile; I thought DC law might be slightly more friendly than California law on this. Now, with the entry of DCFS into our case, I feared I had made a terrible mistake.

"We'll just start with the basics," he explained. "Her biological father may not even be there. The real hearings won't start for another month or so."

"What do we—" I began nervously, but he cut in quickly.

"This is just the basics. Nothing to worry about."

Who says lawyers don't have a sense of humor?

The morning of the hearing, I dressed Amy Joy in her pink dungarees with the tiny butterflies embroidered on the pockets and a matching pink-and-white-striped sweater. As we sat in the small courtroom waiting for the hearing to begin, she amused herself by tugging off her pink booties and putting them in her mouth.

I put them back on her fat little feet. She pursed her mouth and pulled them off again, then grinned mischievously at me. I felt a catch in my throat. This couldn't happen, I told myself firmly. She's mine.

The judge entered, as well as social workers, a lawyer who would be serving as guardian ad litem, and others I couldn't immediately identify. "Mr. and Mrs. Harris," the judge said. "I presume this is Amelia?"

"Yes, your honor," we said.

The lawyer for Greg Clifford, Amy Joy's biological father, had done his research; the DCFS inspectors made David sound like a psychopath. Although the cellphone photo of Amy Joy at the playground was not admitted into evidence, Clifford's lawyer made sure that the judge knew about it. On the way home David was silent. Finally I said, "I'm scared."

"I told you, I'll handle it," he said shortly.

"But how?" I cried. "He had everything—your affair with Mia, your being investigated by the Senate and the Justice Department and everyone else on the face of this earth! And there's no police record on the biological father's abuse of Aviva, so that's just hearsay."

"Except that her neighbor did tell our lawyer that she heard screams and called 911 once," he reminded me.

"Yes, but when the police got there, no one answered the door. And his drug convictions are just possession, and he's claiming that he went through rehab."

He shook his head. "You've been working in these courts for years. How is it that no one cares what Aviva's wishes were? Why isn't the law on our side?"

"The law is. . . ." I stopped. "The law isn't what I thought it would be."

"What do you mean?"

"I thought that I would be helping families in trouble. Instead I'm just helping to tear them apart—and the laws just make it worse."

"But I thought—that's why you went into mediation—"

"Mediation is better, but . . . well. . . ." I shook my head. "Anyway. Why the hell does he want Amy Joy? What would he do with a baby? How would he take care of her?"

"That's what I can't figure out yet," David said quietly. "But I will. Trust me."

"But how?" I cried again. "You keep telling me not to worry, but you're not doing a damn thing that I've heard of! And—"

I shut my mouth, keeping the words inside: It's your fault that he has all this ammunition against us, your fault that we look like dysfunctional headlines from the tabloids instead of the family that we are.

In the same even tone, he said, "Shelley, I know this is my fault, and I'm going to fix it. I promise you."

"No one can promise that," I said bitterly. Not even Clark Kent.

He didn't respond.

But I was grateful for his calming presence two nights later, when the kitchen door burst open and my younger sister stood framed in the headlights of a taxi that idled in the dark street outside. "Thank God you're here!" Dani gasped. Then she burst into tears.

CHAPTER FORTY-ONE

To Do:
Interfaith committee: first meeting
Plumber re hot water
INTERNET!
Draft Qameen proposal for temple

THIS WAS HIGH DRAMA EVEN FOR DANI, who lived her life on the thin line between delirious joy and frothing hysterics. I jumped up and gathered her into my arms while the kids watched wide-eyed.

"What's the matter, honey?" I asked, cradling her shaking shoulders and rubbing her back. "What happened? Are you all right?"

David stood to pull some bills out of his wallet and tossed them at Sam. "Go pay the cab driver," he directed.

Dani lifted her tear-streaked face from my shoulder. "Don't forget the bags," she whimpered. "I'm never going back to New York. I never want to see Josh again as long as I live."

David grimaced. He added another bill to the stack and said resignedly, "Have him bring the bags in too."

Sasha looked apprehensive, and I started calculating beds in my mind while absentmindedly patting Dani and murmuring soothingly in her ear. Now that Amy Joy was here, we didn't have any rooms to spare . . . so that meant that someone would have to share. Sasha and Dani together? Oh, dear. I grimaced too and may have patted Dani a little harder than necessary.

Dani had brought three large suitcases, a Prada messenger bag stuffed with papers, and a laptop. David stared in dismay at the pile in our front hall while I negotiated with the kids in furious whispers. "I can't share with Dani," Sasha wailed. "She's the messiest person in the world and I'll break my neck tripping over her stuff. She'll drive me nuts."

"Well, if you didn't leave everything lying around, so I practically broke my ankle tripping over your stuff when we were in Dis—" Sam hissed back.

I sighed. "Then one of you will have to share with Amy Joy." They both looked stricken.

"Put Dani in with Amy Joy," Sasha suggested wickedly. "That'll send her back to New York fast enough."

I stifled my snort and told David to move Amy Joy's crib into our room so he could set up the rollaway for Dani in the baby's room. He obeyed wordlessly, but his eyes were expressive enough.

"He broke up with me," Dani said disbelievingly. It was at least the tenth time she'd said it, as if saying it enough would make the impossible seem slightly more real. "No one ever breaks up with me!" She emptied her shot glass of whiskey and held it out for a refill; automatically, I complied, and poured an even bigger shot for myself.

David had put Amy Joy to bed and the rest of the kids had retreated to their bedrooms after dinner was cleared, leaving the alternately furious and grief-stricken Dani to my tender ministrations. I had a splitting headache.

"It doesn't sound like there was really much future in it," I said as neutrally as I could. The notion of Dani as stepmother to two boys still grieving from the loss of their mother was obviously unworkable. Not to mention the duties of a rabbi's wife! The sooner it ended, the better.

"I was fine with the boys! I was great! Just because it was what's-his-name's birthday, Josh wouldn't come to the annual PEN dinner with me, and I was receiving an award! I would have been the laughingstock of New York, showing up for my award without a date! I'd told everyone about my gorgeous rabbi boyfriend!"

I sighed. Dani sounded younger than Sasha sometimes. "Dani, if you can't even remember his son's name, it really isn't meant to be. I'm sorry you're hurting, but—"

"I can too remember his son's name! And I remembered his birthday too! I went to Best Buy and bought him the hottest videogame they had—Grand Theft Auto VI, or something like that. It cost a fortune!"

Good Lord. "Dani, how old is . . . what's-his-name?"

"Jason! Umm, Joseph, I mean. And he's . . . ten. Maybe eleven?"

"You can't give Grand Theft Auto to a ten-year-old," I said wearily. "There are ratings on videogames, like on movies; that's for teenagers and older. It's very violent."

"Really?" she looked surprised. "Huh. Well, anyway, I do know his name and it's Joseph."

Suddenly I was too tired to hold my head up any longer. I knew it would be a long night; Amy Joy was a fretful sleeper who snored and snuffled and tossed restlessly. Sasha had complained bitterly when they roomed together in Disney.

"Well, stay here for a few days and relax; then when you go home you'll feel rested and ready to move on."

She stared at me. "Oh, no," she said quickly. "I brought the manuscript with me. That's the other thing—I need peace and quiet so I can do a line edit of the new *Teenage Trauma Trilogy*. It's a disaster and I need to fix it, or we'll all be looking for new professions."

I stared back at her. Peace and quiet? What on earth could she be thinking? I opened my mouth, but taking advantage of my momentary paralysis, she stood up and kissed me on the cheek.

"Thanks, Shelley," she said, tearful again. "I can always count on you." Leaving me frozen in shock, she picked up her whiskey glass and swept out of the room, stiletto heels clacking loudly on the wooden floor as she tapped her way upstairs. I heard Amy Joy cry out in protest from her crib and David's murmured response, and I sank back into the couch again and closed my eyes.

Dani spent nearly an hour in the kids' bathroom the next morning, showering and primping and doing God knows what. Sasha was nearly incandescent with fury. "All of my makeup is in there," she hissed at me for the third time. "I can't go out until I put on my makeup, and I can't put on my makeup until I can get into *my bathroom!*" By the end she was nearly shouting, but Dani was running the water too loudly for her to hear through the heavy oak bathroom door. Sam yelled with rage from our bathroom, where he was awkwardly trying to shower with a Hefty bag wrapped around his cast, "*What happened to the hot water?!*"

I picked up Amy Joy and retreated downstairs to the kitchen.

By Sunday morning I was actually looking forward to the board meeting at the temple, figuring that it had to be less cantankerous than the current state of the Harris household. Dani glared at Amy Joy every time she let out the tiniest peep, which made Sasha gather the baby protectively in her arms and glare back at Dani; everyone was in a state of semi-armed warfare over the bathrooms; and Sasha was fuming over Dani's careless inroads on her nonfat yogurt.

But when I sat down in the temple's small conference room, no one was looking anyone else in the eye, and the rabbi looked downright surly. What now?

Normally our meetings began with a blessing and d'Var Torah, a brief commentary on the Torah portion, by the rabbi. But when he started to speak, the head of religious education cut him off. "We don't have time for that crap today," he snarled. "Let's get down to business."

The head of religious life snapped to attention. "Crap?" he boomed. "Crap, you call it? Why the hell are we all here if—"

The temple secretary interrupted, "Could we at least try not to swear? This *is* a synagogue, you know."

Wearily, the rabbi said, "Fine, let's just skip the blessing this morning. Shelley, Marcy, Stan . . . everyone—we have a situation in the Hebrew school that we need to discuss."

"Situation?" snapped the religious head. "It's a catastrophe!"

"Oh, for God's sake," drawled the interfaith coordinator. "If everyone didn't blow these things out of proportion. . . ."

"Out of proportion!" shouted the fundraising chair. "Why, the—"

I couldn't stand it anymore. "*Sheket! Sheket, b'vakisha!*" I shouted. It was what David had shouted at the unruly kids on the day we met, the essential phrase in every babysitter's and mediator's vocabulary: "Shut up, please."

It worked its usual magic, and everyone fell into a cowed silence. I looked around the table.

"Len," I said finally. He was the treasurer and probably the sanest voice on an issue that seemed to involve a religious dispute. "Can you fill us in on this situation?"

Len took his time, taking off his horn-rimmed glasses and giving them a good polish before launching into his tale. Apparently the kindergarten class had been learning about God's love the previous week. The unsuspecting teacher asked the children, "Who loves you?" "Mommy!" "Daddy!" "My bubbe and zayde!" came the expected responses. Then the bombshell dropped: "Jesus loves me!" piped up one blonde, blue-eyed tot with a discreet gold cross around her neck.

The other parents went ballistic upon hearing of this apostasy. The rabbi launched a hasty investigation and discovered that the girl attended church and Sunday school with her father at All Saints as well as Hebrew School with her mother, so the family was asked to withdraw from the temple. Then all hell had broken loose.

Once I had gotten the facts, I briskly set up an interfaith committee—which I was begged to chair, of course—to investigate the matter. Then I tapped the table for attention and cleared my throat. "There is one other matter," I announced. As everyone looked at me expectantly, I rose and handed the secretary the stack of spiral-bound proposals that I'd prepared that afternoon at Kinko's.

The treasurer glanced at the title page and frowned. "Qameen? Really, Shelley, don't you think we have enough problems of our own without taking on—"

"Never Again means never again," I said quietly.

The rabbi and the head of religious life leaned forward, suddenly intent and suddenly on the same side.

"I've been in touch with leading temples around the country," I explained. "We have a tentative agreement—if Never Again means anything in this world, then it means fighting genocide in Qameen. Now here's what I'm thinking—"

CHAPTER FORTY-TWO

To Do:
Prepare Qameen presentation
Meet with Qameeni ambassador
Take Sharif family to asylum hearing
Get printer fixed for Dani
Get second telephone line
Schedule mani-pedi for Dani

BY THE FOLLOWING WEDNESDAY, the Harris household had deteriorated into a state of guerrilla warfare. Dani was infuriated by the incessant ringing of the telephone: "Am I your secretary?" she fumed. "Why do all these people from Jewish organizations keep calling you, anyway?" Sasha hid her yogurts and trail mix in the garage refrigerator; Dani retaliated by adding extra cheese to the pizza order on Tuesday night. The Internet popped in for a while then vanished again. David and I were exhausted by the effort of sleeping silently (and sexlessly) so as not to disturb Amy Joy, and Sam complained that his friends kept dropping by to ogle Dani as she lolled in a clinging, braless tank top and tiny shorts in the family room with her ever-present cellphone glued to her ear. "It's

March, for God's sake," he fumed. "Who dresses like that in March?"

I recognized the familiar signs of sibling rivalry in Dani regarding Amy Joy. She had reacted the same way when Sam and Sasha arrived, resenting the interlopers who usurped her God-given right to be the baby of the family. Sasha had an attack of that too, when Amy Joy came into our family, but now the twins were her biggest fans. I hoped that Dani would come around eventually.

But I couldn't spare any energy on Dani; today was our second hearing with the judge on Amy Joy's custody case, and I had bigger things on my mind. Dani eyed me curiously as I fussed over Amy Joy's hair and ran upstairs to change my skirt for the third time. "Why are you so upset?" she inquired. "I mean, would it be so terrible if her real father got her back?"

"Her *biological* father is an abusive cokehead," I said icily. "He never wanted her to be born, and he's never laid eyes on her. Her *real* father is David. And if you want to continue sleeping in my daughter's room and hogging the bathroom, you'll *never* say anything like that again. Ever."

Dani drew back, affronted. "Well—"

"I have to go," I said shortly. "If you're still here when I get back, I'll accept your apology then."

This hearing was even worse than the first. Greg Clifford still hadn't made an appearance, but his lawyer was there with two henchmen, and this time they were joined by several clean-cut, missionary-looking men in crisp chino pants and polo shirts embossed with "FAIR" on the pocket.

"Oh, shit," I said.

"What?" asked David.

"It's a fathers' rights group, Fathers Advocating Infants' Rights. Religious right group. I didn't know they were going to get involved."

David looked grim, and my heart sank even further when I saw a news van pulling up outside the courthouse. "You've got to be kidding," David muttered.

A representative from FAIR was allowed to address the judge. He spoke earnestly for fifteen minutes about how the courts should give equal rights to both parents rather than automatically favoring the mother. "In this case, it's a no-brainer," he concluded. "The mother is dead, but the father is alive and well and eager to be reunited with his baby. Amelia Clifford deserves a real father."

I almost choked on my fury. David glanced at me and put a restraining hand on my arm. We had left Amy Joy at home with Dani (God help us all!), and I missed the baby's warm, comforting presence in my lap. The rest of the hearing passed in a daze.

When it was finally over, the representative of FAIR walked over and held out his hand to David. "Ron Hechinger," he said. "Nice to meet you."

David shook his hand. "I'm not sure I can say the same," he returned evenly.

"Fathers' rights are a just cause," the younger man said earnestly. He was fresh-faced and blond, with a conservative haircut and a clean-living appearance that looked right out of a religious playbook. "You're a father yourself; don't you think you deserve as much legal protection as a mother?"

"This case isn't about fathers' rights," David said. "I'm not opposed to your cause in principle, but in this case that's not the issue. The biological father is unfit to care for this child. If it were the mother, the facts would be the same."

Ron shook his head disapprovingly. "You're betraying your fellow men," he chided. "Mr. Clifford is going to be on CNN Headline News with me next week to publicize the assault on fathers' rights that this case represents."

"CNN? Are you serious?" David asked disbelievingly. "Greg Clifford is a drug user, an abuser of women, a man who beat his pregnant girlfriend, told her to get an abortion, and then abandoned her. You really want him to be the poster boy for your movement? You'd better think again."

"That makes him an even more compelling story," Ron said smoothly. "He's found God and seen the error of his ways, praise the Lord. He's reformed."

"Reformed, my ass," David shot back. "I have videotape of him partying, snorting coke, fondling a starlet, and telling her this kid will be his ticket to fame."

"That's from months ago, before he found the Lord," Ron said confidently.

"It's from last week, you idiot!" David snapped.

Ron paused, but one of his FAIR compatriots said, "Well, the video won't be admissible in court unless it was shot with Mr. Clifford's permission. Which I'm sure it was not."

I knew he was right.

David pressed his lips together, and Ron said kindly, "We'll include you and Mrs. Harris in our prayers, that you will see the error of your ways. God be with you." And he strode out the door of the courthouse to the waiting throng of reporters.

The bailiff escorted us out through a back door so we didn't have to run the gauntlet of reporters. On our way home I said to David, "I want to see that video."

"No." He didn't even look at me.

"Why not?" I asked.

"Because it would kill you," he said flatly.

As we pulled into our driveway, I asked, "I just don't understand—why the hell is he doing this? What does he want with a baby?"

David sighed heavily and turned the car off. "I wondered

that too. My investigator managed to chat him up in a bar—she's young and pretty—and he told her the kid would be his ticket to fame. He wants to break into the movie industry, thinks he's an actor because he's had some roles as an extra in Star Wars movies. He's thinking this could land him a reality show."

It would have been funny if it weren't so dreadful. "Did your investigator record him saying that?"

David nodded. "Oh yes, and lots more too. He offered to give her some high-quality coke if she'd—never mind. She declined the offer. But Ron's buddy is right; none of it is admissible in court."

I passed a hand over my eyes and turned to look at my husband. "I don't feel good about the legal case. We don't have any proof of his abuse of Aviva, or his drugs, and the judge won't allow us to introduce his past convictions. Unless he's dumb enough to take the stand—in which case we could tear him apart—" I trailed off, unable to finish the sentence. I couldn't even utter the words.

David looked back at me. "I'm going to take care of it," he said with finality.

I had nothing to say.

It took Dani several days to recover from babysitting. Possibly in self-defense, Amy Joy had slept for two of the four hours that we were gone, but the remaining time had been ugly. Apparently Amy Joy had fallen in love with Dani's glittery, swinging earrings, and the predictable disaster had ensued; I reassured Dani that her earlobe would eventually heal, but we never found the earring.

And I spent a lot of time wondering why I wanted to be a lawyer at all, if the law was going to fail me in its most important test.

CHAPTER FORTY-THREE

To Do:
Temple Sinai follow-up
Call Kerem Shalom Atlanta
Call Chaim Leibovitz Foundation
Find 6-BR rental house

ONE NIGHT, DAVID TRIPPED OVER DANI'S YOGA MAT in the front foyer and exploded. "If you won't evict her, I will," he fumed. So I drove the still-protesting Dani to the train station the next morning, promising that she could come back again in a few weeks for the Passover Seder, and the house settled back into peaceful coexistence.

I could think of nothing but the custody battle; David's legal troubles and my Qameen project shrank in comparison to this all-consuming struggle. So the timing couldn't have been worse for a family vacation—but family vacation it was. The previous summer, before we'd even heard of Amy Joy, we had rented a house for the second week in April on Goose Island, South Carolina for our last precollege family blast—us, the kids, and Neil and Marisa. I never felt less like having a blast in my life, but here it was.

Three days before we were scheduled to leave, though, Dani called me.

"Guess what! I got vacation! So we can come to Goose Island with you too! Isn't that wonderful?"

For the life of me, I couldn't recall inviting her to join us. Besides, we filled the rented house to the rafters with just us and Neil and Marisa; there wasn't a spare bedroom for—wait a minute, did she say "we?"

"We?" I echoed faintly.

"Well, of course; it's a perfect opportunity for Josh and the boys to spend some time with the family. We're so excited!"

"Wait," I said. "Didn't you and Josh break up?"

"Oh, that was nothing," she said dismissively.

I sighed, recalling the drama and hysterics over a "nothing" breakup. "Dani," I started, "I'm really sorry, but I'm afraid. . . ."

"Now what?" she cut me off. "First you kick me out of your house—and now you don't want me on your vacation? I can't believe this." She sniffed, starting to cry.

Oh, crap. "Honey, I'd love to have you on our vacation," I tried again, "but I'm afraid that the house just isn't big enough—"

She cut me off again. "I'm sure you can get a bigger house," she said confidently, tears suddenly shut off. "After all, it's just the four of us—we don't need a lot of space."

Right, I thought, remembering the bathroom battles.

But still . . . how could I go on vacation with one sister and leave the other one behind? Familiar guilt poked its head up again, and I found myself promising to talk to the realtor. Probably there wouldn't be any six-bedroom (six bedrooms! Good Lord!) houses available for rent on such short notice, anyway.

It was raining when we pulled up in front of the rental house on Saturday. The realtor had assured me that we were incredibly lucky to get this house on Goose Island; it was on a small lake and had its own beach plus the required six bedrooms, so we wouldn't have to share a room with Amy Joy, who would be thrilled to see us from her crib and want to play all night long.

The first thing I noticed about the house was the damp. "No wonder this house was still available," said David, coming back to the front hall after a quick tour of inspection. His deck shoes appeared to be squishing on the ancient (gray?) carpeting. "It doesn't just have a lake view, it's actually under water."

"There weren't any pictures or reviews online," I said uneasily. "It was such short notice, we just had to take what we could get."

"Don't take your shoes off," Sasha warned, slipping her feet back into her high-heeled sandals. "The carpet feels like wet sand."

We looked at each other for a moment, then David started to smile. "It's awful, isn't it?" he said, putting an arm around me as we surveyed the living room together. It was carpeted in dull orange, with a lumpy brown sofa and two even browner wing chairs sagging across the room. The television looked like it belonged in the Smithsonian, with two huge rabbit ear antennae stuck on the top. Through the doorway we could see the tiny kitchen, with its orange Formica counter, dirt-encrusted stove, and dark brown cabinets.

"I don't know what Dani is going to say," I said uneasily, pulling away from David's arm. Unable to face the long drive with two lively boys, Dani had plumped for airfare to Charleston; they were renting a car there and driving down this evening. "Did you see the kitchen? No microwave."

"Microwave!" Sam snorted. "There's not even a toaster."

"Well, we'll just have to grill a lot," said David. "I don't know why you're worried about Dani; she wasn't even invited."

"Shh," I said automatically. The door opened again and

Marisa tripped in, wearing the same sandals as Sasha; they must have gone shopping together. Sasha came in on her heels, carrying Amy Joy.

"Shelley!" Sasha announced. "I think Amy Joy has a dirty diaper." Automatically I took Amy Joy and sniffed at her bottom. Sasha was right.

David said firmly, "Sasha can change her. Come on, Shelley, let's go outside and check out the view." Before either of us could protest, he handed the squirming, smelly baby back to Sasha—who looked as if she'd rather take hold of a dead fish—and steered me out through the patio doors to the back of the house.

"Where's the lake?" I asked, peering hopefully through a tangle of trees and underbrush. The smell from Amy Joy's diaper seemed to have followed me out of the house; I must have gotten something on my hands. Yuck.

David shook his head, walking farther into the yard to get a better view. "It must be on the other side of these bushes, but there's a lot of poison ivy here—I don't think—"

Abruptly he jumped back as if he'd been stung. "Jesus H. Christ!" he shouted. "Shelley, get back into the house! Don't let the kids come out!" Waving his hands, he pushed me toward the sagging patio. Six gigantic geese—obviously in the throes of a massive steroidal rage—were hot on his heels, honking aggressively and ready for battle. The damn things were bigger than great Danes. They pecked and batted their heads against the flimsy door for a minute, until David's shouts and threats drove them back to strut around the muddy yard. One squatted and produced a huge steaming pile of what I now realized dotted the yard, no doubt accounting for the smell that I had been noticing.

"Where's that realtor's number?" David asked grimly.

Geese, it turned out, were protected under the Endangered Species Act. You couldn't threaten them, approach them, or try to move them off your property.

"Also," warned the realtor, "I guess I should mention that they can be a little aggressive when protecting their young."

"No shit," fumed David, watching two giant geese head-butt each other while the others nipped at their tail feathers. "They tried to attack me. Now they're attacking each other. We have children here, how are we supposed to use our beach?"

What beach? I wondered. I still hadn't seen any water.

"Well," said the realtor, "I really don't know what to tell you. I'm sure you'll like Planters Beach though, that's the public beach and it's only a few miles away."

David held the phone away from his ear for a moment, visibly counting to ten. "Also," he said, "the cottage is damp, there are no pillows, microwave, toaster, or heavy blankets, and the TV doesn't work."

"Oh, dear," said the realtor. "I don't know how to get in touch with the owners, but I'll talk to our office manager and someone will get back to you."

"When?"

"Well, I can't say for sure," said the realtor huffily. "This is our busy season, you know."

David slammed the phone down and glared at me. "How could you rent a house without looking at it first?" he demanded.

"It's amazing I even found a house with six bedrooms on such short notice," I returned evenly. Amy Joy now propped on my hip, I was rooting through the kitchen cupboard for a non-rusty pot to warm up her macaroni and cheese.

David strode over to the stove and fiddled with the knobs for a moment. "Don't worry about the pots," he said. "The pilot won't light anyway, and I'll be damned if I'm going to blow the place up by lighting a match." Suddenly he grinned. "I can't wait to see Dani's reaction."

Dani, Rabbi Josh, and the two boys arrived after dinnertime. Marisa and Neil had gone out to dinner and a movie; the rest of us had just returned from battling through the traffic to the Kmart in Charleston, where we stocked up on pots, pillows, and cleaning supplies. Then we dined at McDonald's, letting Amy Joy scramble through the playground with Sasha in hot pursuit, while David chomped grimly through a chicken sandwich and then Amy Joy's Happy Meal, and Sasha toyed with her salad. (Sam, speechless with horror at finding himself in a McDonald's, contented himself with three McFlurry shakes.)

We could hear the car coming down the dirt lane to the cottage, because the boys' angry shouts were audible even through the closed car windows. A wiry dark-haired man jumped out and started unloading luggage; Dani, looking like the survivor of a natural disaster, got out more slowly and stretched, looking around in disapproval.

"Boys!" Josh called. "Come help me with the bags."

The older boy shoved the other. "Joseph can do it," he taunted.

Joseph shoved his brother back, and they both tumbled into the mud that passed for a front yard. Dani drew back, her lips pursed.

The man—Rabbi Josh, I presumed—just laughed. "Both of you get up before I throw you into the lake," he said cheerfully.

I decided I liked him.

Dani sighed heavily. "This is Josh, and Joseph and . . . uh . . . Stuart. I need a long hot shower and an Evian spritzer," she informed us. "Then I want to watch *Grey's Anatomy* and go to sleep."

As I considered which illusion to disabuse first, David grinned. "The TV doesn't work. There's no hot water. And we didn't go grocery shopping yet, so there's no mineral water. But if you run the tap water long enough, the color turns much less brown and it's probably safe to drink."

Dani's outraged expression almost made the whole experience seem worthwhile.

CHAPTER FORTY-FOUR

DAVID WENT OUT TO GET DONUTS FOR breakfast the next morning, since the kitchen was a health hazard waiting to explode. We were just sitting down at the undersized dining table when Dani and Josh came down the muddy stairs from their cell-sized bedroom, holding hands and beaming.

"Guess what, everybody! We're going to get married!" And she threw herself into my arms.

I automatically patted her on the back, exchanging glances with David over her head. He rolled his eyes, then stood and went around the table to shake hands with Josh and bend down to the wide-eyed boys.

Sam, following David's lead, was the next to get up and offer his hand. Marisa and Neil murmured unconvincing congratulations, while a tight-lipped Sasha forced a smile. The little boys would practically have to sit in each other's laps, so David put Amy Joy's highchair back in the kitchen to create a little more space. "She can sit on my lap," he said.

Finally we were all seated. Sam was the only one who seemed genuinely pleased at this development. "I might want to be a rabbi," he told Josh, whose chair was squished so close to Sam's that they were practically holding hands.

"I thought you two had broken up," Marisa said, loudly.

"We got back together," Dani said, a little defensively.

"And then Josh proposed, and look—" She held out her left hand, where a tiny little diamond winked in the watery morning light—"we're engaged! Isn't that wonderful? And don't you love this teeny-tiny ring? Josh says it's perfect for a rabbi's wife!"

"Yes! But...when are you planning on getting married?" I asked. Hopefully not until those two boys went away to college.

"August!" Dani squealed. "And we'd just love it if you could plan the wedding for us! Please? We want a vegan wedding, and we want everything to be just right, and I can't think of anyone who would do a better job than you! Isn't it exciting?"

I swallowed. "Dani, August is just four months away," I reminded her. "Weddings take months, sometimes years, to plan. I just don't know—"

"Oh, please say you'll do it!" Dani begged.

Josh spoke for the first time. "I know this seems sudden," he said in his surprisingly deep voice. "But when something is so right, why delay? Besides, my boys can't wait to have Dani as their stepmother. Right, guys?"

Good God. I raised my eyebrows at David, who shrugged.

One of the boys said plaintively, "Can we eat yet? I'm really hungry."

Dani said again, "Will you do it, Shelley? Please?"

"We can figure all that out later," David said firmly. "Right now these children are starved, and we have donuts and cereal to eat."

After breakfast, David and I repaired to our bedroom in a shell-shocked silence.

He was the first to speak. "If you plan that wedding for them, I will have to consider violence."

"Oh, David, how can I say no? Our mother is dead, and we

haven't seen our father in thirty years! I'm the closest thing to a mother she's got."

"You're the closest thing to a mother that everyone's got," he said dryly. "She's a grown woman; she can plan her own wedding."

"Good God, she can't plan her own *lunch*! You know she can't do this."

"Then she can hire someone," he said sharply. "You are not doing it for her."

"A vegan wedding?" I went on, not listening to him. "What are we going to eat, tofu sprouts?"

He laughed. "Cheer up—maybe no one will come when they hear it's vegan. And look at the bright side: They'll probably break up before August anyway."

It rained steadily for the next four days. The front yard turned into a swamp that sucked down one of Marisa's new Miu Miu sandals and a bottle that Amy Joy threw out of the car window in a fit of pique. The backyard was now one giant brown puddle, inhabited by sixteen geese and a few deluded seagulls who apparently enjoyed doing battle with the geese over the scraps of fish that kept washing up from the lake.

After one venture out to search for the lake, Dani stalked in with an outraged expression on her face. "What is with those geese?" she demanded. "At least you should clean up after them. The backyard is one giant goose potty!"

David said, "You can't clean up their poop, since that violates environmental restrictions."

"Very funny," said Sam.

David looked surprised. "It's true. I went to Town Hall yesterday and talked to the environmental protection officer. This is Goose Island, after all."

Sam snorted.

So we played games. At first we played Monopoly. That went well for a day or so, until Sam and Marisa locked horns over whether you could hand in a Get Out of Jail Free card and move on the same turn. Neil, usually the most amiable of men, snapped that Marisa knew all about getting away with murder, provoking Sasha to defend her mother by accusing Sam of embezzling money from the Monopoly bank.

So then we tried Scrabble. But without a dictionary, this eventually deteriorated into a pitched battle over whether "dyne" was a word (of course it was, opined David wearily; no way, argued Dani). Josh tried to settle the dispute by powering up his laptop and trying to connect via dial-up (what's that? Sasha asked innocently) to check the online dictionary, but the power went out—triggering a serious panic since there was no surge protector, and Josh feared he had lost his precious file of ideas for future sermons.

To keep the peace, I offered to keep Stu and Joe at the house while Dani and Josh drove off to find a Starbucks with a wireless connection (good riddance, Sam muttered). Using my best Mom voice, I ordered the boys outside to play football in the mud and fell back against the lumpy sofa. "There must be some game that doesn't have rules to fight over," I said wearily.

"We should play *Survivor*," Sam suggested. "I vote out Dani."

"Really?" David said, interested. "I vote out Marisa. She's much more annoying."

"No," argued Sasha. "We should vote out Sam. He keeps arguing over the rules."

"That's because people keep cheating!" he exclaimed. "I think we should vote out—"

"Never mind," David interposed. "Don't talk unless you have something good to say."

A sullen silence fell.

On Wednesday, the sun finally came out. We had seen every movie that the one-screen Goose Island cinema had to offer, played miniature golf in the damp drizzle until Sam's ball knocked Sasha's off the green and the game deteriorated into shoving and name-calling, and resorted to testing each other on movie star genealogy (David stumped me on the name of Paul Newman's first wife, but I stumped everyone on the middle name of Gwyneth Paltrow's daughter Apple). Stu and Joe, I discovered, loved to hate each other and knew more synonyms for excrement than I had ever thought existed. Marisa, Dani, and Sasha went shoe shopping and all came home with zebra-striped Skechers that I knew they would regret.

But at last, the sun was shining. I packed a beach bag with hats, diapers, three kinds of sunscreen, extra bathing suits, sweatshirts, and wipes. Then I packed a toy bag crammed with pails, shovels, and an inflatable beach ball for Amy Joy's first day at the beach. Finally, I pulled out the cooler and started filling it with drinks and snacks. David wandered into the kitchen, holding Amy Joy, and stared at the bags.

"Holy hell," he said. "Are we going on safari?"

The men loaded my three beach bags, Marisa's two, and Dani's Prada tote into the cars, plus Neil's stack of financial magazines. Then everyone clambered in and I strapped Amy Joy into her car seat. As I closed the door, I straightened up and met David's eyes over the top of the minivan.

"Let's lock them in and make a run for it," he suggested. "There's not a jury in the world that would convict us."

"It took so long to get ready, it's almost Amy Joy's naptime," I fretted. "What if I can't get her to sleep on the beach? Maybe I'd better take her stroller."

"No!" cried David and Sam simultaneously. "Where would we put it?" added Sam. "On your lap?"

"Well," I dithered, and David snapped, "Let's go before Marisa decides to take the DVD player or kitchen sink. I'd like to get at least one hour on the beach this vacation."

We started to get in the car, but then I reminded him about the baby shade tent that we had found at Kmart. So Sam climbed out and went to get it, in the process jostling Amy Joy, who started to scream.

When we were halfway to the beach, Dani said, "Damn! I just realized we forgot Joseph's water wings."

"Only sissies need water wings," contributed Stuart.

"You're a sissy!" Joe shouted, aiming a punch at his brother. Sasha, wedged uneasily between them (to keep the peace, their father had explained), winced and ducked.

We pulled into the beach parking lot, surprised to see a South Carolina State Police cruiser at the gate and two guards at the lot entrance. The officer leaned in through the open window. "Sorry, folks," he said. "This is a residents-only beach. You'll have to go to Planters."

"I thought we were at Planters," said David.

"No, this is Planters Isle. Planters Main is right next door." He pointed, and we all looked down the road to where a long line of cars waited to enter a parking lot.

Sam craned his neck. "But there's a sign on that parking lot that says 'full,'" he said.

"Yup," agreed the state trooper. "Gotta get here much earlier than this if you want a parking space. Guess you'll just have to wait in line."

His mouth set, David swung the car into the line and looked at me. "Let's get the kids onto the beach," I suggested. "We can take turns waiting in the car."

"It must be half a mile to the beach," Dani protested. "What about all our stuff?"

"Come on, we'll manage," said Sam. "Dad, you staying in the car?"

David nodded, turned on the car radio, and leaned back. The rest of us draped ourselves with the bags and chairs, then I put Amy Joy on my hip. "Joe and Stu, stay close to your dad and don't touch each other," I warned. We plodded past the line of cars, then trudged uphill from the parking lot through the dunes.

"I thought I was in good shape," Marisa wheezed. "But this is like trekking through the Sahara with exhaust fumes being pumped into your lungs."

Sam looked at her. He was carrying two bags, the pop-up tent, and a beach chair. Sweat dripped off his brow and his sunglasses were sliding precariously down his slippery nose. "I'll trade with you," he offered.

Joseph started sniffling and whined, "Daddy, I can't walk anymore."

Josh looked at him helplessly, and I sighed.

"Josh, give Neil the chairs you're carrying, and give Joe a piggyback ride," I instructed, giving Neil a look that stopped his protest in its infancy.

With a sigh, Josh handed off the chairs and swung his younger son onto his back.

Surprisingly, Dani—who was staggering wordlessly behind him in her high-heeled Prada sandals—started to smile. "My hero," she said, and Josh started grinning too.

Even Sasha giggled. "We look like refugees. Are we having fun yet?"

We finally reached the beach and set everything up. And an hour later, as soon as David had finally arrived from the parking lot, it started to rain. At least he was there to help us trek back to the car.

—

CHAPTER FORTY-FIVE

To Do:
Hypoallergenic sunscreen (Dani)
Kosher meat (Sam)
Toilet paper
Hide water guns

THE "VACATION" WORE ON. JOSH SEEMED TO have turned over all parenting duties to me, having discovered that my Mom voice was much more effective than his cajoling. So I arbitrated fights between Stu and Joe until exhaustion reduced me to bribing them with new handheld games if they could go one day without blood flowing. The downstairs bathroom flooded, and I had to institute a strict schedule for the upstairs bathroom, limiting everyone to three-minute showers except for the boys, who had chased a ball into the poison ivy and required lengthy soaks in the tub with Epsom salt. At least the Benadryl pills dulled their fighting instincts for a few hours.

On Friday, Rachel drove down for the day with her two children. She had been visiting her in-laws near Savannah and needed a "break." I tried to warn her of the unlikelihood of such an event in our house of horrors, but she came anyway. Her son

Ben—a strapping, husky thirteen-year-old with a bad case of acne and a worse case of ADD—immediately hated Stu and Joe, who banded together for the first time against this common enemy. Her daughter Madeleine went out for a walk with Sam and returned with her lips swollen and her shirt buttoned all wrong; Rachel stared at me accusingly.

Well, at least he's over Sharona, I thought.

In the distance I heard Stuart shouting something unintelligible about "fucking sissy boys" and Ben's roar of rage in return.

Then the upstairs toilet overflowed.

The next day dawned cloudy and cool. I went to a beach aerobics class with Dani, who was semihysterical over a three-pound weight gain. (Marisa's helpful observation: "Now that you're almost forty, the only way you'll lose that is if they cut it off you.") On the drive back, Dani begged me to keep Stu and Joe with me in Washington for the summer, so that she and Rabbi Josh could have a "proper honeymoon."

"You handle them so well," she explained ingenuously. "They like you better than me anyway."

I suddenly recalled David's comment when Dani announced her engagement: "You'll wind up raising those boys too." Ridiculous. And yet. . . .

"Absolutely not," I said. "Under no circumstances."

Dani was first disbelieving, then enraged. "You're always there for Marisa," she threw at me. "You help everybody but me! First you kick me out of your house and now you won't do me a tiny little favor, the only favor I've ever asked of you!" She slammed out of the car and ran into the house in floods of tears.

Slowly, I squished up the narrow stairs to our bedroom. At first I couldn't believe what I was seeing and blinked to clear my vision. But it was really true: David was throwing his clothes into a suitcase.

For a moment, my throat was clogged by a thick haze of fury. Finally I managed to hiss, "What. Are. You. Doing."

I must have looked scary. David said a little nervously, "I know this doesn't look good, sweetheart, but—"

At least he didn't call me "honey." "Doesn't look good?" I repeated. "Doesn't *look good?*"

I thought I sounded quite calm, but he shied back a little.

"It's business," he said quickly. "Really, I swear. I have to be in the Middle East tomorrow morning, but it should only take a couple of days. You'll be okay driving back with the kids on Monday, right?"

Two more days in this house of horrors, without David's calming presence. Driving back with the kids. A ten-hour drive in the packed minivan with a restless Amy Joy, bored and sulky Sasha, lovesick Sam, and nobody but the GPS to talk to.

Amy Joy shrieked downstairs, and I said bitterly, "Talk about rats deserting a sinking ship!"

He opened his mouth to respond, but then pounding footsteps raced up the stairs. "I'm gonna kill you, you little bastard!" Stuart shrieked.

"You'll have to catch me first!" his brother shouted back.

A door slammed and more footsteps pounded up the stairs.

"Shelley!" Sam yelled. "Joe's bleeding, and Amy Joy has a dirty diaper!"

I opened my eyes and turned to face my husband. "I'll see you in Washington," I told him. "You son of a bitch." And I marched out of the room.

So it wasn't surprising that I wound up drinking wine on the sofa with Marisa that night, avoiding the subject of David entirely but telling her about Dani's anger at me. "You did the right thing," Marisa said, seeing my doubtful face. "You've mothered her for years; it's time for her to fly away so you can take care of your own baby. She's a grown woman, for God's sake."

"You're right," I said.

"Really," she went on indignantly. "What nerve, expecting you to take on those kids so that she and Josh can have a lovely little honeymoon!"

I gazed at my older sister, suddenly thinking of the many mini-vacations she and her husband had enjoyed over the years while I took care of her twins. Suddenly I was so angry, I could barely catch my breath.

"Maybe *I* should take a vacation," I bit out. "After all, don't you think you owe me? You, and everyone else. Then maybe someone else could step up, for a change, and—"

"I owe you?" Marisa said incredulously. "Are you kidding me?" She drained her glass of wine, staring at me in disbelief.

In the back of my mind I registered that it was a really, really bad idea to have this conversation after two glasses of wine and David's desertion and a week of bathroom battles. But my hands were shaking with rage and my heart was beating triple-time.

"Who took care of your kids all these years?" I burst out. "Who took them for their shots and helped them with their college applications and went to the emergency room with them and—"

"And why was that?" Marisa cried. Tears were in her eyes too, and her hands were shaking. "Because you're Mother Teresa? Oh, no! It's because you were so crazy after all those miscarriages that you would have stolen my babies if you could have! Wait a minute, what am I saying? You *did* steal my babies!"

Time stopped as we stared at each other, speechless with the guilt and anger and sadness that had lurked beneath the surface for all these years. Finally I whispered, "I didn't steal them. You were sick. You couldn't take care of them."

She sobbed. "And that was just so convenient for you, wasn't it." But her voice was heavy with grief, not anger.

The door opened and Sasha tiptoed in, her eyes filled with tears. "Mom—Shelley—Marisa—please don't fight. Please! I'm so sorry we—"

An apology from sunny, guiltless Sasha was more than I could bear. I fled, running across the damp carpeting and up the narrow stairs to my room.

Almost blinded by tears, I threw my suitcase on the bed and started to fling clothes into it. Sasha's pleading, tearful voice and Marisa's low responses continued downstairs; then someone knocked tentatively on my open door, and Amy Joy started to cry.

Abandoning the suitcase, I picked up my handbag and ran for my car.

CHAPTER FORTY-SIX

To Do:
Nothing

I STOPPED FOR COFFEE, THEN DROVE THIRTY miles to the quiet, idyllic Isle of Palms just as full darkness had enveloped the heaving ocean, and found a Victorian bed and breakfast with a "Vacancy" sign. The sleepy proprietress showed me to a pretty little room under the eaves, and amazingly, I slept.

When I woke up, my cellphone was buzzing insistently. I looked at the display to see nineteen missed calls. Sasha, Sam, Dani, Rabbi Josh, Neil, Rachel, Sasha again, Unknown Caller. No Marisa, though.

I put on my clothes, then deliberately walked out to the back lawn of the B and B, which overlooked the ocean and dozens of sailboats tossing in the breeze. A dock extended into the water, and I strode out to the end, drew back my arm, and hurled my cellphone into the sea.

Feeling much better, I ran up to my room, which was pretty to the point of kitschy, from the ruffled pink coverlet to the beribboned toilet paper cover. David would have hated it.

Obscurely pleased, I picked up my handbag, asked the

innkeeper for directions to a Target, and headed out to buy some clean clothes. There I marched through the aisles, throwing underwear and T-shirts into my basket with abandon. Nine-dollar jeans? I tossed in another pair.

The only time I hesitated was at the electronics counter. The kids didn't deserve to be worried sick, I supposed—though at the moment, I'd have gladly condemned all of them to perdition. With a reluctant sigh, I picked up a limited-use cellphone. If I blocked my caller ID, they wouldn't be able to call me back.

When I got back to the B and B, I placed one brief call to the rental house. Luckily, my brother-in-law Neil answered. "Shelley! We've been so worried! Where are you? Are you all right? When are you coming back?"

"I'm fine. And I'm not coming back for a while. I'm on *my* vacation."

He paused, almost audibly shifting gears. "Is it because of what Marisa said? You know she didn't mean—"

Marisa, and Dani, and David, and . . . I shut my thoughts off. The list was just too long.

"Tell the kids I'm fine. And I'll be back soon—just not yet."

"But everyone's upset!" he protested. "Marisa won't even talk to me, and Sasha was crying, and Amy Joy keeps asking for you—"

Sudden tears sprang to my eyes, and I gently ended the call.

At my landlady's suggestion, I drove to Folly Beach the next morning when the weather cleared. Located down a long flight of wooden stairs from the parking lot, it was an endless expanse of gentle sand dunes, dotted by bright beach umbrellas and weather-beaten lifeguard stands. Waves crested and crashed, rolling across the sand to tease the shrieking children who ran in and out of the cold spray. Farther out a few hardy surfers paddled in the deeper water; every now and then one successfully rode a wave into shore until it pounded into the sand.

I stood at the top of the stairs, gazing at the long, gently undulating shoreline. It was the most beautiful, peaceful sight I had ever beheld, and I smiled as I descended the stairs until my toes met the warm sand. As I remembered my old cellphone lying on the bottom of this very ocean, I smiled wider.

By the time the sun began to set and a cool breeze came in across the blue water, I was warm and relaxed. I unplugged my iPod and closed the book I'd purchased at Target, then climbed up the wooden stairs to my car, where I brushed the soft sand off my legs, breathing deeply with contentment. I hadn't thought once about my family all day.

A week later, my landlady and I were fast friends. On her recommendation I went antiquing along winding, tree-lined roads and bought an utterly useless set of andirons for the fireplace we hadn't lit in twenty years. I drove to Hilton Head and had dinner by myself in a restaurant for the first time in my life, enjoying the devoted attention of my beautifully groomed waiter who confided all the details of his stormy romance with a husky plumber named Vincent. I returned to Target and stocked up on more polyester clothes that would horrify Sasha and steamy chick-lit books that would horrify everyone else. I gave Neil my cellphone number with strict instructions that it was only to be used for a dire emergency, and I sent my family a daily text saying "I'm fine."

Day after day, I went back to Folly Beach. Sometimes my mind was empty as I stared out over the tossing whitecaps; sometimes I thought about all the people who needed me— and how much I needed them to need me. I thought about one sister angry at me because I had taken care of her children, and the other one angry because I wouldn't. I thought about David, and how exciting—thrilling, even—I found the un-David; and yet, I still didn't feel I really trusted him. I thought about Qameen.

And, remarkably, I thought of myself. The first half of my life had a purpose—creating a family and raising my children (I included Marisa and Dani in that). What would I do for the second half? Raise Amy Joy? On the one hand, I thought ahead with delighted anticipation to her first sentence, her first day of kindergarten, her first day of high school. . . . This time around, it would be better; I wouldn't feel like a single parent. David would never head another overseas station again, so he would be in DC most of the time. Seeing his love for Amy Joy, I believed that he would be a full partner this time, reveling in all the events that he'd missed with the older kids . . . her first ballet recital, her first date. . . .

But on the other hand, what did that mean for me? Well—it meant I would have a little more . . . energy. Space. Time. I thought back to that half-forgotten conversation with Marisa; maybe I should do something different for my second act. I thought about David's fierce dedication to his mission; I had applied the same dedication to nurturing our family, and I would do so for the rest of my life.

But—could I do something else too?

And finally, I was ready to go home. I gave my landlady most of my new clothes and books, hugged her good-bye, and set out westward toward Charleston. The road was lined with sandy, scrubby trees and the occasional sign advertising home-made pies or beach rose perfume. But then I crossed the bridge to the mainland and the small road turned into a highway; the roadside stands turned into McDonald's and Burger King, and my fellow drivers were purposeful, business-suited speeders rather than gazers and vacationers. I put my foot down on the accelerator and drew in a deep breath.

After all that, my homecoming was anticlimactic. David met me at the door with a cautious kiss and an even more cautious hello; he didn't even mention what I imagined was the huge expense of getting everyone home without my car. There was a towering pile of mail and FedEx envelopes waiting for me on the kitchen table—a pile that he must have wondered about. But all my attention was on Amy Joy, who crawled at top speed toward me shrieking and holding up her arms to be picked up. I swung her up and rained kisses on her head until she giggled and wriggled with pleasure. "I missed you so much," I told her, wondering guiltily if it really was true.

David took her from my arms and kissed her too. "Who's been taking care of her?" I asked.

"We're taking turns. Dani came up from New York for three days, Marisa took two days off from work, and the kids and I did nights and the weekend. We were fine."

Dani and Marisa had helped out? I felt warmer, somehow, and smiled.

David put Amy Joy down on the floor, and she quickly crawled away to bring me some toys. "Mama! Phone!" And she dropped her toy cellphone in my lap.

"Speaking of which," David began.

"It's in the water off Isle of Palms."

"Oh." He grinned a little. "I guess I'd better call Verizon then, and report a lost phone."

Amy Joy scuttled back with her teddy bear and threw it in my lap. "Boo, Mama! Boo!"

"How many new words does she have?" I asked, almost jealous that I'd missed more than a week of her life.

"Just a few," David said, reading my thoughts. "You didn't miss much."

"David," I started.

"Look, Shelley," he started at the same time.

We both stopped and looked at each other. "I'm sorry," he said simply. "We're all sorry."

"No, I'm sorry too," I said. "This is the life I chose, and it's the life I wanted—I don't know why everything came crashing down on me all of a sudden."

"Well, because nobody ever thinks about—"

Then the kitchen door crashed back against the wall and Sasha flew in, her taffy-gold curls tumbling about her bright face. She flung herself at me and blurted, "Mom—Shelley—we're so so sorry and we know we all take terrible advantage of you and of course you didn't steal us and please say you won't run away again!"

Amy Joy raced over to her and threw her arms around Sasha's knees. "Sasa! Sasa!" she cried.

I disengaged Sasha's clinging arms and smiled at her. "It's okay, Sash, I won't run away again. And you know, your mother isn't wrong either. I did—"

She waved her hand. "Oh, who cares? Anyway, I'm so glad you're back, because I need to go shopping for my college clothes, and I heard that bell bottoms are coming back in again, can you imagine? And—"

She suddenly drew back, staring at me in horror. "Oh, Shelley, *what are you wearing?*"

I glanced down at my Target jeans and smiled.

CHAPTER FORTY-SEVEN

LIFE SETTLED DOWN TO NORMAL AGAIN, or what passed for normal these days as our two trials—the custody battle and David's Senate investigation—loomed. I couldn't think about David's sins anymore; they were dwarfed by the magnitude of our fight for Amy Joy. I worked on the legal side while David pursued his "options." We were teammates, which seemed a huge step up from roommates.

In early May, my simmering anxiety blew sky-high when we got another phone call from our lawyer with more unsettling news. Greg Clifford had hired a publicist and an agent. He was shopping a book deal about his battle for Amy Joy, tentatively entitled *Baby Amelia: One Father's Crusade,* and several publishers were apparently interested. He was hoping for a million-dollar advance.

The lawyer and I discussed seeking an injunction on publication, but both of us knew the only way to get a judge to grant it would be flat-out bribery; unfortunately, Washington, DC, wasn't Nigeria. David disappeared into his office to make some phone calls. When he emerged, he found me in the kitchen. "I'm going out to L.A.," he said briefly.

Anxiously, I looked up from Amy Joy's chicken and noodles.

She was impatient now with my spooning food into her eager little mouth; she wanted to feed herself, resulting in the maximum level of messiness and the minimum level of food ingested. "L.A.? What for? Does this have anything to do with—?"

He ignored my question. "I'm not sure when I'll be back. You might have to go to Rachel's party this weekend without me."

"I couldn't care less about Rachel's party!" I stood up to face my husband, whose face was grim and closed. "David, what are you going to do? What have you found out?"

"He's still a cokehead and a party boy when he can afford it. He still hits women. Amy Joy is his ticket to money and fame, and he's going to play it for all he's worth."

"What are you going to *do*?" I repeated.

"I told you I'd take care of it, and I'll take care of it," he retorted.

And I was supposed to just trust him? Well, the hell with that! I scooped Amy Joy out of her highchair and hurried up the stairs after him in time to see him packing his gun and holster in a black case.

"Why are you taking that?" I asked, proud that my voice was only trembling a little.

He glanced at me briefly. "I always travel with a gun."

He snapped the suitcase shut with a decisive click and swung around to leave.

And that did it.

"David, you fucking son of a bitch, don't you dare go through that door!" I roared.

Shocked, he stopped short.

"Don't you dare pull your spy shit on me again," I snapped. "Talk to me or—or—don't bother coming back!"

I couldn't believe I'd said it; I didn't know if I really meant it. But David looked, unbelievably, frightened. He took a step back into the room and closed the door behind him.

"You bastard," I said, almost conversationally. "What, should I not worry my pretty little head about this? We're past that, David; we're way past that. If we want to have a marriage—a real marriage—then you will talk to me or, by God, I swear I'm done. I'm done with all your secrets and your lies and your—"

I was only surprised that it had taken me this long to get there.

Looking as if I'd slapped him on the face, David held up his hands. "Okay, okay, I get it!"

"So?" I sat down on the bed and crossed my legs. "I'm waiting."

He sat down heavily in the chintzy chair that I had put in the corner near the door, absently swatting aside a few blouses that I had tossed there for dry cleaning. "I'm not exactly sure what I'm going to do," he said slowly, as if with great effort.

"Why the gun?"

"That's . . . irrelevant. I've made lots of enemies, and California is full of Iranians. Mostly good guys, but some . . . not."

I thought I believed him.

"So?" I demanded again. I was still furious, so furious I was shaking with rage.

"I'll start with bribery," he said reluctantly. "We always start with bribery. If it's money he wants, it's money he'll get."

With some relief, I remembered that he was rich. Thank God; surely there could be no better use of his parents' money.

"Okay," I said. "What else?"

"If that doesn't work . . . it'll get ugly."

"How ugly? What do you mean?"

"Shelley—I'm begging you. I just can't talk about what I do. Please don't make me." It was almost as if it hurt him to speak; I watched his throat straining with the effort to repress his words.

I swallowed, my mouth suddenly dry. "You won't do anything illegal," I said.

"I won't get *caught* doing anything illegal."

I studied him, feeling his pain as well as my own. "Okay," I said finally.

"Okay?"

"Okay." I saw that it would be excruciatingly difficult for him to say more, and I was starting to understand that. There was a crack in his wall now; over time, I thought it would widen.

"Thanks," he said awkwardly.

"Be careful!" I cried. But I was talking to empty air; he was already out the bedroom door.

And then, a few days later, he was home. He materialized in the kitchen after dinner, appearing so unexpectedly and soundlessly that I dropped the glass dish of leftover green beans, which splintered into a hundred glittering shards on the kitchen floor. "Shit!" I cried.

David grinned. "Nice to see you too. Sit down." Quickly, efficiently, he cleaned up the mess while I poured myself a glass of wine with trembling hands and sat down to watch him. Suddenly I felt incapable of moving. He dropped a light kiss on my head and asked cheerfully, "How's it going? Where's the baby?"

"Sasha took her up for a bath," I said unsteadily. I didn't even know what to ask. I knew that David was much too efficient, much too competent, to have done anything to Greg Clifford; but why the gun, then?

"Okay. Are there any leftovers? I'm starving."

"David—what happened?"

He glanced back at me from the fridge. "Shelley, everything is fine. It's all taken care of."

The anger flared again. "David, either we're a team or we're not. What the *hell* did you do?"

"Sorry," he said. "I'm not in the habit of discussing operations. But if you really want to know—"

With an effort, I resisted the urge to scratch his eyes out.

"Okay, then. I went to California. Saw Greg Clifford. Threatened Greg Clifford. Scared him to death. Broke the news that he'll never star in a reality show. And then I came home. Op closed. Now—" he swung back to look in the fridge again— "will Sam kill me if I eat his lasagna?"

"You threatened him?" I repeated. "With what?"

"Oh man, there were so many options. Mostly drug dealing though; he had two prior convictions, and California is a third-strike state, so that was very effective." He put the dish of lasagna into the microwave and, with a quick movement, pulled me into his arms. "You don't ever have to worry about Greg Clifford again. He's gone. Amy Joy is ours forever."

And so it proved. Two days later, David was whistling when he came home from work. "The Greg Clifford nonsense is officially over. We just have to go into the lawyer's office tomorrow and sign some papers." He dropped a kiss on the top of my head and lifted the lid of the pan on the stove to peer inside.

"Thank God," I said, my eyes welling up. I couldn't wait to have Amy Joy irrefutably, officially ours.

"There's one thing. . . ." he said.

"What kind of thing?"

"It's fine. It's really not a big deal. I can tell you now if you want, but it's better for you to be surprised tomorrow."

I just looked at him. "Fine," I said. "I trust you."

The next morning we drove downtown together. Pleased at the outing, Amy Joy babbled in the back seat. David spent most of the time on his cell phone discussing the upcoming Lebanese elections, so I had no opportunity to question him.

As we walked into the lawyer's office, Mr. Beecham said stiffly, "Mr. Harris, should we talk privately?"

I glanced at my husband, uneasy again.

"Oh, no," said David. "Shelley should hear everything."

Still stiff, the lawyer turned to me. "Mrs. Harris, I have very good news. Greg Clifford has dropped his case. We can finalize your adoption of Amy Joy today."

Even though I had already known this, the rush of relief that engulfed me was so intense that I staggered. David's arm tightened around me, supporting me, and I allowed myself to sag against him. "Oh, thank God," I breathed. "Thank you, Mr. Beecham, thank you so much!"

The lawyer looked very uncomfortable. "I wish I deserved your thanks, but I am afraid that I do not," he said precisely. "In fact, I have some rather . . . startling news for you about that."

I sank down onto the leather sofa. This, then, was David's "thing." David took Amy Joy from me and put her on the carpet.

"As you know," the lawyer said, "DNA tests are always required in cases of this sort."

"Yes, but we know he's the biological father," I said, mystified. "Aviva hadn't been with anyone else."

Mr. Beecham avoided my gaze. "Actually, it turns out that she was not truthful with you."

"You mean . . . Greg Clifford is not Amy Joy's biological father?" Oh no, did that mean that some strange man could come out of the woodwork now and try to claim Amy Joy? How odd that Aviva would lie to me, though.

"No, Mrs. Harris, the DNA was not a match." He looked at David and I followed his gaze. "There is, however, something else," he said heavily. A small silence fell.

David said dryly, "Apparently Amy Joy's DNA did match someone else."

—

"Who?" I asked innocently.

The lawyer turned away.

"Me," said my husband.

I had to bite my lip hard to stifle a laugh; the lawyer looked at me, confused, and David said quickly, "We'll be going now."

CHAPTER FORTY-EIGHT

SOMEHOW WE GOT OUT OF THE MORTIFIED Mr. Beecham's office without betraying anything and made our way to the car. Once David put the car into gear I asked, "How did you do it?"

David signaled for a turn and shot a glance at me. "It was embarrassingly easy in the end. I just got one of our computer techies to hack into the DNA lab and match mine to hers. I told you I'd take care of it, Shelley."

I opened the folder in my lap and picked up the top paper again. "Final Adoption Decree for Amelia Joy Harris," it read. "Permanent custody awarded to biological father, David Samuel Harris, and adoptive mother, Michelle Mendelson Harris." I closed the file again and looked back at our sleeping daughter, wisps of dark blond hair curling over her soft forehead and her eyelashes drooping against her cheeks as she dozed. I thought about David getting the wrestling coach and ref who had maimed Sam banned from the sport for life, and I thought about him ensuring that Amy Joy would be ours forever—and the ghost of Mia shriveled and popped in my dazzled brain.

He was the father of my children. Forgiveness would never come, not completely, and neither would forgetting. But understanding had come—and I thought it was enough.

"You're my hero, David," I said softly.

—

323

"I love you too," he replied. The shadow of a smile danced around his mouth, and he reached out to take my hand. We held hands like lovestruck teenagers all the way home.

The week after the hearing, I heard Sam's car pull into the driveway and stop with a painful screech of the brakes. I glanced out the window and saw him jump out of the car and come dashing up the kitchen steps, so fast he almost stumbled over his own feet. Sasha followed more slowly.

"I got into Brandeis!" he shouted, hugging me as tightly as he could with only one working arm. "I'm going to Brandeis, Mom—Shelley—and I'm going to do Near Eastern and Judaic Studies!"

"Oh, Sam!" It would be a wonderful place for him, but I suddenly realized that I wasn't quite ready for the twins to leave me yet. "I'm so happy for you. Congratulations!"

He beamed at me. "Sasha didn't get in," he said more quietly. "But she didn't want to go there anyway, right, Sash? She got into the University of Vermont."

I hugged Sasha too. "Thanks," she said, uncharacteristically subdued.

I peered more closely at her. "Aren't you pleased?" I asked cautiously. I had thought UVM a perfect choice for my Sasha.

She shrugged. "Sure. I guess."

Sam scowled at her. "Why are you trying to bring us down? You should be happy! I'm happy; why aren't you?"

"I'm glad you're so happy to be getting rid of me!" she shouted at him. "Finally you're free of the twin sister! Well, good for you!" And she burst into loud sobs.

Sam and I stared at each other in consternation. I couldn't recall the last time I saw Sasha cry—really cry, not like the easy tears at the end of *Titanic*, or the almost-fun tears at a school graduation or bat mitzvah. This was real grief, and suddenly my eyes welled up in sympathy. Sasha would be losing her twin brother's constant companionship, but I would be losing both of them.

"Oh, no," Sam said apprehensively, seeing my face begin to crumple.

Sasha sniffled. "Don't you care at all?" she asked him tremulously.

Being a male, it took him a second to figure out what to do. He put his good arm around his sister and hugged her tight. "I'm going to miss you a lot," he told her earnestly. "But Sash, sooner or later we had to do this. You don't want to go to Brandeis."

"They don't even have a football team," she sighed against his shoulder.

"But I'll come up to UVM so I can see you cheer at their games, and you can come down to Brandeis for weekends," he continued.

She giggled, lifting her head and brushing the tears from her eyes. "Why would I go to Brandeis for weekends when UVM has the best parties on the East Coast??"

The immediate crisis averted, I drew a deep breath and brushed back my own tears.

"Don't overdo the partying at college," I told her, trying to sound firm. "You're there to work, not play."

"Then I don't know why she's going to the number one party school in the Northeast," Sam said dryly, and Sasha swatted him on the shoulder as they both dissolved into laughter.

Just as life at home had settled back into normality, the Norwell Friends auction committee exploded. Our secretary, Allison Paige, had hit the "Reply All" button on an email to me in which she referred to the decorations committee as "prima donnas" and the setup committee as "divas." Then the head of school sent in a lavender pleather coat for the auction, with a note suggesting that its minimum price be set at $2000. And the assistant head of school suggested that he read passages from the three-volume *History of Norwell Friends* during the dinner to inspire donors to give more generously. "It'll inspire donors to run for the exits," responded one of my cochairs. Unfortunately, she hit "Reply All" on that one too.

I mediated all these disputes to the best of my ability, but by the time that we gathered in the cavernous gym the morning of the auction to begin setup, no one was speaking to anyone else. I gave a little pep talk on team unity, handed out supplies, and set everyone to work.

"Shelley," complained the head of setup, "they're folding the napkins all wrong."

"They're hanging posters too high!" wailed the decorations diva. "They should be five feet off the ground, not five feet and four inches."

"We can't find the pirate swords!" shrieked my cochair. "How can you lose one thousand pirate swords?"

I arbitrated the disputes and located the pirate swords under a stack of wrestling mats in the boys' locker room. "Don't ever let me do this again," I ordered David when I ran home to change before the festivities began.

"I told you not to do it *this* time," he said unsympathetically. "You're too damned good at this; that's your problem. Didn't you tell me they want you to be president of the temple next year?"

"I'm going to refuse," I said determinedly.

My husband laughed.

Upstairs I glanced in on the peacefully slumbering Amy Joy and made my way to our bathroom, where I locked the door behind me and sank down on the small cabinet next to the shower. Did I really want to spend the next eighteen years arbitrating disputes about Hebrew school textbooks? The twins' college letters had jolted me into the reminder that soon it would be just me and David and Amy Joy.

Then what? Twenty more years of navigating grief-laden couples through the worst months of their lives? Become the PTO president at Amy Joy's schools and plan a dozen more fundraisers?

And at home, nobody would need me anymore except for Amy Joy. After years of caring for the twins, they'd be gone and I'd be left with just one baby. One *easy* baby.

I stood up and stared into the mirror at my suddenly drawn face. Was it my imagination, or were those worry wrinkles radiating up from my eyebrows? I pressed my lips together and examined the wrinkles at the side of the mouth. Maybe I should have Botox. Maybe I should have plastic surgery. Maybe I should enroll in a program and become an aerobics instructor. Maybe I should go back to practicing law rather than mediation. My shoulders slumped and I turned away. I didn't want to do any of those things.

The auction was a wild success, though. The school treasurer called me with the final accounting as I was in the kitchen preparing our Seder feast: We had raised nearly half a million dollars, every penny of which would go to the school's scholarship fund for needy kids. It was the most successful event the school had ever run, but I wasn't given much time to rest on my laurels; the head of school had already asked me to chair the new Capital Campaign starting in September.

I was still awaiting the results of my Qameen proposal, though, before I thought about the next school year. And the years after that. I was now working with thirty Qameen refugee families, and the temple board had set up a committee to find host families for even more; the response from the congregation had been heart-warming. But I was thinking bigger.

—

CHAPTER FORTY-NINE

To Do:
Final auction accounting
Vegan caterer
Klezmer band? Reggae?
Organic tablecloths
Birthday party for Sharif girls
Organize ESL classes at synagogue
Find host families for ten more Qameen refugees
Call orthopedic surgeon re Sam
Call pediatrician re AJ diarrhea
Call vet re Tinky diarrhea
Car inspection
Call exterminators re wasp nest in attic
Call bank re monthly fee
Call cable company re wonky Internet
Respond to Elie Wiesel Foundation
Find green card lawyer for Abdal

A FEW DAYS AFTER THE AUCTION, I finally forced myself to return Dani's increasingly hysterical phone calls. "Shelley!" she exclaimed. "At last! Why don't you ever pick up the phone when

I call? Are you still spending all your time talking to all those Jewish people?"

She was getting a little too discerning for comfort. "What's so urgent?" I asked.

"I got the names of a couple of vegan caterers for you to call," Dani announced proudly. "And someone told me there's an environmentally friendly linen supplier on Staten Island who doesn't use any detergent or bleach on the napkins and tablecloths."

I could only imagine the smells and stains that would tickle our senses through dinner.

"So you'll need to track them down too."

I sighed. Was she truly serious? "Dani—"

"And we'd like to have a Klezmer band that can also do reggae and hip hop. Doesn't that sound like fun?"

"No, Dani—it sounds impossible." I spied Amy Joy making for the cereal cupboard—her favorite new game was pouring Cheerios out onto the kitchen floor and eating them one by one—and moved to intercept her.

"What? What do you mean?" Dani demanded. Hearing Amy Joy's yells of anger, she added, "Isn't it naptime yet?"

It was nine in the morning.

I distracted Amy Joy with her second-favorite activity—raiding the pots and pans cupboard—and over the noise I said, "Dani, don't you think you should plan all this yourself? Since you're so explicit in what you want?"

"How can you say that?" Dani sounded shocked. "You planned Marisa's wedding for her! And the kids' bar and bat mitzvahs! You're so *good* at it."

"I planned Marisa's wedding because she was only twenty-two—and fragile," I reminded.

"Well, I'm fragile too!" Dani roared.

I looked at the pad that I'd automatically started scribbling on when Dani called: "vegan caterer," "Klezmer band? Reggae?" and "green linens???"—and something inside me snapped. (I seemed to be doing a lot of this lately.) "Dani, I'm afraid I can't do this," I said clearly. "You'll have to plan your own wedding. I'm sorry."

Shocked silence.

"I can't believe you're doing this to me! How can you be so mean? Don't you want me to be happy?"

Her voice was so small and shaken that I felt the familiar tug of love and need reaching out to reel me in again, and I almost—almost—gave in. But then Amy Joy pulled herself up on my knees, beaming up at me with pride that she was standing. I put my hand on her soft head and smiled down at her.

"I'm sorry, Dani," I said again. "But you're almost forty and a successful book editor. Surely you can plan a small wedding. I'm glad to advise you as you go along, but David and Amy Joy and the twins need me. You can do this, Dani. I know you can."

"David needs you," Dani repeated skeptically. "I never met anyone less needy in my entire life than David."

That's what I used to think too. I was silent.

"Fine," she said shortly, and hung up.

And then it was June. There was a lull in the flood of mail and phone calls from my various contacts, as the weather turned sultry and work slackened to a snail's pace. It was Amy Joy's first summer with us, and I dressed her in adorable little pink sundresses and matching hats that always wound up in her mouth or crushed beneath her feet. Her babbling turned into "mama" and "dada" and, ominously, "no!" I loved splashing with her in our neighborhood pool and seeing her marvel at the feel of cool green grass below her chubby feet or the swoosh of wind past her face as I pushed her on the ancient swings in our backyard.

Sasha had proclaimed that we needed a party to celebrate the twins' high school graduation and Amy Joy's adoption, so on the first Saturday night in June we had a houseful.

Marisa and Neil surprised me with a lovely gift—tickets to a ballet gala at the Kennedy Center, with a coupon from Sasha for babysitting. Marisa also gave me a big hug and kiss on my cheek. "I don't know why you want another baby," she said a little mistily, "but you're still the best mother I've ever known." She leaned a little closer and whispered in my ear, "Sometimes I wish you'd been my mother, instead of—well, you know."

Surprised, I hugged her back. "You're not so bad yourself," I whispered back, realizing that it was true. The twins loved Marisa and accepted her for who she was, and she returned the favor, in spades.

After our guests—family plus six other couples and a few of Sasha and Sam's friends—had finally departed, David and I did a desultory job of cleaning up. We had done this so many times that we worked as a well-oiled team, but this time our hearts weren't in it. Finally he tossed the sponge into the sink and put his arms around me from behind. "Let's go to bed," he suggested, nuzzling my neck. "Maybe the kitchen elves will finish the job while we sleep."

I smiled, feeling a thrill of excitement race up my spine. "Let me get ready first."

David looked puzzled. "Get ready?"

I could hardly blame him—after twenty years of plain white cotton, he was in for a shock.

"Come up in ten minutes," I told him, and ran up the stairs. Heart pounding, I rummaged in the back of a drawer for the pink Victoria's Secret bag. Could I really do this?

When David came into our bedroom, he closed the door and paused, looking at me with an unreadable expression. I was lying on the bed in lace-trimmed crimson bikini panties and a silk camisole, which clung to my breasts and outlined the points of my nipples in the cool evening air.

When he came toward me, I braced myself. And when he sat down on the bed and ran his finger down the side of my silky camisole, I shivered.

"God, you're beautiful," he said at last, wonderingly. "How did I get so lucky?"

He leaned down to kiss me, and after that we didn't talk for a very long time.

After he rolled off me and pulled me into his arms, he stroked the tangled hair back from my face and ran a finger over my lips. He said, "You know, after a while, I didn't even want to have sex with you—real, wild sex, you know what I mean, Shells—"

I knew exactly what he meant.

"—Because I was afraid that then I might let go. Let everything slip out."

Startled by his confession, I remembered Rachel's comment after the sexpert night: I never heard of a husband who didn't want more, hotter sex. Then, regretfully, I thought back to all the years of routine, passion-free, once-a-week sex—when he was in town, that is. What a waste.

"I'm sorry," he added. "I'm really sorry."

I wondered if he understood that his urgent need to shut me out of the dark side of his life had crippled our marriage— and for the first time I acknowledged that my urgent need to maintain the happy family facade had completed the damage. "I understand," I said quietly, and fell asleep in his arms.

Then the public phase of the Senate hearings began. David seemed calm about the proceedings, though he had told me he expected to be grilled, filleted, and disemboweled so that the senators could perform for the cameras. His lawyer was an old college roommate from Princeton named Ryder Everett Corcoran IV, who had suggested that I show up for at least part of the time to demonstrate my support.

"Will Mia be there?"

He hesitated slightly. "Yes."

I turned and walked away.

But in the end, Amy Joy and I slipped into the back of the hearing room just in time to see David sit in the witness chair.

"Dadadadadadada!" Amy Joy cried, her little voice clear and demanding all the way across the crowded room.

Everyone turned to stare and, in some cases, smile. "Shh," I said, inserting a cookie into her mouth.

David waved cheerfully at her, and she plucked the cookie out of her mouth to wave it back at him.

Then I saw a face—a stunned, staring face that was for once stripped bare of its professional beauty and charm in shock at the sight of Amy Joy. My baby, who looked so much like David.

As Mia Holloway stared at the baby in my arms, I could almost see the wheels turning in her mind. So David had a pregnant wife at home while he was sleeping with me? she was asking herself.

I gazed back at her, triumphant, the mother of his children and the wife of his home. Our eyes locked for a brief moment, and then she turned away.

"Good work, sweetie," I whispered to Amy Joy.

As I expected, my husband was calm, collected, and utterly impossible to pin down. At one point a senator asked him, "Mr. Harris, don't you have family living in Israel?"

"Yes."

"Aren't they Zionists? Are you a Zionist too?"

"Well, the definition of that term is very imprecise," David explained, settling in more comfortably. "You see, it was first coined. . . ."

After that senator's eyes finally glazed over, another one tried. "Did your brother and his family influence you in any way?"

"I can't think of a greater influence on my life than my twin brother," David agreed earnestly. "Even though we're fraternal twins and not identical, most studies suggest that the bond between twins is. . . ."

After David had lectured on twinship for fifteen minutes, a third senator intervened. "Mr. Harris," he said sharply. "Can we stick to the point here?"

David gazed at him in surprise. "Of course. I was just answering your colleague's question."

They turned the microphones off after that for a brief break, but not before the mics captured a staffer telling the senators that Harris had been trained to withstand torture and extreme deprivation; Senate hearings were no match for him. When the hearings resumed, the questioners had defeated looks on their faces. I almost sympathized.

That night, I said to him, "They're not going to get a thing out of you, are they?"

"It seems unlikely," he agreed.

But the hearings took a more dramatic turn the next day when Mia testified—which I watched from home. Yes, she had had a sexual relationship with David Harris. Yes, he had sent her a computer file with information about the British supplying weapons and information to Hamas. Yes, he had known that she would go public with the information if she could confirm it. Her striking good looks were back again, and she directed several warm, intimate smiles in David's direction. He looked impassive, as always.

On the third morning David came out of the bathroom after shaving and leaned against the door, watching me and Amy Joy lying in bed enjoying an early-morning bottle and Sesame Street. Drops of water sparkled on his bare chest, and his hair looked almost golden in the sunlight. "Are you going to watch the hearings today?" he asked.

"Yes, just like every day."

"Good." He went into the closet and started going through his shirts.

"Why? Is something going to happen today?"

He came out of the closet tucking his shirt into his pants and running a hand through his still-damp hair. "Yes."

At first the hearing seemed uneventful. Various CIA officials testified, confirming the existence of a covert British operation supplying Hamas with arms and information. One senator asked, aghast, "Didn't you know that Hamas terrorists would use those arms against innocent people?" The CIA officer in the stand said coolly, "We were not pleased with the British, but they are our allies. It is a crime to betray secret information about an ally's operation to the press."

I couldn't imagine how David could sit so calmly; I was ready to attack his accusers with my bare hands.

Ryder Everett Corcoran IV stood up. "I would like to recall Mr. David Harris to the witness stand."

"Out of order! Mr. Harris has already testified!" Senator Harland, the chair of the proceedings, pounded his gavel. David had told me that he and Harland were long-time enemies; they had clashed repeatedly over the Senate Intelligence Committee's refusal to approve operations against the genocidal government of Qameen.

"The defense would like to recall Mr. Harris to the stand," Corcoran insisted. The media buzzing in the room rose to a low roar.

"And I would like to remind you that Mr. Harris has already—" The senator's face was brick red.

An aide hurried up behind the senator and whispered in his ear. Harland looked stricken. The aide whispered again, more urgently, and the senator pulled himself together with a visible effort. Tonelessly, he said into the microphone, "Mr. David Harris, please return to the witness stand. Attorney Corcoran may conduct the questioning of the witness."

Pandemonium reigned as David strode across the room and settled himself, once more, into the witness chair. Senator Harland, his face now gray, took a big gulp of water. His hands were visibly shaking.

I leaned forward anxiously, studying my husband. He wore the same dark suit he'd put on in our bedroom that morning, and his dark blond hair still curled up a little on the nape of his neck—but somehow, indefinably, he was the other David. The un-David. A thrill of pride—and desire—coursed through me as I watched.

"Mr. Harris," the lawyer began. "Were you the source of the leak about British intelligence ties to Hamas?"

"No, sir. I was not." The room erupted again, and Senator Harland pounded his gavel and scolded.

"Did you send an email to Ms. Holloway containing classified information on this subject?"

"No, sir. Never."

Pandemonium again.

CHAPTER FIFTY

"Did you communicate with any reporters on this topic?"

"Never."

"Did you speak with any person outside of the CIA about this subject?"

"No, sir. Not until after the leaks were reported on CNN."

"Did you send any emails on this subject?"

David actually laughed. "Of course not," he said. "I've been a CIA officer for twenty-five years; I don't send traceable emails."

At this, even the chairman could not control the spectators, and he called a recess.

I stared dazedly as a commentator started chattering excitedly on CNN and the "Breaking News: Harris Denies Leak" banner popped up on the screen. David had never denied being the source of the leak. Never! (Though now that I thought about it, I couldn't quite remember ever asking him if it was true.)

So was he lying under oath? But how? Why? Surely . . .

The hearings reopened, with the still-shaken Senator Harland once more issuing dire threats to the excited room. Briefly I wondered what leverage David had found to force him to allow the testimony, but I knew he would never tell me. David's lawyer sat down and the senators started firing questions at him, all of which he answered with the same bland blankness. Eventually, they gave up.

At last, David's lawyer announced his final witness. "I would like to call Alan Jones, senior technology analyst at the National Security Agency."

"Alan Jones." A slight Asian man hesitated slightly before giving his name, not even bothering to expect that anyone would believe it was his real name.

"Do you have any knowledge of the email sent to Mia Holloway containing highly classified information about British-Hamas operations?" David's lawyer asked him.

"Yes, indeed."

This time the room was silent, spellbound.

"Did David Harris send that email to Ms. Holloway?"

"No, sir. It would have been impossible for Mr. Harris to send that email."

I dropped my Diet Coke on the floor, and the dark liquid flowed across the wide oak floors and into Amy Joy's laundry. Unheeding, I gazed intently at the TV.

"And how do you know that, Mr. Jones?"

"Because the email was sent at six o'clock on the morning of Tuesday, September first, from a computer located in Malmo, Sweden. And Mr. Harris was, at that moment, in Baghdad. He was, in fact, attending a meeting in person with NSA and CIA operatives, all of whom can testify to Harris's presence. He could not have sent that email."

The room disintegrated into utter chaos, senators barking at aides and reporters racing for the exits so they could use the cellphones and laptops that were prohibited in the hearing room. Only David and "Alan Jones" seemed completely unaffected. David murmured something in Ryder Everett Corcoran's ear, and they smiled at each other in satisfaction.

Then my husband stretched, yawned, and leaned back in his chair.

Amy Joy and I watched CNN as we waited for David to come home. The reporters could talk of nothing else: A story that had sex, handsome spies, secret plots, and hints of family secrets was simply too delicious to let go, so the coverage was endless. For once, I was enjoying the sight of my husband on TV.

Finally one reporter, an ex-CIA officer himself, summed it all up: "This has all the hallmarks of a David Harris operation," he said admiringly. "No harm, no foul, no fingerprints, no tracks. I'd be damned if I knew how he does it."

I couldn't have said it better myself.

David looked quietly satisfied as he relaxed after dinner with a snifter of brandy. "To us," he said solemnly, raising his glass to touch mine. "And to the end of British arms sales to terrorists."

"To us," I echoed. I took a sip of my wine and smiled at him. "Who was that man, really?" I asked curiously.

"What man?

"The so-called Alan Jones."

David shrugged, but his eyes were dancing. "How should I know?"

"For once in your life, tell me the truth," I ordered. I was trying to be stern, but he looked so delighted with himself that I couldn't muster up much real anger.

"I could tell you, but then. . . ."

"I know," I said with a sigh. "You'd have to kill me."

"Well. . . ."

I sighed again.

"Look," he said, suddenly serious. "I really don't want to lie to you anymore, and I really can't tell you about what happened today. So can we drop it?"

I studied his dear, familiar face with its late-day stubble and his ocean-blue eyes, and I felt myself weaken. "Okay," I heard myself saying.

"Okay," he agreed.

"But can you tell me one thing?" I asked.

"Sure."

"Why Malmo, Sweden?" It seemed such a random place for the computer to be (allegedly) located.

He grinned. "We threw a dart at a map."

Part IV

RESOLUTION: NEVER AGAIN

CHAPTER FIFTY-ONE

To Do:
QAMEEN PRESENTATION
Eyebrow wax
Hair color
Buy new suit
Buy new shoes
Manicure
Keep all fingers and toes crossed

I GOT A THICK FEDEX ENVELOPE FROM the American Jewish World Service and hid it under a stack of old photographs in my office so that I could gloat over it in private. All my plans were coming together, but I still had to get through the presentations, and superstitiously, I couldn't share it with David until it was really certain. I was coming to understand some of his secrecy over his "operations." What if the presentation flopped? What if everything fell apart at the last minute?

And then the phone rang—Sasha calling to complain about the "freaky" amount of prep work that her college professors had assigned for the *summer*—and the moment was lost.

The next day, an editorial in the *New York Times* expressed support for David and disgust at the senators who'd hounded him. "The real shame," the editorial proclaimed, "is not that one CIA officer may or may not have released information about an ongoing operation—but that such an operation was ever carried out in the first place. Senators and prosecutors should be going after those "allies" in the British government who decided that providing weapons and information to Hamas was a good idea. His stubborn and principled stance against this operation makes David Harris a man to be admired, a rare ray of hope in the CIA's increasingly tarnished leadership."

The phone started ringing—bookers from all the late-night shows, all the Sunday morning shows, *60 Minutes;* literary agents who promised him a million-dollar advance for his memoir; publicity firms wanting to handle his newfound fame; and a Hollywood agent who wanted to make a film based on his life.

David firmly refused all the offers, of course. Tongue in cheek, he claimed to be tempted only by the TV production company that offered to give him his own reality show. "Just think how much fun we could have with that," he mused. "Sasha could be one of those athletes who kneecaps her rival for captain—or maybe you could kneecap her, Shelley—and Amy Joy would have to be the daughter of China's last Empress . . . and it would kill Greg Clifford."

"But you could earn a million dollars just for writing a book!" Sasha protested. "Even if nobody read it, you'd still get the money. We could donate it or something, if we didn't need it. How cool is that?"

"Not cool at all in the eyes of the CIA," David reminded her. "Anyway—" he exchanged a long look with me—"all I really want is to work for the CIA. That's all I ever wanted."

Sasha asked tentatively, "But David, don't spies do all these terrible things? Like the British who helped Hamas? Why would you want to work with people like that?"

He smiled affectionately at her. "Those terrible things are the exceptions. That's why you hear about them. You don't hear about all the things we do right: keeping nuclear weapons out of the hands of terrorists, stopping attacks before they happen, and preventing . . . anyway. The nature of intelligence is that you hear about our disasters, and nothing about all the good work we do." He leaned back and crossed his long legs in front of him. "And that's fine with me. I never wanted to be famous."

"But now you are," I noted.

He shrugged. "That'll pass soon," he predicted. "Or as we say at the agency, 'inshallah.'"

The following Monday, I put on my new suit and checked my look in the mirror. The new high-heeled pumps matched my dark gray Armani suit perfectly, and the extra two inches of height gave me a confidence that batted down some of my nerves.

When I reached the anonymous, unmarked office down-town, I shook hands with all the serious, important people in the room—people that I had brought together, I reminded myself—from the Israeli ambassador to uber-lawyer Alan Der-showitz to Chaim Leibovitz himself.

When I tapped my laptop to bring up the first slide of my presentation on the screen at the front of the room—"THE NEVER AGAIN PROJECT"—I took a deep breath and dove in.

Afterward, back in day-to-day life, I silently worried. I'd heard nothing but silence since the Great Presentation, and I didn't know what to think. David, completely cleared and diving into work as the director of Clandestine Operations, left for the office every day with a spring in his step and a shine in his eyes. I took care of Amy Joy and the house, and waited and waited.

And then I got the phone call.

My official duties as director of the Never Again Project would begin on September 1, and I had already interviewed some amazingly good nannies for Amy Joy. (If I'd known there were such great nannies out there, I might have done this long ago!) One had a master's degree in child development from Barnard; another had nannied for an ambassador's family for ten years, and had glowing recommendations to show for it. I had decided to work four days a week so I could have three full days with Amy Joy, and I had already hired an assistant and two senior staffers from the mountain of résumés that had poured in since the phone call.

Remarkably, there were investment bankers, teachers, doctors, lawyers, housewives, administrative assistants, and ex-military officers in the pile; I wished I could hire all of them. In fact, I was amazed and warmed by the response; it seemed that the Never Again Project had tapped some reserve of passion in people who had discovered that they wanted their work to have real meaning, rather than a fat paycheck. Just like David, I realized. And me.

Two days later the twins left for camp, and the house felt empty with just me, David, and Amy Joy. On the last Friday in June, the three of us piled into the car and headed for David's first Princeton Reunions since his graduation more than twenty-five years earlier. Reunions were, he had explained to me, a yearly ritual at Princeton, not the every ten- or twenty-year event that less tradition-bound institutions celebrated. But he had been obliged to abandon all his old friends without a backward glance when he joined the NOC program. "I haven't been back on campus since my graduation day," he explained as we swept up the New Jersey Turnpike. "God, I've missed it!"

I glanced at him curiously. It was the first time I could ever recall him expressing regret about the spy's life he'd chosen, aside from how it had impacted our marriage. "You haven't had any contact at all with your college friends since then?"

"No. Not once. Well—until I hired Ryder to represent me at the Senate hearings. He told me everyone thought I was dead when I didn't show up at Reunions."

"People really go every year? *Every year?*" It seemed a little over-the-top to me.

"Well, not every year—but as often as they can. I read the *Princeton Alumni Weekly* online when I can; I remember being in Cairo for my fifth reunion and reading that all my friends were at Reunions—guys had traveled from California and Argentina and China to get there—and there I was, stuck in the Cairo Hilton babysitting an HVD." High Value Detainee. I was proud of myself for remembering the jargon.

"That must have been hard," I said sympathetically, wishing I had known.

He shrugged, seeming to give himself a mental shake. "It's the job. Anyway—" he slanted a wicked grin at me, "I have a lot to make up for."

When we pulled up in front of the Hyatt Princeton, in a long line of Mercedes wagons and Lexus SUVs, he dove into the trunk of the car to retrieve an orange-and-black scarf, which he whipped around his neck. On went an orange-and-black baseball cap. And the crowning touch—a tiger tail that he tied around his waist so that it waggled behind him when he walked.

I pulled the querulous Amy Joy out of her car seat and followed my tiger-tailed husband into the crowded lobby—and found myself in a veritable sea of orange and black. Tiger tails, tiger shawls, tiger hats, and tiger trousers abounded. One baby around Amy Joy's age wore a T-shirt that read "Princeton Class of 2038."

David bounded up to the reception desk, but before he could pull out his credit card, a tall dark-bearded man in a perfectly hideous orange-and-black-striped dinner jacket grabbed him by the arm. "Davey? Dave Harris? Is that you?"

David spun around. "Larry? You son of a bitch, how have you been!" Our bags dropped to the floor with a resounding thump and the two men hugged, drew away so they could look at each other, and hugged again.

"I can't believe you're here!" Larry exclaimed. "I can't believe you're *alive*, actually! Nate's here, and Keith, and Teo, and Mike, and Will, and—the whole gang! Hey, Nate! Teo! Look who's here!"

Two other men in matching orange-and-black dinner jackets came hurrying over. "Holy fucking shit!" one yelled. "Dave Harris! Will emailed me and said is that *our* Davey making all that trouble on CNN, and Keith said no, our Davey would never work for the CIA, but Matt said it was definitely you. And then Ryder said he was representing you, so we knew it was you! I thought you were dead, you old bastard!"

In no time at all David was surrounded by an ocean of tiger-tailed men, all shouting and vying for his attention. Princeton had been coed by the time he attended, I knew, but apparently all his close friends were male. Very male. Resignedly, I went up to the desk and signed in. When I turned around again, my husband was being fitted with a hands-free, tiger-striped beer helmet equipped with built-in straw. "Amy Joy," I said to her, "I think we're in a whole new world."

That night David donned a pair of orange-and-black-striped

trousers, black T-shirt, and his "class costume," the garishly striped dinner jacket. I refused to put on my tiger tail, but Amy Joy was sporting her new "Princeton Class of 2040" T-shirt.

"I've never seen such foolishness," I told him as we boarded the—orange-and-black—shuttle back to campus.

He grinned and threw an expansive arm around my shoulders. "I'm gonna get you a beer helmet. Then you'll get in the spirit of things!"

Under no circumstances would I wear the beer helmet, I assured him. But as the shuttle rolled up University Avenue and into the campus, I began to see the magic of the place through his eyes. A group of young women in Tiger T-shirts stood in the courtyard of a building to the left, their lovely voices blending joyously in a cappella harmony. "That's an Arch Sing," David explained. "And—over there? That statue? Everyone calls it the Flying Fuck."

I scrutinized the statue, a modern expressionist sculpture, and saw immediately what he meant. "Hmmm," I said.

"And most important of all," he continued, "on our right is Prospect Street, where all the eating clubs are. Ta-da!"

Amy Joy giggled as he waved his hand toward the street, which was lined with magnificent ivy-covered mansions. "That's where we party! Come on, Shells, let's go find you a beer helmet!"

The next morning a bleary-eyed David once again donned his grass- and beer-stained dinner jacket for the P-rade. Every class that had ever graduated from Princeton marched in this annual parade, beginning with nonagenarian gentlemen in wheelchairs and ending with the current class of freshly minted twenty-two-year-olds reveling in their first P-rade. Amy Joy and I sat on the grass with a few other mothers and children to watch.

—

"I can't believe this is your first Reunions," said Tanya, Teo's wife. "I refused to come for a few years when the kids were little, but now they love coming too."

We both turned to watch her three small boys, cavorting with a tiger on stilts on the vast lawn of Nassau Hall.

"And," she added, "I can't believe that the famous David Harris finally turned up, alive and kicking! Every year the guys would speculate on what might have happened to him. The more they drank, the wilder it got."

"Did they ever guess CIA?"

"No, but they came close. Mossad was one of the leading theories."

I nodded.

"Mostly, they thought he was dead, though."

"Seriously?"

"Why else would he miss Reunions for twenty-five years?" she asked simply.

It poured that afternoon, and steam was still rising from the muddy ground as we walked to the Ivy Club that evening for dinner. We headed first to the childcare center, where Tiger Teens were running a babysitting service, to drop off Amy Joy.

Without any warning, a group of drunken twentysomethings reeled up the path behind us, shoving me hard enough that I cried out, in both surprise and pain. Quick as a flash, David lunged for Amy Joy and yanked her from my arms. He shouldered past the drunken kids, elbowing one in the gut as he passed, and dragged me into the quiet of a side path. I smiled apologetically at the now-whining kids as they passed. "Was that necessary?" I asked him.

"Never apologize for following your instincts," David said. I remembered that that was one of the "Moscow rules" I'd seen in the CIA museum—always trust your gut—and I smiled at him.

"And what are your instincts telling you now?" I asked.

"To find a babysitter for our baby and dance with my wife."

The twenty-fifth-year reunion class was partying in Whitman Courtyard after dinner. It was a lovely open space, constructed only a few years earlier thanks to the largesse of eBay billionaire Meg Whitman (Class of '77), but the guys complained loudly.

"This wasn't here when we were here."

"In our day, this reunion class got Henry courtyard."

Apparently any change in tradition—even an upgrade—was unwelcome.

In the shadow of red brick, ivy-draped buildings and tall leafy elm trees, we danced to the music of Lester Lanin, a Princeton tradition since the 1950s. Dreamily I drifted in David's arms; he sang under his breath as we swayed to the music. I relaxed against him and closed my eyes.

"Dave! Davey boy! Stop canoodling and get your ass over here!" Will shouted.

David grinned at me and stepped back. "Canoodling?"

"Lester's gonna play some real music now! Right, Lester, my man?"

Somehow I seemed to have stepped onto the set of *Animal House*. The men grabbed their beer helmets and sucked furiously at the straws as the band swung into "Play That Funky Music."

David, dancing furiously while trying to balance his bouncing beer helmet, cupped his hands around his mouth and yelled to me, "Come on, Shells! Come dance with us!"

Giggling helplessly at the sight of my once-dull husband in his beer helmet, orange-and-black dinner jacket, and waggling tiger tail, I took his outstretched hands and danced. We danced to classics like "Good Golly, Miss Molly" and "Twist and Shout" and "Bad Boys." Then the DJ took over, and we danced to Lady Gaga and Madonna and Bruce Springsteen. David shed his dinner jacket, and his T-shirt turned black with sweat; I shed my high heels and danced barefoot on the muddy ground. He swung me in wide circles for the fast dances until I was breathless, and I clung close to his hard chest for the slow dances.

Finally the DJ called last song, and the men lined up solemnly for "Old Nassau." They belted out the chorus at the top of their lungs, saluting with one hand as they sang, "In praise of Old Nassau, my boys, hurrah hurrah hurrah. . . ." Then they broke formation and threw their beer helmets in the air. Everyone hugged.

And for the first time ever, I was with all the Davids—Peter Brooks the superspy, always alert to any danger; David the Daddy, whose first instinct was to protect his daughter; Davey, the tailor's son from Brooklyn and the party boy from Princeton; and the husband who loved me. David and the un-Davids were one.

CHAPTER FIFTY-TWO

THE TWINS WERE HOME FOR ONE last week of freedom before school started, and Sasha began the remarkably complex task of assembling her college wardrobe. I thought she would end up taking her entire bedroom with her, but David promised to pry her away from her seven winter coats before dropping her off at the unsuspecting University of Vermont. Sam was officially seeing Rachel's daughter Madeleine (God be praised!); perhaps the ghost of Sharona, just like Mia, was finally being laid to rest.

And then there was the last great event of the summer before we all settled down to our new jobs and schools: Dani and Josh's vegan wedding. Dani had wavered for weeks over the question of who should walk her down the aisle. At first she'd proclaimed that she would walk herself down the aisle. Then it was to be her brothers-in-law, Neil and David. Then her nephew, Sam. But in the end she asked me and Marisa to take her down the aisle and present her to Josh, whose endless patience with the entire process had gone a long way toward reconciling me to his sons.

As I watched Dani take the hand of her new husband, I was surprised to feel hot tears stinging my eyes. I'd finally talked her down from the 100 percent bamboo gown that she was considering ("Do you want to be scratching yourself all through your wedding?" I'd demanded) and the high-tech hemp clothing she had selected for poor Josh ("Do you want *him* to be scratching himself all through the wedding?"). Dani had never been the prettiest of us sisters—that was Marisa—but she had achieved an edgy sort of chic during her years in Manhattan, and she looked lovely in her simple satin sheath.

Josh couldn't seem to stop smiling. One of his friends from rabbinical school was performing the ceremony, and Josh mouthed the ancient words along with him, gazing at Dani with wonderment.

When I sniffled, David hissed out of the corner of his mouth, "I can't believe you're crying. Or are those tears of relief?"

"Shut up," I hissed back.

He grinned and handed me a handkerchief. "I knew you'd cry," he murmured, and I gave him a watery smile.

I hadn't been able to talk her down from the vegan scheme, though. Hungry after the hours of photo-taking and ceremony, we gathered eagerly around the (hemp-clad) waiters as the cocktail hour finally began.

"Thank God," Neil sighed, cramming two puff pastries into his mouth before I could warn him. "I'm starved." Then his expression changed. "What the hell is this?" he choked.

"I think those are the tofu and olive puffs," I explained. "Not good?"

With a gargantuan effort Neil swallowed down the food and grabbed Marisa's champagne glass for a good long swig. "I thought they were potato pancakes," he said wistfully.

The next round of appetizers was red beet tartare atop tofu croutons, sprouts wrapped in seaweed with spicy wasabi sauce, and smoked bean paste on dandelion-bran crackers.

"What's for dinner?" asked Sam suspiciously.

"Artichoke fettucine with tempeh and soy, tofu and cucumber salsa in squash blossoms, and seitan meatloaf," I said.

"Meatloaf?" asked Neil, his eyes brightening.

"Seitan meatloaf," I corrected.

"What's seitan?"

I had already Googled it. "Well, Wikipedia says 'It is made by washing wheat flour dough with water until all the starch dissolves, leaving insoluble gluten as an elastic mass which is then cooked before being eaten.'"

A short silence followed. Then Sam said sadly, "The tofu puffs may end up being the best food of the evening."

Neil looked like he was about to cry.

When we found our way to the tables for dinner, I breathed a sigh of relief at the sight of a breadbasket in the middle of the table. At least we could fill up on that, if the rest of the food was as inedible as I feared. The four men grabbed eagerly for the bread, biting even before the rabbi had given his blessing.

"Ughwhatthehellisthisstuff," Sam gabbled, his mouth still full of the mealy, chewy mixture.

"Don't speak with your mouth full," I said.

"I can't swallow," Sam choked.

I sighed. "Spit it out, then."

They all looked up hopefully; with resignation I passed around tissues and they obediently spit out the food, then grabbed for their water glasses.

Neil, still chewing valiantly, ground out, "Why does this remind me of nuts?"

"Because it's made with cashew milk," I explained.

Sasha asked, wide-eyed, "How do cashews make milk?"

"That's it!" snapped David. "Pass me a tissue."

So I gave tissues to David and Neil too.

Sam, his gaze wandering around the room, tapped me on the shoulder. "Shelley, you're going to have to deal with Stu and Josh again. They're rolling up the meatloaf and playing baseball with it. Look!"

—

Sure enough, Josh's sons—Dani's stepsons!—had rolled their meatloaf into balls and were batting them at each other with the plastic bats they had used earlier to break the piñata.

"I can't believe those balls are staying together," Sam commented. "What the hell are they made of?"

"I wonder if we could use that stuff in our labs," David mused.

"Oh, stop it, all of you!" I ordered. I always get cranky when I'm hungry.

"I'll go over and stop them," Sam said suddenly. He jumped up, almost running over to the kids' table.

"Me too!" said Neil, and he was off too.

"I think I'll just go and help them. . . ." David murmured.

Astonished, Marisa, Sasha, and I stared after the retreating male backs.

"I don't believe it!" Sasha exclaimed.

"What?"

"They're paying the kids to hand over some candy from the piñata. Look! Sam just bought a lollipop for a dollar."

I craned my neck, hoping David would buy some for me.

Sasha started rifling through her pocketbook. "Look!" she said triumphantly. "I knew I had some trail mix in here."

"I'll give you five dollars for it," I offered eagerly.

"I'll give you twenty!" Marisa jumped in quickly.

"Oh, for heaven's sake," I snapped, my mouth watering. "We'll divide it evenly. Quick, Sasha, before the boys come back and want some."

Still, as we stopped at Ben & Jerry's in Chevy Chase on the way home, my mind was filled with thoughts of Dani in her white satin sheath, dancing in the arms of her new husband. And I looked at my own husband, his face smudged with chocolate sauce and rainbow sprinkles, laughing down at me, and I smiled.

—

Two weeks later David and I attended a dinner at Langley—my first formal event as a spy's wife. For the second time in my life, I walked across the great seal of the CIA in the entrance hall, but this time I was wearing a blue chiffon dress with a swirling hemline and a plunging neckline that made me feel like a glamorous ballerina instead of a Washington housewife. This time there were cameras flashing and champagne corks popping and people rushing up to slap my husband on the back and wish him well. I stood by his side, proud and, yes, a little intimidated, by this man who made love to me and fathered my children, but who was now a famous man, an important man, a man who was going to make history.

I watched as the vice president, a liberal Democrat from California, shook my husband's hand and murmured a quiet aside in his ear. I watched as the CIA director shook his hand and slapped him on the back. I watched as the secretary of state, a former senator with presidential aspirations of her own, kissed him on both cheeks and told him she was counting on him. And then I watched as a tall, dark-haired woman with a visitor's badge clipped on her black gown came toward us to congratulate my husband—Mia Holloway.

Mia, again. I wondered if we would ever be entirely free of her, if I would ever entirely get over that betrayal. Perhaps in time, I hoped, but not yet. Still, that betrayal had precipitated a reckoning in our marriage—a long overdue and badly needed reckoning—and we had emerged as a new, wholly richer David-and-Shelley.

I moved to intercept her. "Excuse me, Ms. Holloway?"

Deprived of her goal, she glanced at me with irritation, but then she recognized me and her face instantly went blank. "Yes?" she said cautiously.

I laid my hand on her arm and moved us slightly to the side, so no one could overhear us. "The next time you need help," I told her, "don't call my husband. Find yourself another hero."

Then I walked back to David. I linked my arm through his so that his upper arm grazed my breast and smiled up at him. He slanted a smile back down at me.

EPILOGUE

The Washington Post, August 10, 2020

"THE NEVER AGAIN PROJECT"

Every major Jewish organization in America and fifty of the country's largest congregations have joined together in an unprecedented effort to form the "Never Again Project," an umbrella group inspired by the Never Again Holocaust Survivors Project, devoted to preventing genocide and supporting refugees from Qameen and other war-torn countries. The group's honorary chairman is Nobel Prize winner Chaim Leibovitz, distinguished chronicler of the Holocaust, and its high-powered board of directors includes Jewish American leaders from both left and right such as Senator David Myers, White House Chief of Staff Howard Kurtzen, and Harvard Professor Alan Dershowitz.

At a reception in Chevy Chase celebrating the organization's new headquarters, reporters met with key staffers. "We're not just an aid group," explained Shelley Harris, the Washington-based lawyer who launched the initiative and who will serve as the new organization's managing director. "We'll draw on the entire Jewish community—doctors, lawyers, bankers, homemakers, students, teachers—everyone can play a part in preventing genocide and in supporting its victims. It's a multipronged effort."

When asked why Jewish organizations are committing such powerful resources to Qameen, an Arab and Muslim nation, Harris simply said, "Never Again means never again. Preventing genocide is the most Jewish of causes, no matter where it happens or to whom it happens."

Harris will have her job cut out for her, noted one longtime observer of the often-fractious Jewish American community. "Getting all these people in the same room, let alone working from the same playbook, will be quite a feat," he noted.

Harris (the wife of David Harris, deputy director of the CIA), shrugged this off with a smile. "I've had a lot of practice holding people together," she said.

Her husband, standing beside her, said, "I can attest to that."

ACKNOWLEDGMENTS

Thanks, as always, to my publishing sisterhood: The long-suffering team at SparkPress (Brooke, Shannon, Crystal, Tabitha, Paige, and Maggie), and my ever-supportive agent, Marcy Posner.

And a huge shout-out to my equally long-suffering family—you put up with a lot from me!

Thanks, always and forever, to my beloved Naomi, Liora, Maya, Gabriel, Eden, Ellie, Cassie, and Lev for making me the happiest, luckiest granny in the world.

Read on for a special preview of

THE LONG-LOST JULES

by Jane Elizabeth Hughes

A SHADOW FELL ACROSS THE TABLE WHERE I sat, devouring a scone and a novel with equal satisfaction. Frowning and shading my eyes against the watery London sun, I looked up to see a tall, dark stranger gazing down at me.

"Hey, Jules!" the stranger said. "I've been looking all over for you!"

Jules! What on earth?

With some regret—this was an interesting distraction—I shrugged my shoulders and turned back to my book. "Sorry," I said. "You have the wrong person."

He gestured to the empty chair across the table from me. "May I?"

"Sorry," I repeated, falling back on all-purpose Brit-speak for *I don't know what you're talking about, and I don't want to talk to you.* "You must have mistaken me for someone else."

He hovered uncomfortably between a standing position and a ready-to-sit position, and I eyed him with a mixture of amusement and curiosity.

"Um . . . I can't believe I finally tracked you down," he said, shifting from foot to foot and trying, unsuccessfully, to look as if he had never expected an invitation to sit. "It's such a pleasure to actually meet you."

"Sorry, but you have the wrong person." I tried again. "I'm not Jules."

He shook his head. "Sorry," he said, now lapsing into Brit-speak for *You are totally wrong, but I'm too polite to say it.* "But . . . well, the thing is . . . well, I believe you are Juliette Mary Seymour, and I've been searching for you for months. You covered your tracks very well, Jules!"

I sighed. "My name is Amy, actually, and I've never heard of Juliette whoever. I don't mean to be rude, but I have to be back in my office in fifteen minutes, and I'd like to finish reading this chapter."

He glanced at my book, a John le Carré classic, and raised his eyebrows.

I held my patience. "Look, whatever your name is, you have distracted me from my problems at work for a few minutes, and I appreciate that. But I'm not the person you're looking for, and I'd like to finish my coffee in peace."

"Oh? What are—sorry, I don't mean to pry—but what are your problems at work?"

"I work with a lot of sorority-ish mean girls, and they . . ." I stopped short; why on earth was I unburdening myself to this stranger?

"And are they mean to you, Jules?" He seemed genuinely interested, but I steeled myself against it.

"Sorry, I'm trying not to be rude," I said. "But I really have to go."

"The thing is . . . um . . . I do apologize for bothering you . . ." Now I saw that his body was tense and coiled, like a panther that has finally cornered its prey and is determined not to let it escape. It was body language that was strangely at odds with his hesitant speech. "You see, I'm Leo Schlumberger, and I'm a historian at Oxford."

A historian! That was the last thing I had expected. He looked more like a Mafia boss than an academic. He was tall and strongly built, with snapping black eyes and a dark five-o'clock shadow that probably appeared fifteen minutes after he shaved. His hair too was black, cut carelessly and curling against the back of his tanned neck. He wasn't quite hand- some—his features were too strong for that—but his looks were compelling. I tended to like easygoing, laid-back men—definitely not stammering Brits who apologized every other sentence.

"A historian? And why are you looking for this Jules?"

"Sorry," he said. "That story is much too long for the remainder of your coffee break. Um . . . may I buy you dinner tonight?"

Despite my curiosity, I reminded myself that I was not the girl he was looking for. "No," I said. "I'm sorry."

"Perhaps we should stop apologizing to each other," he suggested, and, despite myself, I smiled. "Tomorrow night, then?"

"Sss . . . no. Thank you." He muttered something under his breath, but it was too low for me to decipher. The language wasn't English, though, and my curiosity sharpened.

"Really, Jules," he said.

"Stop calling me that!"

"Sorry—Amy. The truth is, I've gone to a lot of trouble to find you, and it's quite important that we—"

As his tone became more urgent, the Britishness slipped, and I heard traces of a more exotic accent in his voice.

Time to end this, I thought. I pushed my chair back from the table and stood up. "Goodbye, then," I tossed over my shoulder as I turned to flee. "Sorry I couldn't help you."

"Hey, Jules!" he called after me, and I paused to look back. "It was great to finally meet you!"

Without another backward glance, I hurried away.

I was slightly out of breath when I got back to my office, having half jogged the ten blocks from the café. There were many cafeés much closer to my building, but then I would run the risk of seeing one of the PYTs (my pretty-young-thing coworkers)—and having them see me eat. Frantically brushing off the telltale crumbs from my scone, I scurried back to my desk and turned on my computer.

"Amy! You missed a call from Sheikh Abdullah," said Kristen R., queen bee of the PYTs. "He wants you to arrange a trip for his granddaughters to the Dubai Atlantis."

I grimaced. As a private banker at Atlantic Bank in London, I was supposed to be managing the wealth of one, fairly minor, branch of the al-Saud family from Saudi Arabia. On paper, my job was to place their billions of dollars in conservative investments to preserve those billions for the generations to come, so that no grandson or great-grandson ever had to lift a finger in honest labor. In reality, the family treated me more like a combination of butler and poodle walker, calling on me to handle everything from buying them a new private jet to finding a masseuse for their horses.

Now, apparently, I was a travel agent. "Which granddaughters?" I asked resignedly. Kristen R. shrugged. Kristen P. looked at me. "Amy, is that *jam* on your collar?"

I knew that the idea of eating anything sugary was horrifying in the PYTs' eyes; it was akin to drinking Diet Coke (only for fat people, they agreed) or eating white bread (only for the unwashed masses). I brushed at the spot, but it stuck to my fingers and settled more deeply into my silk blouse. Damn!

The Kristens exchanged arch glances while I thought of all the clever quips I could have made if I hadn't sworn to play nicely and keep this job. At all costs.

Kristen R. opened the Tupperware container on her desk and pulled it toward her. "Want some of my broccoli sprigs?" she offered. "I'm so full from that quinoa yesterday that I can't eat a thing."

I shook my head. *I would rather eat the bark off a tree*, I thought.

Kristen P. said, "No, thanks. I had a couple of bean sprouts earlier, and I have a hot-yoga session after work today."

The two Matts joined in the conversation, discussing the merits of hot yoga versus spin yoga versus vinyasa yoga, and I tuned out. My coworkers were all in their mid- to late twenties, thin as rails, appalled by any foods other than tofu and sprouts, and obsessed with extreme exercise. The head of our office, Audrey Chiu, was a size negative zero, with tiny wrists and a child's hips. She never ate lunch (or breakfast, or dinner, as far as I could tell), so no one else in the office ate either.

At thirty-four, I was the granny of the group, obsessed with scones and clotted cream. I exercised only because I absolutely had to if I wanted to keep eating. Since lunch was frowned upon and snacks were unthinkable at my office, I was usually hungry enough to gnaw off my arm by the time I got home at night—hence the hike to a café distant enough that I wouldn't be caught eating by one of my colleagues who had stopped in for a chai tea.

In fact, I could tell that my teammates often wondered why Audrey had hired me. Not only was I older than the other vice presidents; I was also cut from a very different mold. To a man (or woman), they had all attended American or British prep schools, Ivy League or Oxbridge colleges, and Harvard Business School (or "the B-school," as they called it, as if it were the only one). All were tall, blond, and genetically thin. I was small, with auburn hair, and slim only because of my grim hour on the treadmill every morning. Even more appalling, I had attended a huge public university, mainly so I could sit in the back of the massive amphitheater and doze while my hand, on autopilot, scribbled notes. Lecturing, someone had once said, was when information passed from the notes of the lecturer to the notes of the student, without passing through the mind of either one in between.

That was my education.

And, this being an American bank, many of my colleagues were from the wealthiest enclaves of New York and New England, while I had grown up all over the world. My playgrounds were Moscow and Amman, Riyadh and Kiev; my schools were whatever American school happened to be convenient to my father's current dwelling.

I turned back to my computer, my stomach already growling. Damn that man for interrupting me before I finished my scone! I emailed our in-house travel expert and asked for assistance on the sheikh's request; then, putting on my meek, demure mask, I called the sheikh to tell him that I was on the job (one of the many frustrations of living to serve the man was his dislike of email).

Then I drew a deep breath. Glancing around cautiously, I pulled up Google and typed in *Leo Schlumberger.*

ABOUT THE AUTHOR

Courtesy of Benjamin Gruenbaum

Jane Elizabeth Hughes is an obsessive reader. Unfortunately, reading novels all day is not an easy career path, so Jane has a day job as professor of international finance at Harvard Extension School. She has also consulted with multinational corporations and governments for nearly three decades and written and lectured widely about international finance throughout the world. With the help of her brilliant agent, Marcy Posner, she published her first novel, *Nannyland*, with Simon & Schuster Pocket Star Books in 2016, and she joined the SparkPress family in 2021 with the publication of *The Long-Lost Jules*. A mother of four and granny of eight (the eldest is only seven, so she's a *very busy* granny), she is fortunate enough to live on beautiful Cape Cod, Massachusetts. Oh yes, and she did work for the CIA once upon a time—so she knows whereof she writes.

SELECTED TITLES FROM SPARKPRESS

SparkPress is an independent boutique publisher delivering high-quality, entertaining, and engaging content that enhances readers' lives, with a special focus on female-driven work. www.gosparkpress.com

The Long-Lost Jules: A Novel, Jane Elizabeth Hughes, $16.95, 978-1-68463-089-9. She thinks he's either a nutcase or an eccentric Oxford professor. He thinks she's the descendant of Henry VIII's last Queen, Katherine Parr. They both harbor deep secrets, but their masks slip as they join forces to investigate the mystery of Queen Katherine's lost baby—endangering their hearts, their carefully constructed walls, and possibly their lives.

Final Table: A Novel, Dan Schorr, $16.95, 978-1-68463-107-0. Written by a former New York City sex crimes prosecutor and current sexual misconduct investigator, this suspenseful political thriller brings readers along for a deep dive into a sexual assault survivor's fight to come out on top—as well as the worlds of high-stakes poker and international politics.

Firewall: A Novel, Eugenia Lovett West. $16.95, 978-1-68463-010-3. When Emma Streat's rich, socialite godmother is threatened with blackmail, Emma becomes immersed in the dark world of cybercrime—and mounting dangers take her to exclusive places in Europe and contacts with the elite in financial and art collecting circles. Through passion and heartbreak, Emma must fight to save herself and bring a vicious criminal to justice.

Pursuits Unknown: An Amy and Lars Novel, Ellen Clary. $16.95, 978-1-943006-86-1. Search-and-rescue agent Amy and her telepathic dog, Lars, locate a missing scientist who is reported to have an Alzheimer's-like disease—only to discover that someone wants to steal his research for potentially ominous purposes.

Girl with a Gun: An Annie Oakley Mystery, Kari Bovée, $16.95, 978-1-943006-60-1. When a series of crimes take place soon after fifteen-year-old Annie Oakley joins Buffalo Bill's Wild West Show, including the mysterious death of her Indian assistant, Annie fears someone is out to get her. With the help of a sassy, blue-blooded reporter, Annie sets out to solve the crimes that threaten her good name.